COCKY SCORE

KENNA KING

Book Cover Design: Star Child Designs

1st edition 2023

BOOK ORDER
The Hawkeyes Hockey Series

Check out **www.kennaking.com** for more books and information.

CONTENTS

CHAPTER ONE

Briggs

"What the fuck do you mean she's suing the hockey franchise?" I ask, the rumble of my voice echoing off my general manager's office walls.

I can hear his assistant, Penelope, jump out of her seat from her desk outside his closed office door.

"She thinks it's a bigger payday... and she's not wrong," Sam Roberts says, his hands pinched at his hips and a stern look on his face.

A Hawkeyes baseball cap in team colors, black and turquoise, covers most of his dark hair.

"It's all bullshit. She's lying," I tell him, leaning forward and planting my fists against the desk between us.

"I know. We got an anonymous package in the mail a few days ago with pictures from the surveillance footage that night that the club refused to give us. It corroborates your story and proves she's lying, but that doesn't mean she can't try to drag our name through the mud in the process."

His eyes cast down on his desk, and he shakes his head.

"She can't get away with this," I say, straightening and beginning to pace in his office.

"Briggs, the legal team is on this thing. With the surveillance proving that you never entered that back room with her, and Altman and Powers being nowhere near the club during the alleged attack, she doesn't have any leg to stand on."

"This just doesn't make any sense. I've been going to that club regularly for over a year. I thought Dixie and I had an understanding... and more than that, I thought we were friends, or at least friendly. With everything we've shared with each other, this just doesn't make sense. Except... I know she needs money. Could she be so desperate that she's willing to end my career for it?"

"What exactly have you two shared? Or do I even want to know?" he asks, the brim of his ball cap riding low, blocking some of his light blue eyes.

The stress of being the general manager of a hockey team is beginning to show in the peppering around the sides of his sideburns and ears, hinting that his age is somewhere in his late fifties.

I ignore his question. I don't want to get into it. My father's illness isn't something I want to talk about if I can avoid it, thus the reason I'm in this mess.

"Let me talk to her," I offer.

"Don't," Sam says, his palm up to stop me. He's a few inches shorter than my six-foot-four, and he's gained a few pounds around his belly since I started at the Hawkeyes five years ago, but he still tries to keep up with us and maintain a relatively built body for a guy no longer playing sports for a living. With the deep timber of his voice, he demands that I fall in line. "Legal doesn't want you making this any worse." His expression almost dares me to challenge him under the bill of his hat.

And I'm stupid enough to try.

"If I could find out what her motive is—"

"Briggs! She's accusing you and two of our other players of some heinous acts against her. You, those players, and this hockey franchise are lucky as shit that the footage inside the club proves her allegations are fabricated; otherwise, we'd all burn for this. Don't go fucking near her, do you understand me? Or your hockey career with this franchise, and possibly your career playing in the NHL, will be over," he barks, leaning forward with his hands on his hips and his eyes piercing across the desk.

Sam is always calm under pressure. That's what made him a killer hockey player in his heyday, and that's what makes him the best general manager in the business now.

His eyes lock on mine, and silence drifts between us for a moment. He doesn't say a word, but I know he's disappointed in me. I can feel it, and my chest squeezes uncomfortably at letting down my GM and the man who took me under his wing when I first started out here as a rookie.

I can't stand the silence anymore. Finally, I ask, "They think I'll make this worse? How much worse could it fucking get? She accused me of sexual assault!"

"Jail time, Briggs, that's how much worse it could get. If a jury believes her over the evidence, you could be in jail for the next twenty years."

"Fuck."

I swallow hard.

"I swear to God I didn't do anything to her that night, or even *with* her."

"I know. I picked you up while you were passed out on the couch in the main part of the club, remember?"

Now I'm the one hanging my head. I forgot that Tyler, the bartender, had called Sam to come pick me up from the bar after I had passed out well over an hour before the sexual assault that Dixie claims happened.

Sam continues, "But even if a jury doesn't side with her, there's no way that if this goes to court, all of our names won't be trashed. It's too good of a story for the gossip blogs and news channels not to go ape-shit over this. I can see the headlines now: *Three large pro hockey players take advantage of a defenseless dancer in a strip club during a lap dance in a private room, out of view of anyone else in the club.*"

With a groan, I fall into the leather chair behind me. "Kaenan Altman wasn't even there, and Lake Powers left hours before. There are too many holes in her story for anyone to believe it."

Light blue eyes under the shadow of his hat look back at me. "People will believe what they want to believe. People love a good witch hunt. We need to do whatever we can to make sure this story doesn't see the light of day. Legal is looking for a way to keep us out of court."

I guess I never considered it would go this far, mostly because it isn't true, and the number of contradictions in her story would leave anyone assuming that Dixie is making this entire thing up, but Sam is right. This doesn't look good.

"Phil Carlton and I have a meeting with Legal this week. We'll see what they've come up with. For now, no more drinking, keep your nose clean and out of the press, and skate your damn ass off. You need to prove to the press that you didn't do anything wrong by keeping your head in the game. Moreover, you need to prove to Phil that you're worth keeping after all this headache is over with."

Phil Carlton, the owner of the team, has been pushing for a more family-friendly image for the franchise, and this is the kind of scandal that would blow up the work he's done to get things on track to bring bright, shiny new sponsorships in the door.

"Sam, I'm sorry—"

"Don't say it, Conley... show me. Prove to the world that you didn't do anything wrong."

How the hell am I going to do that?

CHAPTER TWO

Autumn

"I don't get it. They look like a bunch of overstuffed teddy bears on a pair of thin-ass skates. It defies physics. But also... why in the hell are they wearing shorts?" Erika, the owner of the public relations firm I work for, asks, standing across the conference table from me and opening her box of pork potstickers she had delivered for this meeting.

I chuckle while pulling up a delicious bite of yaki soba noodles with a pair of chopsticks up to my mouth. It's lunchtime in our office, but I'm overjoyed to have been asked to work through my lunch, ...barricaded in the conference room with

Erika and my boss Derek.. She is resolved that we don't leave this office until we find a solution for the new client she got yesterday.

Flutters of excitement fill my stomach at the chance for a second time to show my skill set at the PR firm that hired me right out of college five years ago. As a Junior Public Affairs Associate for Elite PR and Associates, it's not often someone with my limited time here is given the opportunity to brainstorm with the owner of the company. But after I came up with the last solution to link a well-known A-lister actor, who had a bad boy image that was keeping him out of the roles he wanted, with a squeaky-clean up-and-coming star actress who was trying to break out from her childhood star rolls, it shot both of their careers into overdrive. The actor got the lead role in a high-grossing rom-com movie that he would never have gotten booked for if the director hadn't thought that his new actress girlfriend hadn't softened his edges, and she got booked in for an action-hero movie that her fluffy kid's network image would have never landed her.

They faked an amicable breakup after the right amount of time as a couple and are now both getting booked in huge movies. Agents started booking up with us when they saw what we could do, and we gained several big-name clients, putting Elite PR and Associates on the map, although it was doing well before that.

With my big success, Erika is giving me another chance to prove that my idea wasn't a lucky fluke and that I have what it takes to be in this business.

"Okay, I agree, the uniforms don't make a ton of sense, but it's not as if they hired a world-renowned designer like Christian Dior to design a standardized uniform for hockey players. And for the purpose of accuracy, I think it's important to set the record straight that those aren't shorts. They're called 'pants', but they're actually pads," I tell her, placing my half-eaten box of noodles down on the large, lacquered cherry wood stain table and reaching across Derek, who's sitting to my right, for bottled water just barely out of reach.

His charming smile lights up at my failed attempt to attain the H_2O, and his green eyes sparkle back at mine. His jet-black hair is combed back to perfection, like always. He's always put together, and he exudes confidence that is incredibly attractive in a man.

His muscular, tanned forearm peeks out from underneath his rolled-up button-down sleeve as he reaches for one of the fancy bottles that Erika likes to keep in the conference rooms for clients. The bottle label showcases a tropical backdrop that hints to the fact that they're overpriced... and they are, but the water is quite refreshing.

It's probably the placebo effect, but I swear the water does taste better than the bottled waters I buy in the coffee shop downstairs in the building's lobby.

I unscrew the bottled water and take a sip.

"Pads for what?" she asks, her chopsticks frozen in her hand.

"Their junk, for one," I tell her.

Erika snickers as she takes another bite of her food, but Derek grimaces, looking away from me. *That was weird. Does he not like the word junk?*

I turn back toward Erika. "The pads are there to protect against puck hits. And also, I assume, from slicing open their femoral vein with one swift kick from an opposing player's skate blade."

Erika's eyebrows shoot up. "Oh my God... could you image if the blade sliced a little higher and sliced off his—"

"Can we stop talking about hockey players' dicks, please?" Derek interrupts, flashing a quick glance my way, then rubs his forehead, messing up his perfectly styled hair just a little, and stares down at the blank notepad he uses in meetings for client notes. Does it make him uncomfortable to hear me speak about hockey players' 'equipment'? It wasn't as if I was referring to it in a sexual context. After only a handful of dates with Derek, we still haven't gotten to the part where I see *his* 'equipment', but since we work for the same firm and he's my direct supervisor, we agreed not to rush anything. Or rather, I strongly suggested it, and he reluctantly agreed.

Whatever. We're working, and I don't need my concentration focused on office romance issues while my career aspirations are on the line. This over-analyzation of whether or not Derek is bothered by me discussing pro players' dicks would be better served in my bathtub, filled to the brim with bubbles, and my next smutty book read on my TBR all queued up.

I shake my thoughts, putting a bookmark in my brain to make sure I remember where I left off so I can revisit this thought process later tonight.

"Okay, Erika, hit us with it. What are we looking at here?" Derek asks, his eyebrows slightly downturned, his usual indicator that he's ready for business.

He takes a drink of his own overpriced bottle of water, his expensive designer watch catching the light of the new globe chandeliers Erika had installed last year to replace the ones that came with the building originally but were probably designed for a police station interrogation room, not a multi-million-dollar public relations conference room where big contract deals are made.

He quickly scarfs down the rest of his spicy tuna roll and then starts jotting down notes.

"Well," Erika says, sifting through the folder she collected from the client yesterday, "the client is none other than the Hawkeyes."

"The hockey team here in Seattle?" I ask, my eyes widening in surprise and excitement.

Work and play all in one? Oh yeah, I'm going to rock this one. I cross my fingers under the table. *Please let this project come with home game tickets.*

For research... obviously.

"Yes, why? Are you familiar with them?" she asks.

You could say that. My brother's best friend plays for them.

"I've gone to a few games," I admit, shying away from admitting I follow the team religiously.

After all, my family eats, breathes, and sleeps hockey. And not only that, but Briggs's parents still only live one block from my parents in Walla Walla, Washington. They watch most games at my parents' house.

Even though the last time I saw Briggs in person was over five years ago, I see his parents at least once a month during the hockey season when I can make the four-hour drive to Walla

Walla. His parents don't seem to come to Seattle much for home games, and I'm always putting in extra hours at work to prove myself, so I haven't been to a home game since before I graduated from college.

"Perfect! Then I'll have an inside track on the player," she gleams.

"The player?" I ask.

"Yep."

She slides a picture toward the middle of the table where Derek and I can see it.

"Meet our thorn in the side. Briggs Conley."

My heart jumps at the mention of his name. I hate that my throat instantly clogs. I glance back up at both of them to see if they noticed my reaction, but they're both analyzing the picture.

Briggs Conley, my brother's best friend since t-ball days and practically the boy-next-door. He's 100 percent off-limits but also 100 percent out of my league, and he'd never see me as anything more than the gap-toothed little nuisance that used to follow him and my brother around when we were kids.

Is it hot in here, or is it just me?

I unscrew my bottled water again and take a large gulp to clear my throat.

You're a goddamn professional, Autumn. Get it together. He's only a childhood crush.

"Briggs Conley? As in their right-wing?" I ask, willing her to say, "No, it's a Briggs Conley that plays for the Hawkeyes that you've never met, nor accidentally seen his impressive penis one day when your brother pantsed him in front of you and a few of their high school buddies while you were still just a sweet little sixth grader," but I doubt I'll get that lucky. My brother later berated me about being around when it happened, but the damage was already done, and I couldn't unsee *that*. Let's just say every penis I've ever seen since has fallen *short*.

"That's the one. Turns out Briggy boy is the bad boy of their franchise, and he's gotten himself in his last sticky pickle."

I hope she actually meant the phrase 'sticky wicket' because I'm cringing at her wording. Is she referring to him being in a pickle, or is she actually calling his pickle sticky?

Yuck!

And why in God's name is it sticky? Do I want to know? Unfortunately, these are the reasons why PR teams get called in, so likely, once Erika briefs us on everything, I will know *exactly* why his pickle is sticky... and with great detail.

"Tell us more," Derek says, pulling the picture a little closer to him and thus, closer to me. It seems he's left the grimacing behind now that we are on to real work.

I look down at Briggs's team picture and see the familiar dirty blond, blue-eyed dream with a cocky smirk. Only now, he's not a boy from my past. He's a man whose sex appeal has grown exponentially since the last time I saw him.

I take in each feature from top to bottom as if I'm looking over a fine piece of art in a museum, appreciating each brush stroke and each feature. The slight wave to his blond hair that has always made me wonder if it would be curly if he grew it out, those mischievous eyebrows that seem as though he's about to tell me a dirty joke, those piercingly beautiful blue eyes that have me melting with just a glance.

My eyes travel down further to his sharp jawline that seems so much more pronounced in his older age. I continue down his body, taking in his broad shoulders and barrel chest.

He's the boy-next-door that I'm not supposed to crush on, mostly because, as I said before, he'd never go for me with all the drop-dead gorgeous models likely steaming up his DMs, but also because my older brother would disassemble him limb from limb and drop his body in Puget Sound if Briggs ever so much as had a passing thought about me.

As far as I'm concerned, this crush is far too old to fight at this point, and unless I'm watching a hockey game at my parents' house with Mrs. Conley covering her eyes whenever Briggs gets slammed against the plexiglass, I mostly forget about the boy I grew up with.

This crush is like an old familiar ratted blanket that I've had since childhood, stashed in a box on the top shelf of my closet. If I don't see it, I don't think about it, but something about knowing it's still there, neatly folded and tucked away some-where close, is comforting in some unexplainable way. No sense in parting with it now. And anyway, even if I were a stick-thin model, which I'm not, Briggs would still never see me as more than his best friend's little sister.

I've been friend-zoned for a lifetime.

No, wait!

Worse.

I'm 'little-sister-zoned'... for life. That zone is in a realm so far from this galaxy, no one comes to visit.

When Erika's voice cuts through my thoughts, I abandon the image of the starting right-wing hero, whose stats I could list off by heart.

Okay... that sounds a little obsessive... I can actually list all of the players on the roster and their stats. I've never met any of them, but hockey runs deep in my veins.

"The owner of the franchise called me yesterday. They heard about our success with our last account." Erika smiles over at me.

Derek gives me a little elbow nudge. I can feel myself practically blush.

"They want us to pull a rabbit out of a hat with this one." She sighs while pulling another picture from the folder and slides it toward us.

My stomach turns, and I almost audibly gasp at the photo in front of me. I think I'm going to be sick as I stare down at a grainy photo taken in a dark club with an exotic dancer straddling Briggs's lap.

A quick wave of jealousy swirls through my belly. It's been a while since I've felt any type of emotion like that toward any woman in proximity to Briggs because I don't bother to search the internet for him or follow his life in any way anymore. Why keep something in my sight when it will always be too far out of my grasp?

Derek places his index finger on the photo and pulls it closer as he studies it. "I see a man at a strip club... I fail to see the shock factor here," Derek says, looking across the table at Erika and then back over at me sitting to the left of him.

He's waiting for one of us to correct him as if we know something he doesn't, but I have no capacity for speaking as my stomach is lodged in my throat.

Erika nods.

"I don't follow sports that closely, but yes, I believe players have a penchant for partying." I frown at her agreement, but it's not untrue. "And you're right. This isn't newsworthy."

Phew! Not newsworthy is a good start.

I exhale the breath I was holding in with Erika's assurance.

"Okay, so what am I looking at here?" Derek asks, pulling the picture up in his hand and holding it closer to his face as if he's looking for *Where's Waldo?*

"The dancer in that photo claims that Briggs and two other players took advantage of her without consent in one of the private rooms during a private dance that Mr. Conley paid for."

"Oh my God! Please tell me that she isn't going through with this," I spit out without thinking.

Erika gives a tight-lipped nod. "I'm afraid that she is..."

I look over at the conference room door. There is an instant need to run out of the room, lock myself in the ladies' bathroom stall, dial up my brother Isaac, demand he flies home from Vegas, and slap the sanity back into his oldest friend.

I feel like I might lose my lunch with how my stomach is turning with this news.

Erika continues, "But the accusations are the only true portion of this story."

My head spins away from the conference room door and back up at her so fast I just about give myself whiplash. "What?"

Now I'm more confused than ever.

Derek shoots a look at Erika. "She's claiming they gang—"

Erika raises her hand to stop him. "We are not uttering those words and putting that into the universe." She huffs. "One of the players she calls into question wasn't even there that night. He was at a dance recital for his two-year-old daughter with over a hundred guests in attendance, along with his nanny, who could all provide an alibi and social media timestamps that make his involvement impossible. And we have surveillance photos of the second player leaving the club over an hour before the supposed event occurred."

"So, it's just Conley?" he asks.

"Yes. the Hawkeyes' legal team received an anonymous package last week with surveillance pictures that the club owner originally refused to hand over. It includes images of inside the main room of the club. That's where that photo came from." She points to the photo of the dancer on Briggs's lap. "And it also shows an incapacitated, heavily inebriated Conley passed out on a couch in the main portion of the club over an hour before she claimed he ordered a private lap dance for him and his friends." She pulls out the picture of Briggs, alone, passed out, face down on the pleather couch.

I can't even let myself wonder how many years of bodily fluids were attached to that section of couch that Briggs has plastered on the right side of his face. "His general manager later dragged him out." She looks down at her notes. "A Sam Roberts of the Hawkeyes, after the bartender called him to come get Briggs from the club."

"How does the bartender have the phone number for the GM?" I ask, not that this is even close to the most important question of the day.

"Evidently this isn't the first time that Briggs has been dragged out of the club this season. The bartender has the GM on speed dial. Sam also said that he asked the bartender about Briggs's behavior before whisking him off, and the bartender said he had been passed out for hours. However, the bartender has since quit, and the Hawkeyes can't find his whereabouts to corroborate Sam's story."

"Oh God," I whisper, shutting my eyes and rubbing my forehead, deliberating over whether I should call my brother and find out if he knows that Briggs is back to his sophomore year of college, drinking too much and partying, narrowly avoiding losing his full-ride scholarship, all because his college girlfriend broke up with him... or at least, that's what I assume since she disappeared off his social media account around the same time. But I can't call and warn my brother because this information is all in confidence. Erika has already signed a Do Not Disclose contract, and therefore, I can't share any information I receive in these meetings. However, Briggs's reputation precedes him, and I have been seeing more and more tabloid pics of Briggs being the party animal he was in college. Isaac confronted him years ago, and it seemed like it straightened him out. Maybe Isaac needs to come back in again.

"You seem to be taking this unusually hard. You okay?" Derek asks, rubbing my back. I glance up to see if Erika notices his affectionate concern, but she's looking through more items she wants to pass on to us. Not that I think she would care.

Office romance isn't all that frowned upon at this firm. There are a few married couples that work here and one or two couples that have been dating for years. Although a few dates hardly seem as though I could consider Derek and I dating, since I report directly to him, he's more than just a coworker. Not sure how she'll feel about it.

"Yeah, I mean no, I'm fine. It's just that... well, I kind of know him."

"Kind of know him how?" Derek turns to look at me as if not believing that I know a pro sports athlete.

"We grew up together. His parents still live right down the road from mine."

Derek's facial expression changes from questioning the likelihood of my claim to now looking a little uneasy with this new information.

Erika's head perks up from the folder that she's rifling through. "Oh. Do you need to be taken off this project? I can find someone to take your spot," Erika asks, looking at me with compassion as if this project might actually cause me distress.

"Definitely not," I say, straightening my spine and looking as professional as I can. I'm not going to let Briggs's benders be the reason I get taken off a project. "I'm up for this."

"Okay." She nods, a little hesitant.

Derek eyes me for a little longer, and I swear I see the corner of his eye twitch, but I can't be sure. He glances away from me, looking down at his notepad, and then his hand slides off my back and picks up his pen, immediately jumping back into writing notes. He dives into professional mode, and I barely have time to process if something just happened that bothered him. I'll have to wait to find out if the fact that I know Briggs is a problem for him. Not that it matters. I can't *unknow* Briggs.

Unless that little light thingy they had in *Men In Black* is real, and you can erase unsavory memories.

"The stripper's lying, then. Sounds like there's no story here. What do they need us for?" Derek asks, looking down at his notes as if he's making sure he isn't missing anything, and then looks back up at Erika.

Erika pulls more documents from the folder and then slides a photocopy of something across the table to us.

Derek and I both lean in to look over more documents that she starts passing our way as she speaks.

"The dancer is suing the franchise for the alleged attack. And although I'm usually all for believing the woman in this type of situation, the evidence clearly shows that neither Briggs nor the men she claims were in that private room with her were anywhere near it during the time she claims the attack took place."

"So?" Derek says. "It's a wrongful suit. It'll get thrown out immediately."

Erika looks over at us. "Likely, yes. But since the evidence came out, she has backtracked and is now claiming only Briggs was involved. This makes probability a lot harder to deny considering he was in the building at the time."

"But the picture shows he was passed out on camera until the GM pulled him out of the club," Derek says.

"Yes, but that picture is of one moment in time. It doesn't mean that she got the time wrong—and she claims it happened after this picture was taken," Erika says.

She slides over the smoking gun. A receipt tab showing that Briggs did, in fact, pay for a lap dance that night, but whoa, is it just me, or are lap dances expensive? You could practically pay for a first-class plane ticket to the Maldives for that kind of money.

"Holy shit! Prices have gone up," Derek blurts out.

Erika and I both look at him with surprised looks on our faces. It's not as if I'm surprised he's gotten a lap dance before, only that he just blurted it out at work... in front of his female boss.

He looks at me first, his eyes locking on mine. "It was once at a bachelor party."

Sure... once.

"Okay." I reassure him with a nod and a small smile.

Because it is fine. I'm not judging him for a consenting lap dance that he paid for. We're not even officially together. It was only a few dates.

The lap dance that has me concerned has nothing to do with Derek.

My mind is reeling. On the one hand, the time stamp on the surveillance pictures proves Briggs was too inebriated to stand, let alone walk to the back room of his own free will. Plus, with Sam saying that the bartender told him that Briggs hadn't moved since he passed out... we have an eyewitness that he never made it back to the room she claims he took advantage of her in. As far as the receipt, well, paying for a lap dance isn't illegal even if the price seems astronomical, but how he got himself in this position... I'm not so sure that my lifelong crush will survive this.

"There still isn't enough evidence that she would win her case since it clearly shows Briggs never received the lap dance while passed out and the bartender told the GM that Briggs never moved from that spot. But what our client is concerned about now is the damage that will be done by the mere mention of any foul play involving a large jock from their organization against a vulnerable woman."

Derek nods. "Understandably so. The media will have the public burning that stadium down to rubble if they think this occurred."

Erika has finally finished taking out the documents, and at least I know there are no more surprises left in her *Mary Poppins* folder of horror.

"Exactly. Their lawyer has advised them to settle out of court and pay her off instead of dragging the franchise's name through the mud... and Conley's," she adds, "but they are still concerned that she might leak the story anyway."

"Which they could sue her for; defamation of character," I chime in, becoming more and more defensive over the team I spent my weekends screaming over in front of my parents' eighty-inch TV screen and a stack of hot wings, mozzarella sticks, and Mrs. Conley's killer margaritas.

If this lie comes out, the pain it will cost his parents will be immeasurable.

"True. But again, their image is the thing they care about more than money. A good opinion is hard to get back once it's lost. And they feel they can recover the cost if they can keep butts in the seats."

"Where do we come in?" I ask, already chomping at the bit to protect my beloved team... and maybe Briggs. He's been reckless, though, and maybe this is the wake-up call he needs.

"That's the question they're paying us a lot of money to answer. Conley is one of their biggest stars and one of their best players. They want his image protected. How do we get ahead of this?" She walks over to the whiteboard. "Throw out whatever comes to mind. No idea is a bad idea. Let's get them all out on the board."

Derek jumps in first. "We could throw out several different outlandish rumors. So that if the stripper decides to drop her own, it drowns in a sea of others."

Erika writes it on the board as she's thinking through it.

"That's worked for other clients in the past, and it's a good suggestion. I'm not sure it works here since they are trying to save face, and more rumors could start to build a fire, but we'll keep it on the list for now."

She looks over at me. "What do you have for me, Autumn?"

I think quickly through the possibilities out loud.

"Protecting image... improving image... keeping the public in your favor..."

I drum my fingers against the table as I think.

"Oh! How about a charity event... or better yet, several."

"Like what? Give me specifics," Erika asks, facing the whiteboard, ready to write down whatever I call out.

"Doggy adoption at the local pound."

"Okay..." Erika says, jotting it down quickly.

"Car wash to raise funds for underprivileged kids' school supplies," Derek calls out, looking at me for confirmation.

I smile and nod, but I suddenly can't stop comparing Derek to Briggs.

Where Derek is tall, Briggs is taller by several inches.

Where Derek is muscular, Briggs is so much bigger, his presence demanding.

And where Derek is confident... well, all I have to do is watch Briggs skate out on the ice at the beginning of the game, and I can tell that Derek has nothing on cocky-confident Briggs Conley.

Is any of that relevant to me?

Absolutely not, because I'm his best friend's little sister.

Erika is nodding, too, as she writes it down on the board.

"Open rink days for kids to come to skate with their favorite players," I call out.

"Oooh, I like that," Erika says. "I'm going to suggest that one to them even if we don't go this route. A great way to strengthen the Hawkeyes' presence in the community and introduce more kids to the sport. Future players or future fans, either way, a win.

"Okay, good, good. I like all of these, but these suggestions focus more on the team than the player. Although I'm going to suggest they implement these during the negotiations with the dancer's lawyer to keep a positive image out there, they came to us to ask for help on how to improve the party image of their player. Give me something for that."

Derek and I both stare back at each other for a minute.

"Well..." I start thinking out loud. "He's a notorious party boy, right?"

"Right," Erika says, even though I know the man well enough to have seen it firsthand through the years.

"And the reason people will be keen to believe the dancer's claim is because Briggs is known as the wild one of the Hawkeyes."

"Exactly. He needs to be tamed," Erika agrees.

I think about her words for a second, and then it clicks. "Yes! Tamed. Precisely."

"Great," Derek says with zero excitement, his eyes void of interest in this line of thinking. "How do you tame a multi-millionaire playboy who has women throwing themselves at him and people inviting him to party every week, hoping he gets drunk and makes a scene?"

"You make him settle down," Erika answers.

"I'm sure he'll go for that," Derek says sarcastically.

"Not make him settle down... create an illusion that he has," I counter.

"Genius!" Erika beams and writes it on the board.

FAKE GIRLFRIEND, the lettering reads up on the board. I gulp down the thought of seeing Briggs in picture after picture with some bleach-blonde beauty, day after day, whether it's real or fake.

"With who?" Derek asks.

"It can't be the usual types he's seen with," Erika reasons.

My ears perk up. Erika's right. Another buxom blonde with nudes out for any dude to purchase won't work. It will only add to the image that he's a playboy and the relationship is temporary.

"Agreed. She needs to be sweet... wholesome," I add.

"Girl next door vibes..." Erika continues the line of thought.

"Kind of girl he would take home to Mom," I say.

"You mean you?" Derek asks, looking down at his phone as if he had already clocked out on our conversation. He smiles to himself and then looks up, a little surprised when he realizes he said that out loud.

I smile at the thought that maybe he said that out loud because he's already thought I'm the kind of girl he'd take home to meet his mom, but this thing with us is still new, and I'm not sure how I feel about where this is going. Then I hear Erika practically screech with excitement.

"You! Of course! You're perfect."

My eyes flash over to her to find the biggest smile I think I've ever seen on Erika's face.

"Wait, hold on, what?" My eyelids flutter rapidly as I'm sure I misunderstood her.

Me? Fake date Briggs?

Derek stands up immediately. "Now wait a second, I didn't mean her," he says to Erika while pointing at me.

"No! You're absolutely right. She's the ideal candidate. Plus, she's the only one we can trust to keep quiet about it being fake!"

My eyes widen to the size of saucers. She can't be serious.

"How am I the ideal candidate?" I ask, my eyebrows knitting together.

This is a bad idea. My brother will kill him, assuming Briggs will even agree to fake date me, which he won't.

"No way. This won't work. We need to find someone else," Derek demands, still standing and leaning inward, taking the stance of someone ready to stand their ground and battle it out.

Erika glances at him briefly but then ignores his demands and looks back at me to answer my question. "He already knows you. You have history to build on. You know the team and what we're trying to accomplish, plus... you already told me that you grew up on the same street. You *are* the girl next door."

"I can't, Erika."

"Why? Are you dating someone?"

My eyes shift to Derek, and he's looking at me too, but the look of panic on his face has me not sure how to answer.

I look at her. "It's not serious."

I feel him tense beside me, but I wasn't sure how to answer the question because he and I aren't serious. It was a few dates with no agreement or understanding. We have no relationship titles; we've never agreed not to see other people... and we haven't had sex.

"Good, because your job *is* serious, and this client could mean a lot of money for this firm if we get this right and they keep us on retainer. If you land this client... I'll give you the client relations manager promotion and the sparkly new corner office to go with it." She wiggles her eyebrows a little in an attempt to entice me, and it's working.

My heart races at the idea, and a surge of energy rushes through me.

I knew Erika was creating this new client relations manager position because Elite PR and Associates is growing so rapidly that she can't handle onboarding and caring for each client at the level she wants to. She needs help, but I never thought to throw my hat in the ring for it. It's several years still out of my reach. I have so much yet to learn and to prove.

How this is going to fly with Briggs and my brother... I don't know. But right now, that isn't my problem.

"I'll do it."

CHAPTER THREE

Briggs

"Good morning, Adel," I say to Phil Carlton's administrative assistant, stepping off the elevator that leads right into the main lobby of the Hawkeyes corporate offices on the third floor.

I walk up to her massive bar-height desk and grab a butterscotch candy, flashing her my signature grin, sure to get her to giggle.

Adel is in her early fifties, happily married, with shoulder-length auburn hair and kind eyes. She's on the lower end of five-foot, which is probably why she wanted this massive desk during the large remodel a few years back, and no more than a hundred and ten pounds dripping wet, but don't get on her bad side. If you don't have a scheduled meeting with Phil Carlton on the books, your ass isn't getting anywhere near him.

Adel has Security on speed dial, and I've heard she uses it at the drop of a hat. She's a force to be reckoned with, or so it's been said, which is why I try to keep on her good side.

Plus, the woman makes some delicious homemade butterscotch candies to keep me coming back for more. I don't want her to decide to cut off my supply, and now I know how she caught her husband. The easiest way to a man's heart is through his stomach, although... I know another way.

"Mr. Carlton is in conference room number one to the right. He's expecting you. Go on through, Mr. Conley," she says, referring to the largest of three conference rooms in the upstairs corporate offices and down the long hallway past her desk.

"I've told you, Adel," I say as I round her desk and head for the owner's office, "call me Briggs."

"Yes, sir." She smiles back sweetly, but I know we'll have this same conversation the next time I'm up here.

Nothing will change, but I like that I can look forward to something when I come up. Usually getting called up to corporate isn't a good sign unless, of course, you're here to meet with Legal and sign your brand-new contract with extra zeros. Something that looks like I'll be doing here next season.

Unofficially, of course. It's not a done deal, so I can't talk about it yet.

I smile and shake my head as I head down the long hallway, passing by several corporate offices.

The offices up here are the polar opposite of the feeling of the stadium.

Where the stadium illuminates with the bright blue-ish hue of the massive ice rink and the stadium seats are painted in a light turquoise blue with black numbers to match our team colors, the offices up on the third floor have an expensive, darker theme. The floors are covered in dark espresso hand-carved wide wood planks, while the walls are painted in turquoise, black, and white geometric shapes.

The hallway is lined with large glass-framed jerseys of the Hawkeyes' most memorable retired players, along with old photos or memorabilia in glass memory boxes.

Each and every time I come up here, I see something I didn't catch before. A detail in an old photo or a piece of memorabilia hidden in one of the boxes displayed that I didn't see tucked in a corner or something.

I wish I could take a few minutes to try to uncover yet another treasure hidden in this hallway, but Sam called yesterday, saying that they need to meet with me about the plans they've made with Legal about the accusations against me. I'm sure they came up with a way to tell her to kick sand for trying to blackmail me with false accusations. They probably need an official statement from me.

Even though I hate coming in on my only day off this week, I can't exactly say no. They are handling this nuisance for me. It's not as if they have a choice, though. I'm one of their most valuable players. I bring in a large fan base, a significant amount of the jersey sales, and the most fan mail.

Well, actually, Lake Powers, our left-wing, probably has me beat on the love letters from women and men alike. But even still, I doubt I'll be here long, anyway. I'm sure our legal team made her realize what a mistake it was to try to fabricate this story.

I knock quickly on the eight-foot espresso-stained wooden door with a metallic 'one' screwed into it. This is the room Adel told me to use, but why they picked the largest conference room in the office seems odd. We usually just meet in Phil's large office that has an entire sitting area and six TVs with news sports going on 24/7 and a booze cart.

So why the huge conference room?

"Come in." I hear Sam's voice while I'm already pushing through the door. He knew I was coming. I'm sure Adel called to tell him over the intercom.

When I walk in, I'm surprised to see the big conference room holding more than the two people I expected to see.

I quickly look around at the faces staring up at me. I notice a couple of them are from our in-house legal staff. I've had enough encounters with them to remember who they are. Head of social media and Public Relations, Tessa Tomlin, is here too, along with Sam's assistant and daughter, Penelope Roberts.

But then there are three newcomers I've never seen before. One of them is a woman in her mid-forties, good-looking and dressed like she owns something important. A man sits next to her, probably a few years older than me, with dark hair and a well-fitted suit, who's looking at me like I took the last Krispy Kreme donut in the break room. But it's the young woman sitting next to him that I have a weird feeling that I know from somewhere. I can't quite make out her entire face since it's mostly hidden from view, but I must have been staring too long because Sam clears his throat to get my attention.

"Briggs, come on in and shut the door," Sam says, sitting to the right of Phil Carlton, who is sitting at the head of the conference table at the other end in a large high-back black leather conference chair.

Neither Sam nor Phil seem too pleased as they are sporting frowns and worry wrinkles across their foreheads.

What also concerns me is that Sam isn't wearing his Hawkeyes baseball cap. I rarely see him without it on. He's also dressed in slacks and a button-down instead of his usual dark jeans and a Hawkeyes-branded polo. The same polo that all the physical therapists, dietitians, and coaching staff usually wear day to day at work.

I do as he asks... with hesitation.

"Did I miss something? I thought I was just meeting with you two," I say, gesturing to Phil and Sam.

Phil is older than Sam by about twenty years and unlike Sam's roughly six-foot stature and mostly in-shape build besides the last couple pounds he's put on, Phil Carlton is shorter by several inches, with a beer belly and a slight comb-over in an attempt to mask the thinning of his grey hair.

"A few things have changed since the last time we talked," Sam says, standing and walking closer to me. He sees my eyes dart back to the people I'm not familiar with for a moment.

When my eyes lock back on his, he starts again. "Briggs, we're all here to solve a problem, and we need your full cooperation to make this work."

"Sure, Boss, whatever you need." I nod.

"Good, that's the kind of attitude you'll need."

What's that supposed to mean?

"I'll need for what?"

"The woman making a claim against the franchise is still persistent even with the evidence provided, but now you are the only one on the chopping block. She's now saying that Kaenan Altman and Lake Powers weren't there. So, we've offered her a deal to make this go away."

"Excuse me? You did what?" I bark. "She's lying. We have proof. Why won't you just let me talk to her? Something isn't right. I can fix this, just give me a chance."

Phil looks at me. "Briggs, we believe you, and the evidence speaks for itself." He glances at everyone in the room, gaining nods from just about everyone. "We all know. But the faintest hint at this scandal could throw too much of a shadow on you and this franchise, even if the allegations are false. And I've already told you, Legal doesn't want you to make a bad situation worse by speaking with her."

"Even *if*?! You saw the pictures. Altman wasn't even there! He was at his daughter's ballet recital. And Powers left early. This is horseshit, and it makes no sense why she's doing this."

"Why did you pay for a lap dance when you were never planning on using it, and why was it ten times the normal amount that the club usually charges?" a bald man from Legal asks, his pen ready to jot down whatever I say on the legal notepad sitting on the almost black wooden stained conference table with the Hawkeyes logo sealed under a layer of thick lacquer.

I turn to him, taking in the suit he's wearing that probably costs more than most Americans' yearly salary. "That's between her and me, and if you'd let me talk with her, I could figure out why she's blackmailing us." I scowl.

Sam takes a few steps toward me until he's standing right in front of me, his blue eyes softening. "I know it doesn't feel good to handle it this way, but we can recover the loss easily as long as we keep fans paying for tickets. This isn't the first time that the franchise has had to pay for frivolous lawsuits. Last year we had to pay someone for slipping on a piece of ice in the parking lot of a hockey stadium... after it had snowed all day. It's the price of doing business. In the end, it will cost us less to pay this than to go to trial."

"It doesn't matter that I'm innocent?" I say, looking around at all the faces in the room. How many of these people still believe her over me, even with photo evidence?

I look over at the woman who had her face tucked into her notepad, and now she's looking up at me. Full beautiful lips, warm, hazel-colored almond-shaped eyes, and chestnut brown hair that stops just after her shoulders with strands of honey highlights throughout.

She's fucking beautiful, and I wish we were meeting under different circumstances, because damn.

Wait.

My eyes widen, and my heart practically stops beating. Holy shit... it can't be.

Isaac Daughtry's little sister, Autumn?

It's been years since I've seen her in person. Even though her family lives in the same neighborhood as my parents in Walla

Walla, we're not kids anymore. Birthday parties and sleepovers aren't a regular occurrence now with Isaac and I grown and out of our parents' houses.

In the off-season and holidays, my parents come to visit me at my house on Orcas Island in Puget Sound. The last time I remember seeing Autumn was at the Hawkeyes stadium when she and her parents came to watch me play. She was still in college back then. It's been years since I saw her last, but somehow, she looks completely different. Nothing like the little girl who used to chase Isaac and me around the neighborhood, trying to keep up with the boys.

Once in high school, I hugged Autumn when she and her parents came to one of me and Isaac's hockey games. She congratulated me on a win, and I didn't think anything of it. She was still in middle school... a child compared to my eighteen years, but when I bent down and wrapped my arms around her shoulders, Isaac smacked me upside the head in front of her and told me never to lay a finger on his sister again.

"Touch her again, and you're a dead man," I think were his exact words.

It was an easy rule to follow since she was a kid then, and we left for college three months later, both getting full rides for hockey at different colleges.

Now, here I am, having one of the ugliest lies that's ever been told about me shared with someone who knows me from my adolescent years. She knows the man before the money... before the fame. She knows about the Nerf gun wars and the atomic wedgies, and everything in-between. Somehow, it's unnerving that someone who knows me at that level is seeing me at my lowest. A pro athlete who makes his money entertaining thousands of fans every game night and lives for the glory of it all. I'm used to eyes on me... just not hers.

And not that look of pity as she seems to sit there feeling sorry for me.

Don't feel sorry for me. That's the last thing I want.

My eyes shift back to the man sitting next to her, who's still giving me a look like I stole something from him. Also, not an uncommon reaction from people I've never met before. Whether they're fans of another team we've beat, fans of our team that don't like the way I'm playing, or anyone on this damn planet who's found something I said offensive. But I don't have time for his resting asshole face. I've got bigger problems.

All of a sudden, I realize Sam has been talking while I got lost in the past. "So that's the game plan."

My head snaps back to Sam, trying not to look like I forgot he was talking.

"Hold on, what?" I ask, shaking my head.

His eyebrow dips in confusion. He didn't see me get lost in the past and ignore every word he was saying. Thank Fuck.

"What part did you want me to go back over?" he asks, a little annoyance in his voice.

Maybe he did see that I got distracted.

"Better go back over it all," I say.

I didn't catch a damn word, and there's no point in hiding it. He already knows.

"We've hired a PR team to improve your image."

"What's wrong with my image?"

"That's a longer conversation…" Phil pipes up from a leather chair at the head of the conference table, tapping his fingers against the table impatiently.

Sam looks at Phil and then back to me. "Legal is trying to make a deal with Dixie's lawyer, but in the meantime, we need to help boost your public image… just in case."

"In case of what?" I ask, with frustration.

I feel a little guilty for snapping at Sam. He's the best damn GM in the league and he always goes out of his way to protect his players, but this whole thing has me pissed off and on edge.

"In case we pay her off and she decides to spread the lie anyway."

She *still* decides. What the fuck?

"Isn't that what paying her off is supposed to accomplish? We'll sue the shit out of her. She'll be penniless."

I flash a quick look at the legal team, but they aren't nodding like I feel they should be. I know that Dixie can't afford this to happen to her. What I don't understand is that if she needed this kind of money… why didn't she ask?

"Not exactly. The story could fetch a decent amount of money. Especially if they spin that we paid her hush money."

"It's not fucking hush money! She's blackmailing me."

And if you'd let me speak with her, I could find out why.

"Well, technically, she's blackmailing *us*," Sam says, "and we pay your contract salary, so it's in your best interest to let us sort this out however our legal team considers the best of a shit situation."

I lay my hands on my hips and shake my head, breaking eye contact with him. "This is bullshit."

"Well then, you're not going to like this next bit," Sam says.

I look back over at Sam, and then he gestures toward Autumn. "Meet your new girlfriend for the next couple of months."

My mouth drops open as my head turns to look at Autumn. Our eyes lock.

"My what?!"

Chapter Four

Autumn

I sit in my large cubicle the day after our meeting with the Hawkeyes owner Phil Carlton and his team.

I fangirled pretty hard yesterday getting to meet Sam Roberts, the Hawkeyes' very own general manager, who's a legend in his own right. I kept it together just long enough not to ask him for an autograph. But the high came crashing down when Briggs entered the room an hour after the rest of us arrived. Sam wanted to give us all a chance to voice our thoughts about the project before Briggs came in.

It felt uncomfortable and awkward to be a part of the unpleasant surprise that Briggs walked into. We all knew he wasn't privy to the group of people sitting in the conference room when he walked in. It felt more like an ambush than a meeting of the minds to solve the issue of Briggs's reputation.

The look on Briggs's face when it first registered with him had me squirming in the buttery soft leather conference chairs at the Hawkeyes' corporate office.

At first, I swear I saw him give me a once over, and my body lit up with goosebumps at his perusal. I couldn't tell if my body was excited or nervous; it took on a life of its own. I was just along for the ride.

But then I saw the moment when his eyes latched onto my face, and the realization of who I was hit him. The slight glint in his eyes when he thought I was a stranger quickly died replaced with what looked like a mix of surprise and maybe a little disappointment.

Then when he spun around and stared at me with heated blue eyes and a scowl when Sam announced that I was his new *fake* girlfriend... well, I couldn't stop seeing the disapproval in his expression plastered on the back of my eyelids last night as I tried to fall asleep in my tiny studio apartment. I shouldn't even call it an apartment. It more closely resembles the size of a cat litter box than a place to call home, but Seattle isn't cheap, and I'm happy that my job affords me just enough to live downtown and close to work. Plus, I don't have to have a roommate to help with the cost of a place this small.

Maybe with that new promotion, I can consider looking for a slightly bigger place so that I can get a dog, something I've always wanted since my parents never let me have one as a kid. Putting a nice chunk down on my student debt will also be at the top of my list.

"Knock, knock." I hear Derek's familiar voice radiate through my space.

Our cubicles aren't the size of the offices, like Derek's or Erika's, but they're bigger than the ones I've worked in during my internship while in college. They feature a large L-shaped desk, and the best part is that the cubicle walls reach from floor to ceiling, and besides the doorless opening that allows people to enter and exit their cubicles, the space is mostly enclosed. It's the most privacy you could hope for in a corporate office like this one.

However, if all goes well on the Hawkeyes account, I'll be moving to a large office with my promotion.

I turn in my chair to see Derek, dressed to impress as usual, his dark thick hair molded into place and his slacks and button-up shirt tailored to perfection. He leans up against my cubicle wall, his hands casually tucked in his pockets. He's always had this way of looking so cool and confident in any setting, like right now. The only time I've ever seen him shook was at the meeting a few days ago in the conference room with Erika when he was trying to backtrack on his suggestion that I date Briggs.

"Hey," he greets.

His usual grin is back, and I internally sigh with relief.

"Hi." I smile up at him.

"Want to grab some lunch?" he asks, one dark brow lifting in question.

"Yeah," I say, looking at the email correspondence between me and Penelope Roberts, Sam Roberts's daughter and administrative assistant. She's been keeping me apprised of how everything is progressing regarding an apartment that I'll share with Briggs to substantiate the lie that we're a serious couple that's been hiding from view.

She slipped in a few questions about how Briggs and I know each other. She heard that we grew up together and was curious but didn't want to pry if I wanted to keep that private.

Honestly, I'm relieved she asked about me and Briggs and our past. There haven't been any opportunities in my adult life to bring up Briggs Conley and our history... or at least, I've never had a captivated audience before that I could hash out all this history with until Penelope.

Briggs has never come up while talking with new girlfriends because most of them don't give a crap about hockey, and when men I've dated found out that I know Briggs, they ask two questions:

One, did you sleep with him?

To which I reply, "no".

Then that leads to question number two. Can you get me and my buddies season tickets?

To which I reply again with the same answer. *"No."*

After that, the Briggs Conley conversation ceases to exist.

I can't bring it up with my parents because they were there for most of it, so it would seem weird and forced to them if I brought him up out of the blue.

And Isaac will go Rambo the second the name Briggs even leaves my lips. There is absolutely no reason, in my brother's head, why I would utter his best friend's name unless, of course, we're sleeping together. Perfect logic of an overprotective brother.

I type the last few words and send off the email to Penelope to confirm the time the movers she booked will be at my apartment to pick up my things next week to move me and Briggs into our new *shared* apartment.

With Briggs and I likely only having to pretend for two to three months until things blow over, and the shared apartment coming fully furnished, I'll only need clothes and toiletries... along with a few necessary kitchen items for an impromptu baking session if the need hits me. I do my best thinking while whipping up some confectionery treats.

It seemed a bit overkill to send a moving company to help me with the few boxes and luggage I packed. It would only take me a couple of trips in my 4Runner to get it all to the new apartment, but she insisted that this is how things are done in her organization, so I gave in and sent her my address.

"Okay, I'm ready," I tell him, grabbing my rain jacket for the drizzly fall day we're having and then pulling my purse out from under my desk, following him down the hallway of our office and toward the elevator. "Where do you want to eat?"

"Figured we could hit the little sandwich shop a couple of blocks down the way and find a quiet spot to talk if the rain lets up."

That actually sounds really nice. I sort of feel bad for comparing him to Briggs the other day.

Who cares if Briggs is taller, in better shape, or exudes unnatural amounts of confidence? Derek is the one trying, right? He's the one interested and not storming out of doors to get away from me.

The elevator doors open and then close before he speaks. This project is on a need-to-know, and therefore, most of the staff here don't even know that Erika is trying to bring on the Hawkeyes as a client. Their company is listed under a different name in our system, and everything is password protected so that only Erika, Derek and myself have access to it.

"How are you feeling about everything?"

"With the new client?" I ask to clarify.

We're alone in the lift, but it's better to be safe than sorry. Security monitors the cameras in the elevator, so it's not as if we're completely alone.

"Yeah. I didn't expect he'd be happy with the idea we came up with, but I didn't think he'd bolt," Derek says, referring to Conley but not uttering his name out loud.

"He wasn't expecting it to be me." I take a stab at guessing Conley's reasoning.

I shift uncomfortably, the memory again of the cold yet beautiful face of the man I've known since I was in diapers storming out of a meeting once he heard that he was going to be stuck pretending to date me.

Was it a hit to my pride for everyone in that room to witness it? Yes.

Will it stop me from doing my job and earning this promotion? Not in the least.

"Yeah... actually, that's what I wanted to get lunch to discuss."

The elevator doors open, and the instant smell of coffee and chocolate croissants from the coffee shop downstairs fills the elevator immediately.

We both walk out of the elevator and into the lobby of our high-rise office building downtown. The loud whistle of milk being steamed by the barista as a large line forms from employees taking their lunch breaks, and the clacking of shoes against the bright white glossy marble tiles of the lobby from other employees working in this building fills the air around us.

Our office takes up the entire fifth floor with about forty employees on staff, but with twelve other stories, this place is busy every minute of the day from seven in the morning until Security locks up at eight in the evening.

"Discuss what?" I ask as we head for the massive glass doors to the entrance and exit of our building.

He takes a few rushed steps in front of me to get ahead and pulls open the door for me to walk through. "Thank you." I flash a smile over my shoulder.

I take a deep breath the second I step outside. It doesn't matter how long I've lived in Washington; the smell of rain after being cooped up in a stuffy office for hours without a window gives me this small dopamine hit.

I can't prove it, but I can feel the effects.

Once he walks through the door to join me, I pull on my jacket under the cover of the building overhang. The rain must have calmed down since this morning because it's now more of a mist than actual drizzle, but it doesn't bother me to stand in a little bit of moisture while we eat our lunch as long as it isn't a torrential downpour.

We begin our walk, weaving through thick pedestrian traffic downtown, attempting to dodge the puddles of rainwater that have accumulated in areas along the sidewalk. The sounds of everyone's shoes slapping against the wet cement sidewalk is the backdrop noise we'll hear the rest of the way to the sandwich shop, as everyone else is getting lunch around this time too. I'm glad I wore my rainboots today because anything else would be soaked through by now.

Now that we're out of earshot of any employees in the firm, he seems to relax a little, and I almost forgot that I asked him a question.

"Discuss what you're going to say when you tell Erika that you can't date Briggs Conley."

"I'm sorry… what now?" I ask in confusion, looking over at him as we wait for the light to change so we can walk with the crosswalk and move down the next block toward the little shop.

He gives a self-deprecating laugh. "Well, I mean, come on… she can't really expect you to fake date some guy for a promotion. And anyway, you and I might not be serious yet, but there's something going on between us."

The green 'WALK' sign illuminates, and we step off the curb and cross with several other people.

"We went on a few dates, and they were really nice. I liked getting to know you but—"

He isn't going to ask me to turn down career advancement just so he and I can try to see if this thing between us has longevity, is he? I mean, I'd get it if we had been dating exclusively for an extended amount of time and a future with Derek was already in motion, but we're not, and this promotion is everything I've wanted since I picked my major in high school. I want this, and I doubt if the shoe was on the other foot, that he'd give up a promotion to date me.

He fills in the rest of my sentence as we get close to the restaurant's front door. "Which is why you need to tell Erika that you can't agree to the project and that we'll need to find a different fill-in woman to date Briggs," he says.

His deep green eyes look over at me, almost willing me to agree. We stop in front of the little standing-room-only sandwich shop.

"We can just hire a high-paid escort to pretend to be his girlfriend, and she'll probably give him as many lap dances as he wants, and he won't have to pay a fortune for them."

My nose scrunches up at the thought of Briggs getting lap dances from anyone, but it doesn't matter what I think because the reason that Erika doesn't want to go that route is that she wants this fake relationship to feel authentic. And since Briggs and I do have history, a history that we can prove, she believes that will go a long way in selling people on the idea of us and its plausibility.

"Derek," I say slowly.

He turns to face me and reaches out for my hand, and pulls it into his. "Yeah?"

"From the minute I started working here, I've looked up to you." He smiles down at me. "You've worked your butt off to get where you are today. Working your way up to find your spot as the right-hand of one of the biggest PR firms in Washington, and I admire you so much for your accomplishments..."

He beams down at me, basking in my compliments. "It means a lot to hear you say that," he says, rubbing his thumb over my hand that he's holding.

"...Which is why I know that you wouldn't want me to miss my opportunity to do the same."

His smile turns into a frown instantly, and he looks perplexed.

"What are you talking about?"

"I think our timing is off."

Which is true. If Conley hadn't gotten dropped in my lap—ironically by Derek—I'd still be interested in seeing things with Derek progress. But he can't truly expect me to walk away from this offer from Erika for him when we have only gone on a few dates. Can he?

"Are you being serious?" he asks, his forehead creasing with confusion or frustration, I'm not sure.

"This project with Briggs is only a few months, Derek, not a lifetime. I need to see this through. What Erika is offering is—"

He shakes his head. "I know, I know. Operation De-sleaze Conley... It's a huge opportunity for you." He doesn't look back at me. Instead, he watches cars on the roadway slowly passing us by in the lunch rush. Horns beeping in the distance, the ocean breeze whipping between us softly, and the smell of rain from earlier this morning.

I place my hand on his arm. "Thank you for understanding," I say, even though I have a feeling he isn't really okay with this and wants me to put my career on hold for a guy I've only been casually dating for a month. "This could be a huge win for the company as well if I can land the Hawkeyes as a permanent account. We'll all benefit from this."

"Uh-huh," he says, shifting his sights from the traffic to the sandwich shop and releasing my hand. He starts walking toward the shop's front door. I follow behind, even though I'm not sure if I should just head back and grab a yogurt parfait and a coffee at the coffee shop in the lobby of our building instead. He doesn't seem happy about this. Maybe a little breather for him to think this all through and see that I'm right would be good.

I follow behind cautiously, waiting for him to dismiss me, but he doesn't. Instead, he holds open the door for me to walk inside first.

"Thanks," I say, smiling up at him.

He looks down at me with a polite but halfhearted smile and nods. He's never smiled at me like that before. His smiles are usually warm and flirtatious when they're directed at me.

I'm not exactly surprised by his reaction, considering our conversation, but I am surprised that it doesn't bother me as much as I thought it would.

We stand in line, and I'm relieved to see several other coworkers inside. Paul, one of the other managers that works with Derek, gets in line behind us and starts chatting Derek up. The woman in front of me is Erika's assistant, and she turns around to discuss the memo she plans to put out about getting rid of all the paper cups at the water fountain and requiring everyone to bring a reusable one that they keep at their desk. I'd rather listen in on Derek's conversation behind me or watch paint dry, but I'd never be rude to a coworker, and Erika's assistant doesn't have many friends in our firm... for good reason.

She continues...

"This will not only save the company money but also think about how great it will be for the environment." She beams back at me, her strawberry blonde hair pulled back in its usual tight bun. She's about my height and somewhere in her early thirties. She's covered from head to toe in rain gear, but her face shows off her light skin, which highlights all of her unique freckles.

She takes a step forward as the line moves. I take a step as well to keep up.

"That's true, but there will be a lot more dishwashing going on now that people will need to wash out their cups regularly, and that could cut into the efficiency of the staff if they're spending time washing out their cups once a day. People tend to get chatty in the break room. Not to mention more water waste for washing cups."

"Good point," she says thoughtfully, glancing up at the ceiling in consideration. "I'll add that to my report to Erika, and she can make the final call."

I nod back at her as we move again, closer to the cashier.

I think her idea makes sense, but I can already hear the groans of all my cohorts when they realize they will now be responsible for keeping a clean cup at their desk.

Erika's assistant is a bit of a busy bee, which can rub some people in our office wrong, but her heart is in the right place.

She steps up and makes her order, and then it's my turn. Lately, Derek and I have been ordering together when we take lunch at the same time, but he doesn't step up with me. Instead, he hangs back with the employee he's talking with. I can feel his eyes on me, so I know he sees that it's my turn.

I guess he got the message that whatever we were doing before our meeting with Erika a few days ago has now ended, and that's for the best since I need to focus on my job and my promotion. I'm not so sure office romance is a good idea anyway.

I step over to the pickup window, and both my lunch and Erika's assistant's order come up at the same time.

I glance over to find that Derek finished giving his order but went to stand with a couple of guys who work alongside him in upper management.

"I'm heading back with Erika's order," she says, offering up the two sandwiches. Likely one for her and one for Erika. "Want to walk back together, or are you staying?" She sends a quick look over at Derek. Evidently, the office must have caught on to Derek and me spending time together.

Derek doesn't look our way as we both look over at him. He's laughing at something that Paul, the other manager in his department, says.

"No, I'm not staying. I have a large project I'm working on. I'll come back with you," I say, turning to follow her out of the sandwich shop.

"Great! We can discuss my thoughts on bonus vacation pay for employees who ride their bikes to work instead of driving."

Oh joy, it's my lucky day...

Chapter Five

Briggs

I take the elevator up to the corporate office on the third floor and exit the elevator. Adel isn't at her desk, which is a bummer, but it's around lunch time so she's probably taking a well-deserved break.

The homemade butterscotch candies sit perched on her tall desk, but it doesn't taste nearly as good without Adel's sweet greeting, so I walk past without grabbing one. If she's back at her reception desk by the time I walk back out of Sam's office, I'll take one then.

Walking down the long hallway, my sneakers clapping against the espresso wood floors is the only sound I hear. I know the walls here are soundproof on purpose so that private conversations can remain private, but now I realize why Sam asked me to come in at lunchtime.

A heavy feeling tugs at my chest. Is this going to be more bad news?

I glance at the glass shadow boxes of Hawkeyes gear lining the hallways again, buying myself a few seconds longer as I walk past and head for Sam Robert's office.

I glance at a shadow box of the first Stanley Cup that was won under Phil Carlton's ownership. A photo of Bex Townsend, before he was our coach, and the team that played fifteen years ago celebrating on the ice, Champaign spray going everywhere, the players still looking drenched in sweat from a hard playoff game, Bex in the center of the photo holding up the Stanley Cup in his hands, smiling from ear to ear. Inside the shadow box, along with the picture blown up and printed in black and white for dramatics, is the puck from the winning shot that Bex made and the pair of his gloves that he wore when he won that day. The gloves look worn and beaten from the stress of a long season, the winning puck covered in silver marker from all of the players on the winning team signing it. A Hawkeyes shot glass, taken from the bar, also sits inside with one of the players knocked out front tooth from a fight that broke out on the ice during that game.

Phil Carlton likes to tell the story about how his old Zamboni driver spent hours that night, after the game, looking for that tooth, wading through thick confetti paper and red solo cups that had been left behind. He presented the recovered tooth to Phil the next morning in the shot glass he found discarded somewhere in the hallways of the stadium in the aftermath of a huge celebration of fans after the momentous win.

Phil also says that there is nothing better than having a Stanley Cup sitting in your office, but that he spends more time looking at that tooth each time he walks down to his office than he has ever spent looking at the attention-grabbing silver and nickel alloy Stanley Cup that stands at an impressive 35-plus inch tall. When I asked him why the tooth holds more importance to him, he said, *"Sometimes, in order to achieve true greatness... to reach the very pinnacle of your success, you must be willing to sacrifice something of importance. That tooth is a daily reminder for me... and it should be for you too. One day, this sport might ask something of you. It might require a broken ankle, a torn ligament, missing time with your family, or maybe something else entirely. But you're the only one that can make the call on what you're willing to give up."*

That was a few years ago now but it still sits with me, and every once in a while, I wonder when that day will come and what the hockey gods will ask of me.

I hang a right to the third door that leads to Sam's office, twisting the door handle to open it and then walking through. Directly inside is a large waiting room where his assistant, Penelope, has a large desk perched horizontally right outside of her father's office door.

"Briggs!" She beams in that sweet way that Penelope does to everyone.

Her light blue eyes, which match Sam's, sparkle at me as she spins her legs out from under her desk and toward me in her chair. Some kind of ergonomic ball thing. Like those yoga balls that my physical therapist uses to help me stretch out my back.

Her long blonde hair is in a high ponytail, and she's in dark jeans and a Hawkeyes polo.

She's a cute girl who used to be a college figure skater but dropped out of the program for some reason. She still keeps in good shape, skating every morning before we all come in for practice. Not that any of that matters. I don't shit where I eat. And Sam would probably retire any one of his players to a benchwarmer for the rest of their contract terms with the Hawkeyes if they ever made a pass at his daughter.

"Hey, Penelope. He's expecting me," I say, pointing at his closed office door and walking right past her toward it.

"Yep." She beams. "Go right on inside, and then I have a few things for you before you leave."

Things for me? Is it all my shit from my locker because he's going to rip my contract in half right in front of me and light it on fire? I doubt it... I make this franchise too much money, and we're on the cusp of a Stanley Cup win.

"Okay."

I rap on the door with the back of my knuckles lightly, just to warn him that I'm coming in. Never walk in on a man with his door closed before giving him a quick heads up, just in case... well, his *head's* up. A lesson you learn living in college dorms that sticks with you for a lifetime.

I start to twist the door handle when I hear him tell me to come in.

"Briggs," he says, standing from his seated position behind the large desk, when he sees my face appear behind the door of his office.

I glance behind him at the wall full of bookshelves filled to the brim with books, memorabilia, and photos out on display.

"Boss."

I walk up to his desk, but he doesn't sit back down, so I don't take a seat either. I don't think that bodes well for me.

"I brought you in—"

"Before you say anything..." I stop him before he can jump my shit about the way I conducted myself yesterday after they told me that not only are they going to reward fucked behavior by paying off the woman who's blackmailing me, but they are also punishing me with this fake girlfriend shit. They're forcing me to date a total stranger in order to keep my job.

Okay, maybe we're only faking it, and maybe she isn't an actual stranger. Still, he didn't know that, so I feel as though my reaction was reasonable.

However, I shouldn't have walked out on Sam or Phil. Especially since Phil pays my paychecks, and Sam could trade me in a heartbeat and rid himself of the headache of this whole blackmail debacle. Possible Stanley Cup win or not.

"I know that the Hawkeyes are trying to do what they think is best..."

"That's right, we are." He holds my eye contact, challenging me to give a but...

He knows me too well.

"But there has to be another way than making me date a woman that I haven't talked to since I was eighteen years old. She can't be thrilled about this idea either."

Not to mention that her brother's about the only friend I have left from my youth, and he won't take this well. They'd better start looking for a replacement offensive player when Isaac breaks both my kneecaps. I still have enough pride left in me that I'm not going to openly admit to my general manager, and a man I have a lot of respect for, that Autumn's brother could easily beat my ass.

"Do you have an alternative? If you have a woman that you've known for a while and could trust more than Autumn, that might be an option."

"Hell no," I blurt out.

I don't even have to think about it. The list of women I would trust to understand that the assignment would be short-term with no chance of turning permanent is a list of zero. There's not a single woman I've dated over the last few years, and I use 'dated' loosely, that hasn't tried to push for a full-blown relationship with me. And there sure as hell isn't a single one of them that I'd ever consider dating again in an attempt to clean up my image. I'd take early retirement over that mess.

"We could hire an escort or an actress."

"We'd have to pay someone to date me? That's too fucking depressing."

He sighs. "Just as well. If we did that, we would need a nondisclosure agreement and contract. All it would take is the wrong person to see the paperwork, and this story would hit the news for a whole new reason. Autumn is the best fit for the job because she won't require any of that." He shifts his weight and takes a seat back in his chair as if the decision has been made.

"Whoa, hold on," I say, taking a step closer to his desk.

But he doesn't "hold on".

"You know her. You have pictures together when you were kids which Tessa Tomlin told me is social media liquid gold." He places his elbow on his desk from his seated position and holds up his index finger. "Autumn knows the deal." He holds up a second finger. "She's not asking for additional compensation because she wants to help. Which is evidently a pro on the pro/cons list for you and your fragile ego." He lifts a third finger. "And she's the goddamn girl next door, which I am told is exactly the kind of image change you need." He throws up his hands. "There isn't a better fit."

He stops and waits for me to object, but I don't because there is nothing I can say. He backed me into a corner with only one way out.

"Autumn has everyone else's vote except yours."

"Who's everyone else?" I ask.

"The PR company, Tessa, Penelope, mine, and most importantly... the man fronting the bill for all of this, Phil Carlton," he says, reclining back in his chair. "And Phil liked her when he met her. Said 'she's a real peach' and asked Penelope to send Autumn a stadium pass to the owner's box so she can watch the games with the rest of us instead of alone in your seats."

"My seats? She's coming to the games now?"

"As your girlfriend, yes. The media needs to see her. They need to see you two together as often as possible, Ideally, looking like a real couple."

I don't care about the seats. The only people I've ever given them to are my parents or the Daughtry's. I've never had a long enough relationship to warrant giving them to a girlfriend, and I've tried giving them out to friends in the past, but the type of friends I meet these days tend to get a little entitled or drunk and mistreat other fans around them. I don't need that kind of publicity—I have a good enough time creating it for myself if you ask my boss. Not to mention that all of the players' seats are usually filled with the wives and family members of my teammates. People I have to see and deal with regularly. So, we all try to be respectful of one another and not put assholes in those seats.

"Giving her your seats shouldn't be anything compared to living with her."

"Hold the fuck on! What?" I say, stepping up and pressing my fists against his desk as I lean in with adrenaline coursing through my veins. I could not have heard him right.

"You're moving in together," he clarifies, turning away and shaking his computer mouse to wake up his hibernating computer screen as if this conversation is coming to a close and he'll be back to checking his emails soon.

I shake my head, and my eyebrows furrow with his words. I take a deep breath and try to calm my breathing as he goes on.

"Penelope found a large, fully furnished apartment available in The Commons across the street."

I know The Commons. It's the apartment building that all of the rookies and most of the players who don't live here year-round live at during the season. It's only a couple blocks from the stadium, and Penelope negotiated a good rate for our players to rent. I'm there every week during the season for poker at Lake Powers penthouse at the top of the building.

It's a nice place. It's a newer build with much larger apartment sizes than you usually find downtown, along with expensive finishes. It has a doorman, 24/7 security on duty, secure underground parking, and every apartment has a large balcony.

I lived in the building the first year as a rookie, but once I got signed on for several seasons, I bought a condo a little further away. My accountant thought it would be a good investment to own, and The Commons only lets you rent.

My mind flashes to all the mornings when I leave for practice and catch women sneaking out of The Commons with smudged makeup and an oversized shirt after a one-night stand with one of the players on the team. I shake my head, trying not to imagine Autumn in an oversized t-shirt, slipping out of my bed.

"I'm supposed to sleep with her now? I think you all are taking this a little over the damn top. This isn't method fucking acting."

Sam pushes out of his chair and slams his fists on the desk.

Now I've done it.

"Jesus Christ, Briggs, I didn't say sleep with the woman. It's a two-bedroom apartment with separate ensuites. I don't give a shit what you two do or don't do in the privacy of that apartment as long as it's consensual and isn't going to end up in the news."

I glare into Sam's eyes under the bill of that hat he always wears. "You think I did it, don't you? You think I took advantage of the stripper during a fucking lap dance," I say, fuming.

"Holy hell, Briggs. No! Of course, I don't. I picked your drunk ass up off the fucking couch that night. With how plastered you were, there's no way you would have gotten your cock to do shit that night, but I'm getting goddamn tired of chasing your ass around town, getting calls from bartenders so often asking me to come to pick you up that I just received a wedding invitation from one of them last week." He huffs, and that takes some wind out of my sails. I have been a real shit to deal with for Sam. "I've been on your damn side for the last year while you handle whatever shit crawled up your ass and died without making you talk it out with me because, on the ice, you're still as sharp as ever, so you've earned blowing off a little steam. But so help me, Briggs, if you don't get the drinking under control..."

A queasy feeling hits me at the hint of a warning.

"What? You're going to let me go?"

"Do you really want me to answer that?"

I take a step back, crossing my arms and leaning against the wall behind me.

Sam plants his hands on his hips and hangs his head as he sighs. Now his face is completely hidden behind his hat. The black hat with bright turquoise Hawkeyes letters taunts me. The only team colors I ever want to wear.

"I care about you, Briggs, just like every other player out there on my ice. And I will do anything and everything in my power to help and encourage you to be the best player on the ice and the best man you can be off it, but I'm not sure how much I can cover for you anymore. Phil is starting to hear the constant gossip, and you know he likes a 'clean' franchise. No riff-raff, no scandals, and no players showing up for morning skate with bloodshot eyes and a hangover from the night before."

"I know," I say, remembering that I do owe this team a lot.

This was my home team as a kid. The place my father used to bring me when I was little to watch men like Sam Roberts and Bex Townsend, play the greatest sport on earth. This stadium is where I fell in love with hockey and told my dad at the young age of four years old that I would be a pro hockey player one day.

Then eighteen years later, Phil signed me as a rookie, and I've gotten to play my entire career in my home state with my home team. It just doesn't get better than that as a pro athlete. I like to think that this will be the team and the stadium where I'll retire. My number being retired by the organization, and my jersey hung up in the stadium right next to Bex Townsend's, a Hawkeyes alumnus and now our coach.

But if Dixie leaks this false information, and the public decides to believe her, then my dreams will be ripped from me, and the franchise will have no choice but to drop me in hopes that they can still save themselves by cutting association with me. No other team will want to touch me, and I'll be forced into early retirement.

I pinch the bridge of my nose and sigh. "Fine."

"So, you'll do it with a smile on your face and do everything that the PR team and Tessa tell you to do. No drinking until this thing is over, and no seeing other women. No more scandals, Briggs."

Jesus, what in the hell am I signing up for?

"Yes, sir."

"And you'll treat Autumn with the respect she deserves since she's saving all of our asses and giving up her life for months to pretend to be your girlfriend."

Seems like she's giving up more than her fair share, but why...? What's in it for her?

Does she pity me?

Does she feel obliged since our parents are close and I'm her brother's best friend?

Or... fuck. Does she believe Dixie and thinks that our fake relationship is the only way to protect me?

"I will, sir," I say.

"All right. Get out of here," he says, giving a flick of his wrist. "And stop off at Penelope's desk. She has those apartment keys for you."

"Yes, sir," I groan, turning and walking out of his office.

Penelope stops typing as she sees me walk out of her dad's office. I close his door behind me and then turn to my left and walk over to her desk.

"He lives," Penelope jokes.

"Barely," I mumble.

"Here you go." She hands me a large envelope.

I look inside to find a packet of information that looks to be the instructions for entering the building, contact information for the on-sight maintenance dept., things like that, and a lanyard to scan in for the private gated underground parking lot and a key to the apartment.

"Where's Autumn's key?"

Penelope smiles and looks over at the envelope sitting at the end of her desk in an "Outbound Mail" basket and gives it a little pat.

"The courier service should be here anytime to pick it up and take it to her office today."

"Oh."

Why did I care that Penelope was having it delivered to Autumn instead of me making arrangements to meet up with Autumn to get her things? I have no idea. But it was a fleeting thought, and now my concern moved on to how in the hell Autumn and I are going to pull this off when we don't know the adult versions of each other. And damn, did I ever really know the kid version of her anyway? It's been so long since we were all kids running around the neighborhood, and although I don't remember everything, I'm sure I wasn't all that accommodating to her. Not like she's being to me.

My number one concern, though, is still the same. When will Isaac show up to beat my face in, how bad will he beat it in, and will our friendship survive this?

CHAPTER SIX

Autumn

My nerves are on edge as I park my car and climb out of the vehicle. This is the restaurant where my PR team and the Hawkeyes management agreed we would stage Briggs and me getting lunch as a couple.

Erika has already tipped off a couple of media outlets about Briggs Conley having a secret girlfriend that he's been hiding away. There is no doubt that they'll want the exclusive photos.

The photos aren't what has my stomach in knots, though. It's not even the fact that I'm on a date, or rather, a fake date, with Briggs Conley. It's that after Sam Roberts announced me as Briggs's new fake girlfriend, Briggs stormed out of the office, Sam right on his heels.

I have no idea how the conversation went after that. The last thing I heard was that Penelope called Erika yesterday and told her that Briggs is 'coming around' to the idea and that Phil wants us to go full steam ahead. Then I received a package from our courier yesterday with my new apartment keys. Erika suggested that we go public immediately. Or, I guess, public in the social media sense, once the paparazzi taking these photos go viral with them.

A text comes through as I start walking toward the packed restaurant. Erika picked the restaurant for the number of eyes we would have on us.

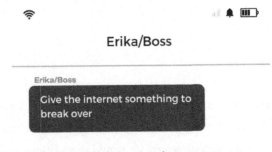

Erika/Boss

Erika/Boss

Give the internet something to break over

Thanks for the added pressure, boss.

I'll do my best.

Erika/Boss

You'll be great.

Erika/Boss

Call me after you get to the new
apartment. Let me know how it all
goes. This is crucial to get right so take
a week or two off to get adjusted with
Briggs. This HAS to work if we want to
nail The Hawkeyes account.

Erika/Boss

And your promotion.

Perfect, keep stacking the pressure on. That should serve as
useful. Not.

I take a deep, cleansing inhale, but the second I round the
corner, I see Briggs standing by the front entrance in a pair of
jeans and a jacket, with a bouquet of flowers hanging lazily by his
side. If I wasn't over-analyzing things, I wouldn't be wondering
if he's using his large glutes to hide the bouquet from the view
of passersby.

Briggs finally sees me walking toward him, and his lip upticks
just a smidge. I've seen Briggs's true smile, and that is definitely
not even close. The barely-there smile he has on now is forced
and guarded. It's for show. For the fans already waving hello to
him as they pass in and out of the restaurant, it's for show for
the media photographers that could be hiding out in any bush,

but the one that kills me is the fake smile he's sporting is also for me.

I dial back my disappointment. He has a right not to be happy about this arrangement. His boss is forcing him to fake date a woman he has no interest in for a few months, and his GM has him swearing sobriety during this time as well. Not to mention, Briggs is the one who faces the consequences once my brother finds out about this. Now that Isaac is a titled MMA fighter after getting injured on the ice and his dream of the NHL faded, my brother isn't the man you want punching your face.

He still has an unhealthy amount of pent-up anger about losing his dreams of a hockey career.

I laid up all night wondering if I should call Isaac and warn him about what he might find on his social media reels later today. But I swore secrecy to my boss and our client. I can't break that trust. Although, I'm not sure coming clean to my brother would spare Briggs's already slightly crooked nose. After a decade of playing ice hockey, you can't expect any of your facial bones to retire in the same position they were when you started playing the game. Briggs is no stranger to broken bones or cracked eye sockets. He lives for the fight on the ice. Shoot, he starts them half the time.

Still, I hope a broken nose is the worst of it because Isaac can be overly protective of the people he cares about. Especially when it comes to me. Our saving grace will be if he's busy training for his title weight fight coming up. He usually ghosts everyone and sleeps at the gym for weeks, cutting out all the noise to prepare.

I look to my left and see a red jeep parked across the street with the driver still inside. They have a camera up to their face, and they're already snapping photos of Briggs standing in front of the restaurant with flowers. It's showtime.

I remember Erika's text, and I know I have to do something...

"Break the internet..."

I still have so many questions about Briggs. Like, why does he think talking to Dixie could fix things? Why does he act as though what she's doing is out of character, like he knows her? Why did it seem like he paid for a lap dance he didn't intend to use?

As of right now, I don't have time to ask him these questions, and they're irrelevant to my ultimate goal. If I want this promotion, I have to make a splash and make the Hawkeyes overwhelmingly happy with the product of this scheme.

"Briggs!" I yell.

His eyes widen as he sees me running down the sidewalk toward him. When he realizes that I do not intend on stopping, he takes a step back with his left leg and braces for impact. I jump into his arms, happy to be in a pair of jeans and a jacket. I considered dressing in something a little fancier for this 'accidental' photo shoot, but then Seattle started spitting rain, and I changed before I left my apartment.

I wrap my legs around his waist and lay a demanding kiss against his warm mouth, pulling his face closer as I wrap my arms around his neck, my chest pressing against his. This is completely out of character for me, and I'd never do this—jump into the arms of a guy I'm seeing and kiss him in front of snapping cameras, but Erika wants a splash... and I want a corner office.

Briggs takes another step back. Not because I overtook this bear size of a man but because I took him off guard. I begin to slip a little, but he catches me, wrapping his free hand under my bum, while the other hand holding onto the flowers I'm assuming he bought me, pulls me tighter against him to stabilize me so that I don't fall.

A man with his kind of power doesn't need both arms to hold me up, and the thought of his corded muscles sends a little shiver down my spine. Or maybe that was just from the cold, wet Washington weather.

He doesn't pull his mouth off mine like I half expect him to, and I need to make sure this stunt works so that they get the photos they need. I throw caution to the wind, hoping Briggs doesn't drop me, and I go in for a second time, and this time, he applies pressure against my lips as well.

I can't ignore how soft his lips are, how plush and supple they feel against mine. I can taste a hint of sour green apple against his mouth as if he had just been sucking on a Jolly Rancher or chewing gum, and he smells like the same subtle cologne he wore in high school.

I can't even believe that I still remember his smell after all these years.

After a few heartbeats, it seems that the paparazzi should have gotten their photo, and I pull back even though I'm curious where this is going, and when I do, I get a one-second glimpse of Briggs with his eyes closed.

He closed his eyes to kiss me?

Does he do that with every girl he kisses?

I only get a split second to admire him like this before he opens his eyes.

His long lashes lay against his tan skin and the little speckles of those freckles I've always loved. His lips are now redder than they were before the pressure of our kiss. The knowledge that his lips are red because of me lets loose a thousand butterflies low in my belly.

When his eyes open, he looks up at me with an inquisitive brow and then sets me down.

"What the hell was that?" he asks with a lopsided grin, his thumb brushing over his lower lip.

"We have to get the people talking if we want this to work," I tell him in a hushed tone, pulling down on my jacket to cover up the sliver of skin that was exposed to the cold elements when I was wrapped around Briggs's waist. Yep, the shiver must have been from the cold, definitely not from Briggs.

"I think you nailed it then." He smirks.

I try my hardest not to blush at his compliment... or at least I think it was a compliment. Maybe he was just teasing me?

I want to ask if he enjoyed the kiss, even a little bit but, of course, I won't.

Then he offers up the flowers in his hand. "These are for you."

They are for me!

They're beautiful, and the bouquet is definitely the biggest one anyone's ever given me, with pink and red roses with white flowers mixed in.

The little girl in me, with a huge crush on him, gets giddy from the thoughtful gesture. But I'd bet money that Penelope told him not to show up without flowers. We need to make this look like a date. We need to look like this relationship is real and serious.

"Hungry?" I ask.

"I just got done with training this morning... I'm starving."

"Good. Let's go," I tell him, taking his huge hand in mine and then spinning around and heading for the door.

It's rather comical how much smaller my hand is in his. It's almost like his hand ate my hand for a snack.

I glance down quickly to see our joined hands, and I can't believe how brave and forward I am with him. I'd never dare grab Briggs's hand if we were in any other situation, but a promotion and the pressure on my shoulders to land this account has me doing things I'd never considered before.

At first, his hand doesn't want to meld together with mine, shaking the little confidence I have in trying to be the dominant one in our twosome to make sure the paparazzi get their photos, but within seconds he grips tighter, and his long legs pass me quickly. Now he's the one leading me inside, and I laugh to myself at the competitive alpha male who has to always be in the lead.

Taking the lead may not normally be in my comfort zone, but I'm not the little five-year-old in pigtails that used to follow him around begging for table scraps of his and Isaac's attention. Begging my mom to help me bake chocolate oatmeal cookies (Briggs's favorite) to bribe them for a chance to play in the tree house with them. I'm the PR superstar that's about to save his dumb ass from career ruin, and in three months, I'll have a promotion to prove it. Then he can go back to chasing women and passing out on random strip club couches.

Yuck... that couch. It still haunts my dreams. Maybe during our short fake love stint, I can convince him to get a tetanus shot.

Maybe if I'm going to be in this close proximity, I should get one too.

His and hers tetanus shots. I wonder if Tessa Tomlin would think that was a great photo opportunity for the Hawkeyes' social account. Cute.

...Not.

Star player Briggs Conley snapped with mystery woman at Seattle Hotspot

...

100k views

View all 1205 comments

1 DAYS AGO

Use QR code to see it in color!

CHAPTER SEVEN

Briggs

What the hell just happened out there?

I'm not sure which one surprised me more, the kiss or Autumn jumping on me and wrapping her toned legs around my waist.

I can't deny that the man downstairs perked up to her nearness. But where did the shy and slightly timid Autumn Daughtry of my childhood go?

I guess I shouldn't be shocked. I get constantly berated every time Autumn shows up at her folk's house to watch a game. My mom calls to tell me how well Autumn's grown up. What a delight and a well-accomplished daughter who sees her parents regularly. Unlike her son, who she sees more in the tabloids than in her call history. I tune my mom out most of the time.

Despite the updates, I wasn't expecting Autumn to be... this confident... this gorgeous.

Even with all of that and the fact that we spent most of our childhood together, I know that agreeing to this is a mistake. There's no way this won't blow up in my face, specifically a fist to the face, care of Isaac Daughtry, but I don't see another option. This is what my team demands from me.

"Will this table work?" the hostess offers, gesturing to a small table in the back corner of the restaurant.

"This is great. Thank you," Autumn says, and the hostess hands us our menus.

I move around Autumn to pull out her chair because, well, I might be an asshole, but I was raised with a few manners that stuck, and since Autumn's parents are still good friends with my parents, I don't need it getting back to my mom that I don't hold open doors and pull out chairs. Especially when Autumn Daughtry's perfectly-shaped ass that was just perched in my hands a minute ago is the one that's going to be sitting in the chair.

Autumn turns her head toward me and gives me a slightly surprised grin as she takes a seat, setting her purse on the ground and under the table. Then she sets the large bouquet of flowers and her cell phone on top of the crisp white tablecloth.

The bouquet takes up half the table, but I don't mind. I'm sort of happy she doesn't just stick it underneath us with her purse.

"Thanks," I tell the hostess as she hands me mine, and then she turns to leave.

Her small black cell phone sits almost between us, and I sort of wish she'd eliminate the distraction. I hate when women check their phones during a date, so I leave mine in my front right pocket. Although, this isn't really a date... right?

She must notice my eyes on her cell. "Does it bother you? It's on vibrate. I just don't want to miss it if it's Erika, my boss, or if Tessa texts or calls with updates."

I guess that's understandable.

"No, it's all right," I tell her, although I'm not sure if I want to be in a public place when the internet blows up.

Mostly everyone in the restaurant can see us at this table, but because of the corner spot, it's less likely our voices will travel as much as in other spots in the restaurant. It's the most privacy we're going to get here. Even though I know that Autumn's PR company and Tessa picked this location for the very public display.

Autumn seems to be taking the task of cleaning up my public opinion seriously. Jumping into my arms and kissing me like we are star-crossed lovers who have been apart for months... maybe years. It took me by surprise, and there isn't much that shocks me these days.

What surprised me even more?

I kissed her back.

It's all for show, I keep reminding myself.

But was it?

The kiss was fine, her lips were soft enough, and it wasn't as if I couldn't hold her mid-five-foot stature compared to my six-foot-four. None of that is why I kissed her back.

Something in that kiss felt like a world I had forgotten about. A time when my life was simpler. When no one expected me to be the life at the party, when women weren't trying to blackmail me for shit I didn't do, and when an entire team wasn't looking at me to bring them to Stanley Cup victory.

Autumn feels like home. That's all it was.

That kiss transported me back to a time when the only plans I had for the day were hopping the back fence of my parents' house with Isaac and spending the day in my neighbors' cow field, catching frogs in the big pond, and then finding ways to freak Autumn out by stuffing the toads in her backpack or tea set and then hoping she didn't tattle on Isaac and get him grounded for a week.

"I thought we could use this time to discuss schedules and discuss the process of us moving in together."

"Is living together really necessary?" I ask, testing to see if this is her idea or someone else's.

Autumn glances around to see if anyone is listening in on our conversation... of course, they're trying, but the closest table is several arm's lengths away. I can see the flashes from cameras snapping photos left and right in my peripheral. She uses her menu to slightly cover her mouth while she speaks. "We're trying to sell an image here. A reformed party boy settles down with a hometown girl. the Hawkeyes rented us an apartment to make us seem serious. Tessa said that The Commons gets paparazzi during game days since so many players live there. She's hoping we get photographed coming and going like a regular couple. It's only for the duration of the project."

"Project?" I scoff, snatching the black cloth napkin from the white tablecloth and putting it up to my mouth to hide my words. "My life is now considered a project?"

"Some people are calling it Operation De-sleaze Conley," she says, attempting to hide her smirk behind the menu, but I caught it. Is she enjoying this?

"Some people?" I ask, likely looking at the 'some people' right now.

"Not me!" Autumn says, putting her hand against her chest, faking insult that I'd accuse her of it. "Not this loving and loyal girlfriend of eight whole mind-blowing weeks of bliss."

"Eight weeks? Why the short timeline if we're faking it, anyway? Wouldn't a longer-term relationship look better?"

"Yes, it would, but if this fake story about you getting a 'special' lap dance gets out"—she says, looking around again to make sure no one can hear her—"and we're out here pushing the narrative that you're a loyal boyfriend, but pictures are surfacing of a stripper giving you a lap dance at a club... it might make a bad situation worse if people start thinking of you as a cheater too," she explains in hushed tones with the menu still blocking her mouth. "Better to say you've reformed since going home to reflect and running into the girl next door and falling madly in love with her." She flutters her eyelashes at me. I know she's doing it as a joke, but my chest tightens anyway.

"Technically, you are the girl next door." I discard the cloth napkin and lean forward.

"Exactly! That's why my firm picked me." She opens up her menu and glances down at the options. "I came up with the idea to get you a girlfriend to brighten up your image, and I was going to suggest an actress or maybe someone inside of the Hawkeyes franchise that would commit to a month or two, but then my boss found out that I'm actually the girl next door and now I'm stuck with you," she says with a slight groan in her voice.

"Stuck with me?!" I ask with a cocked brow, forcing my lips not to tilt up like they want to.

"You know what I mean." She rolls her eyes like she used to when we were kids.

"So, you're the one I have to thank for the fake girlfriend idea?"

She looks up from her menu, her eyes wide at my question, and her mouth drops open just a little like she just got caught.

"Yes, but I can assure you... it's going to work."

"And you offered yourself up as the sacrificial lamb to fake date me?"

She looks back down at her menu, almost seeming as though she'd rather ignore me but answers anyway.

"God, no. That was Derek's idea."

"Is Derek the guy who was sitting next to you during the meeting in the Hawkeyes' conference room?"

"Yeah, how did you know?" She asks, her eyes flashing back up at me.

So the asshole has a name.

Derek.

I shake off her question. A dude fucking knows when another man already wants to kill him for taking his girl. Not that I'm taking her in the typical sense.

So then, if Derek came up with the idea and she didn't have some ulterior motive to date me, what's in it for her?

"That seems like a lot of pressure for your firm to ask you to do that. Put your life on hold to fake date a client."

"And my brother's best friend," she quickly adds.

Shit... yeah.

I rub the back of my neck, thinking about the impending reunion between her brother and me once he finds out about this. "That's true. I'm waiting to get sucker-punched while walking around a corner. Isaac's going to be waiting in some dark alley to pummel me into the ground when this comes out."

"It's going to be fine. We'll think of something, and we should probably break this news to him before he finds out from someone else."

I nod in agreement, but that's going to be tough since we're not allowed to tell a single soul outside of the franchise, although I have no intentions of telling a single one of my teammates. This is humiliating as it is to have a franchise-appointed girlfriend help me clean up my reputation. I'll keep this mess to myself for as long as I can with this group of gossips.

The waitress stops by to take our order, asking Autumn for her order first.

"I'll take the mac 'n' cheese cheeseburger, please."

Her order takes me by surprise.

I'm used to women ordering a light meal while out on a date with me due to anticipation for the main event to follow after, going back to their place because I never invite them to mine.

But unlike most of the women I take on a date, Autumn bringing up that I'm her brother's best friend suggests she already knows that I'm not planning on taking her home tonight.

"That's our best-seller," the older female waitress says, dressed in a black button-up and black slacks, like all of the other staff. "And what side, dear? Salad, soup, french fries, or a fruit cup?" she asks Autumn.

"Do you have curly fries?" Autumn asks.

Really, curly fries too? Not that I'm food shaming, she can eat whatever she wants, I just figured she would bend a little and order a salad. But I'm glad she doesn't because I have every intention of sniping a french fry or two as long as Autumn isn't going to rat me out to the team's dietitian next time she's in the office.

"Sure do." The waitress's graying ponytail nods along with her in agreement with Autumn's order.

The waitress approves.

"And for you, sir?" She turns to me, clicking the end of her pen on her notepad as she waits for my order.

Probably an anxious tick she does subconsciously when she wants someone to get on with their order so she can rush back to the kitchen and put in the order while rushing out to other impatiently waiting customers.

Not that they warrant being impatient. So far the staff seems to be working quickly. They seated us lightning fast, and the waitress came for our order quickly, but people these days feel they are owed instant gratification, and that's just unrealistic to attain.

I worked for the college cafeteria in between classes and practice every year for four years to pay for summer hockey camps with big league trainers, so I know a thing or two about impatient jerks. College kids are the worst. But the experience was worth it and made the difference in getting a rookie spot with a pro league team right out of college.

I sacrificed and put in the work. Is that the kind of sacrifice Phil Carlton meant to reach the highest success?

"I'll take the smoked salmon with pasta. Can you add extra protein to that?" I ask.

The waitress nods and jots down the note and then takes the menu I have outstretched for her.

"And can you bring more sourdough bread when you get a chance?"

I need to carb load to give me the energy for the drills Coach Bex is putting us through this week.

She nods again and takes Autumn's menu before turning to leave.

The waitress takes our menus and hightails them out of there in hot pursuit of an order that is probably ready to be delivered.

I turn back to Autumn, crossing my arms over each other and resting them on the table, leaning in to keep our conversation a little more private.

Is it weird I want her attention all to myself?

"Okay, so besides the fact that we have history, and since I doubt you're doing this just to save your brother's best friend's ass, what's in this for you?"

"Like...?" she asks, playing dumb.

Fine, I'll play along.

"Like, are they paying you a bonus for this shit?"

She looks down at the table and sucks in her lower lip while her hand reaches up to her ear to fiddle with her diamond stud earring. It's funny how no matter how many years go by, Autumn's nervous ticks come back to me. I can't stop looking at her plump lower lip slowly slipping out behind her teeth. The contrast between her pink lips and her bright white teeth is hard to ignore. My mom was right. She certainly has grown up since we were kids.

"It comes with a promotion," she admits.

Is that a look of guilt I catch across her face? It changes so quickly that I'm not sure.

The nervous tick was because she didn't want to tell me that she's using me for a promotion. She shouldn't feel guilty about it. In the world of pro sports, I'm used to being used... and I've done my fair share of using too. Plus, it makes me feel better to know that she is getting something out of this shitty situation.

"Really? What kind of promotion?" I ask, intrigued and also feeling stupid to think Autumn still only plays with Barbies and fills her teacups with the hose water from the spigot out in the backyard.

She's now a woman with a grown-up job, edging for a grown-up promotion. I guess a lot has changed because up until this moment, Autumn has remained in my memory as a seven-year-old with her missing two front teeth and a scowl.

"If I nail this project, I'll get promoted to head of client relations, and I'll get my own team to work on my own projects."

"Oh shit." I nod, surprised at how far she is in her profession. "So after you nail me, you get a promotion." I smirk.

She laughs and then rolls her eyes. I laugh, too, because that was damn perfect, and I forgot how much fun it is to tease her.

"No, smart ass, I have no plans to *nail* you. They won't pay me extra for that." She snickers.

I break eye contact and glance over at the bouquet on the table and then eye one of the perfect white roses nestled among the rest. I slide my thumb and pointer finger between one of its rose petals, rolling its softness delicately against my fingertips.

This is what I imagine Autumn's skin feels like.

"Damn... too bad," I tease, sending her a devilish grin because I can't help it.

She pretends to ignore what I said, but she heard it.

Her phone lights up on the table, but she has it on silent, so the only alert is the screen illuminating. I don't mean to, but I look to see who it is. After all, it could have been Erika or Tessa.

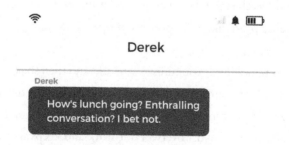

Derek

Derek

How's lunch going? Enthralling conversation? I bet not.

She quickly hits the hibernation button on the side of her cell to hide the evidence, but it's too late.

I pegged him as an ass the first second I saw him in the Hawkeyes conference room, and I was spot on.

She seems a little embarrassed and clears her throat.

"Besides, I'm sort of seeing someone."

Wait... hold up. Aren't we supposed to be exclusively fake dating?

"You're seeing someone? And they're okay with you dating me?" I don't like that my stomach flips with uncertainty at how her announcement hits me. I mean, I didn't figure we'd fuck, considering I value my life, and Isaac will end me, no questions asked if he knows I'm sleeping with his sister.

"It's not serious. We've only been on a few dates. And yes, he's fine with it. He's actually..."

"He's what?"

"My boss, so he understands what I'm doing and why I'm doing it. Plus, he's the one who offered me up. We put everything on hold while you and I are... doing whatever we're doing," she says with air quotes.

I look at her with confusion. "I thought Erika was your boss."

"She's the owner."

"And Derek is the dick who looked at me in the Hawkeyes conference room like I ran over his puppy," I say, piecing it all together.

"He was looking at you funny?" She asks and then shakes her head, deciding against the question. "Yeah, that's Derek, my boss. But he's not in charge of who gets what projects or if we get promotions. He just oversees our work and keeps us from missing deadlines. Erika is the one that makes the big decisions. And even so, there isn't anything in the employee handbook that disallows office romance."

She's been considering a relationship with him.

I instantly don't like this.

"He's not going to have a problem with us living together?"

Anything she says besides, *"Yes, he's very uncomfortable about it and is making me wear a chastity belt,"* is a downright lie.

"We never talked about exclusivity before this, and we haven't..."

"You haven't what...?"

She breaks eye contact with me and looks toward the kitchen. Lucky for her, our waitress is headed our way with our food.

I lean closer across the table, her eyes locking on mine, and I see the unconscious way she bites down on her lip when I do. Then I whisper, "You haven't slept with him yet, have you?"

Her eyes widen, and she shushes me, glancing around the dining room again to see if anyone is watching us... they are but not as many as before. I find that people want to be entertained. If you have nothing to entertain them with, they'll move on. Her eyebrows furrow, but she can't tell me to mind my own business like I know she wants to because our waitress is now standing in front of us with our food.

I smirk to myself. This guy has no claim on her whatsoever, not that I plan to do anything with Autumn anyway, but since we're going to be living together, it's nice to know that she's free and clear.

Her trying to tell me that she's seeing someone is a load of shit. She *was* seeing someone, went on a handful of dates, didn't fuck him, and now the dumb fuck let her go off and date a pro hockey player. A hockey player that is also not allowed to sleep with anyone else until this situation all plays out.

I take back everything I said before...

Two horny adults in a two-bedroom apartment who can't see anyone but each other.

Isaac might as well clobber me now.

I'm a dead man walking.

CHAPTER EIGHT

Autumn

After an 'internet breaking' first public outing yesterday at lunch, Briggs and I are social media official.

God, that feels weird, but it is also a big win and one step closer to my idea being a success. Tessa Tomlin already called me this morning, and we had a long conversation, going over everything she's seeing in the comments and responses from the public. She said that upper management is thrilled with the overall positive reaction from the general public and the Hawkeyes fans. Most people love that Briggs seems to be settling down with the hometown girl.

With the Hawkeyes having a home game tonight, Briggs and I put off the move into the apartment until tomorrow. It still feels so bizarre to be moving into an apartment with him.

Now with a VIP pass that Penelope had a courier drop off early today in hand for the owner's box, I walk through the doors of the stadium and look for the elevator to the private boxes. I've been to more games in this building than I can count. My parents have been bringing Isaac and me here since we were kids, but this is the first time I've been here as a girlfriend of a player.

Wow, girlfriend feels weird to say in relation to Briggs Conley.

Security vets me before they let me in, and as soon as I walk through the doors of the owner's box, I forget that I'm not going to be sitting with a bunch of boisterous fans, lost in the crowd. Nope, I'm upstairs with a room full of people that know Briggs and have no idea who the hell I am.

As I walk through the door of the large owner's box, my senses are almost overloaded with so much to see.

From the team colors represented on every wall and all of the furniture, to the massive food buffet against the right wall that could probably feed the entire stadium of visitors, everything is well-designed and thought out. In the middle of the room, several large turquoise and black couches are set up in different configurations for different groupings of people to sit, eat and visit.

To my left is a massive dark mahogany bar that matches the wood floors with an illuminated frosty light blue bar top. It almost looks like ice from this distance. Jerseys from every player are hung up in different places on the walls around the suite.

A bartender stands behind it mixing up drinks for the maybe thirty people in this room, but I bet this room could hold two hundred comfortably. What catches my eye is the floor-to-ceiling glass windows directly across from the entrance to the owner's box that allow anyone in this huge suite to see the entire stadium from the third floor. Excitement rages at the half-a-dozen bar-style tables with four bar stools set up at each, lining the glass for viewers to sit and eat while watching the game.

I've just found my favorite place in the stadium, and now I'm anxious to claim a bar stool before they all get snatched up for the game.□

In my peripheral, I see Penelope head for me, her long blonde ponytail swishing side to side in her pursuit of me. I've spoken to her the most during this process. She also sent me a massive bouquet of flowers as a thank-you for doing 'extra credit' and agreeing to be Briggs's girlfriend so we could keep the whole thing in-house. The name on the card read: From the Hawkeyes.

I'm sure the team credit card paid for it, but I know it was her idea.

"Autumn!" Penelope beams when she finally reaches me and links her arm through mine as we meet in the middle of the room. A bunch of other eyes are on me too. Some that know me, like Phil Carlton, the owner, who sends me a nod, Sam Roberts, the GM, who smiles warmly, and Tessa Tomlin, the in-house PR guru they hired last year to keep an eye on the guys' social media to make sure they're keeping it all franchise friendly. She's grabbing food from the craft table but sees me and heads our way.

Phew! I'm glad to already have allies in this group. Not that I've ever heard of the Hawkeyes being a difficult group to get along with, and since starting to work with them, they've all been accommodating.

"How was getting in here? Did anyone give you problems?" Penelope asks.

"Nope. I sailed right in. No issues." I shake my head.

"Good," Tessa says, snacking down on something that looks like a pear and brie tart as she walks up. The food looks high-end and delicious. "I bet Security was looking to the skies for flying pigs when you said you are Briggs Conley's girlfriend."

Penelope snickers. "Same thing would have happened if your brother had a woman stopping in claiming to be his monoga-mous girlfriend."

I look over to Tessa. "Who's your brother?" I ask, trying to think through people in corporate that I've met.

Maybe he works in Legal?

Penelope jumps in with the answer first. "Brent Tomlin."

Oh yeah! I obviously know who Brent Tomlin is. He plays for the Hawkeyes as their left defenseman.

"You're right though, long-term relationships aren't on the horizon for my brother." Tessa nods. "Or Powers... or Wrenley... or Altman," Tessa says, listing off more players on the team.

"No," Penelope interjects, "not Altman. He has a sweet little girl. He needs to find a nice woman to marry."

"Yeah... you're right," Tessa says with a sigh.

"Is she here?" I ask. "Altman's daughter?"

"She's standing over at the glass," Penelope says, pointing toward the wall of windows.

I remember now hearing in the news how Altman's daughter was the product of a short fling he had years ago, but the mother never told Altman she existed, until the accident.

I feel bad about how much the news hounded him at the beginning of this year about the whole ordeal.

I quickly scan the room, looking to spot the tiny little Kaenan Altman mini-me.

And sure enough, tucked in the right corner of the room is a sweet little two-year-old girl with the same curling brown hair, wrapped in the arms of a woman around my age, with her tiny little toddler hands plastered on the glass, screaming at the crowd below.

"Who's that?" I ask and nod over to the woman holding baby Altman.

"Oh, that's Isla. She's Berkeley's nanny. She's really nice but a little shy."

"Ah, that makes sense."

"This is her first game. Altman said he's been begging her to bring Berkeley to the games since she started a couple of months ago, but this is the first time I've seen her," Penelope says.

I nod, knowing exactly how she must feel right now.

"I'm going to grab something to eat," Penelope says.

"And I need a drink before the game starts," Tessa adds.

"Meet you girls over there?" I say, pointing to the four bar stools and the table over in the left corner with no one occupying it.

They both agree, and I take a wander over to the glass within a few feet of Berkeley and the nanny.

Right before I make it to the glass, I feel my phone buzz in my pocket. A text from Derek.

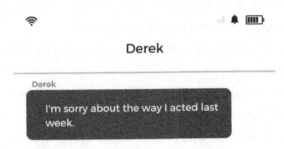

I send a quick response. We work together and I don't want things to get weird between us.

It's mature of him to apologize.

Hmm, some apology this is turning out to be...

I'm not completely sure why I'm reassuring him. It's not as if we're dating right now. And the fact that he told me to pick him over my career has me questioning if I'd consider going out with him after everything with Briggs blows over.

> **Derek**
> You're not the kind of woman a man forgets about so easily.

Aww, that was sweet. Maybe I was too hard on him.

Before I can type back, he sends another text.

> **Derek**
> I mean it's obvious by the way he ate your face in that picture that the paparazzi took of you two outside of the restaurant that he hasn't forgotten about you in the least.

Dang it...and you were so close Derek, so close.

> I'm at the game. I need to focus. I'll see you at work in a couple of weeks after I'm settled into the new apartment.

I tuck my phone in the back pocket of my jeans and turn to my right, where the nanny and the cute little girl are standing.

"Hi," I say, smiling over at the little girl who's being held up by the nanny with her nose almost smashed up against the glass. "She's cute."

"Oh, uh, thanks, she's not mine," the nanny says, glancing at me and then back to Berkeley.

I nod to let her know that I already know.

"Are you a hockey fan?" I ask.

"I've never watched it before. And this is my first time in a hockey stadium."

"Well then, come sit with us," I tell her, nodding toward my new friends who just made it to the table and are looking over at us, waving us over to join them.

"Okay... thank you."

She pulls Berkeley off the glass, and I swear I hear the little girl snarl as the other team takes to the ice.

Yep, that little girl is a future hockey fan in the making.

She and I climb onto the last two bar stools surrounding the small bar-height dark wood table with the Hawkeyes logo laminated under a thick coating of epoxy.

"You've met Penelope and Tessa already?" I ask Isla.

They all nod.

"Great. Well, we will be your guide to all things hockey tonight," I offer.

"Thank you." Isla beams at me and then looks over at Penelope and Tessa's plates. "I can't believe what amazing food they have here. Kaenan said that there would be food, but he didn't say it would be catered." She practically salivates. "I thought it would be dry hot dogs and stale pretzels."

"Absolutely not. The Carltons are the best hosts. Once, one of the players' wives said how much she loves kombucha, and Mrs. Carlton now has a different flavor on tap every home game, and Mrs. Carlton doesn't even come to the games. Today, it's lavender strawberry," Penelope says as she swishes her kombucha in her cup and takes a sip, and then hums her approval.

I see Isla's eyes flash toward the craft table. "Are you hungry, Berkeley?" The little girl nods. "I'll be right back after I get her a plate."

After Isla and Berkeley head for the buffet, Penelope and Tessa turn to me.

"Okay, this might be our only chance to ask." Tessa looks over at Penelope as if they rehearsed that they were going to jump me with questions as soon as I got here. I can see it in their eyes. "How's it going? Is Briggs being a total tool?"

"Yeah, tell us everything. My dad is the GM. I can make his ass do ice burpees for a week." Penelope leans in with an aggressive whisper as though she might enjoy wielding power to cause a player some pain. It's the first time I'm not seeing the sweet, sunny side of Penelope.

But her facial expression has me laughing. She can't do mean. Her face just refuses to look mad or something. Instead, she looks slightly deranged but mostly still smiley.

"Nothing really to report yet. He was a gentleman at lunch and did everything right. Move-in day is tomorrow, so we'll see how that goes," I say, shrugging a single shoulder. "But the minute he screws up, I know where to turn." I wink at Penelope.

"Game's about to start," Sam announces to everyone in the owner's box.

The thirty or so people find a bar stool next to the glass or stand nearby.

The puck hits the ground, and even though we're on the third level, you can see absolutely everything as the ice rink's illuminating blue ice highlights each player. They take off at lightning speed, skating from one side to the other. Defending and shooting. Ref calls and penalty box time. I can't keep my eyes off the game as Penelope, Tessa, and I take Isla under our wing, teaching her everything she needs to know. But through the entire game, there's not a single second when I can't account for Briggs's whereabouts. My eyes are trained on him, constantly looking for his turquoise blue jersey, the same color as his eyes, Conley #48.

There's one moment in the game when he scores a point, and he looks up at the owner's box. Maybe he was looking for Sam's approval or the thumbs-up that Phil lifts high for Briggs to see, but I swear our eyes meet as I'm off my bar stool jumping up and down in celebration of his goal, and my heart warms.

The game ends, and the Hawkeyes narrowly win by one point. It was a tough game against a tough team.

"Let him finish his interview, and then we'll want you to walk out with him so the media can see you leave together," Tessa coaches me while she scrolls through the teams' social media accounts to see what the fans are posting right after the game.

"Got it."

CHAPTER NINE

Briggs

"Conley! Conley! Over here!"

I hear yelling and flashes as I sit in the media room, up on the podium by myself. Sam is off to my right and out of the shot as he makes sure that the media colors inside the lines and stays away from subjects that are outlined by the franchise that the media can't ask.

The other guys wait in the hallway for their required media time. I wait for the barrage of questions I know are coming my way. Hands are lifted, hoping I'll pick them to ask the same question they ask every game.

I pick one of the media outlets I see every week sitting right in front of me. He smirks, happy to be the first.

"Conley, this was a tough game for your team this week. With such a close game, how did you feel about the way your team performed?" Although I typically hate these questions, I could kiss the man for not asking what I know most of these assholes want to ask: who the hell was the woman you were kissing earlier this week in front of the restaurant?

"We knew coming into this game that we were playing against a great team, and they played like a great team. We expected this game to be a challenge to pull out the win, and that's what it was—a challenge."

It's funny how easy it's become after all these years of doing after-game interviews to say something... but not say anything at all.

"Conley! Conley...!" The media room erupts again.

I point to someone further back. He looks like a no-nonsense kind of guy.

"Conley, you were spotted yesterday with a mystery woman." Damn it, I read that guy wrong. "The reports are claiming you've been hiding her away for some time. Care to share some information about the new woman in your life with your fans?"

I look over at Sam, and he nods as if to say, *"Go on, asshole, we pay you well enough for this shit, so don't fuck up."*

"I've known her since we were kids. We grew up together. That's all I'm saying about it. Please respect her privacy." Right... as if they give a flying fuck about that.

The reporter I pointed to tries to ask a follow-up question, but I point to a different reporter when all of their hands go back up.

"Is it true that she's the sister of your best friend since childhood? A hockey player that got injured his freshman year in college? Isaac Daughtry—"

"That's enough!" I bark, standing out of my chair immediately, the chair falling backward to the ground with the force of my movement, but I got what I wanted... the media room goes stark quiet for a second besides the sound of flashing cameras.

Bringing up Isaac is a good reminder of exactly why Isaac's going to be furious about this whole situation. His sister is now a public target, and I let it happen. He won't give a shit that she's angling for a promotion. He'll only care that I didn't protect her the way he thinks I should. He'll think I should be protecting her from being harassed at the supermarket by fans, followed home by paparazzi trying to get a photo of us together, or protecting her from dating a guy like me. "Sounds like you have all the information you need anyway. You don't need me. This interview is over," I say, stomping off the podium.

I want to tell them to mind their own fucking business, but this is what Sam and Phil want. This is what Autumn is counting on. Distract, deflect, and.... de-sleaze Conley.

I get it, okay?

And I'll be the good boy they want and give the media what they're asking for. But if things weren't as they are, if Autumn Daughtry wasn't my fake girlfriend and she and I were really dating, I'd tell them to keep her name out of their mouths and leave her the hell alone. I'd do everything in my power to protect her from the media's scrutiny, which is sure to follow after today. I'd never let them touch her if it was up to me. A feeling I've never felt about any other woman I've dated. Probably because most of those women want notoriety, hoping it will angle them toward a blue checkmark on their social media account or a makeup brand spokesperson deal. But that's not what Autumn wants. This isn't about publicity for her. She just wants to do the best she can at her job and maybe even help me in the process.

Spending time with her yesterday at the restaurant was unexpectedly enjoyable. She's feistier than I remember, jumping into my arms and kissing me without any warning, and now she's all grown up. She grew into that awkward, lanky body. The mouthguard and braces turned that smile into a million watts.

I had her on my mind the rest of the day yesterday after we parted ways, and I woke up wondering when I'd get to see her today. I looked for her all over the stadium when I got on the ice. I looked for her in the stands, in my box seats, until finally, I caught a glimpse of her in the owner's box.

None of that means I have any interest in her. More like curiosity. And if I was ever interested in dating anyone seriously... If I weren't forced into this situation, my plans to stay a bachelor for the foreseeable future would still be in effect. And if I had someone who I'd consider bringing home to Mom to get her off my case about settling down with someone, I wouldn't pick Autumn Daughtry as that person. I can't. There's too much history. Our lives are too entwined for this to work.

Our dads still bullshit in the backyard over the occasional BBQ and beer when Washington weather allows.

If I brought Autumn home for Christmas, our moms would lose their...

Oh fuck.

Our moms.

Goddamn it!

I didn't even consider the shit show that will soon be a barrage of text messages and calls from my mother asking why she's the last to know and when Autumn plans to get pregnant with my mom's first grandchild. I've been too focused on Isaac lighting me up that I never considered how our mothers are going to react the second they see the news. I'm going to have to discuss this with Sam and get a pass on secrecy with my mom. I can't lie to that woman. Not as in I'm incapable of it, more like that woman is a human lie detector test, and she knows when I'm hiding something from her.

I push past Sam, and he follows directly behind me as I exit the media room and enter the hallway. I can sense a couple of other reporters following me out. Altman pats my shoulder as I pass him in the corridor, he's up next, and I know he's been through the wringer with the media as of late with the news of him being a single father to a child he never knew about. Now there's new blood in the water. I hope at the very least this pain in my ass might give him a break. Unfortunately, the media is good at multitasking.

I nod at him and then stare down the hall as I have the exit in my sights with three or four people on my heels. "Conley! Conley...!" I hear behind me, but the second my eyes settle on the beautiful brunette standing at the end of the hall with a sexy smirk across her lips, I'm almost half tempted to try that kiss again... just to wipe that smirk off her face. Yeah, that's the only reason.

I see Tessa to my left as I walk through the hallway.

"They're right on your toes, Conley. You're on," Tessa says so that only I hear it.

Then she disappears in the other direction.

the Hawkeyes want something for the cameras? Fine.

"You played good tonight, Conley," Autumn says as I get closer. She pushes off the wall, and I wrap an arm around her waist, pulling her to the exit with me. I take her by surprise, and it takes her a second to adjust to the large length of my steps and the fact that she has to keep up while I keep her side plastered to mine.

Once we're moving in sync, she gets up on her tiptoes and kisses my cheek as we walk. I can feel the flashes of cameras as she kisses me from the handful of media still following us out.

"Autumn! Autumn...!" the media yells at her. She chuckles and then wraps her arm under mine and around my waist. She has to take two steps for every one I take, but she does a good job at keeping up.

"Looks like they didn't rip you to shreds. You're still in one piece," she says while patting over both of my pecs and then my stomach as if to make sure I'm still in one piece. I don't like the way my body lights up to her touch.

"Narrowly escaped with my life."

She laughs and squeezes my side, pulling her further into me as I pull us closer to the exit. I love her laugh. It's the adult version of the easy-to-laugh girl from my past. "Don't worry. I would have gone in after you... no man left behind. We're in the trenches together, Conley," she teases, gripping slightly on my jacket. I know she's kidding, but damn, does it feel good to hear someone say that.

To no longer be on my own.

To have someone in my corner.

I push the single door open, and she releases me to follow behind. Without thinking, I grab her hand and hold it in mine as I pull her through the door with me. Something about being connected feels more natural than it should.

"Where did you park?" I ask.

"I took a rideshare in. I'll order one now," she says releasing my hand and then grabbing her phone out of her back pocket and stopping at the end of the sidewalk curb directly in front of the players' parking.

I stop, too, and turn directly in front of her, grabbing her phone from her and then sticking it in her jacket pocket. "Then you're with me tonight, Daughtry," I say, leaning in a little closer.

"Is that so?" she asks with a raised eyebrow, baiting me.

There's that feisty girl she shows me every once in a while, and damn, am I getting used to seeing it.

"You're my girlfriend, right? I can't show up to the bar tonight without you. That'll look weird. Especially since you came to the game."

She thinks for a second, looking up at the night sky. It's too overcast to see the stars tonight.

"True. I guess you're right. We could use some more public exposure."

Exposure, yeah, that's what I was thinking too.

"I can meet you there," she offers.

"Not a chance," I say, pulling her hand back into mine and then tugging her toward the players' parking lot and off the curb with me. "You're riding with me."

"Are you kidnapping me?"

"Of course I am, if you won't come willingly."

I look back at her, giving her an eyebrow raise.

"Well, I'd try to make a run for it, but you have a death grip on my hand. And I've never beat you or Isaac in a foot race. I have a feeling the millions a year they pay you in your contract means I'm not going to today either. I doubt they dish out that kind of cheddar for a slow poke."

I laugh. "No, they don't. Otherwise, they'd be a losing team."

I look over my shoulder, and Autumn throws back her head laughing. That feels like a win all on its own.

We walk up to my silver Audi R8 that I bought myself two years ago when I signed a huge endorsement deal with an electrolyte water bottle company. I open her door, and in my peripheral, I see the flashes of cameras. Fuck, I forgot about them. Why the hell did they follow us out here? They never do that shit.

Autumn takes a seat in the black leather passenger seat, and I close her door when I know all of her limbs are safely stowed inside. I round the car and climb inside, ignoring the media's questions as they call out from the cement sidewalk of the Hawkeyes property about half an ice rink away from us. the Hawkeyes rules state that media aren't allowed in the players' parking lot. It's sort of like our safe zone in a game of tag. They can't touch us here.

I start up my car, pull out of my parking spot, and head for Oakley's Bar, a low-key, hole-in-the-wall sports bar that Seven Wrenley found before I got signed with the team almost ten years ago. It's a place that we all go to after a game or after practice, and Oakley, the owner, will kick anyone out who tries to hassle us.

My teammates were razzing me earlier today about the chick who was caught on camera jumping my bones in broad daylight a couple of days ago. The last thing I want to do is put Autumn through the wringer with these guys tonight, but I guess that's what we signed up for, and by tomorrow, we'll see them every day when we start living in the same building as they do. I haven't told any of them that Autumn and I are fake, and I'd prefer to keep it that way until it eventually comes out on its own.

Bring on the shit show.

"Stuck in the trenches" is right.

But something about being stuck in them with Autumn doesn't make it so unbearable.

CHAPTER TEN

Briggs

The second Autumn and I walk into the bar, I feel my phone vibrate a half dozen times. It could be anyone. My agent, one of my teammates, Phil Carlton, or Sam, but Sam's standing a couple of hundred feet from me, ordering a beer at the bar, chatting with Lake Powers, our left-wing, and Ryker Haynes, our center forward and captain.

My hunch tells me that if I pull my phone out of my pocket, I'll find the incessant perpetrator is my mother, who just witnessed the media interview where the media implied that I'm dating Isaac Daughtry's little sister. My mother doesn't have to guess who that is.

No doubt she's calling to find out what my wedding tux measurements are.

I pull the phone from my back pocket. Just as I thought, MOM lights up on my phone. She must have figured texting wasn't working and needed to go to more extreme measures, but if I don't answer, I have no doubt that she'll resort to calling Sam. How in the hell she got my general manager's number, I have no idea.

"Fuck," I mutter.

"What?" Autumn asks.

I hold up my screen so she can read it.

"Oh... yeah... my mom has already called twice since we left the stadium," she says, looking as if she doesn't have a care in the world as she scans the small crowd in the bar.

"What are we going to tell them?" I ask, debating whether or not I should turn to her and shake her for a second to stir some reality back into her.

Does she not get that our mothers are both calling for the same thing? They're undoubtedly going to ask about our relationship status.

"If I knew the answer, I would have already answered her call," she says playfully, nudging me with her shoulder.

My phone stops ringing and then starts back up again.

Finally, I stop and turn to her as we're halfway through the bar. "If I don't take this call, she'll get in her car and drive down here."

Oh damn, I meant it as a joke, but I can already see my mom and Mrs. Daughtry queuing up the *Celine Dion Best Hits* CD in my mom's Ford crossover and headed straight for us. Walla Walla to Seattle is about a four-hour drive, and I wouldn't put it past them to have our entire wedding planned before they get here. "You going to be okay in here by yourself for a bit?"

"I survived a childhood at the hands of you and my brother. I'm made of Teflon, baby." Autumn flexes her biceps, and I chuckle, but then her attention shifts toward the back of the room, and her eyes brighten as she picks up on her tiptoes and waves at someone.

When I look, I find Tessa Tomlin—sister of our left defense, Brent Tomlin, A.K.A. the Hawkeyes' ballbuster—waving back. This isn't good news. Tessa was brought on last year to keep a sharp eye on the social media of both the Hawkeyes and its players' accounts. She's been given a lot of power to jump our shit, and she does, although I have yet to have an incident with her since I don't post much on my social media anyway. Mostly she gets on my case for my poor treatment of the media... even though I'd say they deserve it.

I know she's involved in spreading the social media narrative about Autumn and me and making sure it all serves the best interest of the franchise, which is to make me less touchable by the potential of this scandal. I still wish they would have let me talk to Dixie and figure out why she was spreading these false rumors about her and me. This just doesn't seem like something she'd do. Not that I know her all that well, but I thought we understood each other from the time I spent there.

"You know Tessa then?"

Autumn looks over at me and then down at my phone, which just started ringing for the third time.

"You'd better go. I'll be fine while you're gone."

Autumn walks away, headed in Tessa's direction. I see Penelope walk over and join them.

"I'll introduce you to the boys," I hear Tessa say, "Brent! Have you met Conley's girlfriend?" I hear in the distance as Tessa scoops Autumn in her arm and ushers her through the bar. As the bar door shuts behind me, I hear Brent's voice over everything. "Conley has a girlfriend?! Since when?" I hope Tessa takes care of her, but Autumn is right. Isaac and I probably made her tough enough to handle these dimwits I consider my friends and family.

Well, at least I don't have to make introductions and lie to my buddies. Tessa is more than happy to take it off my hands. I just hope she's emphasizing that she is Conley's *girlfriend, not just a friend*. This whole thing might be temporary between her and me, but I'll be damned if any of them think she's fair game. None of those asshats are going to touch her if I have something to say about it.

I step out of the bar and stand outside in the smoking area. No one's out here right now, so it's a safe enough spot.

I stare up at the dark sky and peer up at the moon, hiding behind layers of clouds but still managing to shine bright enough to be seen.

The day's earlier drizzle is starting back up after staying dry on our way here to the bar. Soon enough, it should be raining pretty hard, or at least that's what the forecast said.

I hit redial, and my phone doesn't even ring.

"Briggs Michael Conley! I've been calling and texting you. I thought you might be dead."

"That's a little dramatic. Don't you think someone from the team would tell you if I died? Besides, I was on national television less than an hour ago."

"Don't you sass me, mister. I was in labor with you for two days, and my hooha ripped—"

"Mom, Jesus! I don't need the details if you ever want me to have kids of my own. Now why don't you just cut to the chase and tell me what is so important that I have eight texts and three missed calls from you?"

Who knows, maybe I'll get lucky, and it will turn out that she didn't watch her only son's hockey game tonight, or at least maybe she skipped the interview afterward. Maybe she's calling because she wants to tell me that she found a suspicious mole on her back and wants to tell me about the Google Ph.D. she just got by self-diagnosing her mole as a tropical disease that was cured over a century ago. But with everything going on back at home with my dad's health, I'm glad she's looking out for her own.

"You're dating Autumn Daughtry and you didn't tell me!?" she practically screams.

I hear another voice in the background... a woman's. No!

"Mom, who's there with you?" I ask, but it's a moot point... I already know.

"Sandy... obviously!"

Of course, Autumn's mom would be at my parents' house right now. Kirk and Sandy Daughtry, Autumn's parents, probably follow my career more than my own flesh and blood. They sure as hell have been to more home games than my parents. My mom doesn't like seeing me get in fights in person. "She ran down to our house barefoot with a bottle of champagne when Kirk told her about your interview. She was in the bathtub when he told her, and she's still in her robe." I can hear the two women in that background giggle with what I assume to be glee.

"Mom... are you drunk?"

"What?! Me?! No, never?! We're just so excited."

"Drunk as a skunk, these two." I hear my dad in the background and the sound of the refrigerator door closing. I picture him walking into the kitchen, grabbing a bottle of water (I assume, since his doctors don't want him drinking), and heading back out to the garage to work on his model airplane. "Congrats on the engagement, son. She's a nice girl."

Then I hear the door to the garage click shut.

Good talk, Dad.

Then his words land on me. *What the hell did he just say?*

"What?! Engagement? What the hell did you tell him?" I hear my voice rachet up an octave. "We're not engaged, and I have no idea where you got that from," I explain to the two tipsy women on the other line, hoping the words "not engaged" really sink in.

I knew they'd blow this out of proportion.

"I had a feeling this would happen!" I hear Sandy yell, ignoring my question. I can already picture her leaning against the opposite side of the island from my mom in the pink fuzzy robe that she's had since Isaac and I were kids.

My mom adds to the ridiculousness of this situation, "It's always the person you least expect. The girl right under your nose ends up being the one."

I shake my head at these two.

"We're just dating. It's not serious."

"The picture of her climbing you like a honey badger and mauling you in public suggests something different." If I hear my mom talk about a woman climbing me like a honey badger again, I'll have my eardrums surgically filled with cement. "And how dare you two keep this from us? It says in this gossip blog that you two have been dating for over two months... and not a single word to either of your mothers? It's as if you two are in cahoots."

"Cahoots? Of course, we're in cahoots. We're dating."

"For shame, Briggsy," my mom says. "Sandy tried to convince me that if you didn't answer on my next ring, we were jumping in the car and driving down to Seattle to confront you two."

Fucking knew it.

I shake my head at the predictability of these two grown-ass women.

"Autumn hasn't answered either. Tell her to call her mother!" Sandy yells from across the kitchen again.

"From the sounds of it, you two are too drunk to drive anything but me crazy."

"Don't tempt me," my mother interjects. "I told your dad he was going to have to be our driver, and you know how he likes it when I change up plans on him when he's already set to work on his plane thingy."

Not only that, but my dad shouldn't be driving them anywhere. He should be resting, taking it easy.

All right, this has gone on long enough.

"Listen, I have to go. My entire team is waiting for me in the bar."

"And Autumn?" Sandy asks.

"And Autumn," I confirm.

"She's not answering her phone. Please tell her to call her mother..." Sandy says.

"All right, I got to go. You two, be careful and tell Dad to take your keys. Autumn and I don't need any impromptu visits from either of you."

I hear my mom cover the receiver of the phone, but I can still make out her excited chatter. "Just think, Sandy, we might have a grandbaby by next Christ—"

Click.

I don't wait for her to finish that sentence. I end the call and take a cleansing breath.

I walk back into the bar, my eyes seeking out the familiar brunette whose mother and mine are wine drunk in my childhood kitchen at almost midnight, probably setting up a monthly diaper subscription that I'll start receiving next month. I should tell them not to bother. If Isaac watched the same interview that Kirk did tonight, they'll be planning my funeral in twenty-four hours. Best friends since we were in diapers or not... bro code clearly states, don't touch the goddamn sister.

If only he knew that I haven't, except for the kiss she surprised me with at lunch... and I guess the peck on the cheek she gave me early tonight as I was escorting her quickly out of the stadium. Still, I haven't touched her the way I'm sure he thinks I have.

If I can't be honest and tell him this is all a lie, how the hell will he think we're not? He'd never buy it if I told him we're being abstinent.

I can hold my own in a fight... I practically do it for a living, but Isaac hits harder than any motherfucker I've ever met, and he knocked out his opponent in last week's fight in the first half... of the first round. I'm tough, I can take a hit... or two, or three, but a hit from Isaac will send me to the ER, no question.

I walk back through the bar doors, and the loud music hits me when the door swings open. The bar is basically one huge rectangle with a bar off to the right and against the wall and three pool tables at the back of the room, all running horizontally from one another.

On practice nights, or nights we just want to go out but not deal with the club scene, this place is quiet, in the sense that everyone who comes here is a regular and mostly keeps to themselves, so no one bothers us. But on winning games nights, this place can get busy with fans wanting to come and congratulate us.

This is one of those nights.

The bar is starting to fill up as I now have to turn sideways to make it through big groups of people to get to the back of the room where all of my friends are... and Autumn.

I see her now, surrounded by Penelope, Tessa, Lake, Ryker, and a couple of other players, all crammed in around a four-top. I don't see Kaenan, but I bet he took his daughter and the nanny home after the interviews.

I walk straight up behind Autumn as she's wedged between a couple of the girls all sitting on bar stools. I take a quick scan of Autumn from behind. She wore a pair of dark wash jeans that hug her bubble butt just right and a pair of heeled booties that give her ass that little bit of lift, although sitting on the bar stool makes checking her out a little more complicated. I still remember what her behind felt like in my hands that day in front of the restaurant when I held her up from falling directly on her rear. When I look up, Lake Powers is smirking over at me like he caught me doing something I wasn't supposed to be.

"Now I know why you've been hiding her away," Lake says as I walk up to the table. "You were afraid she'd realize that you're the least good-looking guy on the roster."

"Sure, that was it," I say sarcastically.

Autumn hears Lake and looks back over her shoulder at me, giving me a cute-as-fuck grin, and then looks forward, joining back into the conversation she's having with Penelope, Tessa, and Ryker.

I know Lake just likes to ruffle feathers when he can, and by now, he's sure to be a few beers in and buzzing with shit talk he's been looking to unload all night. Not as if he didn't do enough of that out on the ice against the opposition during the game.

"I don't see a ring yet," Lake says, getting Autumn's attention. "You've still got time to bail on him and pick a player with better moves." Lake winks at Autumn, and he's damn lucky he's not standing close enough for me to get him in a headlock.

Autumn gives Lake a playful side-eye, as if to tell him she'd never consider leaving me for him and I puff a little in my chest at Autumn having my back in front of my buddies and showing some solidarity even though this thing isn't real.

"Fuck off, Powers. Keep your grubby hands and your athlete's foot away from my girl," I say, coming up behind Autumn where she's seated on a tall wooden stool.

My chest just barely brushes up against her back as I inch closer.

Her back straightens immediately, and it feels like she leans back against me slightly as she takes a deep inhale while the rest of the group laughs at my dig toward Lake.

She looks back over her shoulder again but this time, I'm a lot closer. Her eyebrows raise slightly as she searches my eyes for the answer to her question before she speaks it. "How was the call? You were out there awhile," she says, a little concern in her voice.

"It's official... our moms have lost their minds."

Autumn pushes back and then slides off her bar stool. I step back a few feet from the table to get some privacy. Autumn follows.

"Our moms... as in plural?" she asks, her eyebrows just about knitted together.

I nod. "Your mom asked me to tell you to call her ASAP, but I'd give her until later afternoon tomorrow. I've heard champagne hangovers are pretty rough. Also, it'll give you time to consider a timely question."

"What's the question?"

"Spring or summer for our wedding." I smirk.

Autumn slaps my arm, and the zing of being touched by her hits me again.

"Oh, shut up. They've known about us dating for all of thirty minutes. There's no way that they expect us to get married," she says, rolling her eyes at me as if I'm being dramatic.

If she wants to know what dramatic sounds like, she should give our mothers a call tonight.

A guy tries to squeeze behind Autumn to get to the other side of the bar. I slide my hand around her waist and pull her up against me to avoid him brushing up against her in any way.

Once the guy is clear, she takes half a step back, and I let go of her against my better judgment. I clear my throat and then retort back to her.

"The wedding is the least of my worries. They must be expecting me to knock you up before the wedding because they're planning on a grandbaby by next Christmas." I send her a wink that makes her giggle and shake her head at the craziness of our mothers.

"Whoa, you three covered a lot of ground in a twenty-minute conversation."

"You have no idea," I say and then sidestep around her. "I have to get Autumn home, so I'm going to leave early. Good game, everyone," I say.

Ryker leans out of his chair and shakes my hand. "Good game, man. See you tomorrow for practice."

Lake gives a lazy salute while Penelope and Tessa walk over and hug Autumn goodbye.

I send a quick wave to the rest of my teammates and the coaches and then lead Autumn out of the bar with her hand in mine.

"You need to be prepared for your brother to find out," I say over my shoulder as I weave us through the crowd. Many people pat me on the shoulder and congratulate me on a good game. I smile back in response, but I keep her and I moving forward.

"What? Why? He has a fight in two weeks. He's going to be 'off-grid' focusing until then."

Thank God. That might buy us enough time to get our shit together and come up with a way to explain this whole thing to him in a way that won't piss him the fuck off.

"I hope you're right because we could use some time but it's still going to happen sooner or later."

We finally make it to the bar doors, and I push through them back into the cold, keeping her close as we race through the deep puddles of the mostly dark parking lot. Our parking spot is a couple of rows away from the entrance of the bar as the rain pours down on us.

It must have finally started coming down after my call with my mom, and I went back inside.

I get her settled in her seat quickly and close the door before we both drown in the downpour. I run to my side and climb in, starting my sports car.

"What do we do?" she asks.

I lean my head against my headrest and look over at her. She's soaked, droplets of water dripping off her glossy hair onto her jacket. Her chest is pumping from the mad dash we made to my car. Her eyelashes are clumping together, and her deep green hazel eyes peer back at me. She's beautiful in a way I've never appreciated in the past. Or maybe, I've never seen her kind of beauty before.

"The way I see it, we have two options. One, tell him the truth…"

"Which we can't."

I nod.

"So option two is…?" she asks.

"We move in together tomorrow as we've already planned, and we make him believe this is serious… that I have no plans to hurt you. That this isn't a fling."

"And you think he'll buy it?" she asks, water droplets still dripping off strands of her hair and a doe-eyed look to her like she wants to believe that my idea will work.

We both know deep down… it's a long shot, but it's the only shot we have.

"I have no idea. But I'm about to bet a lifelong friendship on it."

She turns and stares out the front window for a minute. "I guess we don't have an option."

"Nope," I say simply.

"Then I guess you'd better take me home. I have a few more things to pack before the movers come in the morning." She sighs and rubs her hands down her wet jeans. "Tomorrow, we start creating an entire life. Hopefully, by the time he gets wind of this, we'll make it look believable."

I pull out of the parking spot and head for her apartment after she gives me the address to input into my GPS.

I've been down this direction before, but it's not my usual stomping grounds, and I like that GPS reroutes me if there is an accident or slower traffic on a specific route. Since it's a home game night, there will still be more traffic out than usual, until the bars downtown close for the evening.

When I pull up to drop her off, I see the apartment complex is only two stories, with the apartments having access to their doors from the outside, not the kind of secure apartment building with a doorman and secure parking that we're moving into tomorrow.

This is the first time that I'm happy she's moving into this building with me... she'll be safer in this new building.

I'm not exactly sure where this need to protect her is coming from, but I can't stop it, and it only seems to strengthen the more time we spend together.

CHAPTER ELEVEN

Autumn

"Where would you like the box labeled 'cookie sheets'?" the mover asks.

I look up, mid-text in response to my mom. I avoided her calls last night since Briggs spoke to both of them last night while we were at the bar. Now that we're a "couple", he can speak for both of us, right? I guess not, because by 6 a.m. this morning, she was blowing up my phone again, asking how this whole dating thing came to be, if he makes me happy, and what our plans are for Thanksgiving. Turns out nagging moms are immune to champagne hangovers when it comes to prying the truth from their offspring.

I love the woman dearly, and I hate to lie to her. Hopefully, she won't be too mad when the truth comes out that Briggs and I have no real plans to unify our families through wedded bliss.

I can already hear my father's firm voice when I finally tell them. *"Autumn, you're making your mother cry. Would it kill you to just marry Briggs to make her happy?"* Sorry, Dad, Briggs can have his pick of any woman, and he'd never pick me. But his plea wouldn't be completely selfless for my mother's benefit. My dad would also be angling for Briggs's season tickets.

"You can leave that on the kitchen island," I tell him and then head toward the hall to figure out which bedroom is mine.

The first door I see is wide open with two large duffle bags labeled the Hawkeyes on the side and Briggs's number #48 stitched above it. I guess I know which room Briggs is taking. It's a decent sized room with an ensuite. I continue walking down the hallway and find the other door at the end of the hall and to the left. I nudge the door open in surprise to find this room is bigger, with a walk-in closet and ensuite. I can see the freestanding white soaking tub in the back corner from here. Why would he leave this one for me? Did he assume they were both the same size?

I hear footsteps headed toward the hall from the living room. I look over to find Briggs with another bag in his hands, heading into his room.

"Everything okay?" he asks from down the hall, peering past the door jam of the second bedroom.

"Uh, I think you put your stuff in the wrong room. This one is the master."

"I'm only here two-thirds of the week since we travel for games, and women have more shit than men usually. I figured you could use the space." He shrugs. "Plus, you're in this predicament because of me," he says, his eyes casting down slightly.

"It's not *because* of you," I say in an attempt to reassure him.

"Even so. I thought you'd be more comfortable." He shrugs as if it's no big deal, but it is a big deal.

He's practically twice my size. He could use the extra space too.

"Well... thank you." My heart flickers at the sweet gesture.

I watch as he smiles quickly, drops his bag inside the door, and then heads back toward the movers.

The apartment the Hawkeyes rented us isn't far from the stadium. I'll be able to walk to Briggs's games, and since keeping up the girlfriend facade is crucial, I'll be expected to attend all home games. They didn't have to twist my arm. I'm beyond excited to get to sit in Briggs's box seats and watch my favorite sport and my favorite player... er, I mean my favorite team.

I walk inside and head for the closet. It's large, the size of a tiny bedroom, but my heart jumps at the sight of something already hanging up inside.

It's a jersey. A Conley jersey... in my size.

I push my rolling luggage upright, pull the jersey off the hanger quickly and run my fingers over the fabric. Did Briggs do this? I head out of my bedroom to find Briggs.

When I find him talking to the movers, I start walking toward him, and he turns when he senses someone headed his way. He sees the jersey in my hand and smiles.

"I figured you already have a weathered old jersey that you sleep in every night with my name on the back. I thought you could use a new one for the games." A devilish grin stretches across his face.

"You would assume that, wouldn't you? You're right about me sleeping in a jersey... but it's Kaenan Altman's jersey that's all tattered up in my top drawer," It's a lie, but he laughs anyway, and I finally see a piece of the old Briggs I haven't seen since we were kids. "I can't believe you think I'd wear your jersey. Cocky much? It's any wonder how you get that jersey over your massive head," I tease.

"You're right. It is massive. Want me to prove it?" He grins, directing my vision down to his crotch by staring down at it.

I shake my head and try to hold back the laughter trying to bubble out of me.

"No thanks. I've already seen it," I say, quickly spinning and heading back toward my room. I hear Briggs's heavy steps jogging to catch back up to me.

"Hold on, when was this?" he asks, jumping in front of me and blocking my progression toward the hallway.

"Remember that summer, your junior year, when Isaac pantsed you at the pond behind your house?"

"You'll have to be more specific. Isaac and I pantsed each other regularly to embarrass the shit out of each other. Particularly when we had an audience."

True, those two were also hazing each other.

"Okay, well, I was there for one of those times then," I say, trying to turn to his left and get around him, but he counters, blocking me with a grin.

"So you already know how impressive it is." He smiles down at me as he takes a step closer and hovers over me.

The mover walks up to Briggs with an invoice and a pen and offers it up to Briggs in a nonverbal request to sign that they completed their job. Briggs nods and takes the invoice, scribbling his signature on it.

"Oh..." I say, locking my eyes on Briggs and giving him a look of fake empathy. "Is that what you're still working with? I figured once you hit puberty, it would all... you know... fill in for you."

The mover's eyebrows practically hit the ceiling, and he turns swiftly to head back out of the door with the signed invoice from Briggs in hand. He's heard enough, and he knows when it's time to leave. Although, I bet he's heard worse while moving people from house to house. Moving can be a stressful business.

I can't hold back my grin from ear to ear. Besides, Briggs Conley has one of the nicest members I've ever seen in real life, even if I was all the way on the other side of the pond with a few of Briggs and Isaac's friends. It doesn't matter what I say, though; Briggs knows he won the genetic lottery with that thing. Whether or not he's gifted with using it remains a mystery. A mystery I never plan to solve... unfortunately.

I pick up where I left off and swerve around him, heading for my room.

"Very cute," he says, following me down the hallway. I take a left into my doorway. "But you already know how filled *out* it is. However, if you'd like, I can show you how nicely it fills *in*, too," he says, stopping at the door jam and leaning his shoulder against it as I continue further into my bedroom. He's just teasing me, trying to make me blush, and maybe it's working, but I won't give him the benefit of knowing.

"Why don't you clear the idea with my brother first, then let me know what you two settle on? In the meantime, I need to shower. Moving is a sweaty business," I say, headed for the huge bathroom.

"You know he'll kill me if I bring up you and my cock in the same sentence." I laugh as I unzip my hoodie and toss it onto the dresser that stands beside the bathroom door against the wall. "So give a man his last dying wish and let me join you," he teases.

Or at least, I think he's teasing.

I turn around while standing inside my bathroom, taking the bathroom handle in my hand, and smile at him. "All right then, come on," I say, opening the bathroom door a smidgen wider as a welcoming sign.

A giant smirk breaks across Briggs's face, and he takes one step inside the master. I quickly give him an "I gotcha" grin.

"Oh... I mean... I knew you were kidding?" Briggs says, not taking any more steps into my bedroom and rubbing the back of his neck.

Is that a little embarrassment warming those cheeks? It can't be.

"You look better above ground," I tease.

"Right." He nods.

Then I close the door slowly while I watch him stare back at me, tucking his hands in his pockets and smirking.

I turn back to the massive, tiled walk-in shower and flip up the water to scalding hot, a quick daydream flashing before my eyes of Briggs storming through the door and hauling me into the shower with him, undressing me and showing me just how incredibly his cock can fill me.

"Have a good shower," he calls back.

He still hasn't left my room.

"Thanks," I yell over the shower water. "See you at the stadium later. I'll be one of the many girls wearing your number!" I joke.

"Yeah, but you're the only one I'm taking home tonight!" he yells back.

Warmness fills low in my belly and radiates between my thighs at the way he says it, even though he probably meant that only literally because now we live together.

Then I listen for the sound of his feet as he finally walks out of the master bedroom, closing the door behind him.

CHAPTER TWELVE

Briggs

I walk through the locker room, the walls echoing with game-day chatter. Everyone's pumped up for today's game.

"Hey, welcome to The Commons," Lake says, and then pulls on his jersey over his pads. "I was going to come by and bring you a potted plant or some shit so I could come over and get to know this girlfriend of yours that we only met yesterday. Must be fucking serious if you're already moving in with her," he pokes.

Figures he'd bring it up.

Lake isn't an idiot; he knows something's up. Whether or not his flyby plan is to stop into our apartment because he's curious about Autumn or because he thinks he's going to find out that our relationship isn't what it seems, is the question.

I consider Lake a buddy, but that doesn't mean we don't flick shit at each other. He can run his mouth about me all he wants but if Autumn ends up in the middle of it, I'll draw a hard line.

"How about minding your own damn business, Powers?" I tell him, dropping my duffle bag on the bench in front of my locker and opening up the metal locker door to start pulling out my game-day gear.

"It'll be a cold day in hell before Powers learns how to butt the fuck out," Kaenan says, walking up to his locker next to mine and starts to unload his gear out of his bag, which is sitting on the bench that runs along all of our lockers.

He gives me a look and then grunts his annoyance. Lake's been razzing Kaenan about the good-looking live-in nanny that he hired a couple of months ago.

"Shit, you're right. Where are my manners? Why don't you come over tomorrow night for a full-course sit-down dinner with Autumn and me so you two can gab over your zodiac signs? You'll be the guest of honor," I offer Lake.

"Sure, I could go for that... unless you're cooking again."

A few of the guys chuckle. I barbequed on one of our poker nights that Lake usually hosts in his penthouse on weeks that we play at home. I swear I walked away to take a piss. I wasn't more than half a minute, but I burned the burgers and then ordered take-out Thai food down the street to replace dinner.

It would seem I still haven't lived that down.

I turn around and face Lake. "Fuck no, Lake, I was kidding. If I have a choice, you'll never see her again."

I'm only partially kidding. Lake and I talk a lot of shit, but all these guys are the closest thing I have to family, besides Isaac and my parents, but I spend a shit more time with my teammates than almost anyone else during the season.

"Why? Worried she'll like the idea of wearing the number twelve instead?" Lake jokes, referring to his jersey number over wearing mine.

I look over at Kaenan, and he just shakes his head.

"I shouldn't be surprised you're delusional. You've taken too many pucks to the noggin this season. It's a goddamn medical marvel you have any living brain cells left with all that scar tissue."

"Lucky for Autumn, my cock doesn't need brain cells to—"

"Shut up, Powers," Bex Townsend, our coach and fearless leader, says as he steps out of his office. "And get your head in the game. The right head. We need this win just like we needed every win before this, and we'll need every win after this. If you want a Stanley Cup, you'd better start proving you deserve it."

"We're just bonding, coach," Lake says sarcastically, looking over at me a few lockers down and smirking.

Coach Bex doesn't like that Lake isn't taking him seriously and turns to face us, his hands on his hips, scowling at us both. How the hell did I get grouped into this?

"Do it somewhere else. Conley lives at The Commons now, so if you want to chit-chat so damn much, go over to his apartment and have a little slumber party... braid each other's hair, have a damn cock sword fight for all I care, just do it on your own time... not on mine."

Bex is a two-time Stanley Cup winner and a hero among most of us. He retired eight years ago from the NHL but came back as a coach when retirement became too boring for him. The guy is still jacked and looks like a Spartan, even after so many years after retirement. We all look up to him, so his words incite silence throughout the entire locker room.

He's right. Poking fun is all well and good, but tonight is going to be a tough game, and we need our heads in the game. This is our fucking year. We deserve it.

Ryker, our team captain, walks in a minute later with layers of athletic tape wrapped around his bare shoulder and bicep. Something that our in-house sports therapist has been doing for him every game since the start of this season.

Most of us have to tape up ankles, knees, and shoulders before skating out on the ice to play a game. This sport isn't easy on your body, and we all show the signs of broken-down bodies just trying to get one more game in before our bodies give up the farm, as the saying goes.

"What the hell are you assholes doing standing around?" Ryker asks, looking at all of us, still silent from Bex's scolding. "We have a game to win. Get your gear on. Let's go."

We all quickly turn toward our lockers and start layering on our gear, getting ready for a hard game ahead of us. I spend the next half hour getting my head in the game.

Two hours later, the game is tied, and there are only ten seconds left on the scoreboard. This game is as hard as I thought it would be, and every second of it, my mind has been filled with trying to fucking win.

Ryker is making a mad dash with the puck when he sees I'm closer to the goal with no one flanking me. He whacks the puck to me, and I catch it with my stick as I skate full throttle toward the goalkeeper.

An opposing player is right on my heels as I come whizzing toward the goal at full speed. The goalie's eyes are on me, and my eyes are on the sliver of an opening to his left foot in the corner of the goalpost. I pull back on my stick and whack the puck with everything I have. The puck goes flying across the icy surface just as I spin out of the way around the goalpost to not ram right into it, along with the goalie.

The buzzer sounds!

GOAL!

The crowd goes wild. Fans race up to the plexiglass and bang against it. In my peripheral, my teammates from the box jump out onto the ice as my other teammates currently on the ice all hall ass at me with sticks in the air.

We fucking won!

Without thinking, the first place I look is up to the owner's box. Everyone in the owner's box is jumping up and down. Sam,

Phil, Penelope, Tessa... but the only one I'm looking for is the brunette wearing my number.

The second my eyes catch on Autumn, I see her jumping up and down, screaming, cheering, and high-fiving Sam. Her loose waves of soft brown hair bounce with her, along with the jersey she's wearing, as she celebrates with everyone else in the owner's box. I point my hockey stick up at her, and I can see her pound her hands against the glass in response. My teammates ram me into the plexiglass as they all pile against each other in celebration.

"I love you, you motherfucker!" Ryker yells over the crowd, his arm wrapped around my neck in a tight vise.

He's the first one slammed up against me. We break into laughter as the mob of players creates a pile-up of turquoise, white, and black jerseys... our team colors.

"We won!" I yell back to him.

I look up again to see Autumn, and she must know I'm looking for her again because she spins around and shows me my jersey number on her back. She pulls her soft brown hair off her back so that I can see CONLEY #48 spelled out across her shoulders.

Fuck, that looks good on her, and I can't wait to see it close up.

After enough celebration, we skate off the ice and head for the locker room. Now that we've won, the memory of what I get to go home to tonight floods back in. I'm not used to being impatient to get through media so that I can get to see someone waiting on the other side of the stadium doors. I'm usually just racing to get to the bar for a celebratory drink or looking forward to an ice bath after this is all over, but tonight, showing off my fake relationship with Autumn to the media might not be so much work anymore.

I sail through media. Luckily, they got the hint from the last time, and they kept the questions off Autumn and only on the game.

Once I answer enough questions, Sam excuses me and brings in another player. I exit the media room as quickly as I can, and my smile widens as I see Autumn standing where she was last time, at the end of the hall, this time in my jersey.

I stop in front of her and give her body a full scan, using the jersey as my excuse for my inspection of her body.

"You like it?" she asks, stretching out her arms like she's modeling it for me.

"Looks good on you. Now you'd better throw away your Altman jersey," I tease.

"She has my jersey?" I hear Kaenan ask behind me, slapping his hand on my shoulder and then squeezing as he settles beside me.

I look over to find Berkeley fast asleep against his chest as he holds her with his right arm and Isla standing next to him on his left.

"Not anymore, she doesn't," I growl at Autumn more than him.

He laughs.

"Are you coming out with us?" I ask.

Kaenan bends his head down a little and kisses Berkeley's head softly, trying not to wake her.

"Nah, I'm going to take the girls home," he says, giving a quick side look at Isla and then looks back at me. "Good game Conley. See you tomorrow at morning skate."

I see Autumn smile at Isla as the three of them turn and then head for the exit.

"Ready to head to the bar?" I ask Autumn.

"Sure."

I pull her hand into mine, and we leave before the media gets out of interviews, and we head for my car.

I'm looking forward to getting to spend a little time tonight getting to know the adult version of Autumn Daughtry.

CHAPTER THIRTEEN

Briggs

Last night, I spent the entire evening at Oakley's, watching Autumn. It was hard to take my eyes off her. The sound of her voice as she laughed at Brent's dumb jokes he loves to tell, and how she listened so intently to Ryker, Seven, and Reeve as they replayed every second of the game from tonight but from the player's point of view on the ice.

I listened to her conversations back and forth with Tessa and Penelope about how she and I grew up together. I cringed at some of her memories that involved the teasing and pranks that Isaac and I pulled on her. Now that hindsight is 20/20, I wish I could do some of those things differently but she's animated and bright-eyed as she recalls the stories, as if looking back on them is amusing to her now. Not everyone shares in her sentiment, as I got at least one dirty look from Penelope when Autumn retold the story about the time that Isaac and I double-bounced Autumn off the trampoline in my backyard when Isaac and I were twelve. Autumn ended up with a broken ulna in her arm. The image of her tiny purple cast with flowers all over it and little doodles of things Isaac and I wrote on it come to mind. She had to wear it all summer.

I remember that day vividly. I remember seeing a seven-year-old Autumn hit the ground, panic for her safety hitting me instantly as Isaac and I both dove off the trampoline for a crying Autumn. I got to her first and scooped her up immediately off the patchy green grass and held her against my chest as I took off running through my backyard, past the side yard gate, and down the street to Autumn's house, Isaac on my tail as he tried to reassure Autumn that she would be ok.

I still remember my heart racing and the overwhelming need to get her somewhere safe and get her help. Maybe there has always been a part of me that, when it counted, would protect the little girl that lived down the street from me.

Waking up this morning and walking out to the large kitchen to find Autumn in a pair of tiny pajama shorts and camisole making breakfast in front of the range gives this new arrangement its first perk.

I take a seat at one of the bar stools sitting under the large white quartz island. I scan the perfect backside of my new roommate as she works on the other countertop that butts up against the wall, a large wooden hood vent that matches the light-stained cabinets hanging just above her. She faces the white subway tile backsplash, unaware of my eyes locked on her heart-shaped ass.

Yeah... I shouldn't have these thoughts about Isaac's little sister, but they can't be helped. There's something about Autumn that has me curious about what I've missed over our years apart. I want to know what she's been up to since I last saw her. I want to know what about her is still the same and what has changed. Does she still eat her french fries with mustard? Does she hum a tune when she does chores around the house like she did when we were kids? Does she still like the grape-flavored Otter Pops in the heat of the summer?

"Chocolate chip pancakes?" she asks over her shoulder.

Her messy bun on the top of her head bobs as she works to pour the pancake batter onto the hot skillet.

"Yes, please. The way your mom makes them?" I ask, pleasantly surprised at the idea of getting a childhood favorite for breakfast.

"Of course. How else?" she chuckles.

She's still that same girl... I can see it. But she's also this entirely new and confident woman too that sparks my interest. As much as I'd like to deny that, it's becoming harder and harder to do, but I'll do everything in my power not to cross that line concerning her brother and our long-standing friendship.

And also because I'm not sure if she is as curious about me as I am about her. Is she buying her time until she can go back to dating that fucker Derek?

"Smells good," I say, taking a deep inhale through my nose.

Damn, I'm starving now.

"Do you want bacon and eggs, too?" she asks.

Hell yeah.

"That would be great."

I watch as she lays out more strips of bacon on the sizzling pan and then turns to the container of eggs, pulling several out of the carton and setting them by a bowl to be cracked. I stand up and walk around the island to the range where she's diligently working in a silky lavender camisole with black lacy detailing and matching shorts.

I walk up next to her and lean my hip against the countertop, facing her. "Want some help?"

"I'd love some," she says, beaming up at me.

She passes me the bowl along with milk and cheese to add to the mixture once I've cracked the eggs.

I start immediately on my task, quickly cracking the rest of the eggs left in the carton and then whisking all of the ingredients together.

"I'll be leaving in two days to head for Denver," I tell her, still combining the ingredients quickly.

"Oh, I thought your first game out of town wasn't until Friday?" Her eyes roam over the pancakes and bacon to make sure nothing burns.

She starts flipping the bacon over with her fork on the pan as it starts to get golden brown on one side, the sound of popping, sizzling, and the hood vent making us both have to raise our voices slightly to hear one another.

"It is, but I have to leave a couple of days early."

"Oh yeah?"

"Phil Carlton wants a few of us to rub elbows with a large company that's interested in becoming a huge endorsement for the franchise."

Usually, this sort of thing doesn't bother me. I don't mind schmoozing it up with big wig companies to entice them to spend money with the Hawkeyes but with just moving in with Autumn, it's the first time I've ever cared about having to leave.

"That's exciting," she says, flashing a quick smile over at me and then setting her sights on flipping the pancakes with her spatula.

I hand her my bowl of egg mixture, and she takes it, pouring the contents into a prepped pan.

"It is, but it means I'll be gone longer than usual. I just wanted to let you know."

She points to the salt and pepper shakers on my side of the range cooktop, indicating she wants me to use them to season up the eggs as I see fit. I add a nice amount of dusting using both seasonings.

"Okay, thanks for telling me."

She lays out a set of paper towels for the bacon to rest on for the grease to get absorbed.

"Don't worry. I'll clean up the rager I plan to throw while you're gone. You'll never even know."

I chuckle at the thought of Autumn throwing a party. We didn't go to high school at the same time but from the limited information I gathered from what Isaac told me over the years, Autumn is more of a low-key homebody.

"A rager? You?"

She looks at me with a faint look of offense. "What? You don't think I can throw a big party?"

"Could you throw a party...? Yes. Would it be any good...?"

I don't answer before she smacks my arm with the back of her hand. I laugh.

"I'll have you know, your parents' thirtieth wedding anniversary went off without a hitch," she says, a playful scowl across her face.

"You're making my point," I say under my breath.

She turns to me abruptly, her pancake spatula raised in one hand. "Thanks for not showing up, by the way... only son," she says, flicking me shit.

"Well, if someone hadn't planned the party the same day that their only son was playing in his first-ever championship game, I would have been there."

She smirks but doesn't say anything. Instead, she grabs the plate of bacon and the plate of pancakes that she just took off the stove and moves them to the island for us to sit down to eat.

"Yeah, the big screen TV that our dads set up in front of the beautiful ice sculpture I had ordered added to the ambiance of the party," she says, while giving me side eye while reaching back to grab the butter plate and set it with the plates of food on the island.

"I guess my parents hadn't guessed thirty years prior that they might have a son playing in the NHL, headed for a career all-time high, and should have picked a different day to get married," I joke.

"Yeah, you're right. What terrible foresight your parents had," she agrees, laced with sarcasm.

"I fronted the entire bill, at least."

She rolls her eyes as she walks around the island and steps up into one of the barstools, sitting down and staring back at me. "Okay, big pockets, you ready to eat yet?"

I grab the plate of eggs and the orange juice she already has sitting out and head for the other barstool. "Thought you'd never ask."

Autumn

Briggs left yesterday morning for his five-day trip. He texted me when he arrived at his hotel, per my request. I'm overjoyed to feel like a friendship is blooming between us, which is a great relief since the first meeting in the Hawkeyes office with Briggs storming out made me feel certain that this whole thing would be awkward and uncomfortable.

With Briggs gone, I've already made huge headway with a couple of our clients' files that I had been working on before I started working on the Hawkeyes account. Erika told me to leave any accounts not related to Briggs for other staff to take care of. She wants my full attention on landing this project, but with him gone, I have tons of free time... and frankly, I'm bored.

I shoot a text to Erika.

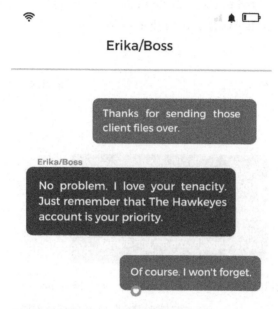

I still haven't heard a single word from my brother, so he must still be in his UFC bubble, and I'd be delighted if his coach decided to keep him there until this thing with Briggs comes to a complete end, but with Isaac's fight scheduled for Tuesday of next week, I have a feeling that by Wednesday afternoon, once his hangover from the night before has gone (win or lose), the news will hit, and I have no idea what to expect. I mean, after all, we're adults now, right?

My mother and Mrs. Conley are in my inbox more than they ever have been. I'm getting daily texts from both of them asking how things are going, wondering if Briggs and I would like to get in on their cruise to Alaska that the four of them are planning next year.

This lying to our parents thing is so much harder than I thought. I'm just glad they don't live close enough to pop over whenever they want and see that we're lying.

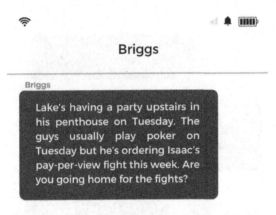

Briggs

Briggs

Lake's having a party upstairs in his penthouse on Tuesday. The guys usually play poker on Tuesday but he's ordering Isaac's pay-per-view fight this week. Are you going home for the fights?

Does he want me to come, or is he just being nice?

I actually haven't thought about it. I've been a little busy as of recently. 😉

I know we need to make it seem real to the public, but does it matter what his teammates think? I'd almost think he'd try to avoid us commingling whenever possible.

Briggs

I get it, me too. Your invited, if you want.

He quickly sends another text as if attempting to entice me.

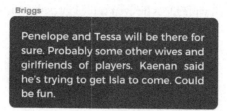

I try to sound even-keeled with my text response, but deep inside... I'm mush.

He doesn't text me that night before he goes to bed, or even the next day but on day three of his trip, when he should be flying out of Denver to meet up with the rest of the team in Texas, he sends off a quick text around ten in the morning.

Is he hoping I will? Does he even care? I guess he must if he's asking.

> I'd be a pretty terrible fake girlfriend if I didn't.

I know that I'm alone in the apartment, but I still check behind me to make sure that no one is looking over my shoulder at that last text. Maybe I should have left the word 'fake' out of the text message. I'm not sure who has access to Briggs's phone.

Could a player on the team see it? Or worse, someone from the media?

Briggs
> The worst.

I laugh out loud at his response.

> Plus I have a bet going.

Briggs
> A bet? With who.

It crosses my mind not to tell him. I'm not sure how he'll react about me betting on the games but then I do anyway.

> With Tessa.

Briggs
> I should warn you. Don't bet Tessa… she never loses.

Briggs
What's the bet?

Should I even tell him? Will he be mad that we're betting for terrible things to happen in the game to his teammates?

> $20 says Brent hits his record penalty box visits this game, and $40 says Ryker gets in a pissing match with the ref and gets kicked out for the rest of the game.

I don't tell him that Tessa has $30 on Briggs ending up being wheeled out of the game on a gurney. This is the Hawkeyes' rival team, so crap is bound to happen as it always does. However, I truly hope that Tessa loses the one about Briggs. I enjoy a good fight on the ice, but just like Mrs. Conley, when it's Briggs getting served up, I close one eye. I can't look away, but only half of me is willing to watch it all go down.

Briggs
> I want $100 on Kaenan breaking a hockey stick over their center forward's head. He hates that guy.

I laugh.

> I'll ask Tessa.

A few minutes after sending Tessa Briggs's bet, she responds back with something along the line of stealing candy from a baby.

> She's in and your bet has been officially recorded, per Tessa.

Briggs
> Thanks for being my bookie.

> What are fake girlfriends for?

There I go again calling our relationship fake over text.

Briggs
> Yet another perk. I'm beginning to see the versatility.

I chuckle and then send off a last text. I know he's busy, and although I have this odd desire to keep this texting going and keep in communication all day, I know he needs to get back to focusing on tonight.

> Good Luck tonight.

Briggs
> Thanks.

Penelope lives in The Commons as well, three stories above me and Briggs's apartment. She calls and invites me up to watch the game with her and Tessa.

These two are starting to become my very favorite part of this whole project. I hope this friendship between me and these women continues after Briggs and I are no longer required to date.

The game plays out fast and hard, all three of us on the edge of our seats the entire night. Ryker ended up getting taken back to the locker rooms by the medical staff after an opposing player hit him from behind after the buzzer and Kaenan ended up spending a good chunk of time in the penalty box for breaking a hockey stick over another player's head... just like Briggs had predicted in his bet with Tessa.

They had to stop the game to clear the ice of broken fiberglass and wood from the splintered hockey stick, and to break up the fight that ensued right after the hockey stick cracked over the player's helmet.

If you ask me, the referees were being a bit dramatic. It's not like the player Kaenan hit wasn't wearing a helmet. Then again, I might be biased.

After it ends, I send off a text to Briggs. I know he won't see it since he still has media, and then they have to get back on a bus and head for the next city they will be playing in tomorrow, but at least it will be there waiting for him when he gets a chance to read it.

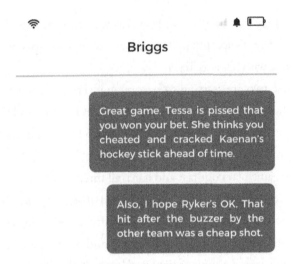

Briggs

> Great game. Tessa is pissed that you won your bet. She thinks you cheated and cracked Kaenan's hockey stick ahead of time.

> Also, I hope Ryker's OK. That hit after the buzzer by the other team was a cheap shot.

I jolt awake to the sound of my phone chiming for an incoming text message and the blue cellphone light glaring up on my pitch-dark bedroom ceiling.

I'm grateful that this apartment came with blackout curtains because the city lights would be too bright to sleep.

I scramble to reach over to my nightstand where my phone is currently charging and a small fan is blowing, making white noise to drown out the loud downtown city noises and sirens.

Briggs

> You're probably asleep but I'm texting you anyway because none of us can sleep, least of all me, we're all on a high from that win.

> **Briggs**
>
> Ryker's ok. He'll rally like he always does. Tell Tessa it's not a bet if it's a sure thing. But I didn't cheat, I just know my teammate and how much he hates that asshole on the opposing team.

My heart flutters seeing his name on my phone.

> She wants to go double or nothing.

> **Briggs**
>
> Tell her to offer up a bet.

> Ask her yourself. This game is a little too rich for my blood. Tessa wiped me out of my latte money for this month.

It's a joke... I'd never give up my latte money for anything! But it sounds better than "I'm not a gracious loser." I guess he did warn me not to bet against Tessa, but it still made the game even more fun to watch having a little money on the hare-brained antics of the players.

> **Briggs**
>
> Did you see me point to the camera after that goal I made at the end of the first period?

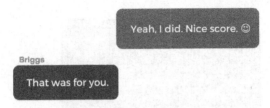

I think my heart just stopped. I re-read that text over and over again. My stomach doesn't flutter any less the more I read it.

My pulse picks up. Why is he being so cute? Before I can say anything back, he sends another text.

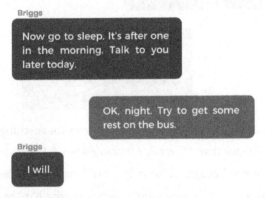

I fall asleep with a smile on my lips. I don't know what all of that was, but I swear, Briggs Conley, my fake boyfriend, was flirting with me.

The next night, Penelope invites me up again for the game. This time, she invites Isla and Berkeley. With Kaenan being gone, Penelope thought it would be a good idea to bring her into our new girls' group, and I couldn't agree more. A bond is beginning to form, I can feel it, and I'm hoping that they'll still want to include me even after I'm no longer associated with the team in the capacity I am now.

the Hawkeyes are dominating this game, and the guys are playing well, despite the fact that Briggs and Kaenan both end up in the penalty box for taking out a player on the other team who intentionally threw an elbow into Lake's face and knocked Lake flat on his back on the hard ice.

You can see from the replay that Lake gets knocked out cold for a moment. His body hits the ice, lifeless for a split second. Coach Bex pulls Lake off the ice and makes him sit out a period of the game.

Luckily, Kaenan and Briggs's alternates are playing well tonight too. Everyone is skating their hearts out, and it's games like this that make me believe the rumors that the Hawkeyes might make it to the playoffs this year.

Briggs is back in the game and scores a goal. The crowd goes wild, and so do we, jumping off the couch and cheering, high-fiving each other and bouncing around with excitement like we're a bunch of middle schoolers at a boy band concert.

"Look at the screen!" Penelope says, pointing at Briggs as he points to the cameraman with his hockey stick.

He skates up, ramming into the side of the plexiglass in front of the camera, and mouths something.

"Did he just say, 'That one's for you?'" Isla asks.

"Pretty sure he said, 'I have to poo,'" Tessa adds with a giggle.

Penelope gives Tessa a playful nudge. "Bull." She looks over at me. "Someone's getting soft on their girlfriend." She sends me a little wink and I can feel my cheeks warm.

"Oooh," Tessa says flirtatiously. "Briggs has a crush," she singsongs.

"Stop it," I tease. "No, he doesn't." Then my eyes dart to Isla, who I forgot doesn't know that Briggs and I are faking it.

She doesn't seem to realize that I contradicted the feelings of a supposed serious boyfriend as she turns back to the TV and watches Briggs skate away.

"That's so sweet," Isla adds.

We watch the rest of the game while snacking down on the pizza that Tessa brought, the pineapple hard ciders that Isla brought, and the Boston cream pie cupcakes that I made.

After the game is over, we keep the TV on. One of my favorite parts of watching the game at home is that I get to see the interviews.

I grab my half drank hard cider off the glass coffee table directly in front of me and scoot back into the dark grey microfiber couch, pulling my legs under my bum and slightly to the right as I snuggle in. No longer sitting on the edge of my seat in suspense over the action-packed game, I can now relax into the interviews and taste the fresh, fruity flavor of the pineapple cider.

Kaenan is up first, and in my peripheral, I see Isla's spine straighten when he comes on screen. She's pretending not to be interested but her body language says otherwise.

"That freaking scowl." Tessa laughs. "Smile! It won't kill you!" she yells at the screen, leaning forward from her seating position directly next to me on the couch.

I see Isla smile at Tessa's comment, and then I look down at Berkeley, who doesn't seem to notice Tessa's outburst but runs to the TV and plasters her tiny little hands on the screen.

"Dadda!" she screams and then plants her mouth against the TV as if to give him a wet kiss.

His interview is over soon, and Briggs steps into view and takes a seat. He points to a reporter to ask their question.

"Briggs, your team seems to have found their groove this week so far. How do you think that will work to your advantage going into Sunday's game in two days?"

"I think we're riding high on this wave, and as long as we can keep up the momentum, we should do well. But we have to remember that we're only ever one bad game away from a loss. Morale is up with consecutive wins. We're feeling good."

He points to another reporter.

"Briggs, you and Kaenan both had some penalty box time tonight. How does that affect your team when two of its top players are out at any given time?"

"Our teammates are talented players. All of our alternates dominated tonight and covered our asses like they've trained to do. But we're a family out there on the ice, and when an opposing player goes after Lake like they did tonight, or Ryker like they did last night... well, Kaenan wanted to make sure they understood that we don't take kindly to dirty hits or hits after the buzzer. And I'll back up Altman or any player out there."

He turns to another reporter and points to them.

"You pointed to the cameraman and then said something into the camera. Care to tell us what you said and who it was for? Could you have been speaking to your rumored girlfriend and the woman who's been spotted on your arm lately, Autumn Daughtry?"

"She knows what I did, and she knows who she is," he says, sending a sexy smirk to the camera. "I'll be home soon," he says to the camera at the end and winks. I feel a waterfall of tingles cascade down my back.

"Oh. My. God!" Penelope yells and looks over me from the other end of the sofa.

Tessa looks at me, too, biting back laughter.

With Isla here, I'm saved from having to dive into a conversation about what is or isn't happening between Briggs and me because, honestly, I have no idea.

The flirting seems to be escalating, but Briggs is a flirt by nature. Maybe this is how he is with every woman he's in close proximity with. After so many years apart, I don't know the adult version of Briggs, but I'm excited that he'll be home in a couple more days—and I'll make the most of that time to pretend this is all real.

CHAPTER FOURTEEN

Briggs

I didn't get home on Monday like I planned. A last-minute meet-and-greet kept me back another day. Instead, I get home around 2 a.m. on Tuesday, the same day as Isaac's fight. Autumn was asleep when I got in, and I didn't want to wake her up. I knew she had an early meeting with Erika, and I had to go to my weekly appointment with my physical therapist, and a meeting with my agent in the afternoon.

Fitting everything in and getting to Lake's on time was cutting it tight.

I hurry through therapy and my meeting with my agent so
that I can get back in time for the fights but my agent was
running late, and now so am I.

I shoot Autumn a text.

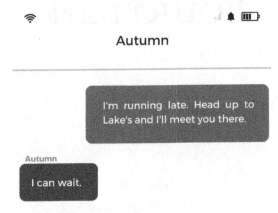

Even though I like the idea of her waiting at home for me
and us taking the elevator together up to Lake's, I can't let her
miss her brother's big title fight if I'm even later than I planned.
Absolutely everything has taken longer than I was expecting
today and the meeting at my agent's office is no exception.

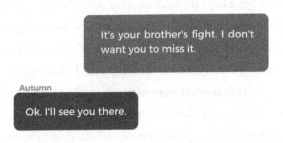

When I walk in the door of our temporary apartment, I can still smell the essence of her... like freshly baked cookies and something fruity like coconut.

I make quick work of changing my clothes from the team-issued practice sweats and t-shirt, to nicer jeans and a V-neck white t-shirt. I wet my hands under the bathroom's rubbed bronzed faucet and then quickly run my wet hands through my thick blond hair to get it to look a little styled. I spray on a small amount of cologne, the same kind I've worn since high school, and then pull on a pair of boots.

I race out of the apartment and head for the elevator. As long as the earlier fights didn't end ahead of schedule, I still have a half hour before Isaac's fight starts.

I blow out a breath the second that the large stainless steel elevator doors shut, and I push the button for the Penthouse floor and then input the code that Lake gives out to guests.

Three penthouses take up the entire top level of the building. One is occupied by Lake, one by Ryker, and one by Coach Bex. Without the code from either Lake, Ryker, or Bex, you can't access the penthouse level. The elevator won't allow you to access the highest level unless you enter it.

When the elevator doors open on the penthouse floor, I step out and head for Lake's apartment door. The landing for this level is different than the others below. Although it still carries through the same high-end carpeting on all landings, the painted solid white doors on the penthouses are wider and taller and the hardware on this floor is a brushed gold finish, instead of the rubbed bronze that all the apartments below have. Where all the other floors have hallways that lead to the many apartment doors on that floor, this landing has a large almost hexagon shape with access to three Penthouse doors and then a fourth that leads to a private gym and a large outdoor rooftop common space for all three penthouses to use.

It almost feels like you're on a game show and you have to pick a door to see what's behind it. Today, I'm picking up door number 802, Lake's apartment.

I push through the door, knowing that Lake keeps it unlocked during events at his apartment. It's not as if random people can access his apartment without the code for the elevator anyway.

Inside, my sights immediately go in search of the beautiful brunette I've been waiting to see for the last few days since I've been out of town.

The heavy door swings back slowly with a soft close feature while I continue further into the apartment.

Reeve sees me first, standing by the large open-concept kitchen, living room, dining room, and balcony that's four times the size of me and Autumn's apartment. He's standing next to Seven, who has his back to me. Reeve holds up his beer and nods at me as a hello. Seven looks over his shoulder quickly to see who Reeve saw, and then sends a nod at me too, then turns back to their conversation.

"Hey man! Welcome," Lake says, standing behind the couch, facing the TV, almost half an ice arena away from me in the large living room.

His hand is working some universal remote that probably controls this entire house.

"Thanks. I meant to get here earlier but... agents." I say simply, taking more steps into the apartment.

Ryker and Brent, who are sitting on the living room couch waiting for the main event to start give a knowing nod at my explanation for my tardiness. It seems agents with no sense of time management run rampant in sports management.

I see Penelope, Autumn, and Tessa standing at the large kitchen island, snacking on the spread laid out in front of them. I head their way, looking to get closer to my fake girlfriend and roommate.

A huge charcuterie board of meats like salami slices and prosciutto wrapped in cheese sits in neat piles. There are cubes of Colby jack and pepper jack cheese, along with a round of brie cheese that looks as though it's still melted, with crispy baguette slices next to it for spreading the brie on. There's a huge array of veggies like carrots, celery, and sliced bell peppers. And fruit galore... strawberries, blackberries, kiwi, and sliced apples, just to name a few. Within each section of food are several dips, both sweet and savory. A little cup with toothpicks to use to stab a piece of food sits in front of the gigantic board.

Lake had to have ordered this because even though he can cook, this is way too far out of his capabilities.

I take in Autumn as I round the island and head for her and Penelope.

She's dressed in a pair of black leather second-skin pants and a cream long-sleeve sheer blouse with a black crop top...tube top... whatever the hell, top... thing on under. She looks sophisticated but also sexy as fuck with a pair of black heeled ankle boots with her shoulder blade length hair down and slightly wavy.

My fists tighten at my side at the thought that she went to work looking like that. Did she see Derek while she was there? She said she was going in today to see her boss so I assumed she meant Erika... but now I'm not so sure.

Autumn sees me heading her way and turns slightly toward me as she and Penelope chat, both of their hips resting against the marble countertop.

I don't think she realizes she does it but I watch as Autumn takes me in with a full body scan just like I did to her. The only difference is that I did it discreetly while she wasn't watching me, and she just checked me out while I watched.

When her eyes meet up with mine, her cheeks redden, and she cuts eye contact quickly with a giggle... she's blushing. She checked me out unconsciously and then got caught.

I can't stop the full-face grin as I take the last few steps to settle up to the girls. I won't call her out though like I want to. Her reaction is cute and I don't want to ruin it by potentially embarrassing her.

"Lake outdid himself tonight. We usually only have pizza, and chips and dip. This is impressive," I say, reaching for a toothpick and then looking around for the exact thing I want.

"Lake didn't do this," Penelope says, pointing to the charcuterie board. "Your beautiful girlfriend did."

"Penelope..." Autumn whispers, stepping forward to nudge Penelope with her elbow lightly.

Penelope gives Autumn a devilish grin. I don't think I've ever seen Penelope make that facial expression. She's usually too damn sweet, so what was that for?

"You did?" I ask.

I'm not exactly surprised; this seems like the kind of thing Autumn would do. The food is organized by grouping and colors. From a bird's eye view, with colorful foods being laid out in swirls and snaking its way through in a well-thought-out design, it looks a little like the Candy Land game board.

Autumn nods, almost a little shyly.

I pierce a piece of strawberry and dip it into a little white ceramic bowl that's labeled cheesecake dip and bring it up to my mouth, pulling the strawberry and cheesecake dip off with my teeth.

Damn... that's delicious.

I nod as I chew. "This looks awesome. Nice work."

"Hey! The fight is about to start!" Brent calls out from the large sunken living room.

"Let's go grab a seat," Tessa says, grabbing her apple hard cider off the drink coaster sitting on the countertop and starts leading the way towards the room with the TV.

A large TV sits inside custom-built exotic wood grain cabinetry that matches the kitchen's cabinets. A huge navy-blue U shape couch fills half of the room and faces the TV. Behind the couch on the opposite side of the wall are big floor-to-ceiling windows with double doors out to the balcony that runs the same length as the large rectangular living room. The city skyline of Seattle is framed perfectly from this view. The same view Autumn and I have, but several levels below this one.

The girls and I head for the living room, following Reeve and Seven who are also in the kitchen on the other side of the twelve-foot island, discussing next week's opposition and how they might change up their goalkeeping position.

I look over our group and realize that we're still missing Kaenan and Isla but maybe they'll show up later.

Even with the couch having ample room for a big crowd,
there isn't enough room for everyone. Usually, I'd just stand
behind the couch. I don't like being anchored to one spot anyway, but I want to be close to Autumn and that's where she's
heading.

The couch is starting to fill up but I see one open spot and I
plop down into it: Brent on my left side, the couch armrest on
the other. It's the end of the U-shape couch which is the worst
viewing spot but I don't care, it gives me a little leverage for what
I'm about to do next.

Autumn looks around quickly looking for an open spot but
there isn't one in sight.

"Here Autumn, I'll go get a chair from the dining room for
me. You sit here," Lake says, putting down his drink to get up
but I stop him quickly.

"It's fine, Lake. Autumn can sit on my lap," I say, shifting
from Lake to Autumn, holding her eye contact to encourage
her.

Her eyes glance one more time around the full couch of
people. They're all looking at her as she stands in front of us
awkwardly. She bites down on her full pink bottom lip for a
second as she hesitates.

I know the shy little girl from Walla Walla wants out of the
spotlight that's shining on her right now.

"Yeah Autumn, sit on Briggs's lap," Tessa says, biting back
what I imagine would be a cackle if she let it loose.

None of the other guys seem to catch on since Tessa and Penelope are the only two other people in this room that know that Autumn and I are fake.

Autumn is now out of choices and needs to step out of the way now that the fight music is starting up and the announcers are beginning to discuss Isaac and the other fighter's long history of hating each other.

She steps close enough for me to slide my arm around her waist and guide her to rest that perfect ass in my lap. She's coming willingly now even though before I wasn't sure she would. I hope it's because she wants to stay close to me too.

Having Autumn here with my teammates and friends feels more natural than it should. And watching Isaac is a reminder that I shouldn't like the fact that our fake relationship gives me the license to touch her whenever I want, but I find it hard to keep my hands to myself now that she is in my lap.

What I failed to consider is the amount of torture that Autumn can inflict in this position without meaning to. Every shift of her hips, every cough or laugh, every time she tenses to her brother taking a hit, it all zings through our connected bodies straight to my dick.

Poor guy is confused as hell down there about what should be going on between Autumn and me. I do everything I can not to poke Autumn in the ass with my ever-growing cock for the entire fight.

Watching Isaac and realizing that those are the same fists he'll send my way if I ever touch Autumn. His opponent's bloodied face only helps slightly to lessen my growing erection and the tightening of my balls as this torment continues.

Maybe this is karma punishing me for having dirty thoughts about my best friend's sister.

After the fight ends with Isaac knocking the guy out cold in the last round, we all leave the couch and wander to different places in the penthouse, none of us ready to go home.

A couple of guys end up smoking cigars out on the balcony while I spend my night around the island with Autumn and a few others discussing what all of our plans for our bye week break in the season look like. The week we all get in the middle of the season for rest, most of us use it for vacation.

I spend the rest of the night finding excuses for my hand to graze over her hand when passing her a drink or press my thigh against hers as we sit on the bar stools around the island.

Not being able to drink means I have the entire night of sober thoughts about the woman I'm not supposed to be interested in. How much longer can I keep my distance, I'm not sure.

The next morning, I wake up and head for morning skate with the determination that tonight, I'll call Isaac and find a way to let him know that I'm dating his sister.

I kill it in practice. We are in the best shape that this team has been in in years.

"Great practice today, Conley. If you keep skating like that, we're bound for a championship win this season."

"No doubt. This is our year," I say back to Kaenan, who's headed in the opposite direction toward Coach Bex's office, with his team-issued duffle bag hung over his shoulder.

I push through the side exit that leads right to the players' parking lot. The heavy metal door slams behind me like it does every time anyone exits. It's so goddamn loud. Someone should install a soft close on it like the doors on our apartments. It's a nice feature.

I reach down into my own team-issued duffel bag and grab my keys as I step off the cement sidewalk and onto the blacktop of the parking lot, anxious to get back to see if Autumn decided to work from home in those tiny little...

Boom!

My vision goes dark, and everything goes black for a second as I stumble back. Did I just get hit by a car? I just about have an out-of-body experience, the confusion slowing down my body's ability to register pain... but wait... yep, here it comes. A searing pain to the left side of my jaw is beginning to radiate quickly.

"What the fuck!?" I say, grabbing my jaw and finally getting my bearings enough to see the perpetrator.

"You had it coming, Conley," Isaac says, still in his fighter stance, his darkening eyes pinned on me.

In a pair of jeans and a hoodie, Isaac looks too ordinary to look as mean as he was in the ring last night.

His buzz cut and bruising on his knuckles that are still up, ready to strike again, make him look like the badass MMA fighter that I already know he is.

He's trimmer right now than he usually is when he isn't getting ready for a fight. He cut weight to make the weight class for this title fight, but he still looks just as deadly and lethal at any size.

I put up my arms in defense. "Whoa! Whoa! Hold on." I look around quickly and notice that none of my other teammates are out here. They're inside talking with Coach, or they've already left after practice. I'm relieved I don't have to stop them from trying to jump Isaac, but I also wish I had at least someone close enough in case this fucker decides to try to kill me. However, if he wanted to kill me, he should have just run me over with his car. It might have been a quicker resolution to his problem. "What are you talking about?" I ask, my jaw already feeling tight and tingling as I try to speak with it.

The adrenaline is still running thick through my body but soon it will settle down and I'll start feeling the effects of that hit in full force.

"You know exactly, asshole. I watched the replay of your interview from last week's game. I told you not to touch my sister," he growls, giving me a good shove with his hands against my chest. I stumble back another step. His shoulders now easing down, he's not going to hit me again... I don't think.

"Shit, Isaac, we were kids when you said that. Autumn and I are grown-ass adults now. I didn't think you'd feel the same way this many years later."

Liar.

Isaac drops his hands down by his sides, although his fists are still clenched, and he takes a step toward me. I don't flinch, but I prepare for the possibility he might hit me again, and this time, I plan to block it.

"You thought I wouldn't want to protect my baby sister from a player like you?" His voice is raised.

"Come on, man, I'm not a player," I tell him, looking around to make sure no one else is watching this go down.

He shakes his head rapidly in disagreement. "Your reputation precedes you, and you forget we went to high school together... I know how many women you've gone through, and I know what you're capable of. You're going to hurt her," he says, pointing a finger at me.

"I'm not that way with her. I love her."

Wait, what the fuck did I just say? He must have hit me harder than I thought because that was straight-up word vomit.

I love her? Love her like my best friend's little sister... sure. But I've never uttered the words I love you to another soul besides my parents. Not even the girl I dated for a year in my sophomore year of college. There's no way I'm in love with Autumn. We're not even really dating.

Even Isaac looks skeptical, and I don't blame him, but I'm pretty sure he'll kill me if he finds out that we moved in together, and I don't pretend to be in love with her. Nope, I've got to sell the whole lie. The only way I walk out of this with my nose in the same place it was before he showed up is to make him believe that Autumn and I are in love, that we're building a future together, and that I plan on never hurting his sister.

His eyes squint, and I can tell he's trying to determine whether I'm being genuine or just trying to keep him from kicking my ass further.

"Prove it," he says finally.

"Prove it how?"

"I don't know. It's your ass on the line, so I guess you'll think of something."

"Fuck... thanks," I say sarcastically. Then, because I can't come up with anything worse than this, I blurt out, "Come stay with us."

"Stay with you?" he asks in surprise, his eyebrows shooting up.

That makes two of us.

"Yeah... we just moved in together. We have a spare room."

Oh, for fuck's sake, Briggs, you're a dumbass.

"You're living with my baby sister?" Isaac asks, taking another step forward, his fists balling at his sides, but if he thinks I'm about to back down or cower, he's forgotten who always had his back out on the ice when we played together. Even if I can't defend myself against an MMA fighter, I'll sure as hell defend Autumn. He's treating her like a child who can't make up her own mind. He has no idea how important this fake relationship is to her career... and to mine.

"I told you, we're in love."

There I go again. Shoving my foot in my mouth.

Isaac stares back at me for a second and then crosses his arms over her chest, "All right, fine. I have to check in with a fighter gym here locally that I'm training with for two days. Text me the address, and I'll head over when I'm done," he says, his six-foot stature of pure muscle finally seeming to loosen for the first time since our odd reunion.

Thank God. I'll have a few minutes to warn Autumn before he shows up and tells her the dumb thing I did, suggesting her brother comes to stay with us.

"Your sister will be glad to see you."

"Yeah... we'll see," he says, looking at my eye and then my jaw. "You'd better get some ice on that."

I don't say anything, instead, I just stare back at him, keeping my feet planted, holding my ground.

Isaac spins around and heads for what looks like a rental Prius. He climbs into the car and I bite back a laugh because he'd just climb back out of the car and give me the beat down he held back from giving me.

Autumn

The second Briggs walks through the door of our apartment, I look over from the spot I'm sitting in the living room, streaming a baking competition show, and see a huge red mark on the left side of his face. I jump off the couch, worried about what happened to him since he left this morning, and head for him as he makes his way further into the apartment.

Did he get in a fight with a player on the ice?

Road rage dispute?

What in the actual hell happened today?

"What happened to your face?" I ask, coming up to him quickly.

He drops his black duffel bag on the ground and looks down at me as I inch closer trying to get a better look at his face. His arms hang down by his sides, so he's not trying to stop me from seeing the evidence. He's watching my reaction to him getting hurt... or at least that's how it feels.

"Your brother showed up to the stadium today and waited for me to come out." He gives a humorless chuckle, and it almost seems like Briggs thinks he deserves this, but he doesn't.

"He did what?! Are you kidding me?" I ask, my voice heated.

I reach out and softly grip his jaw to turn it more to the side so I can see the bruising better.

"It's fine. Could have gotten it from yesterday's game. No one will know the difference." He attempts to reassure me.

"But you didn't get in a fight in last night's game."

He just shrugs.

I can't believe Isaac actually hit him. Why does that hurt me so much? I wish I had been there to defend Briggs; he doesn't deserve my brother physically putting his hands on him just for dating me. I wish we could come clean to Isaac.

"It gets worse," he says, after I pull my hand from his face.

"How much worse?" I ask, my eyebrow cocked and ready for something more unsavory than my brother hitting my fake boyfriend.

"I offered to let him stay in the guest bedroom," he says, and then turns and starts walking down the hall to his right and towards his bedroom.

"You did what?!" I ask, my voice raised higher than I meant to.

When the initial shock wears off, I'm back on his heels following him down the hall.

"It'll be fine, but I'll need to move all of my things into your room ASAP," Briggs says, over his shoulder knowing full well I'm right behind me.

"How am I supposed to lie to him while he's staying with us?"

He turns into his room, and I stop in the door frame watching while he begins shoving things he had unpacked back into his duffle bag, though from the looks of it, he didn't unpack much. He heads toward me with the duffle bags fully packed. I move back to let him out of the bedroom.

"It's only a couple of days, and he's going to be training during the day. We can do this. We'll be fine," he says, standing now in the hallway with his two duffle bags, one in each hand.

I look back at the red bruising that is starting to purple and grey around the edges.

"Right... we'll be fine," I say, rolling my eyes and then spinning away from him towards the kitchen. "My brother is practically like a domesticated house cat. Let me just get you something for that massive bruise he left on your face," I say sarcastically to make a point.

I can feel Briggs's eyes on me as I make my way to the kitchen. He doesn't move from his spot in the hallway except to turn to watch me in the kitchen.

"We'll have to sleep together the next couple of nights. Are you going to be okay with that?" he asks.

He should be asking my brother if *he* would be ok with that. Based on the bruise on Briggs's face... I don't see how this will work out, but whatever, these two knuckleheads worked out this plan so they can duke it out, I guess.

He continues to watch as I pull the freezer door open and grab an ice pack from the bottom freezer drawer.

"Yeah. It's fine. It's just a place to rest for the night, and my brother will be in the room down the hall. It's not as if we're going to..." My cheeks heat at the idea that I just implied that something would happen if my brother *wasn't* down the hall.

It's not as if Briggs would be tempted by me. Not with the kind of women he's used to throwing themselves at him. And I wouldn't dare try anything, either. Not only am I not interested in being rejected by my childhood crush, but fooling around with a client is definitely against company rules. I wonder if living with the client makes the rule null and void.

I walk over to the drawer by the sink and grab a dish towel, wrap the ice pack in it, and head back to him.

"You don't have to worry about me. I'll keep my hands to myself," he says, seemingly a little deflated, taking the ice pack from me and then turning to head back to my bedroom to unpack.

I give him some space and head to the island, where I have my laptop set up for work. I use the quiet time to check in on emails and make a couple of calls with Erika and other clients that I'm still working with. Originally Erika was going to pull me off all of the accounts when I took on this project because she doesn't want me distracted, but without work to do during the day, I'd have nothing to do with my time since Briggs is rarely home between morning skate, the gym, physical therapy, dietitian or doctor visits, social media or team events, endorsement responsibilities... point is, Briggs isn't around to entertain me, and all my friends have 8-5 jobs, and I like being busy.

A couple of hours later, the sun has set, and everything from Briggs's room is now in mine. All of his things hang next to mine in the closet, like a true couple and I don't like that my heart squeezes the first time I walk in and see his large mo-notone single-colored shirts hanging next to my much smaller bright-colored and floral prints. He's spent the last half hour watching the sports channel with an ice pack to his face while he lounges on the couch, and I finish up some notes for Derek on an account we were working on before all of this started.

A loud yet familiar knock pounds on the door. I'd know Isaac's knock from anyone else's. I take labored steps toward the door, glancing back at Briggs for one last *"Are you sure we should do this"* look and he nods in a non-verbal reply.

I'm not looking forward to lying to my brother's face about what's happening between Briggs and me. This would be so much easier if we could tell him what's really going on. He'd still be pissed, I'm sure, but maybe Briggs wouldn't have an Isaac-size bruise on his face right now.

"Isaac!" I say, opening the door and tossing my arms around my big brother's neck before I get a good look at him.

"Hey, little sis," he says, squeezing me closer and lifting me off the ground in a big bear hug. "I've missed you."

"I've missed you too. I wasn't expecting a surprise visit, though. You should have told me you were coming."

He sets me back down and stares over at the living room where Briggs is sitting on the large L-shaped sofa, his arm laid over the low back of the couch and his long right leg stretched out on the sofa, pointing toward us, his other foot still on the ground and an ice pack held against his face. The sounds of the sports channel broadcaster seem too chipper and upbeat for this reunion.

I finally get the first look at my brother since I opened the door. He doesn't look any better than Briggs. In fact, he looks a little like his face got hit by a bus. His buzzed haircut and swollen face from the fight last night make him look as harsh as a true MMA badass, but if you hadn't watched him win that fight last night, you'd never guess that he looks better than the other guy today. The other guy probably got admitted to the hospital.

"Looks like you could use an ice pack too." I chuckle.

Isaac looks past me at Briggs again. My eyes follow his as Briggs and Isaac have a short stare-down, both their faces grimacing at one another. If they were a pair of bulldogs, they'd probably be growling at each other about now..

"Ice packs are for pussies," Isaac says.

"How charming. I love when men use the slang term for a woman's anatomy to imply weakness." I roll my eyes and walk away with irritation.

"Sorry," he says under his breath.

I don't think he is sorry, but maybe at least he'll stop saying it around me.

Even through all of this, I'm still excited to see him. Ever since he moved to Las Vegas to pursue his fighting career full-time, I don't see as much of him as I'd like.

Isaac follows behind me with a swagger meant to piss off Briggs, and from the corner of my eye, I can tell Briggs is growing irritated. I want to tell Isaac to knock off this shit. These two were practically inseparable for our entire childhood, up until the minute they both left for different colleges. Not that they didn't have their differences or arguments, but this is breaking my heart, and I can't stand to see them like this for a minute longer.

"All right, well..." I say to Isaac in an attempt to break the silence. "This is our new place. Let me give you the grand tour."

I pull Isaac along with me toward the large open-concept kitchen to our left. Isaac takes a look around at the state-of-the-art kitchen. "I bet you're in heaven baking in here."

It's true. I packed in preparation for a grand bake-a-thon one of these weekends when Briggs is on the road. I even have everything I need for several batches of ingredients for chocolate oatmeal cookies when the itch to bake arises.

"A little bit, but I have big plans for this double oven and this huge island. I could probably have ten cooling sheets up here with Mom's chocolate chip recipe." I lay out my full wingspan over the top of the island, my cheek resting on the cold white sparkling granite countertop as I stretch out my arms to prove my point about how large the island is since my fingertips don't even come close to touching either end of the countertop.

"That chocolate chip recipe?" I hear Briggs perk his head up a little higher over the couch in the distant living room and look over at me in the kitchen, ignoring Isaac's existence. "Are you going to make cookies tonight? Damn, I could use one right about now."

Isaac looks down at me, too, hope flickering in his eyes... or maybe that's just the look of a man who had to starve himself for the last month to make weight for his fight.

"Mom's cookie would hit the spot after such a long trip coming to see you."

The pressure is beginning to stack up against me.

I guess it's good to see they can agree on one thing.

"Not in your dreams," I tell them both. "I'm not baking tonight. It's late, and I'm tired. I'm ready for a good book and a long bath."

Isaac looks over at Briggs. "You'd better be planning on keeping your pants on for the entire two days I'm here."

Briggs just throws up his free hand in frustration, the other holding the ice pack to his face again.

I roll my eyes and shake my head at my brother's demands. Not because that was what Briggs and I were planning on doing, but because that was the right reaction if I was truly dating Briggs. Damn, I hate this. "Come on, you..." I say gruffly. "Let's get you settled in the spare bedroom."

Briggs stands up as Isaac and I head toward the hallway, but he beats us to it, heading down in front of us.

"I'm tired too. I'm heading to *our* room. Are you coming in soon? I'll run your bathwater."

Briggs stops and turns around, glaring at Isaac, and then smiles down at me.

Perfect, poke the bear, why don't you?

"Watch it, Conley," my brother all but snarls. "There's still plenty of real estate on that pretty boy face of yours for a matching black eye."

Briggs breaks our eye contact and glances at Isaac. Gone is my brother, and in his place is a furious MMA fighter. His shoulders roll back, and muscles flex along his arms. It's only when Briggs looks down at my stomach do I realize that Isaac has put his hand there and pushed me slightly behind him.

I can barely breathe as tension fills the air.

"Twenty-five years of friendship or not," Briggs says with his voice dangerously low. "I'll fight you for your sister if that's what it takes."

What the... where did that come from?

"Guys—" I try to break the tension.

"Glad we understand each other then," Isaac says, turning into the bedroom.

"Isaac—" I try, but he slams the bedroom door behind him.

I turn back to Briggs and give him a lopsided frown, landing my hand on top of my hip to show how I feel about the unnecessary comments he just made to piss off my brother. We were supposed to tread water carefully for the next couple of days, appease Isaac into thinking we're living like nuns in a monastery, and get him back on his way until our "relationship" runs its course and we break up... amicably.

He looks at my cocked hip and chuckles, turning back around and slapping the ice pack back on his face as he walks to the master bedroom.

"That tub is built for two... convenient."

I want to yell at him, *"Not in your dreams,"* but I don't need Isaac hearing a dispute arising out in the hall and deciding to come out to investigate.

Instead, I ignore it and head to the kitchen, where I left my phone plugged in, and I snatch my tablet from my purse with the new romance thriller I've been dying to read.

Tonight, I need a distraction and something that I can count on that ends with a happily ever after.

CHAPTER FIFTEEN

Autumn

"Feel like explaining what happened back there?" I ask as I push through the master bedroom door and close it behind me.

Even with an ice pack to his face, he still looks beyond sexy and cool with his long legs stretched out and crossed at the ankles, leaning up against the large, upholstered headboard, his phone in one hand as he seems to be reading something. Probably reading up on how well the team he's up against next week played or something a sports newscaster said about his team's chances of making it to the playoffs this year.

His blue eyes glance up from his phone and settle on me. "Explaining what?"

I head for the bathroom in search of my anti-aging eye night cream. It works wonders for puffiness. I grab the small blue glass jar sitting by the sink and head back out of the bathroom.

"The fact that you told my brother that you'd fight him for me when we both know that his friendship means more to you than a relationship with any woman, *especially* me."

I raise an eyebrow at him as I walk around to the side of the bed that he chose to sit on. The side that already has my glasses, phone charger, and a small fan to lull me to sleep on the nightstand. I sigh—one pain-in-the-ass problem at a time. The fight over who sleeps where will have to wait its turn.

He doesn't respond. He just watches me as I come closer, dropping his phone on his lap and eyeing the product I have in my hand.

"I don't know why you had to go that far to prove to him we are together," I say, reaching over him and slowly grabbing for the ice pack. I can feel his eyes on me as I bend over him to try to pull the ice pack from his face, but the bed is too tall, and it's an awkward position. I place my knee on the bed to give myself a boost to get closer. "Can I see it?" I ask, referring to the bruise on the left side of his face that I can't reach.

"What's that?" he asks, pulling the ice pack from his face and dropping it on the bed. He looks down at the blue container with miracle powers mixed into every drop.

"It's a secret..."

"And you want me to trust you to put that shit on my face?"

"It's not shit... and what could it hurt?"

"My manhood... my dignity... my—"

"Okay, I get it." I shake my head. "But I swear on Wayne Gretzky and the mighty hockey powers that be that I won't tell a single soul that you wore eye cream tonight, and you can wipe it off in the morning. It'll just help with the puffiness."

He makes a grumbling noise and moves away from me when I reach for his eye again.

"Briggs, stop being such a baby. Your manhood is safe with me."

Briggs looks down toward his dick and then gives me a goofy grin.

"Not that manhood." I tilt my head in annoyance that he had to take it there. He chuckles and finally nods.

"Good boy," I tell him.

He gives a sexy grin.

I lean in again, but it's an awkward position, and I won't be able to rub the gel on very well. Before I can think of a better angle, Briggs turns his torso as both of his hands grip my hips and lifts me. I yelp in surprise, one of my hands pressing against his chest to keep me from losing my balance. He directs my body to straddle his, and now I'm sitting on top of his lap. I don't dare look down to see how close I am to sitting over his cock.

With only a pair of his black athletic sweats that he's still wearing from after practice and my thin pajama pants, there wouldn't be much stopping me from feeling any movement if he got excited while I sat on his lap. Not unlike last night when he pulled me onto his lap during my brother's fight. I did my best not to draw attention to the fact that I could feel him hardening slowly under me.

No matter what happened last night at the party... or didn't happen, Briggs is still off limits, and I know it.

I take a steady breath, and he hears it.

"You okay?"

"Yeah." I nod and try to get back to the task at hand. I look at the bruising, "The ice pack's done a good job. It looks better."

"I wouldn't have used an ice pack if it had been a fight on the ice, but since I've been trying to clean up my image, and I didn't get in a fight yesterday, I didn't want people to think my tiny pint-sized girlfriend got the upper hand in a lovers quarrel."

I just about headbutt him as I burst into laughter at the idea that I could do any damage to him. He grips my hips tighter again to keep me from falling forward, and somehow, I end up further up his lap.

"Oh, dear God, no. Could you imagine the man card you'd have to hand over for that?" I ask.

"No amount of anti-puff cream could help me then."

We both chuckle as I twist open the bottle.

"Do you remember the time that Isaac tried to steal my mom's waterproof mascara because you two wanted to paint black marks over your cheekbones before your first hockey practice to make you look meaner?"

"But it turned out to be her fuchsia waterproof lipstick instead?" He says dryly. "Yeah... I remember."

Something about his lackluster reaction to the memory just gets me. I was probably five years old when my dad brought the boys home after practice. They looked pained over the scarring experience of being razzed by the other kid players. My dad still made them play. He said it was character-building. I guess so because these boys are tougher than nails now.

But the image of my older brother and his best friend coming home with pink cheeks is still tattooed on my memory to this day.

"I'm not sure that was the best memory to bring up before you add more chick shit to my face." He raises an eyebrow at me.

"I'm sorry. I just remembered that," I say, biting back a little giggle.

I can feel his eyes on me as I open the bottle and take a small swipe of the clear cooling gel onto my index finger, trying to get my giggles under control.

"You know what I just remembered?" he asks.

"What?"

"You have a great laugh."

"I do?"

When I look back up, Briggs is still sporting a small smile, and his eyes quickly glance down at my mouth and then back up. "Yeah," he says softly.

A little twinge of goosebumps rolls down my arms at the thought of him wanting to kiss me, but that's crazy, right? I just brought up the exact reason why not. I'm not a hot puck bunny, twisting my long blonde hair at the bar with my tits hiked up to the sky. I'm just the best friend's little sister with embarrassing memories at the ready, wearing a pair of pajama pants and a Nike zip-up hoodie, with my shoulder-length brown hair braided behind me. I look as casual as can be. Not in the least bit dressed to impress.

I reach out, and I rub the gel slowly into his perfectly tanned skin. Up this close, I can see the small little sprinkling of dark freckles against his olive skin. I almost forgot about those. In the summers, even with all the overcast weather of Washington, the beautiful Italian skin that Briggs's mom gave him would somehow absorb the tiniest amount of UV rays, and his skin would bronze while the rest of us stayed stark white. His freckles somehow contrasted with the deepening color, and I would stare at those freckles whenever Briggs didn't notice me. I always dreamed that someday he'd give me the freedom to map every freckle and smooth my finger over each sweet speckle. This is the closest I've ever been, and the desperate little girl in me from years past is begging me not to let this moment go to waste.

I lay my thumb softly against the mostly straight bridge of his nose and sweep my thumb across his cheekbone, using the gel as an excuse for my touch.

He watches every expression I make as I try to laminate every freckle to memory, knowing this might be the last time I have an unobstructed view of them.

"What are you doing?" he asks in a whisper, his fingers slowly tightening around my hips.

"Putting cooling gel—"

"No, you're not," he whispers again.

I desert my quest to find any two freckles the same and settle my sights on his crystal blue eyes that look like crushed ice up this close.

"I forgot how jealous I used to be of your freckles."

"You noticed my freckles? I don't think anyone else realizes I have them." A soft lopsided smile stretches on one side of his ruggedly beautiful face. "Even I forget most of the time."

I swallow hard. Now isn't the time to catch on, Briggs.

"What else did you notice?" he asks quietly.

Everything.

"Nothing. Just the freckles."

I have to do something. We're headed for a dangerous place called the past and my die-hard crush. "I mean... and the fact that you hadn't hit puberty at the advanced age of seventeen."

I fake a grimace and glance down at his crotch.

He lets out that contagious laugh I've always loved, and I can't help but enjoy the fact that sitting on his lap allows me to feel his laugh, too, as his body shakes underneath me. He even throws back his head as if I took him off guard, and I can't help the rise of pride to be able to make Briggs Conley laugh that big.

When he come back around to face me, there's a flirtatious smile stretched across his face, and it might as well be Niagara Falls in my panties.

"Well, I guess now I'm going to have to show you how generous puberty was to me to clear any misconceptions."

"Wait, what? Briggs—" I squeal as he grips both of his burly hands around my waist and hoists me up off his lap, disposing me flat on my back on my *new* side of the bed.

He begins to tickle my waist as he's still sitting up right next to me. I try to push his hands away, but his arms are so much longer and stronger than mine that I'm at a huge disadvantage.

"Admit it's anaconda big."

"What?!" I laugh from the continued tickling.

"Admit it's the biggest thing you've ever seen."

I can't stop laughing, and I barely choke out the words. "I had to use a telescope to see it across the pond."

I snort a laugh as his fingers move quicker as my punishment, and I try to wiggle toward the end of the bed to find freedom from his clutches since trying to fend him off isn't proving fruitful.

"You're not getting away that easy," he says, grabbing my hips and yanking me back toward him. He adjusts his body, and before I know it, Briggs Conley, the man I've had a childhood crush on since the beginning of time, slides himself between my thighs and presses his pelvis against mine. His cock is bulging, and the weight of it against me sends a swirl of excitement through my belly. "Say it or I'll..." he demands in a teasing voice.

"You'll what? Prove how big it is?" I ask, teasing, but then realize what I just said.

Briggs's grin wipes clean off his face as he stares back at me. My smile freezes too, and then slowly dies because something in the air between us just changed. He glances down at our connected bodies, and then so do I.

My chest is still heaving from laughing so hard, and so is his. Our hearts are pumping, and our lungs are desperate for more air.

There's something in his eyes. Something dangerous to his relationship with my brother and dangerous to my promotion.

"Do you want me to?" he asks.

My stomach flips, and I swallow hard. "Briggs... I don't think this is a good idea."

"No... it's not."

He doesn't move an inch, and neither do I. I'm practically holding my breath as he looks deep into my eyes. He feels closer than ever, his lips not far from mine. Then he leans down and presses his lips against mine.

My body explodes in tingles all over as the warmth of his mouth spreads across my own. The kiss is soft, but then he pulls back for a second and looks into my eyes.

"Briggs, this isn't—"

He dips back down and seals our lips together in a demanding kiss. I'm still in shock. This can't be real.

His right-hand snakes up the side of my body, just briefly skating over my breast before his hand wraps around my neck, his fingers plunging into the thick of my hair. He pulls my mouth tighter against his, and I open for him. His tongue dips in, and it's the first real taste of Briggs I've ever had. I moan at the sensation, the taste, the heat.

My verbal approval eggs him on as his hips begin to move, and his hardening cock grinds into the part of me that needs connection even more than our mouths.

I moan again as the pressure between my thighs increases. The probability that he might get me off before he's taken off a single article of clothing is a mortifying and an equally delicious thought.

His hand releases the side of my neck and begins to trail down my body. His fingers dip under my shirt and glide back up my rib cage until his index finger and thumb sneak past the elastic of my sports bra.

He's almost there, his fingers almost secured about my breast, and then there won't be any turning back. I'll beg him to race past third base and go for a home run. I know it's the wrong sport, but Briggs was one hell of a baseball player, too, and a girl can't deny a thick ass in a pair of baseball pants. Briggs used to wear them well.

"Yes," I mutter as his hand almost seems to stall.

"Autumn... are you sure?"

KNOCK!

KNOCK!

"Shit!" I shriek, trying to cover my mouth. I try to pull out from under Briggs, but he grips me tighter and slides me further under him like he's going to protect me if my brother busts through the door. I'd tell him that the only person needing protection is him, but it's a moot point. He's well aware of the dynamic here.

"Autumn," I hear Isaac's voice on the other side.

I try to clear the sex from my voice before answering, "Yeah?"

"Do you have a spare toothbrush? I forgot to pack mine."

I exhale the breath I had trapped in my lungs since the minute he pounded on the door.

"What... too busy cockblocking me to remember your damn toothbrush?" Briggs whispers against my ear.

My stomach flips.

Cock block?

Did he just confirm that we were on the same page only a few moments ago? The heat of his mouth against my ear reminds me that I'm not far from that moment, even still.

"Uh, yeah..." I look up at Briggs, and he looks down at me, still nestled between my thighs. "Hold on, I'll get it for you," I say, attempting to push Briggs off me.

He finally moves off me but not from my weakling efforts. He flops to the side with a groan and lays the crook of his elbow over his eyes in defeat.

I want to ask Briggs what would have happened if Isaac hadn't interrupted us. But I have a pissed-off brother standing on the other side of my bedroom door, and he isn't the patient kind.

Especially when he thinks his little sister is tucked back in a bedroom with the big bad hockey wolf.

I walk out of the room, glancing over my shoulder as I go. Briggs is still lying there on the bed, in the same place and position he was in when he flipped himself off of me. My eyes slide down his body. The view of a decent sized bulge in Briggs's pants has me about ready to punch my brother in the throat for making me miss out. I've always known it was big, but to feel the evidence as he rubbed it against me was pretty phenomenal. I bite down on my lower lip unconsciously until I walk out into the hall, closing the door behind me, and my brother gives me a disgusted look.

"Oh, shut up," I tell him, and power walk down the corridor.

This rental apartment has everything, and I'll bet they stocked a spare toothbrush in the hallway closet. Isaac follows behind me closely. I rip open the closet door, and sure enough, a stack of toothbrushes is sitting on the shelf at eye level.

"Barbie or Paw Patrol?" I ask, showing him the kid's toothbrush options.

He reaches over me and grabs a blue adult toothbrush. "I'll take this, thanks."

"You sure don't need one better designed for a child? Because that's how you acted, flying here unannounced and sucker punching Briggs in the face at his place of employment just because you're mad that we're adults having an adult—"

"Don't finish that." He points at me, a scowl on his face. "I'm your brother, and it's my job to protect you."

"Correction. It's Dad's job to protect me. Your job is to issue me constant flattery and be a complete failure by comparison to my awesomeness... which, by the way, you suck at your job." I roll my eyes. "Congrats on your big title win. Mom and Dad are disgustingly proud of you pummeling that guy's face into the mat."

Isaac wraps an arm around my shoulder. "I'm sorry I made you mad, but in all fairness, I've warned Briggs about touching you... he knows better."

"We're not kids anymore—"

"Even more reason for him to leave you alone and not waste the years where you should be finding a good dude, getting married, and having the grandkids Mom keeps nagging me for."

"Speaking of. Are you done with the ring girls? Anyone serious these days?" I ask.

"Hell no." He laughs. "Come hang out with me for a few minutes. I haven't seen you in over six months."

I look longingly at the master bedroom door, wanting to get back in there and climb back under Briggs, even though I shouldn't. One night could cost me a promotion.

"Don't worry, Briggs can entertain himself," he says, pulling me toward his room.

Yeah... that's what I'm worried about. He should be '*entertaining*' himself with me.

"Okay, fine. A few minutes."

I walk in and sit on the spare bedroom bed. The room still smells like Briggs; the sour apple gum he chews occasionally and his spicy deodorant.

"What's new?" he asks, walking into the bathroom and wetting a toothbrush from his overnight bag. Freaking liar! I should have known.

"Nice toothbrush, loser!" I call out.

He turns to look at me with that stupid grin I want to smack off his smug face.

He adds toothpaste and then walks back out of the bathroom.

"I wanted time alone with my little sister. I gave up a celebration party to be here," he says, and then starts brushing as if I want to watch him brush his teeth. Whatever, annoying brothers stay annoying brothers, I guess.

"And if you would have called first, I would have told you not to bother."

He pulls the toothbrush out of his mouth. "Well, I'm here now, so tell me what's new. How's work?"

"Good. I'm up for a promotion."

He keeps brushing but lifts his eyebrows as if to say he's intrigued.

"I have this new campaign I'm running, and if I save this guy's career, the company he plays... I mean, works for, will become a massive client for our firm. My boss is going to give me a promotion to head of client relations."

My brother stops brushing for a second and stares at me, his mouth now full of foam. "Autumn, that's amazing. They must believe in you," he mumbles with a full mouth.

I nod and stare down at my feet.

"What's wrong?" he asks, and then begins to brush again.

"I have to do something a little unorthodox and not something I would usually agree to do."

My brother's eyes widen to cartoon size. "Hold on." He puts up a finger and heads for the bathroom. He spits, rinses, and then puts the toothbrush away and walks with determination back out to where I'm sitting.

"What are they making you do? And who do I have to kill?"

Aww, that's kind of sweet.

"No." I laugh. "Not like that, jeez. Don't you let out enough of that male testosterone in the ring?"

"If someone is making you do something that you don't want to do..."

"No. It's more like... I kind of have to lie for him," I say, not making eye contact again, worried he'll see Briggs Conley written in my pupils.

"Why?"

"Because he's getting blackmailed for something he didn't do, and I had this bright idea to improve his image in case the fake gossip comes out."

"How would that help him?"

"He has a reputation already of being a party boy, and if we can paint him as a reformed, responsible man, then maybe, if the gossip hits, it won't seem as plausible."

"Is he reformed?"

Good question.

"I don't know."

"Does he deserve your help?" he asks, staring back at me, waiting for my answer, his big, bruised fighter hands pinched at his waist.

I stop and think about that for a second. It's not something I've ever asked when I've worked on PR cases in the past. Is Briggs guilty of what the exotic dancer accused him of... no. But is he going to keep himself out of trouble and get his drinking under control after this all blows over? I have no idea.

What I do know is the real Briggs. The one before all the fame and money, and he is worth my help. The man who pulled me further under him only a little while ago to protect me against my brother, even though he knows my brother would never hurt me. He should have backed away from me for self-preservation, but instead, he leaned in, holding me closer.

Somehow, it feels like he lost his way, but over the last twenty-four hours, I feel a little bit of him is coming back.

"Yes, he deserves my help."

My brother sighs and then thinks for a second.

"Then he's a lucky asshole to have you on his side, and you should do whatever you can to help him."

If only you knew who you were pushing me closer toward.

"Thanks, Isaac."

We chat for another fifteen minutes or so about his life in Las Vegas and how I like living downtown in Seattle, and then I yawn.

"All right," he says dramatically. "I guess you can go to bed. Love you, Autumn." He grins, opening up his arms to signal he wants a hug goodnight.

"Love you, too," I say as I stand, my brother stepping in to give me a quick hug, and then I walk out of the bedroom and head for my room.

I hear my brother's door click closed, and I exhale, hoping that's the last I see of him tonight.

I'm nervous and excited to see Briggs again. I wonder if he'll want to start where we left off or if he's already stripped out of his clothes and is waiting for me naked in the bed.

When I open the door, my smile falls.

He's snoring.

Dead asleep on my side of the bed.

Great. So much for a warm reunion.

I debate just climbing into bed, but I wasn't joking about the bath... I still really want one.

I grab my tablet off the dresser where I left it earlier and head for the bath, flip on the water, and dump enough bubbles in to build a reasonable-sized replica of the Eiffel Tower, which I do right before I start my book.

An hour later, I can't keep my eyes open, and it's time for bed. I drain the water and pull on a cute pair of pajamas that I just bought before I moved in here because, duh, I maybe didn't expect anything to happen with Briggs, but I'm not a hundred years old. I still had plans to flutter around the apartment in cute jammies in front of my old crush. When would I ever get another chance like this?

I walk out and find that in the last hour, while I was in the bath, Briggs discarded his pants and shirt as they are currently laid over the dresser. I find a now shirtless mound of hot muscle asleep in my spot.

If I thought I could move the mountain of a man currently sleeping on my side, I'd attempt to transfer him to the other side, but I'm too damn tired. Tomorrow, I'll beat him to bed and get my spot back.

I roll my eyes and slide onto the wrong side of the bed and pull the covers over me, facing away from the tasty man lying only an arms length away.

I lay down and begin to fall asleep. I'm not quite into full REM when a strong arm and a warm body scoop me up and yank me back against a wall of muscle.

"Briggs?" I whisper.

"No talking," he mutters, half asleep.

"But..."

"Shhh, go to sleep, Autumn."

That's it. No kiss goodnight. No telling me to have sweet dreams.

I'm not sure what happens next for us but whatever it is, I hope every night ends in spooning with Briggs Conley.

CHAPTER SIXTEEN

Briggs

Out on the ice is the place where my mind is the clearest. The world can be going to shit, but my laser focus on my job pulls me out of it. Today is a different story because the only thing I can think about is Autumn and what happened last night. I kissed her, and maybe I shouldn't have, but I couldn't stop myself. Autumn isn't like the women I've met over the years.

This morning, we had an early skate, so I left before she got up, and when I was getting dressed, a text pinged on the phone. I walked out of the bathroom to see who it was, but it wasn't my phone. It was Autumn's. We have the same sound for notifications. I didn't open up her phone, but I didn't have to. The notification was short enough that I could read his text that flashed over her screen.

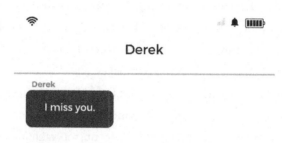

Then a quick second text.

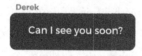

I'm not her real boyfriend, and she already told me that she was seeing someone else. Still, I want to text him back and tell him to stay the fuck away from Autumn, but that's not my call. Instead, I finished brushing my teeth with a little extra vigor than usual and left the apartment, heading to the stadium.

Isaac had already left for the gym. I was glad not to have to see his not-so-happy ass this morning after I came out of the bedroom from sleeping next to his sister all night. The fucking cock blocker.

Autumn's miracle cream did a pretty damn good job of taking away the swelling. Icing it half the day helped it along as well, although I usually sport my battle wounds from a game or bar fight as a badge of honor. Even so, the discoloration was still enough that everyone asked about the shiner since all my teammates already knew I didn't take a shot to the face last game.

I skate out onto the ice, lining up for drills.

I take a deep breath in, loving the feeling of the cold snap against my lungs. Being on the ice is my favorite place. It's a place where I can get away from the world, where I can block out the noise, and do what I do best. Play hockey.

"What the fuck happened to your face?" Reeve Aisa, one of our two goalies, asks, skating up to me and getting in line.

Seven Wrenley, our other goalie, skates up, too, taking a quick look, although he tries not to make it obvious. He pretends he's too old for gossip, but he's never too far from listening in on it.

Lake Powers skates over directly after, undoubtedly not to mind his own damn business. He eyeballs my cheek and whistles. "Damn. Did you get in a fight with a fucking semi-truck? By the look of it, the Freightliner won."

"Shut up, asshole," I mutter, watching the other guys head over.

Lake laughs.

"Hey everyone, check out Briggs's face!" Lake yells to the guys at the far end of the ice headed our way. "Turns out his new girlfriend is a little feistier than he can handle."

"Fuck off, Powers, and start skating your damn drills," Ryker Haynes, our captain, and center, says, skating up to us and spraying ice at Lake.

"Mill your damn gossip on your own time. I don't want to be here all damn day, and Coach said we can go home early. I got a little girl begging to go to the park," Kaenan says, skating up and parking himself on the left side of me.

"More like a nanny that wants to try out your teeter-totter," Lake jabs.

"His tiny otter?" Brent Tomlin asks, skating up to the line with a furrowed brow as if he should take offense. "Who has a tiny otter?"

I'd believe it if someone told me that Brent had taken too many hits to the head, which caused severe hearing loss. The guys can never hear worth shit.

"Don't worry, it's not your otter," I say.

"Damn straight, it's not my otter," Brent retorts. "My otter is huge."

"Jesus. Can we fucking skate already?" Kaenan hollers.

"We've seen your otter, Tomlin. It must have been the runt of the litter," Lake retorts.

"Fuck you, Powers, it's never had a problem cracking open clams!" Brent yells.

"If you assholes don't shut up, I'm making you do burpees til you puke," Coach Bex threatens from the side of the home team bench, his stopwatch in one hand, clipboard in the other.

We hear Coach Bex's whistle, and we all push off the line. Drills have begun, and there's no more room for bullshitting. We'll have to save the rest for the locker room.

An hour and a half later, Coach Bex lets us go for the day. Kaenan is out like a flash, and the rest of us head for our cars as well. I'm looking forward to getting home before Isaac to get in a little one-on-one time with Autumn. Then the walking on eggshells will begin again.

She mentioned yesterday that she has a coffee meeting with Tessa and Penelope this morning to go over logistics and to touch base on how our media campaign is unfolding, but I'm hoping she'll be home by the time I get back, not that she's expecting me home this early.

I need some clarification on what's going on with her and Derek before anything between us continues. Some people might accuse me of being a player, but I don't fuck women with boyfriends or husbands.

I step off the elevator, and the aroma of freshly baked cookies hits me immediately. I know that smell, and it smells like my childhood. Like sleepovers in Isaac's treehouse and cold winters in Walla Walla with warm cookies and hot chocolate.

I input the keycode to our apartment and push through the door as soon as the light turns green. Walking through the door of our temporary apartment, I find a scantily dressed Autumn standing in the kitchen in only a pair of light pink boy shorts and a grey crop top, standing in front of what looks like three batches of cookies laid out on cooling racks and parchment paper covering every inch of the granite countertop.

She yips in surprise, just barely losing the baking sheet filled with freshly baked cookies and spatula out of her hand when the apartment door finally closes, and she realizes she's no longer alone.

She spins around to find me standing in the entryway watching her.

"Oh my gosh, you scared me! You're home," she says, spinning back away from me to where several cooling racks are lined up, full of chocolate chip oatmeal cookies.

She tries to quickly get the last cookies off the baking sheet. "I was about to take a shower after I got back from the gym, but after I started undressing, I decided I wanted to have cookies done and cooled before you and Isaac got home. I thought you two could come to a treaty deal over milk and cookies."

"So you decided to bake naked?" I ask, watching a half-dressed Autumn scurry to finish her task.

"I'm not naked!" she argues, rushing through to get the cookies pulled off the baking sheet, probably so she can escape back to the master bedroom to seek refuge. The ferocity of her spatula-wielding is causing her ass to jiggle in those tiny little pink boy shorts of hers, and I'm fucking mesmerized.

What Autumn Daughtry has is the ass. With just the right amount of perkiness to it but enough volume to make it ideal for pushing up against from behind. I bet it's a little more than a handful for each cheek, and I'm tempted to walk over and test out how much more of a handful it is.

My mouth is watering to the point where I should probably see a doctor to make sure it's not some kind of condition because I'm not sure whether it's the cookies I'm craving or her.

If I was a smart man, I'd make sure never to touch Autumn Daughtry again to avoid imploding my friendship with my oldest friend. This relationship is fake and temporary, so even more reason to make sure we don't fuck anything up in our real lives for when we have to go back.

Too bad I'm not a smart man.

Autumn

Briggs is home!?

I thought practice was much longer. If I had known to expect him, I wouldn't be standing half-naked in this kitchen.

"I thought you were at practice," I say as I feel Briggs start to cut the space between us.

"I thought you had a breakfast meeting with Tessa and Penelope?" he fires back, still coming closer and rounding the kitchen counter and heading toward me.

"I do, but Tessa had to postpone. Something about reaming out Lake Powers for some inappropriate post," I tell him, fidgeting under his watchful eye as he's now right behind me. "We're meeting in an hour instead, so I had time to go to the gym and make cookies."

I can feel Briggs inch closer as he settles directly behind me, dressed in a pair of dark wash jeans that he wore to the fights and a tight-fitting t-shirt from a company that he endorses. His dark blond hair is damp, likely from showering after practice. If I took a step back, my bum would push up against his crotch.

I can feel little goosebumps along my arms. Even the baby hairs around my face tremble with need for the heat of his mouth.

"They smell amazing. Chocolate chip oatmeal?"

I can hear the deep tone of his voice right behind me, and I'm all too aware of how little clothing I have on. My belly flips as I feel his eyes on me.

"Yeah."

"Those are my favorite," he says, another step closer and peering over my shoulder, watching me work.

He's wearing jeans today and the bulge of the denim that covers the zipper slides against my bum ever so gently that I barely feel it but it sends a shiver down my spine.

"I know—" I say softly, almost in a whisper, but he catches it.

Shut up, Autumn.

"You made these for me?" He matches my whisper, the heat of his mouth radiating against my neck.

"I made them for you and my brother. They're his favorite too." I fake a defensive tone.

Not true. He's never been fond of the oatmeal portion. That's all Briggs. But that won't stop Isaac from demolishing a whole baker's dozen in one sitting, along with a half-gallon of milk.

Savages, both of them.

"Hmm. Well, I'm starving, so thanks—"

I smack his hand with the spatula I'm holding as he reaches for a cookie over my shoulder.

"Ouch!" he says, shaking his hand out and smiling when I look over my shoulder.

"They haven't cooled yet. You'll have to wait."

"Bullshit," he says, grabbing the spatula out of my hand and smacking my bum with it.

"Hey, ouch!" I yell back, rubbing the spot where Briggs spanked me with the extra wide spatula I bought specifically for pulling large cookies off baking sheets.

"Be a good girl, and let me eat your cookies, or I'll spank you again."

Umm, can you say that entire sentence again so I can commit it to memory?

"What!? No! You'll have to—"

Before I can finish my thought, Briggs wraps his left arm around my middle and hoists me up against him, my back to his front. He shifts me to the left side of his body, and I try to squirm out of his hold while he grabs two cookies with his other hand and sandwiches them together, taking a giant bite. I can't ignore the fact that Briggs can hold up my entire weight with only one arm and doesn't flinch when I try to wiggle loose.

"Mmmm." He groans, and a zing rolls through my already-warming center.

"Put me down this instant."

Please don't put me down.

And he doesn't. Instead, he takes another bite.

"Damn, these are good," he says, stuffing the last of his cookie sandwich in his mouth. "I almost forgot how good."

He finally sets me back down, and I spin around and punch him in the arm.

"Whoa, little tiger. It's just a couple of cookies," he says, putting his hands up in defense. "You have enough here to feed the entire Hawkeyes team."

"I knew I shouldn't have made you any cookies," I huff.

"Hey now," he says, taking a step closer. "I'm grateful for the cookies... and the view." His eyes brush over my body.

"The view isn't part of the deal," I say.

He takes another step so that my breasts just barely graze against the bottom of his rib cage.

"Speaking of, how would Derek like it if you were walking around half-naked with me in the house?"

"I'm sure he would find that inappropriate of me to do while with a client. But his opinion is irrelevant."

"Because we're living together?" he asks, seemingly fishing, and after what happened last night, I guess I get why he would ask.

"Because he and I put everything on hold until this project is complete, and you and I get back to our old lives."

The old life where Briggs has hundreds of women throwing themselves at him.

There's a little bit of melted chocolate from the cookie in the corner of his mouth. "You've got something..." I lift my hand, and Briggs leans in closer. My index finger glides over the sugar confection and wipes it off his lip while his right hand reaches around my back and his left hand slides along my left butt cheek that's only covered in underwear and pulls me flush against him. I pull my hand back and suck my finger into my mouth, licking the chocolate off my finger that used to be melted against his skin.

"Fuck," Briggs growls, and then before I can register his movement, he squeezes my bum, plastering me tighter against his hard erection.

His warm lips descend against mine with a heated pressure as he backs me up against the island, his lips on mine, one hand in my hair pulling my mouth closer to his, one hand gripping my butt tighter as he pins me in place.

He picks me up and sets my bum on the island.

"My brother..."

He stops and pulls his lips off mine. "Really? You want to bring him up right now?"

I giggle. "I'm sorry... it's just that he could walk in at any minute."

"Then he's going to get an eyeful because I'm still hungry."

"You're what?" I hear my voice shake at the question.

He places a hand between my shoulder blades and then lays me down gently, flat on my back. He hooks his fingers under my knees and lifts them up, placing my heels behind my bum on the counter, and then slides his index finger into the sides of my boy shorts, pulling them down slowly off my bum, past my thighs, and then off my feet.

Seeing Briggs hover over me is a dream. How is this happening?

No one wake me!

"What are you planning to do?" I ask, forced to crab walk back to make room for my heels on the edge of the counter and feeling a little self-conscious to be lying naked from the bottom half while he watches every movement I make.

"I told you... I'm still hungry, and if you're going to make me wait for the cookies to cool, then I'll eat something else."

He turns back toward the cookies on the back countertop, and I watch as he breaks a cookie in half, his index finger scooping up some melted chocolate from one of the melted chocolate chips, and turns to me. "I wonder which will be sweeter. The chocolate or your pussy." He gives a devilish grin that creates another flutter of butterflies through my belly.

I take in a sharp breath as Briggs trails his index finger and spreads the chocolate through my slit. His finger is gentle but there is nothing gentle about the way I want Briggs. My center clenches instantly with a sense of urgency to feel all his fingers on me. Tingles burst at the base of my skull, and I arch into his hand. He then dips his head down between my knees, and the memory of the thirty minutes I spent on the treadmill hit me.

I clamp down on his head with my thighs before he reaches his intended destination. "Wait!" I panic, hearing Briggs's sexy chuckle at my reaction as his head is stuck, sandwiched between my legs. "I haven't showered yet from my workout."

He looks up at me with hooded eyes and dilated pupils; a sexy smirk tops off the full vision of pure sex. "Good. I like a little salt with my sweet."

A mouse squeak of a sound must have come from my throat, and my eyes widen at him. I have no idea what to say back to that. I'm having an out-of-body experience, and I can't be sure. The satisfied look on Briggs's face that he's affecting me as he intends suggests that the sound came out of me.

I'm not usually this timid during sex, and I'm no stranger to oral, but seeing a hockey star between my thighs, telling me he's hungry to eat me, and filling me with chocolate has me a little flustered.

"Maybe I should shower first?"

"Not on your life. I've been thinking about doing this all morning, but I thought better of it... until I walked into this apartment and you made me batches of cookies in your underwear. Now there's no way you're leaving this kitchen without having my tongue inside you."

He doesn't wait this time for me to respond, which is just as well because I have no more words. His fingers glide down slowly from my knees, down the inside of my thighs, and then dig under my bum as he grips on tight, bringing his mouth down to meet them. His tongue gives a long lick through me and the chocolate he swiped there.

I moan softly, my eyelids fluttering closed at the sensation, and I listen for the sound of my exhale, the last trace of resistance leaving my body. I can't deny him now, and I won't. If this is how he wants to repay me for chocolate chip cookies, then I should have made a hundred batches and delivered them to him years ago.

I've always heard the saying that the way to a man's heart is through his stomach. I always thought that was a load of crap. But now I know... it's the way to his tongue.

And God is he good with his tongue.

He bares down as he sucks, licking me clean of any trace of chocolate. My back comes off the granite, arching up and pressing myself further against his mouth.

He hums, and the vibrations just about set me off, pressure building low in my belly, my clit beginning to pulsate, and I can hear my breathing laboring. Just as he's about to pull his mouth off me, his sharp teeth skate across the top of my clit.

"Oh!" I moan out, my fingers desperate to grip the counter's rounded edge down by my heels, my back arching even more dramatically, inadvertently pressing my center closer to the countertop, making it harder for Briggs to get his mouth on me.

His mouth pulls off me because of the angle I caused. I didn't realize how much I needed that short reprieve because I was a second away from coming, and even though I want to, there's something still holding me back. But Briggs isn't on the same page.

"You're not going to shy away from me now. We're too far gone for that," he says, bringing his index finger to my warm wet center and slowly twisting inside me.

"Oh, God." I whimper, gripping his wrist that has his finger inside me.

"Take one more," he says, and adds a finger inside me.

I can feel my body begin to shake with my climax about ready to careen through my body.

I try to steady my breathing, but I can't. I'm at his mercy as he stands between my thighs, watching me, his eyes fixed on seeing me come. It feels vulnerable to be in this position, half-naked, while a fully dressed man eats me and then fingers me to oblivion, but my body is so desperate for release that my brain can only truly focus on one thing. Getting off on Briggs's hand and mouth.

"I'm... I'm..." I inhale a sharp breath, and then Briggs's fingers curl in, swiping over the sensitive spot that isn't always easy for the opposite sex to find, and my body detonates around him.

I moan out an inherent jumble of words as my body shakes in his hands and my orgasm takes over.

He stands there, soothing me still with his fingers until my shivers finally stop.

I look up at him between my thighs, a look of need in his eyes.

"You're beautiful when you come," he says.

"Thank you... for that," I stumble out the words, unsure of what to say.

"Yeah, well, thank me later. We're not done."

"Huh?"

Briggs slides his arms around me and pulls me against his chest. Instinctively, I fold my arms around his neck, and my legs grip around his waist, and they wrap around him. His long legs move out of the kitchen and swiftly carry me past the living room, heading for the hallway.

"Where are we going?"

"You said you need a shower... so do I."

"Didn't you already shower at the stadium?" I ask but the question isn't relevant.

Shut up, Autumn. You're about to shower with Briggs Conley. This is your goddamn fantasy come to life.

"Yeah, but we'll both need one after what I'm going to do to you."

My center squeezes down hard again at his promise.

I look back at him and the devilish grin he's sporting, but I don't know what to say. Briggs is talking dirty to me, and it's the best thing I've ever heard.

"What do you say? Want to shower with me?" he asks with a cocky grin.

I suck in my lower lip and wet it, the thought of it already making me wetter.

He continues down the hall.

The master bedroom is not far from us.

"Are you going to make me beg?" he asks when I don't answer him right away.

"After what you just did to me in the kitchen, I think I'm the one who should be begging."

"Hmm," he says. "You on your knees... I could get into that."

He opens the door to the bedroom and then closes it, locking it behind us since my brother could come back at any moment. Then he walks over to the bedside table, still not putting me down and opens the bedside table, reaching in and pulling out a condom.

"You put condoms in here?" I ask in surprise, glancing down at the contents of the drawer that only contain an unopened black and gold box of condoms.

When did he do that?

"It's best to be prepared... just in case." His lip turns up on one side in a lopsided grin, and then he carries me to the shower.

How long has he thought we might... oh my God.

More warm liquid coats me, and I'm sure he can feel the wetness against his shirt as he carries me into the bathroom.

He opens the shower door and walks us in.

"Our clothes!" I remind him, even though I only have my crop top on... mostly disheveled.

But he's still dressed in a shirt and jeans. We must have left my boy shorts out in the kitchen.

He gives a sexy smirk and presses me against the shower tile wall, setting the condom in his hand on the tiled ledge by the shower head designed for shampoo and conditioner bottles.

I watch as he lays the gold-foiled package down. The anticipation of the moment when he'll open the package has my belly flipping with excitement.

I'm so distracted staring at the condom wrapper that I don't see his hand reach down for the faucet as he flips on the shower water.

"Ah!" I scream as the cold water hits us first. "Briggs!"

"That's exactly how I want you to come next time. Scream my name just like that."

He presses his mouth to mine to stop my rebuttal, and finally, the water turns warm.

I pull up on the hem of his soaked shirt, and he grips the back of it, pulling it over his head. I glance down at the hard edges of him, the hills and valleys of Briggs's cut torso. He watches me as I scan every inch. When I look up into his eyes, he smiles down at me.

"What?" I ask.

"Nothing. It's just a different way you look at me."

"Different how?"

Is he referring to other women looking at him naked? I hate thinking about Briggs with anyone else, but that is the reality of it. It's one of the reasons I have a job right now. But I won't let that deter me. This is my chance with him, and it might be the only one he gives me. I push the thought down deep.

"I don't know." He thinks for a second. "You sure I'm not just a space to mark off on a game of sex bingo? B25, screw pro player." He's teasing, obvious by the glint in his eye.

I shake my head. "Who in the hell would I play sex bingo with?" I poke back.

"Somehow... that answer isn't reassuring. Or maybe I'm just a guy you're screwing because of his big bank account." I still see the twinkle in his eye as he says it... he's not serious.

And thank God for that, otherwise I would have to set the record straight that I'm not a gold digger. I'd have to admit that I will still want this even if he was penniless.

"Oh, Mr. Conley..." I use my best bedroom voice, reaching between us for the button of his soaked pants. "I think you just figured me out."

"Oh yeah?"

I grin, his lips almost on mine again. I nod. "Uh-huh."

My fingers find the button to his pants.

"All I care about is your big..." I feel the button give way, "...big..." I pull down on his zipper, "... big bank-a-cock account."

He chuckles and presses me tighter against the shower wall so that his hands are free to push his jeans down.

They're wet and an already tight fit for his thick, powerful hockey player thighs used for moving through the ice.

He bends down, miraculously keeping me still in place while his hands yank down his jeans. He makes it look effortless, but I feel the force he uses to push them down, and I remember exactly whose arms I'm in. A badass hockey god with skills in so many different arenas.

He kicks off his jeans and toes them to the side corner of the shower, away from us. Then his fingers trail up my sides, creating goosebumps over every inch he touches. He hooks his finger into my sports bra, pulling it up over my head. Now I'm fully undressed, and Briggs only has on a pair of boxers.

"Any last words before we do this?"

"Make it worth the ass beating my brother will give you."

Briggs's mouth crashes over mine and kisses me so passionately I'm not sure if my mouth has ever been taken the way Briggs is right now.

He pushes down his boxer briefs until I hear the loud thud of his wet boxers on the tiled shower floor, and then he pulls his large cock between us, the tip pressing against my belly button as the shaft slides between my cleft every time one of us moves. I break away from his kiss to look down. I've waited too many years to be this up close and personal with this man's erection to not be impatient.

He looks down quickly, and then I can feel his eyes on me again. "What do you think?"

"He's beautiful."

Briggs chuckles at my response. "I don't know if he's beautiful—"

My eyes dart up to his. "I do."

I watch as water drips down his dark blond hair and then over his jaw. It's not just his cock that's beautiful; there's something about this man.

He stares down at me, his eyes searching mine. It almost feels like he can see that I'm different. That my intentions with him are true, not like the other women he has been with. This feels like the moment. This feels like the first time he truly sees me... understands me.

"Put that inside me," I beg softly.

I'm no longer the girl out in the kitchen, wondering if this is a dream. I know what I do to him, and I know what he does to me, and we both know the potential consequences for no longer resisting this pull.

And I don't care.

He bends in and kisses me again. One hand gripping onto my left thigh, the other around the side of my neck, holding me into place for his mouth to devour me.

He releases my lips and reaches for the condom on the soap shelf, his eyes searing into mine as he rips it open with his teeth and then rolls it on, never breaking eye contact.

He presses me tighter against the shower wall to anchor me in place to free the use of his hands. I whimper softly every time the head of his cock slides along the crack of my bum on its own accord, bobbing slightly under me.

"You okay? Am I hurting you?" he asks of his body smashing me into the shower tiles.

Nothing has ever felt better.

"I'm good... yeah." I nod in reassurance, barely able to think of a coherent thought.

He presses his left palm just above my head as his other hand reaches around my thigh and grips his sheathed cock.

My arms tighten around his neck as he guides his engorged cock with his right hand and lines it up with my opening. Then he presses it against me.

I moan out when the tip of his cock pushes inside. Even with my legs still wrapped around his waist, he's so much taller than me. He pushes more of his length further into me, and I whimper at his size.

He presses the side of his mouth against my temple, and now that he's inside of me, his right hand comes back up from guiding himself into me and grips around my left thigh, squeezing tight. "That's it, Autumn. Take me," he says, sinking deeper into me with every powerful thrust.

I'm so full I think I might burst at the seams.

"I can't." I shake my head, my voice shaky. I bury my face against his neck.

"Yes, you can. You were fucking made for me," he says, his voice becoming labored, rocking into me again. "But I'll slow down if you need me to. I don't want to hurt you. I'd never hurt you."

His proclamation causes my heart to squeeze, and my arms grip him even tighter.

I shake my head again. I don't want him to stop... ever.

"That's not an answer." Keeping the same rhythm but not increasing any deeper penetration. "I need you to tell me if you want me to stop."

"You're not hurting me. Please don't stop... don't ever stop."

We stare at each other for a moment as he continues to pump inside of me. An unspoken question feels like it passes between us. What part of this is fake, and what part of this is real?

I can feel our hearts beating rapidly against each other. Did I say too much? Did I give too much away? And then, before

I can ask, he kisses me ferociously like he can't get enough. It almost feels like an answer to that question.

His tongue seeking out mine, he thrusts in again, once, then twice, and fully seats inside me. I cry out at the fullness, but he consumes my sobs, swallowing them whole.

There's tenderness and aggression in how he's kissing me, in how he took me against the countertop in the kitchen earlier, and how he's taking me now against this shower wall.

I don't want this to end. This feeling of being with him. This feeling of his cock buried deep inside me.

Is it stupid to feel so connected to him right now when I have no idea how he feels? Maybe, but I can't stop myself from sending a prayer that we stay like this forever. Slipping and sliding over each other's naked bodies as he owns me.

I'm out of time to overthink it all because my brain is turning to mush. With my first orgasm making my clit extremely sensitive, it's not taking long for my body to begin to vibrate for a second time as the warning signs of my climax are building in ferocity.

I want to hold out for longer. I want to keep going like this for as long as Briggs is willing to hold me against this shower wall, but I can't stop how my body is reacting to him. It's too many years of pining in secret for this man. There's no manual off switch to turn down the chemical reaction I'm having to finally being taken by Briggs Conley.

"Briggs..." I whimper.

"Come... I want to feel you pulsate on my cock the way you did on my fingers."

My eyelashes flutter closed as I concentrate, and then I feel Briggs's warm mouth on my breast. He swirls his tongue over the hard nub of my nipple and then sucks down hard, and just as I get a grip on what he's doing to my body, his teeth bite down on my nipple, and my body clenches down on his cock as I ride him as hard as I can from this position, egging him on to give me more... to give me faster. I want everything he has to give me, and he answers my wordless desperate plea.

His hand comes off the wall and snakes between us. My legs have to squeeze around him tighter to accommodate his large forearm between us, pushing me away from him slightly, but the work is worth it when his index finger presses against my clit.

His finger circles over the sensitive nub as his lips clamp down on my nipple. His finger applies even more pressure my clit and my body starts to shake as it starts racing towards release.

That's all it takes. My climax bursts from its confines, and I cry out Briggs's name as my center clamps down on his cock.

"Jesus," Briggs growls. "Fuck."

His thrusts increase in pace and penetration, chasing his orgasm after mine. I grip my arms tighter around his neck, trying to hold on as Briggs uses me for his own pleasure.

He presses into me, his hand bracing against the shower wall again after he releases my clit. His other hand grips firmly around my right thigh and just before he comes, he lays his forehead down on my shoulder and groans out in pleasure, spilling his warmth inside of me.

I feel the pulsation of his tip lodged deep, and I wish he wouldn't pull out. I want to stop time and enjoy the feeling of his cock twitching as if he is as completely undone by his orgasm as I am by the one he gave me, but we both have things to do today. I have no idea what time it is, but I guess that I should be meeting with Tessa and Penelope soon, and my brother should be back at any time.

Briggs lets my legs slip down his body while he protectively holds on to me to make sure that I don't fall too quickly. Once my feet hit the ground, he kisses my shoulder, and we both sigh in relief. Finally, we ripped off the bandaid of this sexual tension.

A loud bang sounds from the entry of the apartment. Briggs and I both look at each other, both breathing quietly, trying to listen for more sound.

"Hello? Anyone home?" I hear the faint echo of my brother's voice in the kitchen. Probably going straight for the cookies. That should give us some time.

"At least this time, he had the decency to wait until after we finished."

I swat at Briggs's shoulder. He laughs and takes a step back.

"How thoughtful of him," I tease.

Briggs takes a full scan of my naked body, the first time he's seen me fully naked and not smothered under his.

"If he hadn't just walked in, I'd suggest we go again."

"You do have a death wish."

"I can handle your brother."

"The point is that you shouldn't have to. And if you and I hadn't gotten pushed together by our jobs, what's the likelihood that this would have happened?"

"Slim to none. I would have avoided touching you at all costs."

"Right—"

My stomach drops at his statement. I knew it. I knew Briggs would never have gone for me if it wasn't because of this arrangement and the fact he couldn't touch anyone else without looking like he was cheating on his—fake—girlfriend.

"But now that I know how you taste"—he takes a step forward toward me, his eyes searing into mine, the look of a hungry man— "it would have been a damn shame to have missed out."

I hate the flutters that erupt from the look in his eyes, especially since he seems to be telling me that he wouldn't have done this if it wasn't because we're required to live together during this fake relationship.

I react in defense to make myself seem less affected by his admission. "You're Shakespeare incarnate with that speech," I say, rolling my eyes playfully and walking around him and out of the large walk-in shower, grabbing a towel off the shelf on the wall to the left. He's only talking about sex... that's all.

I walk out of the bathroom in search of clothes, and it hits me... the underwear Briggs took off me. Oh damn! But I can't storm out there now in a towel. I have to get dressed and quickly.

I glance over at the clock sitting on the nightstand on the side I slept on last night. Crap! On top of everything, I'm about to be late for my coffee meeting with Penelope and Tessa about how our fake relationship is working toward improving public opinion.

I quickly make it over to the walk-in closet and grab a thong, a pair of jeans, a long sleeve black thermal, and a blue down Columbia vest.

Next, I grab a pair of socks, my Hunter rain boots, and a Patagonia hat to cover up my dripping wet hair. I don't have time to dry it so I'll have to tie into a bun on the elevator trip down to complete my wet rat, just-got-railed-by-a-hockey-god look. Now I'm all set.

I throw on my outfit choices quickly. Briggs finally walks into the closet, one towel hung low on his hips, one towel he's using to shake out his wet hair, and my anti-aging night gel slathered under his eyes. Minus the eye cream, Briggs is a walking wet dream.

"Hoping to stay youthful?" I ask, adjusting my jacket.

"I like the cooling sensation, and yes, it might have worked yesterday. No harm in a little self-care."

I smirk and shake my head as I try to make a quick exit. Briggs throws out an arm and wraps it around my waist to stop me, pulling me back against his hard chest.

"Where are you going?" he asks, his mouth pressing against the back of my ear.

"I told you, I have a meeting with Tessa and Penelope this afternoon. Plus, I have to find my underwear we left out there."

Briggs releases me quickly. His eyes flare wider for a second, his tongue darting out to lick his lips quickly, the realization that my brother might find them first has just dawned on him.

"Where did you leave them?" I ask.

"On the island," he says tight-lipped.

"You left my dirty underwear on the island... where we prepare food?" I ask, my eyes flashing at him.

"Hey. First of all, there is nothing dirty about you, except for the way you like to be fucked." He smirks.

My cheeks must turn bright red because Briggs chuckles a little.

"Still... my brother is out there."

He looks past me towards the bedroom door. "True. I'll get dressed quickly and meet you out there."

"Okay," I say, leaving him in the closet and taking steps toward the bedroom door, smoothing my drenched hair back and pulling it behind me, twisting it up and then twirling it into a bun low against my neck.

I set off to find my boy shorts... then find my brother...

...in that order.

CHAPTER SEVENTEEN

Briggs

I can't wrap my mind around what just happened between me and Autumn. The sex on several surfaces of this apartment was fan-fucking-tastic, and I want to ask her when we can do that again. I know later tonight, I'll find myself alone in bed with her, and the question will have to wait, or maybe I'll get an after-hours showing. I'd be down for that. As of right now, I'm picking up anything that looks clean off the floor and throwing it on over my bare body so that I can help Autumn cover up the scene that transpired.

I think I remember leaving the underwear on the countertop before I wrapped her sexy body around mine and hauled her to our bedroom, but I was mesmerized by her, so they could be anywhere.

Boxers, a t-shirt, and jeans are all I need, and I'm back on the chase to find Autumn somewhere in the apartment. I'm preparing to be met with a fight. Since Isaac thinks we're dating, he can't be all that surprised if he suspects that we got down and nasty in the kitchen. And fuck, we did.

Now, offering Isaac a place to crash to see that Autumn and I are a happy couple is screwing with the plans I have for her. Mostly keeping her under me for as long as possible. I'm becoming addicted the more we're together and it's not just the sex... I could feel the need to be with her growing a little more each day, even before I took her on the countertop.

We should have gone straight from the shower to the king-sized bed in the master. I wasn't done with her and I'm still not.

I hear Autumn's voice and her laugh, then I hear Isaac's voice, and he seems to be in a good mood too. Good, maybe she found the underwear before he did.

"Hey," I say, walking into the kitchen and seeing Isaac leaning against the island with his forearms holding him up. A plate of cookies and a gallon of milk sitting out in front of him.

"Hey," Isaac says flatly, taking a bite of cookie and washing it down with a glass of ice-cold milk the way he always did when we were kids. He's still not happy to see me, and I'm becoming tired of this disapproval. At first, I understood his position, almost accepting of it, but now...

I glance around the kitchen island, but no panties. I check over the countertop on the face side where all the cookies are lined out of baking sheets, and again... no panties. I look over at Autumn, and she shrugs at me when her brother isn't looking as if to say she has no idea where they went.

Oh well, no panties, no problem. Works for me. Maybe I brought them back with us to the bedroom and forgot. My hands were very busy at that moment. Who knows what I grabbed in a frenzy to get Autumn back to the bedroom?

I walk over to the cabinets above the cooling cookies and grab a glass. I set it on the island, and the gallon of milk is still sitting out. Isaac eyeballs me for a second. He grabs the handle on the milk like he's about to deny me milk... milk I paid for, but then he seems to shake off the look and releases the carton, sliding it over to me with irritation.

"I have to head out. I'll be back in a couple of hours," Autumn finishes.

"Fine," Isaac says.

He looks over at my wet hair and then over at hers. "You two leave enough hot water for the rest of us?" His hand balls into a fist on the granite countertop, but he looks more like he's trying to check his anger than planning to use those knuckles on me. This is progress.

I look over at her, trying my hardest not to toss my bedroom eyes at her. Her cheeks turn a little rosy under her brother's accusation, but she recovers quickly.

"You're making it fucking hard to leave you still standing, Conley," he says, peering up at me with fire in his eyes.

Autumn steps forward and dips down to Isaac's eye level. "You know, you could always stay somewhere else."

"I'm fine here," he says, meeting her eye contact.

A swell of pride hits me, seeing her go toe-to-toe with Isaac to defend me... to defend us.

"Then I suggest you stop threatening my boyfriend in our home, which he generously invited you to stay in after you cold-cocked him."

I try to hide my smirk. Good girl. Glad to see her setting some limits on how much he can walk on her. I guess he and I both used to walk on her as kids. My chest squeezes uncomfortably tight. I'm regretting that now.

With Autumn out for the afternoon, that means Isaac and I will have to play nice while she's gone. What a weird alternate universe, where being with Autumn is easy... the girl I used to groan about when Isaac's mom said we had to include her in our shenanigans. Now it's my best friend that I need a buffer to stay in the same room with. Who knows, maybe with Autumn gone, it will feel more like the old days.

"Okay, I have to go. I already texted the girls and told them I'd be late, but I need to get down there," she says, sending a glance my way.

"See you tonight?" I ask her.

Maybe if I'm lucky, Isaac will decide to stay out all night so I get his sister to myself this evening but since he's training... I doubt it.

"Yeah." She smiles over at me.

"Good."

A knock sounds at the door, and her eyes dart over to me first.

"I'm not expecting anyone," I say.

Autumn and I look at Isaac, and he shrugs and shakes his head with a mouth full of cookie. Seems he isn't expecting anyone either.

She turns and walks toward the door, but I don't like this idea.

If she wasn't expecting anyone, I should be the one to open the door. I've yet to get a crazy fan or a stalker, but Isaac and I are the public figures in this room, and if it is a crazed fan or worse, it should be him or me dealing with them, not her. Maybe I'm being overprotective, especially in a building with a doorman and security, but that feels like it fits under my new job description as a boyfriend, fake or otherwise.

Even if Autumn and I weren't living in a fake relationship, and she was only here visiting with her brother, I'd still feel as though I share the responsibility with Isaac for her safety while she's in my presence.

I frown for a second. Had I always been this protective of her and never noticed it? Is it because she is the little sister of my best friend or because she is Autumn?

Even as I ask the question to myself, I know the answer. It's because it's Autumn. No one—not even Isaac—could protect her better than me.

I pass her up with my longer stride, beating her to the door. "Wait there," I tell her and point toward the end of the foyer. "I'll see who it is."

I open the door, and when I see who it is, I'm about ready to slam it in the asshole's face.

Derek.

Autumn's boss and the man who texted her at 6 a.m. this morning.

The boss that she *didn't* sleep with. *Didn't* being the operative word here. A bit of information I got when she attempted to tell me they were in a relationship.

They were most certainly not. No dude in his right man who saw long-term in his future would let a knock-out like Autumn go out and date another man. I sure as hell wouldn't, even if it meant she came home with the Powerball winning numbers. Some things aren't worth the money.

"What the fuck do you want?"

Oh shit, did I just say that out loud? That was unintentional, but now that I've said it, I won't take it back. I meant it. He shouldn't be here. Autumn is mine, not his... at least for the next few months. And I'm going to soak up each second of it.

"Is Autumn here? This is the address she sent us in an email," he says, pressing up on the balls of his feet to try to get a look over my shoulder, but it's a feeble attempt. My six-four has at least four to five inches on him.

"What do you need her for?" I ask, not opening the door any wider.

"Derek?" I hear Autumn say, coming behind me and attempting to pull the door wide and out of my hands. I let her because if I don't, she'll ask why and the only reason I'll have is "I don't like looking at his face when I know what he wants to do to you." I doubt she'll find my reasoning compelling enough to agree to deny him entry. Although, I'd bet she's denied him entry enough times if they've gone on dates since he never sealed the deal.

"Hey!" he says, side-stepping past me and walking toward her. Fucking bold move. "I wanted to come to check on you since you've been working from home."

"A phone call would have sufficed," I say under my breath.

Autumn hears it and gives me side-eye, then she turns and heads for the kitchen quickly, bringing Derek with her, probably hoping to let him know that the three of us are not alone and not to spill the beans. Although if there was anyone I'd like to come clean with, it's Isaac.

"Have you met my brother? He came into town from Vegas to visit." She offers up her brother, and Isaac walks around the island, his chest half-puffed already. Half of me hopes he'll deck Derek right on the spot. That would probably get rid of the guy once and for all, and I wouldn't have to get my hands dirty, but Isaac's not a hot head going around hitting any man who make eyes at his sister... just me. In fairness, I broke the bro code.

"Nice to meet you. I'm Derek," he says, reaching out and shaking Isaac's hand.

Isaac's eyebrow is turned up for a minute. He thinks this is weird, that's obvious. Isaac doesn't have much of a poker face.

Derek turns to Autumn. "Didn't realize we were meeting family already."

What the fuck did you just say, asshole? And in my damn apartment where I just fucked the girl who I'm supposed to be dating. Your ass is the one who sold off your 'girlfriend' for a payday from the Hawkeyes. There's no way she'll go back to dating him after this is all over. She deserves a hell of a lot better. Thinking on how much I've fucked up over the last year, she deserves better than me, too, but a future between us isn't realistic anyway, not with Isaac already ordering my headstone. It probably reads:

Here lies the worst friend on the fucking planet.

I hope his dick decays first.

Briggs Michael Conley

Autumn looks a little uncomfortable about his comment, and I should fucking say... where the hell does he get off coming over unannounced to our apartment while we're trying to look like a couple?

"Already?" Isaac asks. "I thought you've been working together for the last four years since Autumn graduated from college?"

I fold my arms over my chest, a smirk brushing across my lips. I'm not offering this wanker a lifesaver. He can tread his way out of the deep end he threw himself in.

"Uh, we've been working together awhile. But how often does upper management meet the families... I mean, really?" She gives a tight laugh.

Isaac's right eyebrow is furrowed, a tell that something seems off, but he's not pushing the subject. Autumn turns to Derek quickly. "And you already know my boyfriend, Briggs Conley," she says, gesturing toward me in an attempt to change the subject.

He looks at me with that same look he did at the first meeting we all had in the Hawkeyes' conference room, where I was basically forced to fake date Autumn, which Autumn told me was his idea. I guess I did owe the guy a little since he was the one that got us together.

He barely looks over at me. "Right. Hello again," he says, avoiding shaking my hand, but I reach over anyway. If he doesn't take it, he'll look bad in front of Autumn and Isaac, and he knows it. He reaches out and takes my hand, and I put a little extra pressure in my squeeze until he flinches.

Autumn's eyes connect on something on the floor, and I follow her line of sight. Her boy shorts lying on the ground under the island. They must have fallen off the island during the encounter. I see Derek follow both of our attention, and he clears his voice the second he realizes what they are. I'm closer than Autumn, so I quickly pick them up and slide them into my back pocket when Isaac turns to put his milk glass in the dishwasher.

Derek clears his voice even louder that time. I think the only thing worse than seeing evidence that your not-girlfriend is getting laid by someone else is to see that same dude putting her panties in his back pocket.

It might have been an unintentional marking-my-territory stunt, but now that it's done, I couldn't be happier.

Fuck him. She deserves better than a guy offering up his girl as a fake girlfriend for someone else. Who knows, by the end of this, I might even help her forget his name.

Autumn tries to divert Derek's attention from the event. "I was just headed out. I have a coffee meeting this afternoon, and now I'm late for it."

"Oh! I'll walk you out." Derek beams. "I'll just take a cookie for the road," he says, grabbing for a cookie that Autumn made for me. You can do a lot of shit to piss a man off, but take one of his cookies that his fake girlfriend made for him without asking? Now, it's war.

He bites into the cookie as he tries to usher her out of this apartment as quickly as he can and away from me, I'd suspect.

"Did you make these?" he asks her. "They're amazing."

I want to make an excuse to head down with them, but I still don't know what's happening between Autumn and I. The door clicks shut after them and it sounds like a coffin shutting on the possibility of something more between us. What happens if this whole thing just blows over after our contract is done?

Does she want Derek over me? The idea of it makes me want to connect my knuckles with a sheet of ice. I'd rather get body checked against the Plexiglass by the opposing team without pads on than watch Autumn go out with that dick.

CHAPTER EIGHTEEN

Autumn

"This was a surprise." I smile over at Derek as I hit the call button for the elevator.

"I haven't seen you much since you've been working from this apartment. Erika is adamant that you stay laser-focused on this project... but... I've missed seeing you around the office."

"I wish you would have called or texted first."

I look down the hall to ensure no one is listening to us. The coast is clear. "My brother doesn't know that Briggs and I are doing this to clean up his reputation."

"Operation De-sleaze Conley," Derek says, shaking his head like something tastes bad in his mouth.

"Right..." I say.

I might have said it to Briggs in an attempt to cut him down a peg, but I didn't come up with it; Derek did. But now, from a closer vantage point, I can see that the Briggs I've known since I was a kid is still in there.

The question still remains. Why is he back to self-destructive drinking and partying? And how did he get himself in this mess with the exotic dancer? If he doesn't tell me, I may have to do a little digging myself.

The elevator door opens, and Derek gestures for me to go first. He's been chivalrous on the few dates we've had. Picking me up instead of meeting, opening doors, pulling out chairs, offering me his coat, and refusing to let me pay, even though I offer.

I hit the ground floor button, and the doors close. He and I stand side by side, staring back at the elevator doors from the inside. I can see both of our oddly warped images in the metallic material of the elevator, but it's not perfectly reflective, so I can't make out either of our expressions.

"So... Briggs," Derek says.

We're both facing the stainless-steel doors, and I watch Derek rock on his heels with his hands in his pockets.

"Yeah?"

Was there more to that comment, or are we just calling out any random person's name? Maybe I'm more irritated with him showing up unannounced than I originally thought.

"You two getting along?"

"So far, so good. It's been an adjustment."

"But he's being respectful...?"

Huh? Respectful? Like leaving the seat down on the toilet and passing gas in a different room than the one I'm standing in? Or respectful in that he's not tossing me up on the kitchen island and devouring me because he felt like it?

But really, I don't want to get into it with Derek right now. I have a meeting with the girls that I'm late for, and Tessa seems anxious to get together ASAP. I'm worried something might have been leaked already.

"Sure, I guess."

"He's not pressuring you in any way, is he?"

I look over at him. I can't hide my look of confusion.

"Pressuring me to pretend to be his girlfriend? He's the one that didn't want—"

"No," he interrupts, shaking his head. "Pressuring you into more than what you signed up for."

He saw my panties on the ground, but I also live there, and he's never been inside my apartment. For all he knows, I'm a slob. Or I could have been folding laundry on the kitchen island, and those pair dropped from the stack.

I'll admit, though, Briggs tucking them in his back pocket was incredibly hot, and I can't deny that I'll be fantasizing that he leaves them in his pocket all day.

"I don't know what you're referring to."

"Sex, Autumn. Is he pressuring you into sleeping with him?" He huffs as if annoyed that he has to spell it out for me.

"Derek, I don't think that's any of your business."

"I'm your boss, Autumn. Of course, it's my business. It would be highly inappropriate for you to be involved in a sexual nature with our client."

I take a step to my left, further away from Derek, and turn to face him, crossing my arms against my chest in a protective stance.

"I will say this again. What Briggs and I do in that apartment is none of your business. This whole idea was yours, and Erika loved it."

"We've been on several dates over the course of a month, and I never so much as got to second base. But you let some manwhore hockey player that you've been fake dating for three days screw you?"

My hands tighten around my biceps. I want to reach out and smack him, but we're in an enclosed elevator still, and even though I don't think Derek would physically retaliate, I'm not willing to roll the dice for instant gratification.

I'm not a tiny little thing, although Briggs's arms have a way of swallowing me whole and making me feel Tinker Bell-sized. But Derek is still bigger than me and pound for pound stronger than me.

"You have no right to speak to me that way."

Angels must exist because the elevator doors open right then, and I lunge out of that elevator car and speed walk for the door.

I hear Derek as I increase the distance between us. He isn't following after me.

"I came here to ask you out on a date!" he yells.

"I guess you know where you can shove your invitation!" I yell over my shoulder, pushing through the glass doors and out onto the public sidewalk, free at last.

I know I could call my brother or Briggs, and they'd come down to give Derek a good talking to, but I'd prefer they both stay out of jail.

If I nail this account, Derek will be a peer and no longer my boss. We'll work in different divisions of the firm, and luckily, on different floors too.

Briggs

"So… how's the gym?" I ask, reluctant to make contact, but we're both awkwardly standing in the kitchen now with Autumn gone.

"Good," he says without looking up, his arms folded over each other and leaning against the island as he stares down at his phone. A plate of cookie crumbs is all that's left of the mountain of cookies he devoured.

"Good," I say back.

"How's the team playing?" he asks, again, not looking up as he types a text.

"Good," I tell him.

"Good," he responds with zero interest.

Silence sets in, and this is easily the shortest conversation Isaac and I have had in our entire lives.

"I'm heading out to meet a friend at the bar," he says, leaning up and tucks his phone into his front pocket.

"At two in the afternoon?" I say.

Isaac finally looks up at me. "Interesting coming from you."

I stare back at him as he rounds the island and heads for the front door.

Why are you so against this?

"My sister deserves better than a drunk who passes out at God knows where for God knows how long."

"That's not who I am."

"It might not be who you'll always be, but it's who you are right now. And my sister needs a real man who will provide for her, protect her, help her accomplish her dreams, and give her the family she's always wanted."

"And you think I'm not that man."

He turns and faces me straight on, taking a couple of steps closer to me. "No. I don't think you are."

There have been very few times in my life when someone has used words that hurt me as badly as those do.

He turns around without another word and leaves the apartment, closing the door on his way out, leaving me with more questions and uncertainty about where Isaac and I stand and whether or not this feud over his sister will end our friendship, fake or not.

Will he be relieved to find out we faked the whole thing and his sister was never truly in danger of ending up with me? Or will he hate me for lying to him and making him fly out here to defend her and protect her from a man he finds to be inadequate and lacking to ever deserve his sister? I guess we'll find out in a few months.

CHAPTER NINETEEN

Autumn

Finally, Serendipity's Coffee Shop where I'm meeting the girls comes into view under the bill of my hat. I decided to walk since I didn't want to take the elevator down to the garage with Derek still with me. I wanted a quick getaway, and the lobby served that purpose. Plus, the doorman is on the lobby floor, and I wanted to know he was nearby, just in case. Besides, the café is only a couple blocks away, and the rain doesn't bother me.

Raindrops are beginning to spatter on the cement sidewalk, and I'm glad to be nearby before it really starts coming down because the best way to tell someone from the Pacific Northwest that you're not a native is to carry around an umbrella. Also, your choice of footwear is as follows:

Year-round: flip-flops.

Hiking: Birkenstocks or Merrell's.

Dec – Jan: rain boots.

If you are not dressed for an impromptu hike, your closet is not chock-full of all things Patagonia and Columbia gear, and you do not have a crippling coffee addiction... just pack up and go back home. You won't last here.

I really hope to God that Tessa doesn't have bad news to share because I could use a break after what transpired in the apartment with my brother and then the weirdness in the elevator with Derek.

The smell of freshly brewed coffee and pecan caramel sticky buns hit me right to the face as I open the heavy red door to the quaint little café that is anything other than a closely guarded secret. This place is booming with customers trying to get a sugary fix on their lunch breaks, or in this case, a post-work sugar rush. The aroma almost feels as though it pulls you in, kisses you on the cheek, and wraps you up in a warm fuzzy blanket. Nothing better on a rather drizzly day in Seattle. The red door acts as a beacon on an otherwise colorless and gray afternoon as the fog decided not to lift completely today.

"Autumn!" I hear and then follow the sound to a lively waving Penelope sitting at a table in the back corner, Tessa's head down in her phone, texting rapidly. Oh no, please don't let that be related to Briggs.

"Hi," I say, grabbing my wallet out of my purse and setting my purse under the table. "I'll be right back. I need coffee before I melt," I tell them. Tessa looks up quickly with a smile, but that's all she gives me as she dives back into her phone.

Weird... and unnerving.

I order my coffee, and of course, a sticky bun, and head back to my table with my number for my order.

"Okay, I'm here. I'm sorry I'm late," I tell them.

"No biggie. I'm just happy to be out of the office, and Tessa has been text-shouting at Lake for the last twenty minutes."

"Text-shouting?"

Penelope grabs Tessa's phone from her.

"Hey!" Tessa objects, but it's too late. Penelope is already turning it to show me.

Penelope holds the phone closer so I can read the conversation between Lake and Tessa, and sure enough, there is a long conversation between them, all caps and exclamations. I don't think I see a single lower-case letter in the entire thing.

Tessa grabs at the phone, and Penelope lets it go. She and I look at each other and bite back a chuckle. I feel bad that Lake and Tessa's rivalry hits my funny bone, but it just does. I should be a better friend to Tessa since I'm still the new girl in the threesome—if you count Isla, the foursome—and I should take her side over Lake's, but the way she carries on about his misdoings, the more I wonder if Lake's inability to just grin and bear her, falling in line like all the other players on the roster, is what's getting under her skin.

His social media posts can be tasteless, with scantily clad women on his boat at his lake house during the off-season.

Sometimes with emojis covering up what would be their bare nipples. But he has ten times as many followers on his social media as Briggs... mostly women, because with that sexy grin and a nickname like Magic Stick, how could he not?

Tessa slams her phone on the table just as my coffee and sticky bun come out to the table. "Okay, I'm done, sorry," she says.

"No, it's fine. Do whatever you have to."

"Absolutely not. I invited you both here so we could hear how things are going with Briggs," Tessa says, saying his name teasingly and wagging her eyebrows at me.

"Ooh, yeah!" Penelope says, taking a bite of her bear claw and leaning in. "Do tell. How's living with all that testosterone? Please tell me you're in a one-bed type situation... and that the heater broke, so you have to use each other as a heat source."

"You need to stop reading so many romance books, Penelope. You think everything is a trope."

"It is! Give me any relationship, and I will name their trope."

"I think I'm going to like this game." I nod and lean in closer.

"You read smut?" Penelope asks, almost giddy.

"Who doesn't?" I joke.

"Tessa doesn't read dirty books."

"Let's just call it what it is... literary porn." Tessa takes a sip of her coffee and then continues. "Word dicks. But I prefer my porn the old-fashioned way."

"Tessa!" Penelope says with shock and then turns to me almost as if she half expects me to realize I sat at the wrong table.

I hide my grin as I take a sip of my coffee. "Oh yeah, how's that?"

"Visually stimulating," she says with a smirk. This isn't the first time these two have debated this because Tessa knows she's riling Penelope up.

"Well, excuse me for liking to read my porn... like a dang lady." Penelope huffs, only pretending to be upset.

A smile peaks out when she sees I'm chuckling at these two.

I look around our surroundings to see if anyone heard our conversation. Of course, there's a man, slightly advanced past middle-aged, reading his newspaper two tables away. I see him peeking over his paper for a minute. Then I hear a chuckle, and he goes back to his reading again.

"We got off track," Tessa says. "We need all the sexy details about your sleepover with the right-wing hottie."

"Hold on. I thought we were meeting about work-related things."

"We are, but I believe in an even-keeled work/play balance."

"She totally does." Penelope nods vigorously and points a thumb at Tessa using her other hand to take another sip of her drink.

"Okay, fine. Work first," I tell her.

If they want details, I want what I came for first. I want to know if risking my brother's ability to ever trust me again and causing a blow-up with a coworker is worth the risk. I need to know that this fake relationship is changing public opinion for the better and that no rumors have started surfacing.

Tessa picks her phone back up, growling at a new text she got from Lake but clicks out of the messaging app, even though I'm sure it's killing her not to respond back to Lake right away.

She scrolls through her phone for a second, and then she must pull out a report she compiled because she starts listing off key points.

"I got the reports from apparel, and they are reporting an increase in Conley jerseys and merchandise by 18%."

"Is that good?"

"It's a giant jump for sales in general but huge for only a few days." Penelope nods.

"Yeah. It's promising news," Tessa agrees, still looking down at her phone.

"What else you got?" Penelope asks.

"His social media account grew by almost ten thousand new followers between the day your restaurant kiss surfaced and the blow-up he had at the reporter after the game last week."

I cringe at the fact that Briggs might have hurt his reputation by defending me, but in this case, it sounds like it actually worked to his benefit. The public is intrigued by him... they're talking. I just hope it's mostly good.

"Is that good?"

"Really good. And the comment section is looking promising too. Naturally, with social media being the animal it is, there is always a few dim wits who want to see Briggs crash and burn, but overall, people have good things to say about his girl-next-door wholesome new relationship. The narrative is going the way we were hoping, and people are rooting for you two."

People are rooting for us? I bite down on my lip a little but then try to cover it up by tearing off a piece of sticky bun and plopping it in my mouth before either woman sees the effect that comment has on me.

Oh damn, that's a good pastry.

Almost better than sex... well, better than sex with a normal man. Not better than sex with Briggs.

Sex with Briggs is more like getting to eat a whole truckload of sticky buns with zero calories.

My mouth begins to water again but not for the sticky bun. Though, I can't let that happen again. If I want this promotion, and I do, I'm on a 100 percent Briggs diet... except in public when we have to show affection.

I clear my throat and try to focus back on work. "And if the false allegation story drops tomorrow? How would that affect us?" I ask.

"His reputation is still a drag, and your relationship is as fragile as a glass egg. If the story drops, I suspect the glass will shatter. We need more time to solidify his new public image."

I nod, disappointed but not surprised. I knew well enough that public opinion takes a while to alter.

"What about the sponsor deal?" Penelope asks, turning to Tessa.

"What sponsors deal?" I ask.

Tessa makes a lopsided frown. "It's not a given yet."

"My dad was talking about it with Phil Carlton. Sounds like Briggs's agent thinks it could be a great opportunity."

"It's a very family-focused company."

"You think they'll go with someone else?"

"I just think they haven't seen enough of Briggs out of the party scene to gamble on their reputation too. Briggs would need to really prove he's a changed man before they'd consider him."

"But the sponsorship aside, you think things are looking good?"

"Yes, but the best thing we can hope for is that hiring your firm was simply a precaution. I hope that Briggs doesn't have to base his entire career on whether or not this woman gives a four-page spread on this story. If she does, then we'll see if this safety net you're creating holds."

"And if it doesn't?"

"the Hawkeyes may have no other choice than to separate themselves from the dumpster fire and drop Conley."

"What?!"

"That might not even be the worst of it for Conley. She could drag him through a criminal case," Tessa says.

"But she won't win. There's not enough evidence. And if the team drops him, he'll look even more guilty, and no other team will pick him up," Penelope jumps in. I know this is part of Tessa's job to consider all the possibilities, but I'm glad to have Penelope feeling as defensive over Briggs as I do.

Tessa looks over at her. "You're right. It will ruin him."

Damn it. I hate that she's right.

"I have to go." I stand quickly.

"Where are you going?"

"I need to think. I need to talk to my boss."

"Wait! You didn't give us the dirty," Penelope objects.

"I know, I'm sorry." Sort of. I'm not exactly sure how much I should tell them about what's going on between me and Briggs. This friend group is new, and they are all employed by the franchise, whereas I was hired for a job. A job where client fraternizing is frowned upon, and I can't imagine Phil Carlton would like that he's paying me while I'm having hot shower sex with one of his most valuable players. He'll want my head in the game, not under the sheets. "Rain check?"

"It's already raining." Penelope pouts, then all of a sudden, gasps out of nowhere like some thought just came to her. "Enemies-to-lovers. That's your trope," she says and looks at Tessa.

"What are you talking about?" Tessa says with a scrunched nose.

"You and Lake."

"Lake and I hate each other. That would never happen."

Like a scene from a movie, Penelope and I slowly look over at each other, and both grin huge.

"I'd buy that book," I say with a smirk.

"Me too," Penelope beams.

"Over my dead body." Tessa huffs.

"Drinks. Tomorrow night," Tessa demands like she's not asking.

"Okay," I say, grabbing my purse from under the table and grabbing my to-go coffee cup off the table. I pick up my empty plate where the heavenly pastry confection once sat and look over at the self-busing station. "Text me," I say over my shoulder as I head for the red door and set my plate in the dirty plates bin by the trash and recycle cans for the staff to get later.

I head for the door, pull out my phone and dial Erika. When she picks it up, I jump straight to it.

"Are you in the office?"

"Yeah."

"Good, I'm coming in."

I hang up and pull up the rideshare app since I didn't bring my car to the café because of Derek.

It's time to pull out the stops to protect Briggs's career and help him get that huge sponsorship. Briggs is one of the hardest-working pro hockey players in the league, and I'll be damned if some woman thinks she's going to use Briggs for a payday and ruin him while she's at it.

I can't do anything about the franchise wanting to pay off her entitled ass, but I can do the one thing I'm good at—protect Briggs's pro hockey dreams.

CHAPTER TWENTY

Autumn

"Autumn." Erika smiles as I walk through the open door to her office. I close it as I walk through. This case I'm working on is on a need-to-know basis. "Just the woman I wanted to see." She smiles.

"Really?"

"Since you've been working from your joint apartment with Briggs, I haven't seen you over the last few weeks. How are things going?" She smiles and gestures for me to sit in the chair on the other side of her desk.

She sits in her tall, white leather office chair.

"I just left a meeting with Tessa Tomlin about what she's seeing on social media. It seems as though we're getting traction."

"Ooh, you know I love traction." She gleams.

"I do. And he could be up for a large sponsorship with a company that could help turn his image around, but they want a certain type of athlete that mirrors their brand."

"Aw, I see. And you're concerned he doesn't have the right image for the brand?"

"Right. So I wanted to talk to you about what we could do to attempt to push him toward winning them over."

"I'd love to discuss this. Getting a household name brand to 'vouch' for him could go a long way in changing his image."

"I agree." I nod.

"Okay, take the day and get me a list of your ideas. I will go through them and see if I can build even further on your list. Maybe I can pull out a favor or two to get big exposure on him."

"That would be great. I'll go back home right now and jump on it," I say, standing out of my seat, amped to get to work on ideas.

I make it out of the office without running into Derek. It was almost the end of the day, and he probably already went home. I head for my apartment, the one I still have on lease since Briggs and I won't be dating and living in a team-paid-for apartment forever.

I can't go back to the apartment where Briggs and Isaac are currently. For all I know, World War Three might have broken loose, and it could be a blood bath. Briggs put himself in this position, inviting my brother to stay with us, so he'll have to be the one to get himself out of it. I have bigger fish to fry, mainly ideas on how to fast-track turning Briggs into America's sweetheart and how to resist him for the next few months to keep my promotion. No matter how great Briggs is in bed, this is all temporary, and I don't want to throw away everything I've worked for to get me here. I have to try to keep things professional with Briggs.

Briggs

It's been over an hour since Isaac got back from the bar around midnight and headed to his room to turn in for the night. I sit on the bed, debating whether or not to call Autumn. I don't like that I haven't heard from her since she left this afternoon. Now it's almost one o'clock, in the morning and she hasn't even sent a single text to let me know she'd be home late.

I can't take the silence anymore, and I'll only stress more if my text goes unanswered.

I pick up my phone and dial her number.

"Hello?" I hear her groggy voice, relief hitting me that she's not in some car accident on Highway 99 or something.

"Hi."

I try to think of something else to say, but I run the danger of sounding like a real boyfriend asking where she is or where she's been. I'm not sure that any of that is technically my business.

"Hi," she echoes. "Everything ok?"

"Yeah. It's just... it's late," I say.

"It is?" I hear her voice further away, probably pulling her phone from her ear to check the time. "Oh shoot, it is."

A bit of vindication that I'm not overreacting hits me.

"Are you coming home?" Nerves prickle at the back of my neck at the thought that she might be at Derek's and isn't coming home tonight to sleep next to me.

"Yes. I am." I hear her yawn. "I lost track of time."

"Where are you?"

Please don't say Derek's.

"At my apartment."

Alone? But I can't ask that. Can I?

"Your apartment? Why?"

Did she need a break from me? The thought of that is deflating.

"I'm working on some ideas to get you more public favor."

"What kind of ideas?"

"A toy drive for kids in foster care, a golf tournament for international health aid, a meet-and-greet for a new children's cancer facility—"

"I'd do that," I say quickly.

"The cancer wing for the hospital?"

"Yeah. When is it?"

"Uh..." She seems a little surprised that I picked something so quickly, but this one means something to me, and I want to do what I can. "It's the day before you leave on your next out-of-town game. That will make for a long week, and it's a little last minute, but Erika has a friend at the hospital that could use a celebrity pull to bring in more donations."

"I'll do it. What do they need me to do?"

"Just show up, sign autographs, and take pictures with fans. There's a silent auction, too. If you could sign a hat or something, that would go a long way."

"Tell Erika I'll be there. You'll come with too?"

"If you want me there. It will be a good chance for us to be seen out together."

"Of course, I want you there." I tell her

I can practically hear her smile over the phone.

"Well, the hospital will be elated. I'll let Erika know. You just made my job easy."

"Haven't I made your job easier since day one?" I tease.

"True. Just an absolute delight since the second you stormed out of our first meeting," she gives back.

I rub my jaw. A light stubble is starting to form.

"I'm still sorry about that."

And I am.

"It's fine. I'm just playing."

I have to ask the question because she still hasn't given me any reason to understand why she couldn't have done this brainstorming here in this apartment where I wouldn't have wondered all afternoon if she had ended up hanging out with Derek.

"You could have done your work here and bounced these ideas off me in real time. It probably would have saved you some energy."

"I could have, but it's quieter here. No distractions."

She thinks I'd bother her?

"I'm a distraction?"

"If you recall, you stopped me from finishing a project earlier today, and I ended up on the kitchen island and then in the shower." She snickers.

I can't stop the smile spreading across my face. She thinks I'm *that* kind of distraction. I'll take it.

"Sorry. Would you rather I'd left you to take care of your *cookies* on your own?"

She laughs, and my smile widens. "It was a great distraction, but I still have to do my job."

Good to hear we're on the same page about what we did together earlier today.

"I appreciate what you're doing. I don't think I've said that yet," I tell her.

There's silence for a moment on the other line.

"You do?"

"Yeah. I'm sorry again that I was a jerk at the first meeting and stormed off. This whole thing sort of sucks."

"Oh... right."

Damn it, did she think I included her in the sucking part? She's turning out to be the only thing I look forward to these days. Well, that and skating.

"Shit. Not you; the whole thing with Dixie and my bosses on my ass. And I have to lie to everyone who means something to me."

She can probably relate to all of this. And I guess her promotion is just as much on the line as my job. But she doesn't face public humiliation... or worse, someone lying about me because they think I'll make a good payday.

"I get it," she says.

More silence.

"You still there?" I ask.

"Yeah."

"Are you coming home?"

"Yes. I'm grabbing my things and walking out the door."

"Okay, I'll stay on the line until you get to your car."

"You don't need to do that."

"I'm going to. Now leave your apartment," I demand, anxious to have her inside this apartment.

She huffs. "You're bossy."

"Yep."

I hear her grab a set of keys off some counter or desk and some rustling around that sounds like a backpack or a laptop bag in the background. A few seconds later, I hear a loud bang like she just closed the door to her apartment, and then the sound of a key locking the door behind her.

"Did you leave?"

"Yes. Jeez. Must you know every move I make?" she says playfully.

"If that's an option, then yes, I'd like to know your every move."

"I was kidding," she says flatly.

"I'm not."

Then I hear the sound of her heavy breathing as she walks down a flight of stairs. I saw her two-story building when I dropped her off at her apartment when she attended her first game as my girlfriend. I'm glad to know what her apartment looks like and that it seems to be in a good neighborhood.

"I don't like that you don't have a doorman."

"I don't need one."

Bullshit, you don't.

"Besides, much good that did since Derek sailed right on past him."

A discomfort hits me in the chest at the thought that maybe she ditched the girls and spent the whole day with him today.

"What happened after you two left?"

Silence on her end. I have a feeling she didn't mean to say that out loud.

"Nothing happened. I was just making a point."

I don't like her answer, but I'm not going to press her about it right now. She's only a small cellphone button away from hanging up on me and deciding to stay at her place tonight, but I know she wouldn't because Isaac would ask reasonable questions as to why, if we're a supposedly happy couple, his sister kept her apartment and opted to stay there instead of with me. It's too risky.

"Where are you now?"

"I just got to the parking lot. Relax. My brother doesn't even hover this close."

I ignore her jab.

I hear the sound of her opening her car door. It shuts, and then a few seconds later, her car revs to life.

"Okay, nosy... I'm on my way home."

"Call when you get here. I'll come down."

"You don't need to."

"It's late."

"We have a locked private parking garage with cameras."

"Someone could still be down there. The parking garage is for all tenants."

"We have security," she argues.

"Not standing around in the parking garage this late waiting for you to get home."

Home. That slid off my tongue pretty damn easily.

She doesn't say anything back, so I say it again.

"Call me when you get close so I have time to take the elevator down to meet you."

"Okay," she says softly.

Relief hits me again.

She hangs up first; if she hadn't, I probably wouldn't have ended the call.

I would have stayed on the line and listened to the noises of the street as she drove and the rhythm of her breathing. Then I'd know when she was pulling into the garage when the beep sounded as she used her lanyard to open the underground garage gate to get into our apartment parking.

Autumn
Twenty minutes later...

I push send on my call log that says "Briggs".

"I'm pulling into the garage. I'll be up in a minute," I tell him when he answers.

"I told you to call before you got here so I would have time to get down there."

"I'll be fine. I'll see you in a minute." Then I end the call before he can reprimand me over the phone.

I pull into the garage after the gate slides open for me. I hang a right and head for the two parking spots reserved for our apartment, but when I pull up to it, there's a tall, brooding man standing in it dressed in a pair of basketball shorts low on his hips, a white t-shirt, and flip-flops he usually keeps by the door. His arms are crossed over his chest, and he doesn't look happy.

How in the world did Briggs get down here so fast? A fire station pole straight from our apartment on the sixth floor probably wouldn't have even beat me to my spot.

He steps out of the way as I pull into the parking spot.

I barely have the vehicle turned off when Briggs opens my door.

"How did you—"

"I was already down here. I figured you'd do this." He scowls while he holds my 4Runner's door open for me.

"Do what?"

"Be a brat and not listen."

I snicker at the name he calls me.

"Look," I say as I step out of the car and do a full 360-degree turn. "I'm in one piece. Told you I would be."

"Let's go, smart ass," he says, reaching around me and into my car, pulling my laptop bag out of the passenger side, and then closing the driver's door.

I scoot out of the narrow walkway between my car and his as he follows me. He takes large steps and begins to pass me but then reaches for my hand, taking it into his. He slides his fingers between mine, lacing them together, and it feels like an electric current zipping up my arm and bursting around my heart.

I should pull my hand from his. I should find an excuse to release my fingers from his own, but I can't bring myself to do it just yet—one more night.

He pulls me along with him until we get to the elevator, and then he lets go to hit the call button on the elevator lift.

The elevator opens immediately since it's late; this was probably the last place it was. Dropping off Briggs so it was already here.

It starts moving as soon as Briggs hits level eight. The doors shut and then shoot us up.

Briggs looks over at the pajamas I had already put on while I was at home. My face is cleaned of all my makeup, and my hair is braided for bed.

"Were you planning on sleeping there until I called?"

He's frowning. Does he not like the idea of me sleeping at my apartment for one night?

"No. I needed a brain break around 9 p.m. and decided to do my nighttime routine. I wouldn't have stayed there. My brother would have asked questions in the morning."

"Okay." He nods and then stares back at the elevator doors.

"Speaking of. You look no worse for wear than when I left you. Did everything go okay?"

"Yeah. We had a great heart-to-heart." He smirks to himself.

I'm guessing that's his way of telling me that they didn't talk.

The second the elevator stops and the doors open, Briggs wraps his fingers around mine again.

He leads me out of the elevator and down the hall to the apartment we're living in temporarily. He opens the apartment door and pushes it open for me, leading me through the door jam. He still doesn't release my hand.

He walks over to the kitchen counter and lays my laptop bag on the island. I look over and notice that none of the cookies are lying on cooling racks and that the entire kitchen has been wiped clean.

He cleaned the kitchen?

"Where are the cookies?" I ask, partially expecting him to say that he and Isaac ate their feelings this afternoon after I left instead of talking them out with each other.

"I put them away," he says, and points to the tower of Tupperware that was furnished with the apartment, all stacked nicely beside the fridge before he turns toward the hallway, bringing me along with him like the caboose to his steam engine, following his path exactly, only one step behind.

A man who uses Tupperware. Why is that a total turn-on?

He leads me down the hallway and toward the master bedroom. He pushes through the door that was left cracked open and pulls me through with him.

"You said you're ready for bed?"

"Yeah," I say, staring at the bed that he leads me to. "Teeth brushed and everything."

"Do you need to pee?" he asks.

I laugh. "No, I went right before you called."

"Okay then, get in," he says, pulling back the sheets on the side I slept on last night.

It seems like an odd request, but I'm exhausted. I yawned the whole drive over and was excited to get to climb onto this expensive memory foam mattress, so I go along with it.

I climb in and pull the sheets over me, but then Briggs yanks them back. When I look back toward him, he's pushing into my personal space.

"Scoot over," he instructs.

"Why? What are you doing?" I say as I start scooting.

"More," he says, following me on his knees further into the bed.

Before I know it, I'm settling into my usual side of the bed, and Briggs slides in under the sheets, pulling me back against him, sliding his arm into the gap between my neck and my pillow, and then his other arm wraps around my middle.

"Is this why you wanted me home so badly? You can't sleep alone?" I tease. "Do you want me to check under the bed for you like my mom used to do?"

He grumbles.

"It's almost one in the morning. Go to sleep."

"This feels like déjà vu."

He leans in and kisses the back of my head. "Go to sleep. We'll talk tomorrow."

When I don't say anything more, he hums his approval. The kind of sound I make when I'm so incredibly comfortable under a warm blanket with a pint of mint chocolate chip ice cream. My heart squeezes at his reaction to being snuggled up with me.

This feels just as decadent, but I can't get used to this if I want my corner office... not that Briggs is even offering a reason for me to turn down the promotion. As far as I know, this is all temporary, and I'm guessing so is the sex.

A few moments later, he speaks against the back of my head, his mouth pressed against my hair.

"You're right... I can't sleep alone. Where would I put my hands?" he says, and then squeezes me against him tighter.

I bite down on my lip to stop myself from squealing with glee.

But he's right... we do have to talk. Mostly about how after tonight, sex is off the table.

Erika was clear.

It's Briggs or the promotion.

And I already know which one makes the most sense.

CHAPTER TWENTY-ONE

Briggs

Today the team has the day off. We leave town in two days, and tomorrow Autumn and I are going to the hospital's fundraiser and grand opening of the new children's cancer hospital wing.

Isaac leaves today, and I almost want to ask him to stay to look after Autumn for the three days I'll be gone on the road, but he has a life back in Vegas, and Autumn doesn't need a babysitter.

I roll up to the curb in my sports car and look up at the large warehouse building. Sampson and Sons Gym is the MMA training gym that Isaac is training at today.

I get out of my truck and head for the army-green metal door, pulling it open. The music and the smell hit me right away. The music is blaring, and the smell of sweat and old musty warehouse permeates the space. If I thought the hockey locker room smelled of twenty sweaty ass players after one of Bex's notorious 'sweat drills', I had no damn idea.

There's light streaming in from the small windows at the top of the vaulted ceilings and one large stadium-sized light hovering over the three practice rings, laid out in a V-shape, one ring directly in front of me and two in the back. All three are currently in use. The one directly in front and the one in the back left currently have a fighter and a trainer working on combinations and jabs. But the ring in the back right has two men sparring. I see Isaac is one of the two men, and I head in his direction.

An assistant coach or someone who works for the gym makes a beeline for me. I figured someone would ask me who the hell I am and what I'm doing here. These gyms are invitation only, and with very few people working out inside at any given time, they can spot an outsider immediately.

"Can I help you, man?" a guy about my age says, walking up to me, flipping a gym towel to lay over his shoulder.

"Here to see Isaac. I'm a..." *What are you now, bud?* "A... friend. He's staying with me," I tell him.

The guy looks over at Isaac and then back at me. Seeing me for a second time must have refreshed his visual because recognition flashes in his eyes.

His demeanor changes; he eases slightly and then smiles. "Hey! You're Briggs Conley, the hockey player, right?"

"Yeah," I say, looking past him at Isaac as he puts a combo on his sparring partner, and the older man standing down on the ground is yelling more directions at Isaac with his erratic hand gestures. That must be the world-renowned gym owner and coach that Isaac came here to train with.

"A lot of people are saying this is going to be the Hawkeyes' year."

"I hope they're right."

"Well, good luck. Isaac's in the back corner," he says, and then turns and heads for the front ring.

I head for the back right ring. The second I put my hands on the ring's ropes, the coach notices my presence, but he does the same as the coach before. His eyes flash over at me once, but he ignores me until it registers who I am.

"Conley?" he asks, and turns to me, putting out his hand to shake mine. "I'm Tim Sampson, owner of the gym."

The guy can't be taller than five-foot-seven, likely bald, but I can't tell under his ballcap with the gym's logo on it. He looks like a dude who could have been pretty lethal back in his day. For his age, probably in his sixties, the dude is still jacked.

"Good to meet you."

"The pleasure is mine," he says, his eyes darting between me and the two fighters in the ring, "Benji, stop letting Isaac get that close to you. You have a longer wingspan than he does," he tells the other fighter, who's currently getting his shins kicked the shit in by Isaac.

This time, Tim doesn't turn to look at me, he just crosses his arms over his chest, and we stand side by side as we watch the two fighters.

"I'm a big fan of the Hawkeyes. Been following the team since the eighties when the stadium was built," Tim says.

"Do you come to any games?" I ask, watching Isaac go for Benji's legs for the takedown, but Benji narrowly escapes the move.

"Close, Isaac, that was very close. Next time you need to distract with a right kick to the outside thigh and then come down with that leg to launch forward. Your opponent is less likely to see it coming, and you have speed on your side!" Tim yells at Isaac.

"Haven't been to a game in over a decade, but I've been meaning to take my grandson," he says, still watching the fighters.

"Let Isaac know when you want to come down for a game. I'll put some tickets down at will call for you."

"Tickets... really? That'd be great. Thanks."

"Just extending the hospitality. Isaac said that he's getting more out of these three days than he has in a long time." More like that's what my mom told me yesterday when she called to check in. She heard it from Autumn's mom while they were getting side-by-side pedicures.

"He's a gifted fighter. His talents would have been wasted as a hockey player." He glances over at me, quickly realizing he might have offended me, although I doubt this guy cares much about offending people. "No offense," he adds.

"Yeah, well, my left jaw would have to agree with you," I say under my breath.

He glances over at me and smirks. "I heard some grumblings about a sister." He adjusts his weight and then looks back out at Isaac. "You the screwball responsible for why Isaac's fighting so well?"

"Responsible for it?" I ask.

"Every fighter needs motivation. Someone to visualize when they're putting the hurtin' down on their opponent."

Fuck, I hope that's not me.

"I sure as hell hope not."

He chuckles. "I wouldn't want to be on the receiving end of that guy's hate either."

Isaac goes for the kick and then the takedown that Tim suggests after sparring for a few minutes. Tim launches forward toward the ring.

"Yes! Yes! Now grab for the left leg! Get control, Isaac!"

This is where Isaac excels. Being a wrestler in high school, once he gets his opponent on the ground, it's pretty much over.

"Pin him. Pin him."

In a few seconds, Isaac has the fighter's shoulders pinned to the floor.

"All right, all right," Tim says, breaking off Isaac from turning the other fighter into a pretzel. Isaac pulls back and stands, giving his hand out to Benji and helping him up. Both of them are dripping sweat, staring over at Tim. Isaac's opponent doubles over with his hands resting on his knees, probably to keep himself from collapsing, Isaac's hands resting on his hips as if unfazed. And if he wasn't breathing like a cheetah was on his ass, you'd never know that his training affects him at all. Tim's right. MMA is where Isaac belongs.

"Take a water break. Catch your breath," Tim says.

Isaac's opponent nods and looks relieved for the break. Isaac seems uninterested in breaking at all. His attention finally falls on me as he realizes that I'm standing here too. I didn't tell him I was coming.

"Hey," he says flatly, and walks to the end of the ring, ducking under the ring ropes and climbing down off the ring. He grabs his towel and water bottle off the dark-stained cement floor and wipes his face before he takes a drink.

"What are you doing here, Conley?"

"Heard you're kicking ass down here."

He takes another drink of water and looks over at Tim, but Tim is busy taking a minute to talk to another fighter. Since Isaac has no excuse for getting back up in the ring, I go in for more.

"How are you feeling in there?" I ask.

He looks behind him, back at the ring, and then turns back to me. "Ready for another fight. My agent called. They're lining up a fight in a couple of months."

"That's good news, right?"

"Yeah," he says, and then takes another drink. "So, what are you doing down here?"

"I told you. I wanted to see you in action."

"You didn't need to."

"We're still friends, Isaac. We always will be, even if you hate my guts right now and you were visualizing beating my face in."

"Visualizing beating your face? If I wanted to do that, I'd just do it."

Nice.

"I'm not the motivation you need in the ring?" I ask

"What the hell are you talking about?"

"Tim said every fighter needs motivation... someone to hate."

"No, you're not my motivation, Jesus. You think I hate you that much?" He asks squinting back at me.

"Feels like it."

"I'm not happy about it, I think I've made that clear, but prison orange doesn't look good on me."

"Funny," I say, looking over at the other fighters to avoid showing how frustrated I am that he's still on this same track. I have to be patient if I want to keep our friendship. If I show any real fight in me, Isaac will push back harder.

"Your face looks better. My sister must be taking care of you."

"She is," I say, burying my hands in my pockets.

"Make sure you do the same."

"I plan on it."

"Just be careful, Briggs," he warns, but it feels more like a plea.

"With what?"

"She's had a thing for you since we were kids. It's one of the reasons that I always warned you off her."

She has? I hide the smile at the thought of Autumn liking me. It gives me more motivation to tell her that I think something is happening between us.

"Why would you do that?"

"You know the fuck why."

"No, I don't."

He gives an irritable sigh. "You've never been ready for a girl like Autumn."

"Are you saying that I don't deserve Autumn?"

"That's not what I said. I just said you've never been in a place to care for my sister the way that she deserves."

Does he still feel that way?

"I care about her. I want to make her happy. Do you trust me now?"

He thinks for a second. "Jury's still out, but our mothers seem hellbent on the idea."

I chuckle. "Yeah, I've heard."

He laughs. "Better they're on your ass than mine."

"Just wait. Your day is coming too."

He nods, and then Tim and Isaac's sparring partner walk back over. "I'd better get back to work."

"Want to do dinner at the apartment? I want to use that expensive grill out on the balcony before Autumn and I move out of the place."

Isaac gives me a confused look. "Didn't you guys just move?"
Oh shit.

"Uh, yeah, but it's a short lease, and we might look for a place with more room." Liar. "Your sister wants a dog."

What the actual fuck? Why am I lying more than absolutely necessary?

"She's always wanted a dog, but my parents wouldn't let her. Now you're going to cave? You're getting soft in your old age, Briggs."

"It's not my age, it's your sister." That came out without even thinking, but it's true.

He looks at me, but I can't read what he's thinking.

"I'll see you later tonight for dinner. I'll be here late since this is my last day of training before I leave in the morning."

"Okay, a few of my teammates would like to meet you if you don't mind them coming down; they all live in the building. Autumn is going out for drinks with the girls."

"The girls?"

"A couple of women that work for the Hawkeyes. She's become friends with them while coming to my games."

"She's making friends with people at your work? Fuck, you two are getting serious, aren't you?"

I hope so, but we haven't talked about it. There's still the conversation of Derek and the need to get Isaac's blessing.

"Yeah, we are."

I pull my hands back out of my pockets, my right hand gripping my keys.

Isaac sees the keys in my hand. "You can stay and watch for a bit if you want."

"Really?"

"Sure."

Isaac climbs back up the ring and ducks under the ropes. I stay for another hour and talk with Tim while we watch Isaac put into motion everything that he's been learning over the last couple of days. He looks even sharper than he did in his fight last week. He's improving with the help of Tim Sampson, but I hope he doesn't make coming to Seattle and staying with us a recurring habit.

Staying with us. As in a future where Autumn and I are still together. The thought lingers as I leave the warehouse.

A few hours later, Isaac is sitting in a patio chair, and I'm getting the grill ready out on the balcony of the apartment. I hear the door open to the apartment and peer through the glass door of the balcony to see Autumn coming through.

I watch her walk into the kitchen and drop her purse on the kitchen island. "Autumn!" I yell to get her attention.

Her head whips over to find me looking over at her with a plate of seven raw steaks in one hand and a pair of tongues in the other.

She smiles over at me and then heads toward us.

She peaks out the door before walking through and sees her brother sitting in the chair. I can sense her tense up slightly.

"Hey, sis," Isaac says, lounging in the chair with his feet up on the table and a beer in his hand.

"Hi, are you boys getting along?" she asks.

I look over at him, and he looks at me.

"Look, no new bruises on your boyfriend's pretty face. Happy?"

Autumn looks over at me and takes a few steps toward me, softly putting her hands on my jaw and twisting it slowly side to side to ensure he isn't lying.

When she confirms that I'm no worse for wear, she hums in approval. "He is pretty, isn't he?"

I wish my hands weren't full and her brother wasn't here. I'd wrap my arm around her back and pull her to me, laying a kiss that I've been thinking about giving her all day.

She looks up at me, and I give my best "I want to lay you out on our bed and lick every inch of you" smile. She bites down on her lip and rubs her right earlobe with her perfectly painted pink fingernails. Her tell.

"I should go get ready. I have drinks with the girls."

"Yeah, I remember."

"Okay," she says, her eyes not leaving mine for a second.

"Abandoning me on my last night," Isaac pokes.

"Next time, give me some notice that you're dropping in to harass us, and I'll be sure to move my whole life around yours," she fires back with sass that I love.

"What fun would that be?" he asks.

She turns to look back at me and rolls her eyes.

"Do you need a lift home? I could come get you," I tell her, praying she takes me up on my offer. But before she can offer, Isaac pipes up.

"Don't you take drinks from strangers or leave your drink unattended," Isaac chips in. "In fact... just don't drink at all."

"Why don't you just lock me up in a tall tower?" she asks.

"Don't tempt me," he says back.

"He's right, though," I agree.

"I've been a female for the last twenty-six years of my life. Thank you for your unsolicited advice, but I'm more in tune with the dangers I face every time I step out of this apartment than either of you knuckleheads could fathom."

"Just be careful, that's all," Isaac says back with pleading eyes.

"We will. I'm going to get ready," she tells him and then looks at me. "Don't have too much fun without me."

Not a chance if you're not here.

I smile down at her. "We won't. Lake, Reeve, Seven, and Ryker are coming down to level six tonight," I say, referring to our apartment. Everyone else's apartments are above us by a story or two.

She walks back into the apartment. I follow her movement down the hallway through the glass windows.

Once she's out of sight, I remember why the hell I'm out here. I slab the steaks on the grill, along with slices of pineapples and halved peaches that I'll sprinkle with brown sugar and cinnamon once they have a nice grilled flavor.

"Want a beer?" Isaac says, getting up out of his chair and heading for the kitchen.

"No, I'm not drinking," I say, hoisting up my long-neck root beer.

"My sister has done a number on you, hasn't she?"

You have no damn idea.

"Something like that," I say, taking a sip of my cold drink.

A few seconds I hear, "The hell you're going out like that."

I look up from the grill and see Autumn and Isaac in the foyer of the apartment. I can't see well enough through the glare of skyscrapers against the balcony windows. I head inside to find Autumn standing with annoyance, her hip popped to one side with her hand planted on top. Isaac stands with a scowl looking at her.

"There's nothing wrong with it," she argues.

"Your shirt practically shows your belly button."

"Can't you find something else to do with your time? Get a hobby, Isaac."

"What's going on?" I say, stomping through the kitchen and heading toward them.

Isaac points at Autumn's top. "She's wearing that." He grimaces.

I look over to see Autumn in a pair of jeans as tight as a second skin, a pair of high-heeled boots, and a top that's... oh, shit.

My dick perks up a little at the plunging neckline of Autumn's top. It's not down to her belly button like Isaac is squawking about, but it's down past her perky tits, and fuck, she looks good. I can see the indent of her breastbone and the top of where her stomach starts. I want to fucking pull her to me and lick a line from where the fabric dips down her perfect body to the top of her collarbone and then bite down on that beautiful neck while I strip her naked from head to toe.

"She looks good," I smirk, taking another full scan of the gorgeous woman who will be in my bed later tonight, the ideas of what I plan to do to her already forming.

She smiles back at me.

"You're going to let her go out like that when you're not around? I hope you're cool with every dick in that bar staring at your girlfriend."

Oh fuck, he's right. I didn't think about that. I was too busy thinking of taking off every article of her clothing when she got home, hoping for her to be a little tipsy and handsy.

"He's right. You should change."

"Screw you both. I'm leaving," she says, and then turns and heads for the door.

Isaac throws up his hands and stomps off in the opposite direction, back out to the balcony.

I jog behind her to catch up. "Wait, hold on."

She puts her hand on the apartment door and then turns to look at me, an annoyed look in her eyes. "What?"

"You're just going out with the girls?"

"Yes."

"Are you meeting anyone else out there?"

"Like whom?" Her eyebrows furrow in question.

"Like..." I'm going to be in trouble for asking, aren't I? "Like Derek."

Her eyes turn into slits like she's trying to see through me. "You should be careful. You're starting to sound like a jealous boyfriend."

I take a step forward. "What if I am?"

Her eyes widen, and we stare at each other for a beat.

"Briggs!" Isaac calls out from the balcony. "I'm flipping the steaks. And do you have A1 sauce?"

"Yeah," I yell over my shoulder.

Just then, a knock echoes through the foyer.

The guys.

Autumn opens the door, and sure enough, a handful of my buddies walk through the open door, all of them unable to keep from looking down at Autumn's shirt as they pass by.

Shit, the dicks at the bar are going to be all over her.

A notification flashes on her phone that her Uber is downstairs. "I have to go. They're starting the meter. I'll see you tonight, though. We can talk?"

I check back at the balcony and see that all the guys are far enough away and distracted with introductions, meeting Isaac the MMA fighter we all just watched a couple of days ago on pay-per-view.

"Yeah. I'll be the dude in your bed," I say, taking another step and bending down to kiss her.

She melts into me and drops her hand off the door handle. I press her back up against the door and deepen our kiss, slipping my tongue into her mouth. She moans and grips my shirt at my chest height and pulls me closer. My hands slide behind her and grip her ass with both hands.

Then they travel up her backside and sneak under her shirt, my fingertips gliding over the bare small of her back. I can feel the small dimples that sit just above her ass, the curvature of her spine, and the warmth of her skin against mine.

"Briggs! Steaks are done, and we're starving. Let's eat," I hear Isaac say.

She pulls her mouth off mine and giggles. "You'd better deal with the grown toddlers on our balcony."

Our balcony. I like the sound of that.

I pull back just enough to lock my eyes with hers. Isaac's words from today echo in my head.

"She's had a thing for you since we were kids."

If the blackmail hadn't happened, would I have missed out on this woman? I think I would have.

I want to ask her if Isaac's words are true, but she's right. Now isn't the time.

"Don't you want to take him with you?" I practically beg.

"Nice try," she says, putting her hand back on the door handle and twists it. "He's a buzzkill and all yours."

The door creaks open, and now I have to step back and let her leave, but I don't want to.

I watch her dip out through the door, smiling over her shoulder at me and then closing the door behind her. She's gone, but it still smells like her, and I take a long inhale.

I walk back to the balcony as Isaac and the guys are all sitting down to eat at the long outdoor patio table that seats eight, but five big dudes make this table look like it was built for children. We barely all fit.

A couple of hours later, my buddies take off back upstairs. We have an early skate in the morning, and everyone wants a good night's rest.

Isaac is standing at the balcony railing with a beer in his hand as he looks out over Seattle.

"I'm leaving tomorrow, and I need to let you know... that I know," he says.

That was cryptic.

"You know what? That you're a dumbass?" I say as I step up to the balcony and mimic his forearms resting on the balcony railing.

"Funny, asshole," he says, sending a glare my way. "No, that you're not dating Autumn."

"What are you talking about? Of course, I am," I say.

"Hold on to that denial. I'm getting to that next. That's not what I want to talk to you about. There's another reason why I came here besides you fake dating my sister and lying to me about it."

"You already knew about Autumn and me?"

"Not until the first night when she told me."

She told him?

"And that pencil dick Derek stopped me on my way back up this afternoon to confirm my suspicions."

"What the fuck?! How... when?! What the hell did he say?" I tense up and grab for my phone to text Autumn and ask where that asshole lives.

"Just chill for a second. I want to talk to you about your dad." He takes a pull off his beer and then looks up at me. "It's back, isn't it?" he asks softly.

I look down at the street six stories below us.

"It's sophomore year of college all over again. You're drinking."

"I stopped, so leave it the fuck alone."

"Autumn told me about the partying."

Did he tell her what he suspects is going on?

"She did?" I ask.

"Not in so many words. I've seen the gossip column and social media about you partying, and Autumn said that she's helping repair someone's career and has to lie to people she cares about. It wasn't hard to piece it together after that."

I don't respond. The idea that Autumn is feeling guilty for lying to people we both care about and love is a punch to the gut. It's not as if I don't know that she and I are both lying, but it hits harder when hearing that she's not happy about being put in this predicament because of the way I've been handling the news.

"How bad is it?" he asks.

I hang my head.

"Stage three."

"How's he coping?"

"Fuck, man," I say, shaking my head and trying to hold back the wetness in my eyes trying to break through. "He's the strongest man I know. How can this be happening? I thought he won last time. Why is it coming back?"

I stare out at the skyline. I can't look at Isaac, my oldest friend and the only person I've ever confided in about how hard my dad's cancer struggle has been on me.

"I don't know. And I know I'm not the asshole who should be saying this, but burying yourself in booze and women isn't going to take the hurt away."

"What do you mean? You still bury yourself in booze and women."

"Fuck yeah, I do. But for the fun of it." I give a halfhearted chuckle, and then so does he. He's trying to lighten the mood. "But you're doing it because you feel out of control and want to forget for a few minutes about what's happening in your life. The problem with that is… you're just wasting time because he's still here. You're grieving the loss of a living man. You need to wake up and look around you at the things you still have, like your dad."

"It's hard to see him like this. He's sick, and every day there's more bad news, and he keeps this bright outlook. It's just not fucking fair."

"It doesn't seem like Autumn knows."

"I haven't told her." I admit.

"She thinks the drinking is because..."

"Because I'm a hockey player who likes to party. It's easy enough to let her believe that than to tell her the truth."

"Don't do that," he says, shaking his head.

"Do what?"

"Push my sister away."

"That's fucking confusing," I say, giving him a lifted brow.

"I just mean that she can help you through this."

"But don't touch her." I clarify.

"...Or I'll kill you," he says, finishing my thought. "Listen, I'm not happy that you're using my sister to improve your image, but she needs this to get her promotion. So... fuck it. I guess do the damn thing until this shit is done with. I'll stay off your ass and keep your secret from our moms."

I shake my head in disbelief. "You will?"

"Just until this whole thing is over in another month or whatever the hell. She gets you out of the situation, and you get her the job she wants. But that's it. I'm only agreeing to this because Autumn deserves that job. I don't give a fuck about your career in the NHL. You get me?" he says, looking over at me. "Then you two break up and find a way to tell our moms in a way that doesn't crush their souls. And we never talk ever again about how you fake-dated my sister."

"And what if I don't agree to your terms? What if I don't want to break it off after?"

He straightens his posture. "Don't push your damn luck with me. And Conley?"

"Yeah?"

"Go the fuck home and see your dad," he says, pushing off the railing and heading back inside the apartment.

I guess the heart-to-heart is over.

This wasn't how I saw this conversation going tonight. I hoped I was going to convince him to see that I was making her happy. That all his misconceptions about me not being boyfriend material for Autumn would be obvious over the last couple of days.

Isaac was clear. He'll let us get what we need out of this arrangement, and then it ends. Otherwise, he'll be back, and our friendship will be over.

CHAPTER TWENTY-TWO

Autumn

"I think he could be my soulmate," Penelope says about the email pen pal that she's had since college who is now slipping back into her inbox... out of nowhere.

"I hope he is Penelope, you deserve love, but soulmates are too farfetched an idea for me. There are too many damn people in this universe for only one person to be your soulmate," Tessa says, taking a sip of her raspberry lemon drop.

Although I would tend to side with Tessa on this, I think Penelope truly believes in it, and honestly, I could use a little happily ever after discussion right now.

"If he's your soulmate, then you need to force him to meet you, once and for all," I encourage.

Things with Briggs seem to be coloring outside of the lines, and even though I've enjoyed every second of it, Erika's warning has me knowing that this thing with Briggs and I can't keep going on if I want the promotion.

I should have told him last night when I got home from my apartment, but being locked up in his arms while I slept was too good to let go of. And then this morning... I still wasn't ready. Then he kissed me before I walked out the door to head to the bar, and I just about texted the girls to cancel so that I could get one more shower sex session in before we have to call it quits, but with my brother in the apartment, and Briggs's teammates showing up, I lost my chance. I have to tell him tonight that we have to stop the physical portion of this because it could cost me everything I'm working for.

I'm glad to be getting a few hours with these girls to blow off a little stress before heading back to my apartment with Briggs.

Penelope invited Isla to come out with us, and since Kaenan is leaving for a few days with the team, he told her to take the night off. I'm glad she's here too, but with her here, we can't discuss what's happening between Briggs and me. I could have used Penelope and Tessa's input on what I should do and what they think Briggs wants.

"I agree," Isla says. "Demand the things that you want, and don't be scared if stating your true feelings might ruin everything because one day, your ex might drag you back to Colorado." Isla clinks her glass with all of ours and then downs her drink like a shot.

"Uh, you okay over there?" Tessa says to Isla with concern.

"That was oddly specific," I say.

"Do you have something on your chest?" Penelope says, "Spill. That's what girls' night is for."

"I don't think I should talk about this out loud. He's my boss." Isla's eyes go so big as saucers that she just let the cat out of the bag.

The three of us gasp but smile at each other. Tessa called this. Isla and Kaenan have a thing for each other, but they're trying to hide it from each other because pretty much anyone in proximity to these two can see it.

"We've got all night," I tell her, grabbing her empty drink and heading for the bar to get her a refill. She needs liquid courage. I walk up and set the empty drink on the bar as the bartender walks up.

"What can I get you?"

"She needs a refill." I toss a thumb over my shoulder. "Liquid courage, please... something fruity that goes down easy."

The bartender gives me a weird look.

Tessa walks up behind me with two more empty glasses, probably reordering too. She leans in to see what the bartender and I are discussing.

"She's about to tell us about a secret love affair with her boss, but she needs a little push." That doesn't lessen his scowl. "We already know who it is. We just want her to finally admit it and free herself."

He still seems displeased.

Tessa decides to chime in. "Please, for the love of God and all that is holy in this world, our dear friend needs help, and we need you to wave your magic fairy tequila wand to assist us in unburdening her on girls' night."

He takes the empty drink glasses and then looks back over at our table. "Fine, but I'm watching you two."

It's good to know the bartender is looking out for his customers… can't be mad at that.

"Great, now make it a round for the whole table… thanks." Tessa beams and does her innocent girl head tilt, sliding a black metal card toward him.

The name on the card reads Lake E Powers.

"Lake E Powers?" I ask.

"I know, right? What could the E stand for? Elmer? Enrique?" she says, debating the possibilities. "Penelope won't tell me. She says it's against confidentiality policy for her to tell me anything inside Lake's file."

"Why don't you just internet stalk him like a normal person?" I suggest.

"What fun is that?"

"No fun, I guess." I laugh. "So, why do you have it?"

"Because I bet him that I could pickpocket him without him knowing."

"Did you win?"

"Well, we're here, and I'm buying us all drinks with it." She smirks.

"Does he know?" I ask of my crazy friend.

"He'll know soon enough." She gleams.

I shake my head and then take a quick look around the bar, mindlessly looking over the other patrons in the bar, when my eyes catch on a woman in the back.

She almost looks like...

I swear that's...

She sees me, and our eyes connect, and then she bolts for the bathroom hall.

Shoot, it is. But how does she know who I am? I only know who she is from the photos that I've seen of her from the surveillance photos from Erika and Sam Roberts. Maybe she recognized me from gossip magazines or social media.

"I'll meet you back at the table. I need to use the restroom," I tell Tessa, and then speed walk to the restroom.

I push through the bathroom door but don't see anyone at first.

I walk through the line of bathroom stalls until I find the only one closed. I consider it a strike of luck that no one else is in here.

"Dixie?" I say softly.

I'll be embarrassed if it's not her, and I came in with guns blazing.

"Dixie, I know you're in here."

Still no response.

"I just want to talk to you."

"Are you going to hit me?" she asks, her voice echoing in the metal stall.

She thinks I'll hit her? Well, yes, actually I'd like to, but I won't. I don't want to spend the night in jail for assault, and I still don't even know the real story because Briggs is tight-lipped about it all.

"No, I'm not going to hit you."

Still no movement.

"Okay, how about if I just ask questions and you answer them? I just want to know what's going on. Briggs seems to think this whole thing is out of character for you. I just want to know your motivation for doing this to him."

"He said that?" she asks.

"Said what?"

"That he thinks this is out of character for me?"

Yes, but he has to be wrong.

"He did. He wanted to talk to you, but the franchise won't let him."

"This is all so fucked up." I hear her voice break as she seems to start crying.

Who blackmails someone and then cries about it?

"What's fucked up?" I ask.

"Briggs is a good guy. This shouldn't be happening to him."

"I agree. So why are you doing it."

"Are you wearing a wire?" she asks.

What the hell?

"No. Why?"

I hear the sound of the metal lock sliding loose, and then the door opens slowly.

She opens the stall door and then looks at me, her eyes red and blotchy like she hasn't slept in days, and I can see new tears that have fallen. What is happening to this woman?

She walks over to the sink and washes her hands even though I don't think she used the restroom, but bathrooms are dirty, so washing her hands is smart.

I watch her meticulously wash them, and the silence is killing me.

"Dixie—"

"My name isn't Dixie. That's just my stage name."

"Okay..."

"It's Samantha."

"I'm Autumn."

"I know. I've seen pictures of you and Briggs online."

That's what I figured.

"As his girlfriend, I just want to know why you're blackmailing Briggs but crying over the injustice of it. I don't understand."

"It's not me."

"What do you mean it's not you?"

She looks around the bathroom to make sure we're alone, but right as she's about to say something, two women walk in. They both smile at us and now it's my turn to pretend that I'm washing my hands.

The two women are chatting about the scowling bartender while they reapply lipstick. Well, at least it wasn't just me that had him frowning. He just does that, it sounds like.

After a minute or two, they turn to leave.

I step closer to her. I want to get this information before the next person comes in to use the facilities.

"Someone else is blackmailing Briggs?"

"Yes. My boss."

"Who's your boss?"

"The owner of the club."

"I don't understand. Briggs is a big client. Why would he want to lose out on business?"

"He thought it would be a big enough payday. He has a drug habit, and he said he'll lose the club if I can't get a cash infusion."

"So he came up with the idea to blackmail Briggs?"

"Yeah. He's been seeing the lap dances Briggs has been paying me for and figured Briggs wouldn't miss the money."

I want to ask her about the lap dances that it seems Briggs pays for but doesn't use. However, that's more of a personal question, and I need facts about the blackmail portion. I'll ask about the lap dances if I get the time.

"But when Lake Powers came in with Briggs, he thought he could sue the franchise instead and get more money."

"But Briggs wasn't involved?"

"No."

She hesitantly looks around the room again.

"What's wrong? Why are you so anxious?"

"I need the money from my job. If my boss finds out, he'll fire me and blackball me from all the other clubs. I have a little girl to look after. I need that money."

"I'm not going to tell anyone. Then did you send the surveillance photos?"

"No. My guess is that Tyler did. The guy who used to bartend for the club. He likes Briggs. The owner fired him because he said he wouldn't lie about seeing Briggs and the other players walk into the back room with me."

"What's the club owner's plan now?"

"He gambled all the money away, so he plans to sell the story to a gossip magazine next week."

"Next week!? But you signed a document that says you won't sell the fake story. the Hawkeyes are going to sue you for breach of contract."

She starts crying again and stares down at her shaky hands.

"I know. I'm scared. I didn't know about his plans to sell to the gossip magazine. But he said there's enough money to protect me as long as I go along with everything."

"And you believe him?"

"What other choice do I have? He says no one will believe me. I have a daughter I have to think about. I need the job, she's sick, and I'm all she has."

"Cancer?" I ask softly, not completely sure if I should even utter the words.

She nods. The lap dances Briggs didn't take. Is it possible he was helping her? His dad had cancer once, years ago, when I was still in high school. Luckily, he beat it. I see why Briggs would want to help Samantha's daughter.

"What about the money that the Hawkeyes sent you?"

"It went to an account that the bar owner set up. I never saw a dollar of it. He said he needed it all to keep the club going and keep me employed."

"What happened to the bartender?"

"He quit when this was all happening. I think he moved to Portland, Oregon."

I think for a second.

"Samantha, are you willing to help Briggs if I can find a way for you to do that?"

"Yeah. I'll do whatever I can," she says adamantly.

"Give me your number, and I'll text you mine. We'll stay close. I know a new charity that could help you with expenses for your daughter."

"Really? You think they'd help me with everything I've done in my past?"

"I know the president, and I think you're the perfect family for this."

She smiles at me, wiping her tears.

She and I walk back out of the restroom, and I head back to the table, trying not to race right out of the door, and head directly home to tell Briggs what I found out. To tell him what's on its way. It turns out Briggs was right. He should have gone to talk to Dixie... er, Samantha. Maybe this could have all ended without Briggs and I having to fake date.

That thought hits me. Suppose the owner hadn't decided to blackmail Briggs. In that case, my PR company might never have been called, Briggs wouldn't have needed a fake girlfriend, and I would probably still be dating Derek instead of heading home to Briggs.

What an odd turn of events.

"OK, I'm back. What did I miss?" I say, sliding in next to Isla on the bench.

"We thought maybe you got a job in the back," Tessa jokes. "You were gone forever."

"I'm sorry. I ran into a friend," I say, looking over to find that Samantha isn't here anymore. She must have gone home.

"Recap!" Penelope declares. "Tessa wants to find a way to get rid of Lake's body without anyone tracing it back to her. Isla wants to rip Kaenan's clothes off with her teeth..."

"Whoa, I didn't say that," Isla interjects.

"...And I have met the man of my dreams, but I've never met him. The only one we're missing is yourself, so now stop holding back and give us all the juicy details."

I glance over at Isla and then at them.

"Penelope told her," Tessa smirks and takes a sip of her drink.

"Well... she's a part of our core group. It was essential."

"I wish I had your logic when I asked the Hawkeyes if I could avoid lying to my own parents and my brother... who, by the way, hit Briggs when he found out we are dating."

All three of them echo an "Ooh."

"I'm sorry." Penelope sinks into her chair and gives a pitiful smile.

"It's okay. But I should probably go. Briggs and I are supposed to have 'the talk' when I get home about where this is going, and I have to tell him that my boss just told me I have to choose between him or my promotion."

They all gasp, and Penelope reaches out to stop me from standing up.

"You can't drop that on us and then leave," she says.

"I'm sorry, but I have to."

I look toward the door as I make plans for an escape through the crowd when the door opens, and a familiar man walks through it.

"Uh-oh," I say as I watch Lake scouring the bar. I've got an idea of who he's looking for.

"What?" Penelope perks up, looking around.

"Someone's in trouble," I say, glancing away from Lake and looking at Tessa.

"Who... me?" she says with confusion.

She follows my eyes and sees Lake. His eyes latch onto hers, and his face turns dark.

"Welp, that's my cue to go," I tell them, grabbing my purse and slipping back out of the bench seat.

"This was fun. Another night next week?"

They all nod, and I pass by Lake.

"Go easy on her," I whisper to him.

"Like she does to me?"

Okay... good point.

I look back just as I exit the bar to see Lake hovering over Tessa; his hand outstretched as if telling her to give him his card back. He must have had a notification that told him someone used his card at the bar.

Dang, I wish I could stay to hear this. Oh well, they'll have to give me the details at our next girls' night.

CHAPTER TWENTY-THREE

Autumn

I text Briggs when I leave the bar in the rideshare I ordered.

Briggs

Coming Home. Just Leaving.

Then I send a text to Penelope because I can't resist.

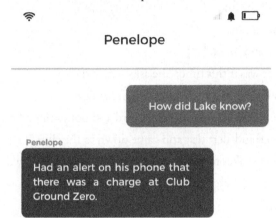

Knew it.

The car drops me off at the front door of our building, and I see Briggs standing outside in a pair of gray athletic sweats, a dark blue zip-up hoodie, and a pair of flip-flops. My heart picks up speed. We have a doorman, but he came downstairs to be here when I got to our building.

He steps forward when we pull up, opens my door, and takes my hand to help me out of the car.

Briggs dips down and makes eye contact with the driver. "Thanks for bringing her home safely." And then gives the driver a wave before shutting the door.

Briggs slides his hand into mine and then leads me through the front door as the doorman holds it open for us.

"Did you have fun with the girls tonight?" he asks, glancing over his shoulder at me as he leads me through the large entrance of the apartment building.

"Yeah. Lake showed up as I was leaving, though. I think I missed all the juicy drama." I playfully huff.

"What drama?"

"Lake and Tessa."

"What was it this time?" he asks with a sigh.

I guess their history is longer than I realize.

"She pick-pocketed his credit card and bought us all drinks. He got a fraud alert text and came down to the club."

He just shakes his head at the shenanigans of those two.

"How did things go with my brother tonight?"

"Fine."

"Just fine?"

We stop in front of the elevator, and he stalls for a second, "He told me I need to tell you why I've been drinking."

"Is it because of a breakup like sophomore year?"

"What?" He looks back at me with confusion. "No."

"Oh, I thought that girl from college broke up with you for partying too much."

The elevator doors open, and we walk through. He pushes the number to our floor, and then the elevator doors close again and begin moving us up to the sixth floor.

He begins to speak again. "She did break up with me for drinking too much, but I was drinking too much because my dad got cancer, and I didn't know how to handle the pain and depression that came with it. It's just as well. If someone leaves you at your hardest times... it's better to know early on. I didn't shed a tear for that relationship."

I lay my hand on his right arm and squeeze a little. "I didn't realize that was the reason. I'm sorry about your dad and that you didn't have any support from your girlfriend."

"And now he has it again," he says softly, almost like he doesn't want me to hear it.

"Hold on, what did you just say?"

He stares back at the elevator door and doesn't look at me.

"My dad has stage three cancer."

"Oh, my God! Are you serious?" I ask, turning towards him immediately. "Is he getting treatment? How's he feeling? How's your mom doing with this?"

A million questions barrel through my mind.

"Better than me," he says flatly, still not looking at me.

"When did you see him last?"

"It's been at least six months."

"No! What? Why?"

I can't believe he wouldn't see Mr. Conley more. They've always had a great relationship, and Mr. Conley has always been so proud of Briggs. It's hard for me to believe that Briggs doesn't go see him every chance he gets.

"Because it's tearing me up, and he just seems to brush it all under the table. He's always trying to lighten the mood, and it makes me feel like when I'm around sulking, I just remind him that he's sick. That's not helpful when you're trying to recover and having someone around who keeps begging you not to die."

"Briggs, he loves you. You need to be there."

The door to the elevator opens, and he steps out. I follow closely to his side.

"How long has this been going on?" I ask as we walk down the hallways toward our apartment door.

"I've known for a little over a year."

"The drinking..." I say softly.

"Yeah."

"This all makes sense now. I didn't know any of this."

"Your brother knew. That's why he came."

"Not because of the last TV interview that he heard about us dating?"

"That too. He was multitasking," he says.

Another puzzle piece comes to mind.

"Wait, hold on, is that why you've been paying for Samantha's daughter's cancer treatment?"

"Who's Samantha?" He finally looks over at me for a brief second.

I shake my head. I didn't realize he didn't know her real name.

"Dixie. Is that why you were paying for lap dances that you never received... to pay for Dixie's daughter's treatment."

We come up to our door, and he spins toward me, stopping in front of me before he opens the door for us to enter.

"How did you know that's what the lap dance receipts were for?"

I guess now is when I tell him I ran into her at the bar.

"I ran into her at the bar tonight."

"What?" His eyebrows stitch together, a slight scowl on his face.

He's not happy about my news.

"I sort of chased her into the woman's restroom."

"Why? What were you thinking?" He demands to know, taking a step closer.

It's not as if she's dangerous and might have shanked me in the bathroom stall... or wait, would she?

"I wanted to know why she's blackmailing you. When she saw me, she ran. She knew who I was. My reflexes kicked in, and I went after her."

"What did she say?" he asks, leaning in to hear me more closely.

"You were right."

"About what?"

"That you should have gone to see her like you told the Hawkeyes."

Although then, you and I might never have been. This thing between us would never have happened, and I would have remained your best friend's little sister for eternity without you ever noticing.

But I don't say any of that out loud.

"She told you why she's doing all of this?"

"Actually... she told me *who's* doing all of this."

"You lost me."

"Her boss, the owner of the club. He's the one that made up the story about what happened that night and told Samantha that if he didn't get the money, he'd lose his club, and she'd lose her job."

He turns to the left and away from me, running his hands through his hair.

"Goddamn it," he mumbles. "Her crackhead boss is the one pulling the strings? How didn't I think of that?"

"Do you know him?"

"No... but I've heard he's shady as fuck."

He stares at the wall as I'm sure a million thoughts are going through his head.

"She told me that the bartender lives in Portland. I'm going to call Erika in the morning—"

"Whoa, whoa." He spins back around and places his hands on my shoulders. "You are not going out looking for Tyler."

"Erika has the very best private investigator on retainer. He can help me—"

He cuts me off again. "Listen to me. You need to let the Hawkeyes' legal team deal with this, okay? This is not only not your problem, but I leave tomorrow morning for four days, and I need to know that you're home safe. Not running into dingy bars looking for a guy who may or may not want to be found. Do you understand?"

"He must be a pretty decent guy if he called Sam to come to pick you up when you'd pass out and quit when he found out what was happening. And Samantha thinks he's the one that sent the pictures to the Hawkeyes."

"It's possible. I always thought Tyler was a good guy, but I still don't like the idea of you wandering around Portland. Let the legal team figure this out... please."

"But the Hawkeyes haven't found this guy, and I got more information in ten minutes than they have over the last several months ."

"Autumn, don't make me beg. Promise me you'll let someone else pursue this lead. Not you. Otherwise, I'm packing you in my suitcase, and I'm bringing you on the bus with us, and trust me, traveling with a bunch of dudes is no vacation."

"You wouldn't do that."

"I wouldn't do what?"

"Pack me in your suitcase."

"You're right. I'll just toss you over my shoulder like this," he says as he grips around my waist and hoists me up. I squeak out a sound of surprise as he flings me over his shoulder. "And use you as a body pillow so I can sleep better in the hotel."

He reaches for the apartment door and opens it, walking inside with me still folded in half over his shoulder. He flips me back over, slowly and gently, making sure my feet touch the ground, and I cover my chest, making sure my boobs don't fall out of my low-cut top.

His eyes cast down at the low V of my shirt too.

I love the feeling of his eyes on me in a provocative manner, but I know better than to let these feelings grow.

He reaches back for the door and engages the deadbolt lock. Then he heads into the kitchen, and I follow. If we're quiet, Isaac shouldn't be able to hear us.

Briggs presses a hip to the counter and then folds his arms over his chest.

"So, you were going to see Samantha after you heard about your dad?"

"Sort of. The club isn't far from my apartment, and when I found out about my dad, I didn't want to drink alone. I started going where the lights and the music stayed on all night. Where I don't have to go home to the dark and think about my dad and wonder how much time he has left, wonder if he's scared, and what my mom will do when he's gone. What I will do when he's gone."

He looks away, and I see his Adam's apple bob with emotion like he's pulling back the tears.

"Briggs," I say, placing my hand on his chest.

"I go to where the music is so loud, I can't think. And I drink until I pass out in a place where I know Dixie and Tyler will make sure I don't get fucked with while I'm out."

"And the lap dances?"

"One night, the club was slow. She came out and sat next to me at the bar where Tyler was serving me drinks, and he and I were talking. She asked why a guy like me comes in night after night on his own and sits at the bar, never watching the show. I told her about my dad, and then she told me about how she needs this job as a single mom to a daughter who's fighting childhood cancer."

Is that why he agreed to the charity fundraiser so quickly? He still wants to help her daughter even though she didn't even bother to warn Briggs about her boss. Or maybe he's doing it for his dad.

"Oh, jeez. That's sad that she has to carry the burden alone."

He nods.

"She said it's expensive driving to and from treatments. The travel costs and missing stretches of work to be with her daughter. She was disappointed that it was a slow night because she had a payment to the hospital coming up, so I paid for a lap dance that night but told her I'd rather talk instead. I started doing that once a week when I'd go in, even if she was too busy to sit and talk with me. Tyler would ring it up on my tab and make sure she got the money before the end of her shift."

"How thoughtful of you," I say sarcastically.

As if paying for the lap dance was the best he could do. She needs out of there and away from her slimy boss but still make money to support her daughter. That's what she really needs.

But I can't be to upset with him. At least he was doing something to help her.

"I've never gotten a lap dance from her. I swear. And I'd never lie to you. I hope you believe me."

"I do."

This is so different than what I'd thought. I would have never guessed that this is why he paid for lap dances that he never used.

"I'm sorry to ask this. I'm not trying to be heartless, but..."

"Is she telling the truth?"

"Yeah."

He thinks for a second. "I asked Tyler one night about the story she told me. He confirmed it was true."

"So you pay for lap dances that you never get."

"I have probably over a 100 saved up." He shrugs.

"Cute." I roll my eyes.

"I have no intentions of ever cashing them in," he says, pulling me against him. "I'd rather get a lap dance from you."

"Why am I the one giving the lap dance? What if I want one?"

"Autumn," he says, running his fingers up the side of my neck. "Anytime you want me to dance half-naked on you, I'd be more than happy to oblige you with my best moves."

"Wait, why aren't you fully naked? I want my money's worth."

"Fuck, I'll get naked and grind on you anytime you want," he says with hooded eyes. "I'm sorry I put you in a position to believe the worst in me," he says.

"I never believed any of it. Not for a second. I just couldn't understand why you were hurting so bad that you were drinking like that."

"It wasn't my smartest decision," he says, biting down on the inside of his cheek.

"And I don't understand her motive. Why would she black-mail a big, hot hockey player already giving her money to take care of her daughter?"

"That's what I've been wondering too. I wanted to go see her and ask what the fuck, but she filed a restraining and a do-not-contact order against me. The team lawyers don't want me touching a damn thing with this case even though... I don't know. Something just didn't seem right. And now I know my intuition was correct. I'm glad you got to the bottom of this," he says, and then looks at the clock on the stove. "But it's almost two in the morning. We need to go to bed. I'm leaving early, and so is your brother."

"Okay, let's go," I say.

He smiles and then wraps an arm around my waist and pulls me in front of him, kissing the top of my head and pushing me gently toward the bedroom. "I'll call Sam tomorrow and see if I can meet with him and Legal."

"Good idea. Let them handle everything from here, though. Please don't get involved past this."

"I'll do my best," I say, noncommittal.

He squeezes my sides from behind, and I yelp.

"Shh, you're going to wake up your brother." He chuckles, even though it's his fault for tickling me.

He follows me into the bedroom and then stands in the door jam of the walk-in closet as I strip out of my jeans and shirt in exchange for silky pajamas that I'll admit, I got because they were a little sexy, and I wanted to torture him a little. But now that we've had sex, I'm a little surprised he's only standing there watching instead of touching.

I pull on my silky pajama shirt over my bare breasts, and he doesn't seem happy that I cover them up.

He goes silent for a second while he seems to mull it all over.

"Your brother knows we're faking it."

Where the hell did that come from?

"You told him?" I say in shock.

Why would he do that after all this work we've put in? We're almost at the finish line. My brother leaves tomorrow.

"I didn't. Derek came by today and gave us up."

"Derek came by? Here? You're kidding."

"Nope."

"That's a violation of our contract with the Hawkeyes. He could get fired for that... I could get fired for that. What did my brother say?" I ask, my arms folded over my chest.

"He agreed to keep our secret until this ends."

Until this ends...

There it was.

I've heard it many times before this, but hearing it again just solidifies what I already know.

"And you agreed to this?" I ask.

He just looks back at me and doesn't speak for another second.

"It's this, or he said he'll come back. He didn't have to say it, but our friendship won't survive a second fight over you."

I nod. I won't let this crush on Briggs end Isaac's relationship with his best friend. It's wrong of me to want it, and it's naive to think Briggs wants a relationship with me after this, anyway.

I need to remember what I'm doing this for.

My promotion.

CHAPTER
TWENTY-FOUR

Briggs

"I still can't believe the turnout they had today. That was amazing. The charity president said this was the best turnout he's had in years." Autumn beams, walking in front of me through the master bedroom.

She heads for the bathroom and I walk into the master closet. I'm ready to get out of the slacks and button-up I decided to wear for the pictures with fans. It was a great turnout and it has me wondering how I can do more for the organization.

"Want to change out of these clothes and watch a movie? It's only just after eight p.m.," I ask.

"That sounds fun," she says, still in the bathroom.

She walks out quickly and finds me in the closet and backs up to me with her hair pulled over the side of her shoulder.

"Can you unzip me, please?"

"Absolutely," I tell her, remembering when she asked me to zip it up for her earlier. My fingers graze over the back of her neck, the sweet smell of her coconut shampoo and hair spray wafting across my nose. I love the smell of her. She doesn't know it, but I stole her pillow and changed it out for an identical one, packing the pillow she's been sleeping with into my luggage for my trip tomorrow. I'll sleep like a baby in the hotel with the smell of her on my pillow.

I remember Isaac's warning that this is temporary. But how the hell am I supposed to honor 'temporary' when she fucking looks like this?

I haven't considered the idea of permanent in a long time. Every relationship since my girlfriend in college has been temporary, and I've preferred it that way. Now, temporary has my heart racing at its inevitable ending.

I pull the zipper of her dress down, slower than necessary, but I like her this close, and I want to keep her like this as long as I can before our time runs out, which now that we have a real lead on the blackmailer... could be sooner than later.

Isaac left this morning, and with the spare bedroom open again, I have no reason to get to sleep next to her tonight. Different bedrooms are how we started this cohabitation, and it only changed because Isaac was here. Does it mean I have to go back now that he's gone?

The zipper finally ends at the bottom of her floor-length, body-hugging, floral dress she wore today.

She looked incredible at the fundraiser, but now with her back bare for me and the white silk panties enticing me to run my fingers over them to feel if they are anywhere near as soft as her skin, I'm positive I've never seen anything as beautiful as Autumn.

I bite back a guttural groan at the increasing pressure of my growing erection.

"Thank you," she says, grabbing her pajamas and then heading back for the bathroom off her side of the closet shelving. "I'm going to use the bathroom and brush my teeth. Then I'll be ready for the movie."

I unbutton my shirt and then hang it up. Next comes my slacks as I pull them down my muscular thighs. Slacks aren't the easiest thing to wear with large legs and a narrow waist. Everything I buy has to be tailored, and since we wear slacks and button-down shirts for post-game media, I have to wear them more often than I'd like.

I pull on a pair of sweats and a T-shirt to wear while we watch the movie.

When I turn around to walk out of the closet, I'm not expecting Autumn to be staring back at me in her tiny pajama shorts and thin silk top that leaves very little to the imagination.... just how I like it.

Was she checking out my ass?

I smile, and she looks up at me, her cheeks warming in that cute light shade of pink that's hard to see in this dim closest lighting, but I know it's there.

"Ready for the movie?" I ask.

"Yep." She nods, playing with the hem of her super short silk shorts.

"What do you want to watch?" I ask, taking off my watch and laying it on the closet shelving on my side of the closet.

"Anything that won't mean you're offended if I fall asleep before it's over."

"Fair enough. It's been a long day," I agree.

We walk out of the bedroom and down the hall towards the living room.

She flops down on the couch while I grab the remote off the coffee table.

"My feet are killing me," Autumn says, her left foot in her hand as she rubs the arch.

"You wore four-inch heels and didn't sit down once during the hours we were at the fundraiser. And how many times did you climb the stairs to run around and get things for the charity staff?"

"I was happy to help, and there were a ton of people to meet. I met a couple of people who have connections to some hot companies that might be interested in having you endorse some athletic products. It was a great networking opportunity."

"Are you my agent now?" I smirk, walking over to the couch and plopping down next to her feet, lying on the sofa, and she analyzes them.

I find a movie that I think we could go either way on watching or not. Truth is, I'm beat too, and I have to get up at the ass crack of dawn to leave town on the team bus.

"No, but you need all the help you can get." She gives me a challenging look as if there's no way I can object to the truth.

"Ouch," I say in response. "Here, give me that foot," I say, reaching over and taking her delicate right foot into my hand and pulling it to rest on my thigh.

"You want to give me a foot massage?" she asks, her nose scrunching a little.

"Sure. You deserve it. You spent the whole day taking care of other people when you didn't have to be there. You came because I asked you."

She readjusts her seated position and tries to relax. "Okay, if you're offering. Thank you."

I turn a little sideways on the sofa and start to slowly rotate my thumb on the balls of her feet. She watches my hands as they work.

"How's that?"

"Good. Really good," she says.

I move my thumb to the spot between the middle of the pad of her feet and press firmly. Her eyes roll to the back of her head, and she lets out a moan that has blood rushing to my cock again.

"Oh..." she says.

She moans again and then tosses back her head and hums an approval. If she keeps up with that, she'll be getting a hell of a lot more than a foot massage.

"Harder..." she whispers.

Fuck me.

This woman is hot when she's getting a massage. Note to self: give Autumn as many foot massages as she wants.

"How about this?" I ask for more instruction.

I want to know how to make it good for her.

Her head comes forward now, and her chin almost rests against her chest as she's reclined back, her eyes still closed as she enjoys my fingers.

"How about your calf?" I ask.

"Yes, please," she says, and I start to work my fingers up her leg.

I massage, and the moans get more frequent, so I inch higher, not realizing it.

I look down a few moments later to find my hands halfway up her thigh. She looks down, too, and then looks back up at me, our eyes locking.

I continue to inch up, our eyes not flinching away from each other. Not even to blink.

She's still leaning back against the armrest, her eyes now on my hands. She's watching... waiting. My hands slowly make it to the top of her thigh.

"How much farther are you going to let me go?" I ask her.

"How much further do you want to go?"

"If it was up to me, I wouldn't stop until I was three fingers deep inside you."

She lets out a labored breath.

"Would you like that, Autumn?"

She nods. "Yes."

I sit up and kneel on the couch, giving me a better position by hovering over her. I reach down and adjust my ever-growing hard-on, and she watches, her tongue darting out to wet her perfect lips.

My fingers finally graze her pajama bottoms, and I push past them until my fingers find the wetness of her panties.

Her eyes roll back again at the small touch from the pads of my fingers. A small moan escapes her lips again when my index finger pushes her panties out of the way, and I run my finger up the full length of her from bottom to top.

Goddamn, I want to take all of her.

I look into her eyes as they open slowly, and she looks into mine.

My index finger runs again along her clit, preparing her for my touch before I sink my index finger completely inside.

"Open wide for me, Autumn. I want to watch my fingers disappear inside of you."

She gives a small gasp as my finger slips inside her soaking center.

"Open wider if you want more," I instruct, watching as her knees fall further apart, and I have a perfect view of my fingers disappearing inside something that feels so much like mine. Like every inch of her belongs to me. It's a feeling I'm struggling to fight. "That's it, good girl," I praise because Autumn Daughtry deserves to be praised... she deserves to be worshipped, and I'll be damned if I let our short time pass without me showing her what she deserves in the bedroom.

Complete and utter adoration, because any man who holds Autumn and doesn't fall to his knees has no fucking clue what he has in his hands.

"Since you did what I asked, I'll give you another one. Would you like that?" I ask her.

She nods and swallows hard.

I sink another finger inside of her, bottoming out to the knuckles slowly as I massage the insides of her.

Her sounds become louder and more desperate.

"Briggs... oh God." Her eyes are fluttering closed again.

"One more? You want another one?"

She nods as she squirms in my hands.

I stretch her tight velvet smooth channel with my third finger and begin to rub the spot I know she needs, wishing it was my cock inside her but happy to at least be touching her. If she lets me, this will only be the start of everything I plan to do to her tonight.

I won't let another minute with her be wasted. I won't allow another second to go by where she has to wonder what I want... who I want.

It's her. Maybe it always has been.

"You're fucking gorgeous laid out for me," I tell her.

I can feel her body tightening around my fingers at my words. Her soft breathy whimpers are giving her away. She's not far from coming on my fingers and I want it too.

"Pull up your shirt, Autumn. Let me see all of you," I demand, knowing she's not wearing a bra under that silk pajama shirt.

I can see her hardening nipples. I'm convinced she's been purposely going braless in her pajama shirts since we moved in together.

She does what I ask and her fingers pull up on the hem of her shirt, pulling it up over her bare breasts and exposing my own personal paradise. She pulls her shirt off and over her head, then her eyelids flutter open, staring back up at me.

"That's what I want, Autumn. You... all of you."

She reaches down and grips my wrist that's between her thighs, anchoring me to her, and then begins to rock hard against my hand.

"Are you going to let me fuck you tonight?" I ask, ready to bend over her and suck down on her perfect rose-colored nub if she agrees.

She nods. "Yes... please."

I lick my lips and then bend down, my free hand supporting my weight so that I can hover over her. I blow softly over her nipple at first. I watch as her nipple tightens even more and then I flick my tongue over it.

Autumn moans and arches into me. I'm teasing her and she loves it, just as much as I love doing it.

More of her arousal coats my fingers and they work in and out of her.

"Your mouth..." she gasps out. "I need it," she begs.

I grin to myself and then press my lips around her perfect nipple and suck down on her. She whimpers and then rocks against me faster like she's chasing her climax and that's when it hits. Her muscles grip me like a vice as her orgasm swirls through her. Her breathing labors and she moans out my name.

Fuck, I've never heard my name sound like that, and now I don't want anyone to say it unless it's her. No one will ever do it justice again.

She's holding on to me as if to keep herself from falling.

"I got you," I tell her. "Let it roll."

After a few more moments, those stunning hazel eyes open again.

"I think you're trying to ruin me for anyone else," she teases.

"You're damn right I am," I say matter-of-factly.

She looks up at me to gauge if I'm joking, but it only takes her a second to realize that I'm not.

Not even a little.

"Are you ready for bed?"

She looks over at the TV, noticing that neither of us has bothered to watch a second of it.

"Yes."

"Good. Me too."

That night, I spent the rest of the evening inside Autumn, giving her two more orgasms, and one for myself, until we passed out at some time well after midnight.

CHAPTER TWENTY-FIVE

Briggs

I didn't like leaving Autumn at dusk this morning and the warm master bed that we both ended up sleeping in together last night, but getting the first win under our belt for the three games was a great start. I'm fucking tired, and after going through media tonight, the smelly bus with its cramped legroom and slightly worn-down chairs is a welcome sight. The only thing I want to do right now is get on board and get settled for the long drive ahead with my noise-canceling headphones. But first, I want to call Autumn and see how her day went.

I pull out my phone to dial her, but when I see it's almost one in the morning, I think better of it. I don't want to wake her up.

I reach back to slip my phone back into the pocket of my athletic sweats when my phone starts to vibrate in my hand.

Autumn calling...

Relief hits first at the sight of her name displayed on my phone.

"Hello."

"Hi... sorry, is it too late to be calling?" she asks.

"No, not at all. We're just loading onto the bus," I tell her as I get in line behind a couple of other guys.

The driver starts grabbing our duffle bags from us to load them underneath the bus. "Thanks," I tell him as he takes my bag from me.

"You guys played a good game," she says.

"Did you see that slapshot I made?"

"Yes." I can practically hear her smiling.

"Did you see me point to the camera?"

"Yes." She chuckles.

"That was for you."

"Really? Because I think the cameraman thought that the kiss you blew to the camera was for him. He probably fainted with desire."

"Probably."

Autumn breaks out in giggles at my simple agreement. "But he was about as wide as he was tall and hairier than my uncle Fred, who looked half chimp... not exactly my type."

"Oh really? What's your type?"

"Who's asking?" I ask, flirting back with the girl I'm falling for.

"Every puck bunny on the planet."

"Well, I don't care about the puck bunnies, but I'll tell *you* what my type is, if you're interested."

Reeves, who's sitting one row ahead of me on the other side of the aisle, looks over at me with furrowed eyebrows. I give him a 'get lost, asshole, I'm talking to my girlfriend' look, and he shakes his head, puts his noise-canceling headphones on, and then pats his pillow into place so he can try to fall asleep.

"I might be interested. For research, of course."

"Right, for research," I say, watching as the bus finally pulls out of the parking lot of the stadium we're leaving. "Turns out I have a thing for strong-willed brunettes who make killer chocolate chip cookies."

"Oh, that is noteworthy information," she says.

"Could you find some use with that information?" I ask.

"I'll see what I can do."

"Good." Now that question I've been waiting all day to ask. "How did your meeting with the Hawkeyes legal team go today?"

I hear her sigh. "All in all, it was a good meeting. They felt that the lead was promising. They're going to dig more into the owner of the club, and they have their team out looking for the bartender to get a confirmation on his side of the story."

"Thank you, Autumn."

"I didn't do much."

"No. Thank you for everything. Not just chasing down Dixie... which, again, I want to make sure you promise you'll never do again..."

"You can't stop me," she says under her breath.

I sigh briefly and then continue. "But... for just being here through this, having my back."

"I'll always have your back, Briggs. No matter what happens after..."

After... *fuck.*

"Thank you."

There's a short silence.

"How long til you get to the hotel?"

"Four and a half hours until we get to our hotel, but probably six hours before I'm asleep in my bed."

"Can you sleep on the bus?"

"I'm going to try after I get off the phone with you."

"Then I'll let you get some rest."

"Will you stay on the line for a little bit?"

"While you fall asleep?"

"Yeah... would that be okay?"

"Sure. I can do that. I'll put my phone down on your pillow, and you can fall asleep to the restful sounds of my snoring."

"You don't snore."

"I don't?"

"No. But you do fart in your sleep."

"What?!" she yells.

"I'm kidding. I've never heard you fart. But you must. Everyone does."

"Go to sleep, Briggs, before I hang up on you."

I chuckle, and then I can hear a small laugh on her end too.

Soon, the low lights of the bus, the rumbling of the road, and the sweet sounds of Autumn breathing while she's safe in our apartment all work to lull me to sleep.

Four hours later, I'm abruptly woken up as the bus hits part of the curb on its way into the hotel parking lot, swaying the bus enough to jostle me awake. My phone drops from my ear where it was nestled between me and my pillow for the last four hours. The call is still running. She never hung up.

"Autumn?" I ask quietly, trying not to wake her but wondering if she can still hear me.

"Hmm?" she hums half a wake.

"I just got to my hotel. Goodnight. Sweet dreams."

"Night," she mumbles.

Then, reluctantly, I hang up.

CHAPTER
TWENTY-SIX

Autumn

With the amazing success of the charity event that Briggs helped with a couple of days ago, and his interest in getting more involved by fundraising on his own with his big network, Erika thought we should get together and run through logistics.

"Well, I said it once, and I will say it again, that was a hit. The hospital loved him, the president and the staff of the charity loved him, and, of course, the fans loved him."

"He did great, didn't he?" I beam.

"Incredible. And you said he wants to start his own charity and raise funds for my friend's organization to open more children's cancer wings?"

"Yes, he's passionate about it. He wants to do everything he can, and I thought we could help him get his charity on his feet. In the off-season, he can be more hands-on."

"That's great. I love this idea. If any other Hawkeyes players want to start a charity, we can help them too."

"I'll let Tessa know. I have a feeling she'll devour this new service."

"Perfect. I spoke with my friend who held the fundraiser at the hospital, and he is going to come in next week so that we can strategize with how Briggs's new charity can assist them."

"That sounds great. I think Briggs would like to be here for that as well. If we can schedule it for a time we both can come in together, that would be ideal."

"Yeah, um, that's something I wanted to chat with you about while you're here."

I look at her and don't like the more serious look in her eyes.

"Derek came to see me a couple of days ago..."

A chill runs down my back at the mention of his name... and not a good one.

"And...?"

"He said he went by your apartment, and he felt that your relationship with Mr. Conley has become unprofessional and that how you're handling this account would make you a poor choice for the Client Relations job."

That freaking jerk! Office romance gone bad, I should have figured, especially after he showed up and talked to my brother.

I want to blurt that bit of information out to her, too, but that might not help the situation. I try to keep a level expression on my face.

"And what do you think?"

She looks up at me and smirks. "Regarding Derek... I think jealous men are whiny bitches."

I laugh out loud. Erika does like to tell it how it is.

Then she clears her voice and starts again. "However, as your boss and the owner of this company, I feel as though I must remind you that we have a strict policy about employees fraternizing with clients."

"Erika, I..."

She holds up her hand to stop me.

"Before you lie to me and yourself, let me finish."

I nod, folding my hands over one another as they dangle at my thighs. I've never gotten in trouble at work before, and I have no idea what she's going to say.

She sighs and looks down at her desk as if working through her thoughts. "It isn't lost on me that both the Hawkeyes and I have asked a lot of you. We've asked you to date a man that you have a long history with, and then we've demanded that you and Briggs live together to cement the lie. We've even asked you to show intimacy every time a camera might be in focus to make our story more believable. And you have delivered everything we have asked of you with the utmost care." She purses her lips. There's a 'but' coming. "So it seems hypocritical for me to now ask that you remain professional and not allow the potential bond between you two to grow. As it has, based on the way he looks at you in the photos I'm seeing online."

"The way he looks at me?" I ask, curious to get someone else's perspective on what I think I see and what is real.

She tilts her head slightly with a smile as if she knows what I'm asking for. Can she read minds? I'd believe it if it were true.

"No man looks at a woman like that in obligation." She smirks.

"But I could date Derek or any other employee, and you'd be okay with it?" I ask, hoping she sees the double standard.

"The reason employees can date each other but not clients is simple to explain. If two employees become romantically involved and it ends poorly, I might lose a good employee due to a bad breakup, but I won't lose a million-dollar account. And our reputation could be jeopardized if anyone thinks we sleep with our clients to keep them or to earn their business. Do you understand?" she says, with an almost empathetic look in her eyes.

"I do."

She nods.

"You've done good work, and you've put your life on hold for this company and the Hawkeyes. You're an asset here. But I do have to hold the line to make sure that I give fair treatment to all of my employees. If you choose Briggs, I'll have to ask for your resignation... as much as it pains me to say that."

My resignation. They want me to quit after what I've done? I have a mixture of feelings running through me, but it's not as if I didn't know the rules. I read the employee handbook when I got this job. I just skimmed through the employee/client relationship because I never assumed it would be relevant.

"Even though I own the company, I have a board to answer to, and they'll expect this of me."

I nod. "I get it, Erika. I know it puts you in an awkward position."

"Can I say one more thing... as a friend? I know it may seem that I'm trying to sway you one way or the other, but I do want you to be happy."

I smile up at her. "Sure. What is it?"

"Just... tread lightly. You've known him far longer than me, but from an outsider's view, just remember that we might be trying to change his public image, but he earned that reputation he had well before we showed up. Don't give him a chance to prove to you that he earned it fair and square."

"I won't," I say simply.

"I hope not."

"Anything else?"

"Only that I hope you pick us. You are a real talent, and you'll be difficult, if not impossible, to replace."

"Thank you," I say.

She nods and then turns to her computer. She's a woman with a lot more on her plate than one employee who's been dangerously walking the line of breaking a company policy. I mean, technically, I guess I have. But this whole thing has become one big, blurred line, and I have no idea if I'm still straddling it or if I'm miles away from it now. I walk out of her office and close her door.

No losing your heart to the cocky player.

Later that night, Briggs calls.

"Hey, I should be home tonight. How did your day go?"

"Fine," I say, short.

"Just fine."

"Yeah."

"Is everything okay?"

I think for a second, and the silence grows.

"Autumn—"

"I spoke to Erika today."

"Okay, what happened?"

"She told me that Derek came to see her. Evidently, the same day he came to see my brother."

"What did the asshole say?"

"That you and I are having an unprofessional relationship."

"And Erika told him to mind his own fucking business, right?" he asks.

I can hear the slight edge to his voice that seem to come out whenever Derek is involved.

"Not exactly."

"What did she say then?"

"That it's against company policy to have a romantic relationship with a client."

"You're kidding me, right? This was their damn idea. They've asked us for PDA everywhere and anywhere there are cameras around."

"I know..."

"Did you tell her she can eat a dick?"

"Briggs!"

I know he's mad but it isn't like I didn't know the rules. I've always known that staff can't get involved with clients and I never thought that anything would happen between Briggs and me.

"Fine, did you at least tell her she can't have it both ways?"

"No, I did not tell my boss and the person who writes my paychecks that she is giving mixed signals... she already admitted to it."

"So what exactly did she say?" he asks.

"That you and I return to a professional relationship and only show affection in public when we have to, or I need to turn in my resignation letter."

"You're fucking kidding me. They're making you choose between your job and me?"

His voice increases a little. He's upset. I get it.

"Yes."

I can hear him huff in the background and the line goes quiet for a second.

"What do you want to do?" he finally asks.

What do I want to do? I want you to be home so I can run into your arms and feel safe for one second.

I want to stop being scared of telling you how I feel about you because I'm terrified that this being temporary is what you like about this arrangement most of all. It's not easy to walk away from a promotion you've always wanted when you're not sure if the boy that you've always wanted, wants the same thing.

"I'm not sure."

"Which means you're picking the job."

"Wait, I didn't say—"

"I got to go. We're getting on the bus to come home. I'll see you in the morning."

"Hold on, Briggs—"

But it's too late. He hung up.

I think to text him but if anything has proven that talking over the phone isn't working, it's that conversation. I need to see him in person.

Briggs

I'm finally back home and asleep in the spare bed after getting back around three in the morning. After what Autumn told me yesterday, I have to guess that the odds of us being together after Operation De-sleaze Conley is null. The disappointment of hearing her say it over the phone still hasn't softened, but I guess on the bright side, Isaac won't be coming back to kick my ass.

My phone starts ringing, and I'd like to huck it across the room, but I think better of it and check the caller ID.

Mom calling...

Shit.

She knows I just got home. She wouldn't call before ten in the morning on the day after game day unless she had a reason.

"Hello," I answer, trying to clear the grogginess from my throat.

"Hi, sweetie. Are you back home from this weekend?"

"Yeah. We got home early this morning."

"Oh... right, I'm sorry to be calling this early. Go back to sleep and call me when you get up."

She has something important to tell me. I can hear it in her voice. A feeling of dread sweeps over me. Would it be too much to wish back to the days when she was calling to nag me about proposing to Autumn instead of what she's probably calling about? I'd give anything for that to be the reason for my mother's early morning call. I'd even take an hour-long conversation about not wearing my jock strap and cutting out all foods with yellow color dye to increase my sperm count so she can get a grandbaby over the likelihood that this conversation is going to lead to my dad's illness.

"No. Mom... it's okay. I'm up," I say, sitting up in bed and rubbing the sleep from my left eye.

"I didn't want to tell you until we were sure. Until the doctors were sure..." She stalls.

"It's okay, Mom, take your time."

I hear her sigh. "He's not responding to the treatments anymore."

"Jesus..." I say, slamming my eyelids shut and running a hand through my hair.

"They have one more thing they want to try, but it's not a sure thing, and there are a lot of things that have to go right for this to work."

"Okay! That's good news, right? What is it? We'll try anything. I'll pay for anything. Tell them money isn't an object. I'll drain every last dollar I have, Mom," I say.

I can hear the hope in my voice, and so can she.

"I know, Briggsy. Thank you, baby. But you know Dad wouldn't let you do that," she says.

"Then we don't tell him. So what is it? What can we do?"

"He needs a bone marrow transplant."

"I've heard of that. That should be easy, right? They have a whole bank of people willing to donate."

"It's not always that simple—"

"Then I'll donate. We're blood." I argue.

"Yes, the doctor would like us all to test and see if any of us are a match. Sandy and Kirk are here this morning to test, and your uncles are getting tested as well."

"I'll come tomorrow. Okay? I'll tell the team I have a family emergency."

"That would be good. Your dad would like to see you."

"Autumn and I have a meeting with Sam Roberts this morning. I'll get it cleared."

"Autumn's going in with you to see your general manager?"

"Yeah." Shit, I didn't think that through. "She's helping with some charity work I'm doing, and the Hawkeyes are lending a hand."

I hate lying to my mom, but that wasn't a lie. We are working on charity work together, and the Hawkeyes said they'd help out however they could.

"That's so great, honey. Bring Autumn with you, will you?"

"Sure, Mom. I'll ask her to come if she can."

Although now... coming with me could cost her a job.

"Love you, Briggsy."

"Love you, Mom."

She hangs up, and I jump out of bed in search of Autumn. I need to see if she can come with me tomorrow, and now with the news of my dad, there's no way I'm sleeping anymore.

Autumn

I hear a knock on my door while I'm putting on my mascara.

"Come in." I watch for the door to open, but I know who will be on the other side, although I wish he was still sleeping. He'll have only gotten four or five hours of sleep at this point. When I see his face come into view around my bedroom door, I'm instantly on alert by the look on his face. "Why are you up this early?"

He just wanders into my room and takes a seat on the bed, not uttering a word.

I holster my mascara wand back into the tube and set it on the counter. I make a cautious exit out of my bathroom and toward him in the bedroom.

"What's going on?"

I walk to stand in front of him, and I reach for his hands which are lying almost lifelessly in his lap.

He looks down at our joined hands.

"My dad is sick."

I nod. This much I already know from him telling me last week.

"Okay?" I ask, encouraging him to go on. I know that's not the only reason why he's up and sitting in my room.

"My mom called. I need to go home. I need to get tested as a bone marrow donor."

"Oh my gosh... Briggs."

He looks away and down at our hands, his thumb running over the top of mine.

"I'll get tested too," I offer up immediately.

That catches his attention, and he looks up at me.

"You will?"

"Of course I will," I say, squeezing his hands.

"Will you go home with me?" he says, looking into my eyes and then looking back down to watch his thumb continue its sweeping effect over mine. "I think I need you."

That brings me down to my knees as I settle in front of him. I need him to see me when I say this, and I need him to understand.

"I will go wherever you need me to go. I will be wherever you need me to be. I'm at your full disposal. Tell me what I can do for you."

His eyes meet mine, and it guts me how sad he looks.

"I think I should head home after we meet with Sam."

"I think that's a good idea. You won't be able to focus on anything else here anyway."

He nods.

"I have a meeting with Erika right after we meet with Sam. It's critical I go, or else I—"

"No," he interrupts. "It's fine. You should go. Get it cleared with Erika. I don't want you getting fired for this. I'll drive up ahead. It might be good for me to get some time with my parents before you get there anyway."

Now I wish I hadn't said that my meeting with Erika is important. Nothing is more important than us getting up to Walla Walla and seeing what we can do there.

"Are you sure? I can reschedule. You're more important than anything else. And if she fires me for going to spend time with our family... well, then she does."

"Do you mean that?" His eyes search my features to determine authenticity.

"Of course I do. Do you want me to prove it? I will..."

"No," he says, brushing a strand of hair behind my ear. The left side of his lip curves up in a slight smile. "I'll go up ahead. I've been avoiding this for some time now, and my dad deserves some one-on-one time with me."

"I'll be right behind you, Briggs. Two hours, tops. I promise."

He nods and then stands up, holding my hands still in his.

"I'm going to go pack, so I'm ready to leave after our meeting with Sam."

"Okay," I tell him softly.

He pulls me gently into him with our joined hands and kisses my forehead.

And then I watch as he exits my bedroom, not looking back as he leaves, and then shuts the door behind him softly.

The feeling that I need to go with him is strong, but this meeting with Erika involves the intel she said she just heard from her private eye. I need to hear what she has to say before I leave town.

While in the privacy of my bathroom, I make one quick phone call... to my brother.

I know Briggs won't call him, not with everything going on between them, with me smack dab in the middle of it. And even if I weren't, Briggs has been unpredictable when it comes to handling his father's illness. That is undisputed because it's the reason behind the whole blackmail mess to begin with, so I have no idea if he'll call Isaac on his own accord and tell him what's going on with Mr. Conley.

I quickly call my brother and catch him up on this morning's events.

"So, can you come?" I ask.

"I have an interview with a radio host tomorrow... shit, Autumn, I'm not sure. But I'll try, okay?"

"He needs you, Isaac. More than he ever has before."

"I know... I gotta go. I have calls to make if I'm going to work this out."

"K, love you."

"Love you."

CHAPTER TWENTY-SEVEN

Briggs

Walking down the upstairs corridor of the stadium toward Sam's office makes my stomach unsettled and my hands restless. I have no idea what news he has or what came of Autumn's lead.

Has Dixie been helpful in uncovering the rat that's been pulling the strings this whole time? Did Legal find the bartender? And if so, is he willing to help us uncover the smoking gun that could put the club owner away for a little bit?

I cross my fingers that something will come of this meeting... something that leans in my favor and the favor of the franchise.

I walk through the first door, opening it wide for Autumn to walk through behind me, holding it open for her until she's cleared the door jam. Penelope is sitting at her desk and jumps up to give Autumn a hug.

"Hi, you two. He's available now. Go ahead and go in," she says to us both.

"Thanks, Penelope," Autumn says back to her.

I knock on the door and hear, "Come in."

We both enter, a little unsure but ready to hear whatever news he has to tell us.

"Thanks for coming in this early after you just got home. I know you boys worked your asses off this week."

"About that, sir. I wouldn't ask, but... I need a couple of days off."

"Oh...?" he asks, his eyebrows furrowed in question.

I've never asked for time off during the season.

"Yeah," I say, and then glance over at Autumn, like I need the reassurance that she's nearby before I say it. "My dad is... well, he's... really sick. He's been sick for over a year, but my mom called this morning, and it's getting worse."

"Oh, I see..." he says, as the last puzzle piece to the answer to my reckless behavior finally fits into place. "I wish you would have told me sooner. I could have..."

"You could have what?" I say more defensively than I mean to.

This is why I don't want to talk about this out loud. What could he possibly do? What can anyone possibly do? That's why

I took to drinking and partying. I can't do anything... and with the doctor grasping at straws, it would seem no one can, least of all my general manager.

"I could be here for you. I could listen when you need to talk. We're a family, aren't we? We're here for each other, and we're all here for you."

I know he's right. And he didn't deserve my attitude. He's done a lot for me. He's gone to bat to keep me on the Hawkeyes roster more times than I can count.

"You're right," I say.

Autumn takes a step closer, and I feel her hand slip into mine. How does she always know what I need? And when I need it?

She squeezes, and I run my thumb along her thumb.

"Take the time you need, Briggs. Be with your family. Let us know if there is anything we can do to help facilitate more time for you to spend with your dad."

"Thanks, I appreciate that," I say, taking in a large inhale. "You called us in for something?"

"Yes. Legal had a breakthrough." He smiles. "They got a call from the DEA... evidently, the club owner was also attempting to extort money from a congressman with questionable photos of him with several strippers. The congressman is, of course, a married man and up for re-election."

"Oh my God." Autumn gasps.

"How does that help us?" I ask.

"Well, for one, the DEA is going to take down our opponent for us. We're no longer playing defense. Now we're on the offense with a strong player on our side. And because of Autumn's brilliant work convincing Dixie to testify, as well as her lead on Tyler, the bartender, ending up being fruitful, we have a large bargaining chip to offer the DEA to get in on the charges."

"You're kidding?!" Autumn says with glee.

I look over at her, and she gleams back over at me. I squeeze her hand to let her know I'm both grateful and proud of her.

"Nope. They didn't have quite enough witnesses and people willing to speak out against the owner, but when we offered up our sources, they agreed to add us to the suit, and once they unfreeze his accounts which still contain well over the amount of the funds we gave 'Dixie' and he's convicted, they'll send back the funds."

"That's incredible," I say.

"Since our accountants have already written off those funds as 'cost of doing business,' we'd like to donate the funds to your new childhood cancer charity."

I look back at Autumn for what feels like the hundredth time, and she and I share a smile.

"Thank you!" She smiles.

"That's very generous. That money will do a lot of good for families that need it."

"We know it will, and we're glad to be a part of it."

"And the other good news about all of this..." he says. "You two don't have to fake it anymore."

"Excuse me... what?" I say, hoping I didn't hear what I thought I did.

"You're off the hook, Ms. Daughtry. We appreciate everything you've done, and we look forward to working with you and your firm on a regular basis as a full-time client."

I feel the blood drain from my face. I can't bring myself to look at her. Will her expression be one of relief? Happy to finally be rid of me and her obligation? She can now go back to keeping her job and getting her promotion with the corner office she wanted so badly.

In my peripheral, I can feel her looking at me, waiting for me to look back at her, but I can't. Her hands are still in mine, and she hasn't let go. It's the only thing keeping me upright.

Finally, she turns to Sam.

"Thank you, sir. It's been a pleasure working alongside your wonderful team for the last month. I look forward to a long relationship with the Hawkeyes."

"Yes, we do as well. And I believe congratulations are in order. I heard you had a promotion coming at the end of this project, if I'm not mistaken. Erika mentioned that we might be working with you as our new client relations manager."

I can feel her eyes on me again, but I only stare out the window of Sam's office.

"Yes. I was up for a promotion. Thank you."

"Well," Sam says, looking at me, probably wondering why I've suddenly gone mute. "That's all I have for you two. You're free to go, and I will let Coach Bex know that you will be out for a couple of days of leave."

I nod, keeping Autumn's hand in mine. I can't let go of it, even though I probably should. She no longer has any reason to hold mine, but she doesn't pull away from me, and that feels like the first good news I've gotten since I stepped into Sam's office this morning.

I walk out of his office with her in tow. We pass by Penelope's desk, but I pull her at a steady pace behind me.

"Oh… okay, bye," Penelope says as she watches us leave.

"I'm leaving for Walla Walla, but I'll call you on my drive up," Autumn says while keeping up with my pace.

She's still coming to Walla Walla with me? After Sam told her she was free of me?

We start back down the corridor, hand in hand. We step onto the elevator, and that's when I finally find my words during the two-level elevator ride.

"You're still coming with me? Even though we're no longer required to be connected?"

"Of course I am. You asked me to come. I'm coming, and I'm going to get tested too… remember?"

Now my head was spinning. Is she coming for me or to help my father? And why does it matter which one if it's possible she could be a match?

The elevator dings, and now I have two blocks to clear my head and ask any questions I need answered before I climb into my truck and head for Walla Walla, because once we get there, I doubt anyone will give us privacy to talk out the end of our fake relationship.

When we finally reach our building, she follows me down into the underground parking structure, where both of our vehicles are packed with the luggage we loaded this morning before we went to meet with Sam.

I'll be heading on a four-hour drive home, and she'll be heading to her offices first to meet with Erika, no doubt to discuss her promotion which keeps her out of my grasp.

We stop in front of my truck, and I turn to her.

"Autumn, I need to ask you a serious question, and I need a God's-honest-truth answer."

"Okay," she says with hesitation. "What is it?"

I bite down on my lower lip for a second as I think about how to word this.

"Do you have feelings for me?"

"Do I have feelings for you?" She parrots my words back at me as her right hand reaches up and rolls her earlobe.

I blow out a breath and try at a different angle.

"If your firm didn't have a no-client-fraternization clause and your brother didn't want to kill me for looking at you, would this"—I wave a hand between us—"be ending today?"

Her arms cross over the front of her chest. She is uncomfortable with the topic, and that makes two of us, but I have to know where I stand before we go play house with my parents. We still haven't discussed how we're going to break the news to either of our moms and with what's going on with my dad, now doesn't seem like the best time.

She reaches her hand up to her earlobe and rolls her opal stud earing around in her fingers, her tell, as she stares down at the cement floors of the parking garage, thinking. "Would my answer change anything? Because all of it would still count against us. My brother will never approve of us, and my boss won't bend the rules for me, and I understand why she can't. She doesn't want a company mutiny due to favoritism."

I look down in disappointment. It's what I thought her answer would be.

I nod.

She gave me an answer to let me down lightly. She loves her job, and she's never made it a secret that she was only doing this for the promotion. I owe it to her, for everything she's done, not to make any of this any harder on her, but I still have one last request to make.

If I can't bring her home as my real girlfriend, can I at least bring her home as my fake?

"We're about to go home to our families, and it would mean a lot to me if we could fake this for a little longer… just until we get back to Seattle. My dad's health—"

"Of course," she blurts out, uncrossing her arms across her chest and laying a single hand on my left arm. The contact feels good. "I would never want to compromise his health. We can fake it while we're in town. We'll find another time to tell them," she agrees.

I sigh in relief but also a little crack forms in my chest that the end will still come.

This wasn't the answer I wanted, but it'll take one big elephant off my chest for the next few days while we try to get my dad well.

"Thank you," I tell her. She smiles, nods, and takes a step back as if I'm going to climb into my car and leave, and she should give me space.

I don't fucking want space.

I want her.

I want her in my car for the next four hours.

I want to spend the next 240 minutes explaining why being together is the only right choice for us.

I want to use up every one of the 14,400 seconds to think through every possible scenario that would lead to us being together, for real this time.

But she's already pulling away from me, from this.

I look into her eyes as she looks back at me. She hasn't turned around and climbed into her own car. She's still standing near, waiting for something. That has to mean something, right?

"This might not be what you want to hear," I start, and I can see her tense and brace for the impact of my words. She doesn't know where I'm going with this, and I can see it on her face. "But if given the opportunity, I'd do anything you asked me to do to be with you."

There's shock on her face. I've shocked her into silence, but silence isn't what I was going for. I want her to run into my arms. Kiss me and tell me that we'll do whatever we have to to be together; fuck everything else.

But she doesn't.

She just stares back at me.

A blank look on her face.

"I should go," I say when the silence stretches on for a painful length.

I don't deserve Autumn Daughtry. That I'm sure of, and now I'm confident that she knows that too, just like Isaac does. She has a future ahead of her. A shooting star and I won't be a part of it.

I open the door of my car and slide in. Still, there's a part of me that hopes seeing me get in my vehicle will break loose the fact that I'm leaving. That this moment between us... this small window that's closing quickly shouldn't be squandered and left with unspoken words but to my disappointment, she still says nothing.

Finally, I pull my door shut and buckle up, then put my car in reverse. As I back up, I watch as she grips herself tighter and takes a couple of steps back to get out of the way of my tires.

I can feel her eyes on me, but I can't look up at her.

I'm leaving Seattle, headed for Walla Walla, and I'm leaving my heart punctured and bleeding at her feet on the cement floor of the underground garage.

Now I'm relieved to have the four-hour drive alone. I'll have time to get my shit together before she and I have to play the happy couple again... in front of an audience of people who know us best.

CHAPTER TWENTY-EIGHT

Autumn

He wants to be with me?

The little girl in me still can't understand it. I keep replaying his words in my head, but I'm no closer to comprehending them.

Yes, we've become closer than I've ever imagined we would in all the years I've known Briggs, but still, why would he choose me when he could choose someone else? He could have anyone. Why risk losing your oldest friend? Why risk the possibility that the Hawkeyes might not like that I work for the PR company they hired? And what if it doesn't work out? Then it was all for nothing.

My brain runs over every thought, every scenario in which this could play out.

Why would he risk it?

I step up into my 4Runner, my gear for the next couple of days already packed and sitting in the back seat.

I need to keep my thoughts on Erika. She has news for me, and based on the information I got from Sam, I have information for her as well.

Once I arrive at our offices, I feel like a live wire of emotions as I trudge through the main office floor, headed for her office.

The door is closed, but this was the meeting time that we loosely discussed.

I knock since her door is usually open. She likes to keep an "open-door" policy and keeps herself available to the staff, although that usually means she struggles to get her work done since the staff takes full advantage of being able to pop in whenever they please.

"Come in," I hear her say.

I walk in and stop in my tracks to find Derek sitting in one of the chairs opposite her desk and only a few feet from me.

"Oh, I didn't realize..."

"No, it's fine," she says, directing me to take a seat. "We had our meeting scheduled first, but since Derek came by to discuss a few matters, I thought he might as well stay and hear how things are going."

"Uh, okay," I tell her, although now I'm not as sure I'm prepared to tell her what I want to in front of Derek, especially after everything he's done. And I still haven't told her, despite Penelope, Tessa, and Isla telling me that I should.

"The good news is that my private eye has made contact with the bartender, and he seems happy to be of service to the Hawkeyes..."

"I should stop you there," I tell her, putting up my hand quickly and with a smile. "I've just come from Sam Roberts's office."

"Oh?" she asks with intrigue and a smile of her own.

"Sam was contacted by the DEA yesterday, and they're working on a case already against the club owner. With the information and the corporations of Dixie and the bartender, the DEA has agreed to allow the Hawkeyes to be included in the suit."

"I had no idea." A glimmer of excitement is broadcasted across her face.

"It looks like the Hawkeyes will be getting the money that they paid the club owner as well, and they are going to give those funds to the new charity that Briggs is setting up."

Erika sits back in her chair. "Well, well, the student has become the master."

I can feel my cheeks warm at her praise.

"I don't know about that. The funds aren't a sure thing, and it could take a year for assets to be released or liquidated before the Hawkeyes ever see those funds."

"Still," she says, "I'm impressed. You have gone way above the call of duty for this client."

"She's something, isn't she? I told you she would be when you hired her," Derek says, reaching over his chair and setting his hand on my thigh.

Yuck!

I'm grateful that we are still in the thick of winter, and I'm not in shorts or a dress so that his skin isn't directly touching mine, but the heat of his hand radiating through my jeans has me ready to smack his hand off my leg and demand he never touches me again.

However, I still want a job here, and I don't want Erika to think that there may be issues between Derek and me that would lead to one of us being let go. I love this job, and I still want to keep my role here.

"Thank you," I say as I pretend to readjust in my seat, folding my right leg over my left and just narrowly pulling my leg out of his reach. I tug a strand of hair behind my ear to distract from the motion of my thigh as I do it.

"I guess this means you no longer have to slum it with the jock," Derek says, ignoring the fact that I just rejected his assumption that I want his hand on me. "I'll come back with you to your apartment and help you pack."

I'm just about to tell him, "Not in your goddamn dreams," when Erika looks over at me.

"That's right... your contract terms have ended if the Hawkeyes are no longer in need of your services."

She seems happy with this news, and why shouldn't she be? We did what we promised them we would do. Briggs is now practically America's sweetheart, and the club owner is going to be up to his neck in government officials that he won't have time to go after Briggs anymore.

So why does the idea that Briggs doesn't need me anymore sting so bad? Especially after what he just admitted to me.

Maybe because being his fake girlfriend is something I'm familiar with, I know what to expect, but the idea of being his real girlfriend has me unsure of the unknown. My brother's reasoning that he's not equipped to give me the life I want has me less worried that Briggs will underdeliver on my expectations and instead leave me worried that the life I want won't be something he'll want to stick around for.

He said he wants me, but at what cost?

A relationship with a lifelong friend?

And what happens if it does all go to hell like Isaac predicts it will? Then what? Do I lose Briggs altogether?

Erika continues. "I think congratulations are in order. I believe I am looking at our new client relations manager," she says with a grin.

Derek is ginning too. "I knew it would all work out."

Oh, did you, Derek?

Was that before or after you told my brother in an attempt to get me either fired, in trouble, or worse, hope my fake boyfriend got his ass beat by my brother?

I won't say it out loud even though he deserves it because that's not who I am. I know I'll feel bad if he gets fired because of his jealousy. That could change Erika's mind about coworkers dating, and I don't want this to affect others who have been making it work without drama like ours.

Instead, I stand up out of my chair. Something just doesn't feel right about this, like something is missing. This win doesn't feel like I thought it would. Mostly because I don't have the person at home that I would want to run home to and share this news with.

He's currently traveling on I-5 headed to our families' homes without me while I stand here discussing a promotion that isn't worth losing him for.

Whoa. Did I just answer the question I've been wrestling with for the last month?

I look down at her from my standing position.

"Erika," I say, turning and walking around to the back of my chair, grabbing my coat off the back. "I'm eternally grateful for this opportunity. I can't even describe what an honor it is to be offered such a highly coveted position. However, I have to respectfully decline the offer, and I will turn in my resignation letter next week."

"What?" Derek says, instantly shooting out of his chair. My eyes abandon Erika's as I stare back at his outburst. "You're declining?! You went through all of that for nothing! And you're quitting?"

"Not for nothing, Derek," Erika says.

When my eyes travel back to hers again, I see a knowing smile across her lips.

"I am disappointed. We will certainly miss you, but I hope this is the right move for you."

I nod and smile, sensing that she'd offer it again to me in the future. "Yes. It is. I can't give him up."

"I'm envious of whoever gets you next. I'll call down to HR and let them know that you deserve a one-year stipend package and a sterling reference letter."

"A year?! Wow, thank you, Erika."

"You deserve it for what you did for our client. The promotion would have been reimbursement for that, but since you're not taking it, this should give you enough time to find a place to land."

My phone starts to ring, and it's Isaac.

"Shoot, I need to go. Briggs and I are headed home to see our families for a couple of days. His dad is sick, and I want to be by Briggs's side."

"What?! Why? You're not together anymore. You don't need to go!" Derek shouts, his face scrunching up in confusion.

Erika and I both ignore him.

"Of course. Safe travels. And Autumn, if I can ever be of service to you in the future, please let me know."

I smile back at her as I turn to leave.

Derek tries to follow me out while Erika calls him back. "Derek, we have more to discuss."

"Hold on. I'll be right there," he tells her with irritation in his voice.

He jogs behind me to catch up. "Autumn, hold on," he says as he's directly behind me. His hand reaches around and tugs on my bicep to stop me. "What is going on? It's over between you two. The project has ended. You're not his fake girlfriend, so you don't need to go with him anywhere."

"That's the thing, Derek. I'm beginning to realize that there was nothing fake about us at all. You and I are the only thing that's over, and it was over before it ever really started," I say, pulling my arm out of his hand. "Move on, Derek. I plan to," I say over my shoulder.

"He's just using you, Autumn!" he yells after me in a room full of my coworkers. Jerk. "He'll get bored. All those assholes do."

I walk out of my office, a little shaken by his words. Words that he didn't need to say because they are the ones that have lived rent-free in my mind since this entire thing started, but I have to believe what Briggs told me today in the parking garage. I have to believe what he's shown me with his late-night texts while he's on the road, the sexless cuddling where he never pushed for more, and the fact that he's protected me every chance he's gotten, just like my brother was always worried he wouldn't.

I've given up what was required to keep the door open for us by closing others; Derek, the promotion... but the last door, I won't close that one. I can't close the door on a nearly twenty-five year friendship.

I just won't.

What I can do is beg and plead with my brother to reconsider. To give Briggs and me a chance to prove to him that he won't hurt me. And that even if he does, their friendship can survive it and that I'm not made of glass. I won't break if Briggs drops me, but I can't miss the chance to find out where this could go if Briggs is willing.

I hop back into my 4Runner and hightail it to Walla Walla. No matter what happens, I still want to be there for him. I still want to be in his life.

CHAPTER TWENTY-NINE

Autumn

I spent the last four hours thinking about what I was going to say when I got here and then about the same amount of time rehearsing it too, but the second I walk through the door of Mr. Conley's hospital room, a strange feeling comes over me seeing Briggs sitting by his bedside.

I'm relieved to see Mr. Conley with good color to his skin and his usual bright smile that looks so much like Briggs's that it makes my heart hurt a little.

Now, everything that seemed so important, like my brother's approval or the promotion I just turned down, no longer feels important at all. And the things that have me feeling unsure and hesitant, like whether or not this thing with Briggs has staying power, seem like the only thing in the world that matters. Life is short, and we all only have this one life. Taking the chance and spending it with the one you want to be with is worth the risk.

...Right?

Briggs is sitting on the bed next to his father with his back turned to me when his father sees me standing in the doorway and cranes his neck around Briggs, flashing me a welcoming grin. The same grin that holds a warm place in my heart. The same one that would beam back at me when I would come racing over to the Conley's house to find Isaac and Briggs to play with them. Mr. Conley would whisper the boy's super-secret hideout location so that I could find them quicker. They never found out that Mr. Conley was my informant, and it's been our little secret ever since.

"Well, hello, beautiful. Come in," Mr. Conley says.

Briggs's neck whips back to watch me as I enter the room, but my eyes are still locked on Mr. Conley.

"Mr. Conley..." I start.

"Oh, don't let all of this fool you, sweetheart. It's just a formality. They're a bunch of money-hungry doctors trying to pay off their student loans that want to run every test known to man so they can bill my insurance," he says, and then winks with another warm smile. "Bleed 'em dry, I say. I certainly paid enough in my union dues working for the railroad. It's time those insurance funds came to use. Never been sick a day until this damn stuff."

I plaster a smile to keep the welling of tears at bay. "Well, you look fabulous. They must be taking good care of you."

I'm not lying. For a man with stage three cancer, he does look better than what I was bracing myself to see.

"Yep. They let me have all the Jell-O I want. And if you promise to take my lump of a son out of my hair for an hour or two so that I can finish my new show, I think I can talk one of the nurses into bringing you some of the green apple flavors. They ration those ones out as if they're made with pure gold, but I'm in good with the nursing staff," he teases.

"That sounds delicious. I'll take you up on that."

I finally look at Briggs with concern that his father thinks he's a lump. That comment has me worried too.

When my eyes connect with him, his eyes look so sad, even though I can tell the rest of him is putting on a good front. I want to run to him, toss my arms around his neck, and kiss away his hurt. Actually, I want to through my arms around both of them and squeeze them tight.

We should have come sooner. I should have demanded we come home when he first told me about his dad and Briggs's struggle with coming to terms with the fact that the cancer is back.

"Hi," I say with a little wave.

"Hi," Briggs says back.

I look back at Mr. Conley because, oddly enough, he doesn't look near as miserable as Briggs and doesn't make me want to burst into tears.

"What show are you watching?" I ask as I take a couple more steps inside and crane my neck to the opposite side of the room as the bed to find a TV mounted to the top of the wall.

Instantly I can tell it's a soap opera, and I bite back a giggle.

"It's called Harbor Bay Med, and all the nurses have me watching it. It's addictive, and right now, one of the patients was in a car accident with her ex-husband, but she's the leading surgeon in the hospital, and she needs to do the procedure to save her ex-husband's life even though she can't even remember her own name... or his."

"Mom's letting you watch this trash?" Briggs chuckles.

"She can't watch me every minute of the day, son."

We all laugh, and it's the first time since I've been here that Briggs looks like himself.

Just then, I feel a whoosh of air, and a man in a white coat comes walking in.

"Do I understand I have someone who would like to get tested as a donor?"

He looks like a doctor, but I'm not sure.

"Yes. Me," Briggs says, standing up off the bed.

"And me," I say, raising my hand.

He looks down at his chart quickly while Briggs catches my attention. He's staring back at me, and I can't read his expression, but I'm just happy he's looking.

"Okay, great. Follow me," he says, looking at both of us and then turning back toward the door and exiting. Briggs's long legs eat up the distance as he follows the man out of the room, and I jog quickly to catch up.

"I'm Mr. Conley's oncologist, and I don't usually walk down donors to the labs, but since we're in a hurry to get the results back, I'm going to walk you down personally, so they know that these results need to be expedited."

"Thank you, Doctor," Briggs says, following closely behind.

I finally make it right up behind Briggs and look down at those big capable hands. All I want to do is slide my hand into his and feel his pulse beneath my thumb on his wrist.

I want him to know I'm here for him.

I throw caution to the wind, and my hand dives for his, intertwining our fingers.

He looks down at our hands and then back at me again, a small smile pulling up on the left side of his mouth as he tows me behind him now. He turns his head back to watch where the doctor is leading us and squeezes my hand in return.

"How long will the results take, do you think?" I ask.

"We should have it back tomorrow. It's just a Q-tip swab on the inside of your mouth, making the expedited request relatively easy."

When we get to the lab room, the doctor leaves us with the technician and gives clear instructions.

We both get our swab tests, neither of us letting go of the other's hand the entire time.

After we finish our swabs, we head up to Mr. Conley's room, still hand in hand, but he's fast asleep. We stand there together, side-by-side, watching Mr. Conley sleep but not daring to go inside and wake him. My phone has been vibrating since I put it on silent when I got here. I pull the phone out of my pocket with my free hand to see that it's a text from my mother.

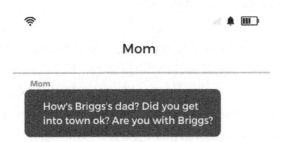

I can feel Briggs peering over my phone and reading the text.

"My dad's asleep. This is a good time for you to go home and see your parents. My mom says that he's usually out for hours. It might be a while."

"Where is your mom?" I ask. I realize I haven't seen her yet and would feel better leaving him if she were here to keep him company.

"She had to take my grandmother to her hair appointment across town. She'll be back in an hour."

"That's fine. I'll wait with you until she gets back."

"You don't need to. I have hours' worth of opposing team game reels that Coach Bex just sent me since I'm missing our team meeting. I have to watch and study them before our games next week and take notes. It'll be good to focus without any distractions." He smirks.

"Distractions?" I ask. My heart plummets.

I'm a distraction? I wanted to be a help. I wanted to ease his burden.

"It's not an insult, Autumn. It's a compliment," he says, turning to me, letting go of my hand, and placing his hands on my arms as he spins me to face him. "I can't think of anything but you when you're around. Shit, I can't think of anything else when you're not around either."

"Really?"

"Really." He gives a guarded smile, probably because I said nothing after he told me he wanted to be with me. "Which is why having some time to process this alone while he's asleep is a good thing for me. It's been a long time coming, but I'm finally where I should have been over a year ago."

"Instead of those clubs?"

He nods. "Instead of drinking in hopes this would just go away, but it didn't, and I might have just lost a whole lot of time with my dad that I'll never get back. Sitting in here while he sleeps just so I can be near him is a small thing, but it's me taking that time back."

I nod.

"I get it now."

He smiles and brushes his thumb over my cheek softly.

"Thank you for coming. My mom stays the nights here with him, so I'll leave when visiting hours are over and head for their house tonight. Then, maybe you would want to come back with me when visiting hours are open again in the morning? We could come to see him when he's fresh, and maybe they'll have our test results."

"Yeah. I'd like that."

"Okay."

"Will you call me when you get home?"

"Yeah. I will," he says, releasing my arms, and I hate the loss of his heat against my skin.

Then he moves into the room quietly.

I don't want to leave him here, but I get what he needs. He needs time with his dad. He's no longer on the self-destructive path he was on when I first came into the Hawkeyes fold and became his fake girlfriend.

When I get to my parents' house, I spend the last few hours of daylight helping my mom in the backyard. It's winter now, but in a couple of months, she'll start planting for her spring garden in her raised beds outback.

I hate the silence of no correspondence from Briggs, but I know this time is important, and I don't want to be the distraction that he says I am, so I do what I always do when I'm excited, nervous, bored, or need to focus and think through a problem... I bake chocolate chip oatmeal cookies.

CHAPTER THIRTY

Briggs

It's been a fucking day today when I finally pull into my parents' driveway.

Visiting hours were over a couple of hours ago, but I drove around after I left the hospital.

It's after eleven when I walk through my parent's front door. The smell of home and my childhood hits me instantly. It's been years since I've been home—my parents visit me in Orcas Island for holidays instead, because I've wanted to use the home I spent millions of dollars on and only get to use in the off-season. They've always agreed and never given me flack for it, but now

I'm starting to feel the stomach-turning that typically follows regret.

I walk through the entry and then into the kitchen, which runs along the back of the house. The ambient lighting of the solar garden lights my dad installed when I was a kid illuminate enough of the backyard that my eyes latch onto the back fence.

Something in me forces my legs to keep moving. I grab the flashlight off the counter where my dad has always kept one, and before I know it, I head out the back steps of my parents' back patio and I climb over the six-foot wooden fence. I don't scale it as easily as I did when I was a hundred pounds lighter and fifteen years younger, but I jump over into the field from the top of the fence and head straight for the pond. It's the place that has always brought me the most peace when I was stressed during playoffs in high school or during my SATs.

I find a spot to sit and stare out over the pond. If today was a long day, tomorrow will be longer. I can only hope that when we show up tomorrow, we get good news, and I'm a match because I don't like the idea of putting Autumn through the process. I can't protect my dad from this, but I can protect someone else I love.

I love...

It hits me hard when I realize it.

I love Autumn... and she doesn't want to be with me. But she did show up for me today. If all she'll give me is her friendship, I'll take it. I can't blame her after what she's seen from me. The partying, the drinking... Dixie... even if the Dixie situation looked worse than it was.

I haven't given her the best reasons to count on me... to believe in me.

An hour passes, and my attention catches on movement on the fence by my parents' house. When I realize it's not a cat but instead a beautiful Autumn struggling to climb out of the backyard, I jump up and race to her before she falls flat on her face.

"My shirt's caught on a nail," she says, frustrated as she struggles to hold onto the fence while balancing a plate full of cookies wrapped in saran wrap and a throw blanket that looks like it came from the back of my parents' couch over her shoulder. She sways a little as she tries to keep her balance. "I don't have any hands to get myself unstuck."

"I got you," I tell her, reaching up over the other side of the fence and feeling for the nail since I can't see it from the side of the fence I'm on.

I get it loose and free her.

"Here," she says, attempting to hand me the cookies so she can figure out how she's going to get down.

"You hold on to the cookies," I instruct, putting my hands on her hips and then lifting her up and off the fence.

A little squeak comes across her lips, and I chuckle again.

Yep, I'm fucking in love with this girl.

"How did you find me?" I ask with amusement.

"When you didn't call to let me know you got home safe, I got worried, so I went for a little walk and was planning on leaving the cookies for you on the doorstep so you had some when you got home, but then I saw your car in the driveway." I set her down, and then she hands me the plate of cookies, and it takes all my willpower not to consume every last bite in seconds.

"Thanks," I tell her, and then we both start for the pond.

"The door was unlocked, and then I saw that the back door was left ajar. Your flashlight flicked against the big willow tree in the field."

"Oh." I nod and glance over at the tree as the wind blows softly through its dangling branches.

Then I watch as the wind blows through her chestnut color hair, a shiver rolling through her. We're both in jackets, but the wind is adding to the chill in the air.

I click off the flashlight, not wanting anyone else to see us and join our twosome. I want Autumn all to myself tonight now that she's found me out here. The moon is bright enough outside with the lack of overcast skies, which is unusual for Washington but its timing couldn't be more perfect for some star gazing with the only woman I care to do it with.

We get to the pond, and she pulls the blanket from her shoulder and pulls at its folded edges. Once she has the blanket pulled apart, she goes to lay it on the ground.

"What are you doing?" I ask quickly, stopping her.

"I thought we could sit on it. The ground is probably wet."

"Yeah, but you're cold. You should wrap it around you," I say as I sit back down in the spot where I was before she showed up.

My jeans are wet, and so is my ass, so there's no point in saving it now. Not when she's cold. And I'm used to being in cold environments. Blame it on the career choice.

"Here, give me the blanket," I tell her, while I pull off the down vest I have over my hoodie. I don't need both.

She looks down at me in question but does as I ask.

"Come here," I instruct, laying out my waterproof vest between my thighs and opening my legs wider for her to sit between them.

She does as I ask again, without question, stepping between my legs and sitting against my crotch.

Maybe I should have rethought this since my cock twitches at her nearness.

I whip the blanket out over her and cover her up to her neck with it, pulling her against me for more warmth.

"How's that?" I ask.

"Better, thanks, but are you warm enough without your vest?"

"I'm fine, but if you're too cold, we can go back inside."

"Nope, I'm right where I want to be," she says, settling her head back against my shoulder.

I'd stay here all night if I thought I could keep her against me like this.

I pull her even closer and set my cheek against the side of her head.

"How was your meeting today?" I ask.

She seems to hesitate to tell me. Does she not want to tell me that she got the promotion? Does she not believe that I'd be anything other than proud of her, even if it is one of the reasons keeping us apart? Or, at least, I think it's one of the things keeping us apart. I don't want to consider the idea that she kept quiet in that garage because external forces aren't the reason we can't date. Maybe she really isn't interested in me, and she's only here because she's a good person and I asked her to come.

"It went well. She offered me the promotion," she says, still looking straight ahead.

"That's amazing. You deserve it."

I wrap my arms around her a little tighter to emphasize my sentiments and to seem sincere. It's true, she deserves the job even if it means I can't have her.

"Thanks," she says with a lack of enthusiasm and lifts her head off my shoulder.

I don't like that small gesture of pulling away. She thinks I'm not happy for her, and that stings a little. Of course, I'm happy for her, and if the plans I've set in motion follow through, her promotion and her brother will no longer stand in our way if she'll give me a shot.

"I'm proud of you, Autumn. I hope you know that."

She cranes her neck back and looks at me. Her lips are so close, and with the moonlight casting a glow across her cheek, I do everything I can not to dip my head down and kiss her.

Her eyes cast down to my lips, and she sucks in her bottom lip. She's wavering on self-control just as I am. She turns back to face the pond to break the moment, but at least there was a moment... a string of moments all day. Between holding my hand and baking me cookies. Climbing over the fence and bringing a blanket to sit with me. Gazing longingly at my mouth like I am at hers. There's more than physical attraction and more than friendship here, and that's all I need to know to push forward with my plans.

The last piece of the puzzle is to find out if she wants the same things I want.

"Can I ask you something?" I ask.

"You have my undivided attention." She finally leans her head back against my shoulder.

"Is there any reason other than the promotion and your brother that has you unsure of giving us a shot?"

She goes silent, but she doesn't tense like she did in the garage. I hope this is a good sign.

"You never noticed me before this. I've always been your best friend's nuisance of a sister. Then I walk back into your life, and it's all different." She takes a deep inhale and then blows it out. "I want to believe you when you say you want me, but..."

"You're worried we don't want the same things like your brother keeps telling you. You think I'll change my mind when the new wears off?"

She nods. "I guess... yeah."

"Okay, so you don't trust me then?" I ask.

"That's not exactly what I said. I'm just not sure why you're now willing to have a committed relationship after living like an aged-out frat boy living in a sorority."

"Hey. I'm no saint, but I've never been *that* bad."

She looks back at me and gives me a "don't insult my intelligence" look.

"Okay. How about I haven't been that way in a while. The drinking and partying though... yes, I'll admit that it's been a recent couple of years of mistakes."

"And now, all of a sudden, you want a woman you forgot even existed until one month ago, and you want to give all of your freedom up to date me."

"I think that's what you're stuck on. You think I'm giving something up?" I hope to God this is her biggest hesitation because this one is easy to solve. "There is nothing about the life I was living before you that held any appeal to me, Autumn. Losing you is the only thing I'd consider a loss. The other shit is trivial... unimportant, things I used to pass the time or fill the empty parts of me."

She looks back up at me, her eyes darting between mine to gauge my sincerity.

"You fill the parts of me that were void. And the parts of me that I thought were already full, overflow when we're together. There is no scenario in which my mind changes about us or that I feel I'm giving up anything to be with you." She looks back at me over her shoulder. I have her attention. "And there is nothing I'm not willing to give up to be with you... nothing."

"I..."

"Don't say anything... please," I stop her. I'm not ready to hear her turn me down. I want to spend tonight believing I still have a chance with her. Tomorrow is going to be a long day, and the potential of losing her is too much on top of everything else. "Take the night and think about everything I said before you answer."

She nods and then responds, "Okay."

"Let's get you inside. It's cold out here."

"Only if you're ready to go in."

"I am," I say, pulling her up and then standing next. "I can walk you back to your parents' house if you want..."

Even though the thought of her leaving guts me a little.

"It might seem weird to them that we're living together in Seattle, but we won't stay together in your old room in an empty house," she says, looking down at the ground as we walk.

"You want to stay?"

Please say yes.

"Is that okay?"

"Hell yeah," I say, practically pulling her across the field and heading for the fence.

CHAPTER THIRTY-ONE

Autumn

Waking up next to Briggs after everything he said last night, it was nearly impossible not to tell him that I turned down the promotion and am giving up the job altogether to be with him. But before I do that, I have one last thing I need to get squared away. I need to convince my brother to keep an open mind about me dating Briggs.

I just can't stomach being the reason these two have a falling out. I need to try first with my brother before I tell Briggs how I feel. Otherwise, Briggs is acting like he'll happily send my brother a picture of his middle finger and tell him to F off. I can't risk it.

When we walk into Mr. Conley's hospital room, armed with a full breakfast in our bellies and a double shot latte for me and black coffee for Briggs, the doctor is already in the room. The look on Briggs's mom's face tells us everything we need to know.

"None of us are a match," she says softly, rubbing Mr. Conley's shoulder.

Mr. Conley, of course, looks unaffected and is sporting his usual happy smile. He just shrugs.

My breakfast wants to make a quick exit back through my mouth at the news. This was not how I thought today was going to go.

"Don't lose hope yet," the doctor says. "We're still reaching out to the donor program to see if they can find us a match. We just usually like to test family first since it's the easier course of action."

"So, what's the next step?" Briggs asks.

We all look at the doctor for his response.

"We're sending Mr. Conley home tomorrow, as planned, and we'll wait to get all of the test results back as well as wait to hear if we have a match from another source."

"What can we do in the meantime?" Mrs. Conley asks.

He looks at Mr. Conley, speaking to him directly instead of speaking as though he's not in the room.

"It's most important that you eat healthily, keep up on all of your vitamins, and try to avoid anyone who is sick. We don't want you fighting off a cold if we find a donor and decide to move forward. We need you in tip-top shape for the transfer."

"Is it okay to have visitors at the house?" Briggs asks.

"Yes, just make sure they aren't sick before they come over. Research has proven that cancer patients with a good solid support system and positive thinking are far more likely to heal and recover than those without a support system and a negative outlook." The doctor looks over at Mr. Conley. "Keep doing the things you enjoy and spend time with the people you love. It will improve your health."

"Thank you, Doctor," Mr. Conley says.

"All right, well, I'm going to go check on a couple of other patients, but I'll be back to check on you in a bit," the doctor tells Mr. Conley.

I hear a knocking on the door, and when I look over, my heart leaps to see Isaac standing at the door.

"Isaac!" I yelp and race to him, throwing my hands over his neck and give him a giant hug. "You're here!"

"Of course I am." He squeezes back. "Hello, Mr. Conley," he says over my back.

"Isaac, what a surprise," Mr. Coney says. "What are you doing here? I thought you have a fight in a couple of weeks. Shouldn't you be training?"

Isaac releases me and heads over to Mr. Conley's bed.

"Well, I heard there might be some donor testing I could get in on, and I didn't want to miss my chance."

"You'd like to be tested?" The oncologist was just on his way out after writing a few more notes on Mr. Conley's chart.

"Yes, sir. I flew over from Las Vegas on the first flight out this morning when my sister called me yesterday."

"You didn't need to do that—" Mr. Conley attempts to argue, but my brother raises his hand to stop him.

"We're family. That's what we do," Isaac says, and then looks over at Briggs.

Briggs walks over, and they embrace for a manly hug that ends in a lot of back-patting.

"It means a lot to me that you're here," Briggs tells Isaac.

"I'll always show up for you. You know that."

Briggs nods in agreement.

"Follow me, and I'll take you down to the testing," the oncologist says.

This is my opening, my chance to talk to my brother alone and convince him to give Briggs his blessing so that we don't have to go against my brother on this. I already gave up my promotion. This is the last thing I need to secure before telling Briggs that I want to be with him too.

"I'll come with you," I tell Isaac, quickly making my way out with Isaac and the doctor.

Once we're settled in the lab room, waiting on the nurse to come in and swab Isaac, I take the empty room as my opportunity.

"I can't tell you how happy I am that you're here. This means a lot to the family... it means a lot to Briggs and me."

"I know. That's why I canceled a podcast I was supposed to be on this morning to promote the fights."

"You did?" I say with a little guilt.

"It's okay, Autumn. They rescheduled, and I don't give a fuck if anyone thinks it's unprofessional. They can go fuck themselves. Nothing is going to keep me from being here."

Isaac throws his arm over my shoulder and pulls me in for a quick side hug.

"How are you holding up, though?" he asks.

"This is harder than I thought, but seeing Mr. Conley in better shape than I thought he would be in keeps me hoping."

"How's your job? What did they say when you wanted to leave on such short notice with everything going on with Briggs and the project?"

"It's over, actually. The club owner was the one who was blackmailing the franchise and Briggs. Turns out he pissed on the wrong senator, and he'll be doing some time."

"Oh shit."

"Yep."

"That means you and Briggs aren't fake dating, or whatever the fuck it was? Did your boss give you the promotion?" he asks, then looks over at me with furrowed brows. "Wait... if you're not fake dating Briggs, why are you here?"

"Yes, Briggs and I aren't faking it anymore." His eyes narrow at the way I word it. "And yes, I was offered the promotion, but I turned it down. I'm turning in my resignation when I get home."

"What the hell? Why?!" he asks with confusion.

"Why do you think?"

He looks away and shakes his head. "What are you thinking, Autumn?"

"That I love him..."

"Jesus, Autumn. You're going to regret this. That Derek dude was a better fit."

"Will you let me finish?" I snap.

Isaac looks at me with surprise. I don't often get angry with my brother, and it takes him off guard.

"Derek is a terrible person, which only further confirms that you are in no place to tell me who I should or shouldn't date. You can't even pick a semi-normal woman for yourself, and you're pushing me to date a man who went against company policy and ratted to you about my private relationship with Briggs. Not to mention the horrible things he said to me while I was trying to do my job."

"I didn't know. I'm sorry. Want me to go beat his ass?" he says, his eyes softening toward me.

"No! Keep your fists in the ring where they belong. Stay away from Derek." I shake my head at my brother's desire to try to fix everything with his fists. "As for Briggs, he has done nothing but take care of me and protect me during this entire process, showing me more respect and patience than my own brother at letting me make my own decision as a grown woman."

He looks past me for a second.

"Maybe..." That's as close to "you're right" as I'm ever going to get with him.

"Damn straight, I'm right." I huff, realizing that I just cursed at my brother. A rarity for me. And he didn't technically say I was right, but I'm taking it how I want. "And yes, maybe you're right. Maybe there is a slight possibility I *might* be disappointed about giving up the promotion and the job someday down the road. But I know with every inch of my being that I *will* regret giving up Briggs, and that's the one regret I can't live with. Do you understand?"

He looks down at his athletic pants. "I guess."

"The only thing still holding me back is that I can't let Briggs give up his friendship with you even though I know he will if you push him to do it. He'll choose me if you force his hand, and I don't want that to happen. Please, I'm begging you, don't make him choose. He needs you right now with everything going on with his dad."

He nods again, not looking at me still.

"You know... I've never seen Briggs want a woman so badly that he'd be willing to give up anything for her." Isaac looks up at me.

"Please tell Briggs you approve."

My phone vibrates with a call. I pull the phone from my pocket and see it's Erika. She wouldn't call after telling me I had the day off unless it was an emergency.

"Shoot, it's my boss."

"Take it. It's fine. I need some air."

I nod, give him a quick peck on the cheek, and then hightail it out of there. Downstairs has the worst reception, and I'm lucky to have even gotten this call.

I run up the stairs, not wanting to risk losing her in the elevator.

"Hello," I say, a little out of breath.

"Hi, Autumn. Is this a good time to call? Am I interrupting anything?"

"No, actually. Now's a good time. Is everything okay?" I say with concern.

I think quickly about the accounts I've been assisting with over the past month, even though I've been taken off most of them to focus on Briggs. Could she be calling about those? Maybe she needs me to do a few things before I officially quit.

"Oh... yeah, everything's fine. After you left, I called Phil Carlton and Sam Roberts and had a nice long conference call with them. They are beyond grateful for the work we've done for them, especially you, and they confirmed that they will be signing on as a client with a huge retainer."

"That's great news," I say, happy to have been there to help facilitate the win.

"But that's not all..." she says, excitement in her voice. What could be better than this? "They want more hands-on assistance with turning each of their players into golden boys, at least in the eyes of the media, like you did with Briggs, that they're asking if I would be willing to create a liaison position for you so that you can work day to day in an office on the Hawkeyes' premises."

"What!?" Where is this coming from? I don't get it.

"Sam says that you, his administrator Penelope, and their in-house PR manager Tessa Tomlin all work together seamlessly, and they want to offer you your own office next to Tessa's where you two can work together."

"They came up with this idea?" I have no other words. I can't even fathom this. Did Briggs do this?

"I was a little surprised too, but it does make a lot of sense since we will be working so closely with the team and all the players. You'll have a better feel for each team member and how the Hawkeyes operate to better serve them and have a closer working relationship with Tessa. You two could feed off each other."

"And I'd still work for you?"

"Not exactly, which is how this works out, and my board members are happy too. You'll be a liaison working between the two companies, so you'll technically be an independent contractor. You'll be in contract with me. Of course, I'll require you to sign a non-compete contract, meaning you can't work for any other PR firms, and on occasion, I might need you to work on a plan for another client if we need your expertise."

My expertise? My grin widens at her compliment.

"I can't even believe this. This offer seems too good to be true, but I don't think I can accept this offer either, with Briggs and I deciding to stay together. And what about Derek? Will he be working on the Hawkeyes account too?" I ask, not wanting any further contact with the man.

"I'll get to Derek in a moment, but first I spoke with Sam discreetly about the situation. I hope you won't feel that I over-stepped."

I don't say anything because that will depend on Sam's an-swer.

"He said that he assumed that you and Briggs were getting closer, and he feels that you are the reason for Briggs cleaning up his act. He has no problem with you two dating."

"Really?"

"Yep. Sam said he wants to be sure you get a raise for this and to charge it to the Hawkeyes, so I'm doubling your pay."

"What!? That's more than the promotion pay I was going to get."

"I know, but I think you're worth it, and you'll be wearing a lot more 'hats' over there as our in-house PR director. I have a feeling that you'll earn every dime with those boys on that team."

A new wave of relief hits me. I can't even describe the cloud nine I'm bouncing around on. And it gets me out of the office where I no longer have to see Derek regularly.

"Thank you, Erika. I won't let you down." But then a thought comes to mind, and I have to ask. "Did Briggs have anything to do with this?"

"Absolutely not. Sam Roberts thinks you're a genius, and Tessa likes working with you. This all came about based on your own merits."

I smile as I walk down to the far end of the hall, where there is a small sitting room and no one in it.

Then I remember I have one other question that she hasn't answered yet. "You mentioned Derek."

"Right, yes. You'll no longer have to worry about bumping into Derek when you're in the office. He was terminated after you left."

"He was?!"

That's surprising. Even with the crap he pulled yesterday in front of the staff, he's still very good at what he does.

"Sam called me the day before you came into the office and told me that he had heard from Penelope that Derek told your brother about the fake relationship... something you failed to mention..."

"I'm sorry, Erika. I just didn't want to cause issues."

"I understand. However, what Derek did was considered a breach of contract, and Sam said that if I didn't fire Derek, Phil Carlton would void our contract with them."

"What? Are you serious?"

"Yes. And understandably so. Although I should tell you now, I don't like not knowing what's going on under my nose. I was blindsided by a client when my best employee could have warned me that this might be coming."

I didn't consider it from that angle. Then again, I told Penelope, Tessa, and Isla in confidence. I can't be mad, though. Penelope was trying to be a good friend, and her action did ultimately eliminate Derek from us further having to work together.

"It won't happen again, I swear."

"Good." She clears her throat. "I agreed with Sam that Derek should be terminated and that I would have done it sooner had I known. Sam was understanding, and no damage was done, but that's why Derek was in my office. I called him in to let him know that his employment was being terminated, but you walked in early."

"I apologize. I wasn't sure I would have the nerve to turn down the promotion if I didn't do it right then."

"It's not a problem. I let him go after you left."

"I'm sorry it had to come to that. I hope our drama won't make you retract your open policy for office romance."

A pang of guilt hits me.

"It won't. He was jealous about your relationship with Briggs, but he was aiming for your promotion behind your back. It came with a better office and a bigger salary than his."

That little shit.

"No wonder. I kind of feel stupid that I thought he wanted me to turn down the project because he wanted to date me."

"He's always been a selfish dick, and you're a catch. He wanted both, so don't sell yourself short."

"Thank you, Erika, for everything."

"Think about the position and let me know."

"Let me bounce it off Briggs, but I think he'll like this option."

"Take care. You'll start first thing on Monday morning at the Hawkeyes stadium if you decide."

We hang up, and I stand looking out over the hospital parking lot on the second floor of the hospital, reflecting on everything that's happened over the last month.

CHAPTER THIRTY-TWO

Briggs

I walk out of the hospital room when Autumn and Isaac's parents come to visit. The hospital room is large, but with five grown adults, it's a little cramped, and I could use a little breathing room to digest the fact that I'm not a match for my dad, and Isaac is downstairs, unaware that I'm about to give him an ultimatum of our friendship.

The sound of the elevator pings and it grabs my attention. I've been waiting patiently for Autumn to come back to the room after leaving with her brother to get his test swab, but disappointment sets in when it's not Autumn but Isaac instead.

"Hey, man," Isaac says, strolling over to me, one hand in his pocket.

He looks as though he doesn't have a care in the world. His usual demeanor unless he wants to put his fist through my face, obviously.

"Hey, how did it go?"

"Easy enough. They said they'll have the results tomorrow. They'll call your parents since your dad is going home today."

I nod. "Listen. I know this isn't the best time... or the best place to have this conversation, but we need to have it," I demand.

"You're not going to back off my sister, are you?" he says, calmer than he's ever been when discussing his sister and me together.

"Not a chance in hell. I told you I'd fight you for her, and I didn't realize until now how much I meant it. Beat the shit out of me if that's what it takes... I'm not backing down."

He still stands with his hand in his pocket, and the way he's taking this has me on alert. Is he going to sucker punch me when I'm not expecting it? Fuck it. He can do his worst—I'm not stopping until I get this all out.

"I called my agent a couple of days ago. I'm looking at other teams for next season."

His eyebrows furrow. "What the fuck? Why? I thought they unofficially already offered you a spot."

"They did. Three more years and double the pay."

"I don't get it." He shakes his head, staring back at me.

"Autumn can't take the promotion if I play for one of their clients, so I'm eliminating the barrier between us."

"Whoa, hold on," he says, shaking his hands out at me. "Have you talked to my sister about this?"

"Not exactly. She'll tell me not to do it so that I don't have to give up anything, but she doesn't get that she's the only thing I *won't* give up. I don't want to tell her until I land somewhere so that I know where I'm going to be next year, but I think it will be soon. My agent already has several teams interested."

"Okay, Briggs... Jesus. I get it now, all right?" He looks away from me and runs his hand over his buzzed haircut. "You can date my sister; just don't piss away your contract. Call your agent and tell him you changed your mind."

"Not until your sister agrees to be with me."

"She already quit the firm to be with you!" he says, frustrated.

"No, she didn't. She would have told me."

"Well, she just told me downstairs."

"When did she do this?" I ask, my mind running a mile a minute.

When did she have time to do this since we've been here?

"The meeting she had with her boss before she left for Walla Walla."

She turned down the promotion yesterday and didn't tell me. Why?

"Why didn't she tell me? I would have told her not to. I don't need to play for the Hawkeyes. I can play anywhere. She should take the promotion."

"Fuck if I know. Go find her and ask her yourself."

Shit, he's right. But where is she?

Then he turns and heads down the hall to my dad's hospital room. I hear his parents celebrate when he walks into the room.

They haven't seen him in months, and as much as I'd like to get in on that reunion, Autumn and I have a lot to discuss.

I race down to the elevator that Isaac just exited and jump in once the door opens for me.

This hospital is three stories, and she could be anywhere, but my guess is one of the two stories below me.

I decide to stop at level two, and when I step out of the elevator, I find a mostly quiet hallway with Autumn standing a hockey rink length away by herself, staring out the large floor-to-ceiling windows out at the hospital parking lot below.

"Autumn!" I yell to the end of the hallway and begin to move quickly toward her.

She spins around when she hears my voice. "What's wrong? What happened?" The concern is coating her angelic face as I get closer.

She probably thinks there is something wrong with my dad, but at this point, there isn't any news on that front, so I'm using this time to right something that never should have gone wrong in the first place.

"Isaac just told me you gave up your job. Why would you do that?" I say, taking the last few rushed steps to her until we're toe to toe.

I place my hands on either side of her shoulders. I need her close. I need to see her when she tells me why she gave up the one thing she spent the last five years of her career to achieve, only to turn it down the minute she got it.

Isaac may have told me the reason that Autumn gave him, but I need to hear it from her.

"That big mouth." She huffs, looking anywhere other than up at me.

"Autumn," I say softly, trying to get her attention, but it doesn't seem to work. "I called my agent two days ago, right after you told me what Erika said about not dating clients. I told him to find me a new team."

Her eyes flash up to mine, her eyebrows furrowed, and a frown bends those pretty pink lips in the opposite direction I was hoping they'd curve at my news.

"the Hawkeyes aren't offering you a renewal? I thought there was an unofficial deal already. Why would they put in all this work with improving your image if they—"

"They did offer me another contract. A bigger one," I confirm.

"Then why are you leaving Seattle? Why a new team?"

"Because I want you, Autumn. And if playing for the Hawkeyes means I can't be with you, then... fuck it. It's not worth it to me anymore. I'll play for someone else. I'll live here in the off-season, and maybe you could work remotely. Maybe travel to be with me for home weeks wherever I get placed. We could spend the holidays on Orcas Island, or we can go wherever you want when I'm not playing. I just want to be with you."

A smile flashes across her face, but she bites down on her lip to cover it up. The fact that her natural first reaction is to smile at the plans I'm making up in my head for us together gives me hope that I'm on the right track.

"Briggs, you love that team," she says, her hands finally reaching out to touch me. My hands drop from her shoulders to wrap around low on her back as her hands connect against my chest.

Jesus, I'm addicted to the feel of her.

We both watch as her hands come up and smooth over my pecks.

"Not more than I love you," I admit.

This isn't the moment I planned to tell her, but now that I'm sure it's true, I need her to know.

Her eyes connect back up to mine the second the words leave my mouth.

"You do?"

"There's no other way to explain it. I'll give up anything for you to belong to me," I admit.

"For me to belong to you?" she asks, her cheeks blushing as her smile widens.

"Yeah. Because I've belonged to you for a long time now... and I think it's only fair." I smirk.

She laughs as her hands smooth up over my chest and wrap around my neck. I bend down to kiss her. The feeling of having done everything I need to ensure we don't leave this hospital as anything less than together feels good. There isn't a single iota of doubt in me that wishes I wasn't giving up my team for her.

I've already decided I'm willing to give up more if I have to. None of it will feel like a sacrifice to gain a life with her.

She softly speaks against our kiss. "What about my brother?"

"He gave his blessing upstairs outside of my dad's hospital room."

She pulls back from our kiss to look at me. "He did?"

I simply nod, watching her reaction.

"Then I should tell you that I came up here from the lab room downstairs because Erika offered me a job."

"She offered you a different job or the same one?"

I don't care if this still means I need to sign with another team. I meant what I said. I'll give up anything, but what does this new job entail, and does it have some stupid as fuck rule that she can't date a man with the last name Conley or some other ridiculous thing that would attempt to sabotage our newly formed and permanent relationship?

"A different one."

"What is it?"

"It's a freelance position with an office next to Tessa Tomlin's in the Hawkeyes stadium."

"What would you do?" I ask, hope blooming in me at the idea that Autumn and I might both soon be working for the same team, and if that's the case, I'm calling my agent and telling him that I want the fact that I'm allowed to date Autumn as part of my new terms for re-signing.

"My job would be to help each player in the franchise individually, and I'd help turn the franchise into the family-friendly image that Phil Carlton wants. They want me to try my hand at a little bit of elbow rubbing to get players more lucrative deals."

I chuckle, thinking about Autumn running around at the fundraisers, schmoozing with big-time companies in the sports realm.

"We already know you're good at that. My agent received two calls from the people you talked to at the fundraiser. I have a phone interview with one of them next week to endorse some high-end athletic wear. It could be big."

"Really?!" She beams.

I nod again.

"Well, the best part of this new job is since I'll be freelance, I can date whomever I want," she says, tightening her arms around my neck and pressing her breasts further again my chest.

I dip down and take her lips again.

Why the hell can't we be home in our apartment when this conversation is happening?

I need her stripped down and bare for me, laying naked on our master bed where I can devour every inch of her body.

My hands trail down to her perfect ass and I grip it with both hands and pull her against my growing cock.

She moans into my mouth on our next kiss.

We're in a goddamn hospital out in the open where anyone can see us, but I'm about to sit in that waiting room chair by the window, unzip my pants and pull Autumn on top of me, seat her on my pulsating erection, and claim her.

For a split second, I consider the terrible idea of searching out an open hospital room or abandoned broom closet to cement this verbal agreement we just made. Physically claiming Autumn is the only train of thought I have right now, and my desperation has me considering leading her downstairs and taking her in the back of her 4Runner parked downstairs. The thing has tinted windows, and if I lay the rows of seats back, I might be able to fit in the back with Autumn.

If we get caught having sex inside, we run the risk of getting kicked out of the hospital that my dad might still spend many more days in. I don't need Security denying me access if he's ever admitted again.

Autumn

He told his agent to find him another team? My heart melts. He was going to give up a team he loves and a group of guys who have become as close as family to be with me.

This is not what I expected. I could never live with myself if I let him sign with a different team to be with me. He has dreams of retiring with this team and because I love him as much as I do, I'd never let that happen.

With Sam's request to Erika, and Erika's creative ability to solve an issue, even when it comes to my employment, neither Briggs nor I have to give up anything. We get to keep everything. Even if something happened in our future and one of us had to switch our job situations out, there are plenty of Public Relations firms in Seattle and with Erika's letter of recommendation that she agreed to give me with my resignation, I could find something else.

"Come on," Briggs says, pulling his mouth off mine and his hands off my bum.

He reaches for my hand and links them together, pulling me behind him.

"Where are we going?"

"Somewhere I can get these clothes off you."

"Briggs...." I giggle as he pulls me towards the elevator. "We have more than enough time for that now. Let's go see our family."

"Our family," he whispers to himself with a smile while pushing the button the elevator call button. "I like how that sounds. You're right, we should go see them," he says as the elevator opens and pulls me through with him. "Can I announce that you're my girlfriend when we walk in?"

I chuckle. "Everyone already thinks we're together."

"I know but now that we're not faking it anymore, I want to tell everyone that we're together," he says, looking over at me and squeezing my hand as the elevator doors close. It starts moving up to the top floor.

"OK," I smile back, loving that this is important to him.

"Hey Autumn..." he says, wrapping his arms around my waist from behind and bending down to press his lips against my neck, right below the soft spot behind my ear.

"Yeah?" I ask, my eyelashes fluttering at the sensation of having his mouth on me.

"Will you move in with me?"

My heart squeezes at his request. "We already live together," I remind him.

"I know but our lease on the apartment that Penelope got us ends next month and I want us to stay together even when our time at the apartment is up."

"Where would we live?"

"I don't care. We can live in the penthouse I own across town during the season and my house on Orcas Island in the off-season. Or we could live in your studio apartment for all

I care, I just want to call the same place home. I want to be wherever you are."

My smile stretches so big that it almost hurts. Usually, I would think this is fast to be moving in together, especially after becoming a couple all of twenty minutes ago but we already live together so what would be the difference now?

"Ok," I agree. The doors to the elevator open when we get to the next level. We walk out into the hallway and I can see Briggs's dad's room at the end of the hallway. "But can we stay in The Commons? I like being close to all of our friends and I'm going to be at Penelope's for all of your away games anyway to watch you play."

Briggs pulls out his phone and starts typing with one hand.

"What are you doing?"

"Texting Penelope to see if she can help us find a bigger apartment on her floor."

My brows furrow together. "Does any of that matter as long as we're in the same building?"

"I like the idea of you on the same floor as Penelope for when I'm away. You two can look out for each other."

"Ok, I get that. But why the bigger apartment? It's just the two of us and that apartment was huge as it is."

"We'll need room for the dog."

"A dog?" My ears perk up.

I've always wanted a dog but I didn't peg Briggs as an animal person.

"I like the idea of some huge man-eater around to protect you when I'm not home. I was thinking of a Doberman."

"Really? Because I'm thinking a French Bulldog who wants to curl up and watch chic flicks on the couch with me while I eat ice cream and fast food when you're away sounds more my speed."

He shakes his head and grins. "What's that tiny dog going to do if someone breaks in?"

"Kill them with cuteness." I beam up at him.

We walk up to the hospital room, and everyone's hugging. Mrs. Conley and my mother are crying happy tears. My dad pats Mr. Conley's shoulder as they share a smile. Everyone seems to be celebrating. My brother and the doctor are discussing something amongst themselves off to the side.

"What's going on?" Briggs asks.

"Isaac is a match," my dad says.

"They're going to start treatment immediately!" Mrs. Conley says.

I look up at Briggs but he's looking at Isaac.

Briggs pulls me along with him as he heads straight for my brother, wrapping his free arm around Isaac's shoulder. The two collide in an emotional embrace.

"Thank you," I hear Briggs whisper to Isaac, his voice thick with emotion.

"We're brothers, Briggs. I'll always have your back."

"I know you do. And I have yours."

Isaac pats Briggs's back as their hug ends.

Briggs turns to the other people in the room, the rest of our family. We both face them, hand in hand.

"I guess this is the best time to announce since we're all here...." Briggs stops and looks down at me, something flashing in his eyes like a new idea just came to him, and his lips uptick to one side.

Then he turns to me and gets down on one knee.

I gasp out loud and my eyes go wide as saucers. I hear both of our moms shriek with excitement and run to each other embracing as they watch this take place.

I glance up quickly to see an unreadable look on my brother's face but I think I see a slight smile.

I'm not hallucinating because everyone else is seeing the same thing I am. This big hockey player down on one knee still holding my hand.

"Autumn. I know this started as fake—"

"Wait, what?!" our moms say in confusion and unison.

"...and I didn't know it right then, but I realized that it stopped being fake for me the second you jumped into my arms at the restaurant that first day."

Tears begin to well at the realization that all that doubt over the last month was for nothing. He wanted me too.

"Someone once told me: *'It's always the person you least expect. The girl right under your nose that ends up being the one.'* And I wasted a lot of time not taking that advice."

"That's right," Mrs. Conley interrupts, "but actually, it's always been your dad that knew that you two were perfect for each other. Since the minute she started showing up at our house and he told her where you boys were hiding," Mrs. Conley tells Briggs.

"Hey! What?!" Isaac objects and shoots a playful shocked look at Mr. Conley.

Everyone in the room starts laughing.

Mr. Conley just shrugs and then sends me a little wink.

Briggs glances over at everyone in the room with a disapproving frown. "Ok, I'm proposing over here, can you all shut up?" he teases but the confirmation that's he actually proposing has butterflies fluttering in my stomach.

Briggs turns back to me. "I love you and I'm sorry that I made us both wait over twenty years for me to realize that I always had the one." He bites down slightly on his lip as he pauses before he asks the real question. "Will you stop the wait from continuing any longer and marry me?"

"Yes!" I nod vigorously. "Of course I will. I love you too. I always have."

He stands and pulls me into him. I toss my arms over his neck and tighten my squeeze on him.

"I'm sorry I almost missed you," he whispers against my ear.

"It wasn't our time then," I whisper back and then pull back to see his face. "But it is now," I tell him and then he leans in and kisses me passionately, pulling me against his chest, my feet dangling off the ground.

He sets me back down when my brother clears his throat—obviously, Isaac's had enough of our PDA.

"I didn't get a ring... since, up until an hour ago, I wasn't sure if we were real or not."

"Uh, is someone planning on explaining that to us?" my mom says.

"Nope," Briggs says, smiling down at me.

My mom looks at Isaac and he just shrugs.

"Well, in that case, I believe I have something for you," Mrs. Conley pipes up.

We look over to find Mrs. Conley looking down at Mr. Conley and he nods in confirmation.

Mrs. Conley walks up to us, smiling at us both, and then turns to me.

"We could never have dreamed up a better wife for our son and we can't wait to add you to our family." She smiles, rubbing my arm and then her right hand reaches for the heirloom wedding ring that was Briggs's great grandfather's, brought over from Italy when he immigrated here. I've never seen the ring off her hand my whole life.

It's a large two-carat solitaire. Simple in design but perfectly classic. I've always admired it as a kid, the way it sparkles effortlessly in any kind of lighting.

I'd never admit it but I used to imagine wearing the ring when I was younger. Daydreaming of what it would feel like to wear the Conley ring and to belong to Briggs.

It feels too surreal to now be offered everything I've dreamed of.

"If you'd accept this ring, Mr. Conley and I would be honored for you to carry on the tradition and pass it on to your firstborn."

My throat clogs with emotion. The Conley family accepting me so instantly into their family within a minute of Briggs's proposal and the idea of building a family with Briggs...my heart is bursting at the seams.

I look at Briggs for approval and he nods. "If you want it but we can get you something else if you—"

"No," I practically shout, my eyes widening at the thought that he thinks I would want anything else. "This is exactly what I want."

I turn to Mrs. Conley, and she beams back at me, pulling the ring off her hand, and separating the diamond-encrusted band from the solitaire.

"I'll hold on to the wedding band since he bought that for me to go with the heirloom," she says, slipping the band back on her finger. "Maybe you two can pick out a wedding band together," she says, handing Briggs the engagement ring. "Here, put this on your fiancée's hand."

Hearing that title makes me want to jump around and scream into a pillow like a lovesick teenager.

"Then you'll have something new and something old," my mom says, walking up to us.

"You'll just need something borrowed," Mrs. Conley says.

"How about my last name." Briggs winks.

"No... that's something I plan to keep," I say, turning to face him.

He nods with a grin and then pulls my left hand into his and slides the ring onto my finger.

"It's a perfect fit."

"That's because it was always meant to be yours. Just like you were always meant to be mine." Briggs says.

And then he seals this moment with a kiss.

The END

Want an extra BONUS chapter? Get Briggs and Autumn's
Two Years Later – THE WEDDING, here!
https://dl.bookfunnel.com/v8gislsh50

Thank you for reading Cocky Score!

To read the next book, Filthy Score, you can find it on Amazo
n.com or on my website. www.KennaKing.com

Use this QR code for the amazon.com store!

Keep up with Kenna by following here: KennaKingBooks

Made in United States
North Haven, CT
17 August 2024

56204347R00225